Rolling Pigeons

Minneapolis

FIRST EDITION FEBRUARY 2026
Rolling Pigeons. Copyright © 2026 by Dan Roettger.
All rights reserved.

This is a work of fiction. Characters, names, incidents, organizations, and dialogue are the products of the author's imagination. Historical figures and the scenes in which they appear have been originated or expanded fictionally by the author.

No part of this book may be used or reproduced in any manner whatsoever without written permission except in the case of brief quotations used in critical articles and reviews.

For information, write to Calumet Editions,
6800 France Avenue South, Suite 370, Edina, MN 55435

10 9 8 7 6 5 4 3 2 1
ISBN: 978-1-962834-70-4

Cover illustration: Vince Cook
Cover and interior design: Gary Lindberg

Rolling Pigeons

Dan Roettger

Minneapolis

Chapter 1

It was Mary Kay Schlueter's first day off for some time. Since the morning had dawned fresh and clear with no sign of rain, she decided to do her laundry and dry her things the old-fashioned way, outside on the line. She worked the midnight to seven shift at St. Jude's, and after weeks of driving home in bright sunshine, only to have to shield herself behind double-lined bedroom curtains in order to sleep, the extra effort of hanging her clothes in the sun would seem like no work at all.

Besides that, a nurse's uniform just wore better when dried naturally. Only sunshine could purge the material of hospital stink, which brought with it a sense of illness and disease. For Mary Kay, sun-dried uniforms meant you could begin work without the pervasive stench of fear that, by the end of the day, would saturate the garment and even blend with your skin.

She stepped out the basement door of her two-bedroom brick home, and as always, found it difficult to maneuver between both the wood and screen doors, edge onto the tiny landing, and thump up the concrete steps while holding the basket of damp laundry in both hands.

A husband might have made things easier by moving the washer and dryer upstairs into the mud room, but since divorcing three years ago Mary Kay had rejected any such liaison that might allow her even that small service. She knew it was harder for nurses to sustain relationships, and it was especially difficult for intensive care nurses on rotation. She wasn't up for the effort anymore; it wasn't worth looking for a new career just to facilitate dating. The few encounters with men she'd had since the divorce were merely functional, and after having performed their function Mary Kay had cleared them out as mechanically as she swept the kitchen floor.

To get as much sun as possible Mary Kay performed almost all outdoor chores in a one-piece, black bathing suit. After reaching the top of the basement steps with her second load of whites, she set the basket down on the grass, adjusted the tight-fitting suit, and surveyed the surrounding corn field.

At the far end of the hundred-acre field Mary Kay could see Frank Tochtrop's twin silos spearing skyward, and she was just able to distinguish the silver roof of his barn against the powder-blue horizon. With the twin silos the only visible evidence of an outside world, Mary Kay had grown used to the calming sense of solitude the backyard provided. But it would last only until fall, when the corn walls would be torn down by the giant roaring combine that always munched away at her enclosure, exposing her for all to see.

With the house still penned in by corn, the backyard looked like a sculpted habitat at the zoo. The brick barbecue pit, the rotting, abandoned doghouse in the corner, the aboveground propane tank up against the corn, and the three-stranded clothesline running across the middle of the yard created an ersatz environment for its sole human inhabitant.

After a minute, Mary Kay picked up the clothes basket and began adding to the clothesline where she'd left off—a couple more uniforms, two blouses so thin you could see through them, a slip, then the first of two bedsheets. Opening the sheet fully in front of her, she draped it over two lines to give it more air. The light breeze filled the sheet like a sail and caused the bottom to angle out a few feet toward the corn. It was a queen-sized sheet, and it blocked Mary Kay's view of the field.

As she moved over to hang the second one, she saw a man standing in the space for the next sheet, not four feet away.

The sudden appearance of a man in her yard caused Mary Kay to scream. She continued screaming because he wasn't wearing a stitch of clothing.

Nothing looked malicious about him. In fact, for an instant, just before Mary Kay began screaming, he grinned proudly, almost as if he didn't know the difference between acceptable and non-acceptable behavior.

As soon as the screaming started the man's smile turned into a grimace, as if he believed the woman would calmly go about her business. In truth, the sudden apparition so terrified Mary Kay that all she could do was scream bloody murder. It did little good, since only the rows of corn stood witness.

Since the panic-stricken woman didn't seem to be calming down, the man grew flustered and more confused. He bent low, like an umpire motioning with both hands out and palms down, as if to implore the lady to please be quiet… please lady, be quiet. She took it as an aggressive gesture which inspired her to move, but instead of making a mad rush to the house, her panic disoriented her, causing her to edge around the wall of hanging clothes. It was the first and only barrier, meager as it was, between her and the naked man facing her on the opposite side.

Mary Kay was just shy of thirty-eight and had been a hospital nurse for eighteen years, which meant she'd seen a lot of naked, older men. But in most cases, she was the one in control, the men generally supine and embarrassed. This man was standing, his body still fairly firm and, judging by the cut of his erection, was certainly not submissive. Torn was a better word for the way the man looked now. Torn between the desire to get himself fully in front of Mary Kay or run away as fast as he could.

For a moment their eyes met, and Mary Kay recognized a third feature, one she had seen many times from the end of a hospital bed.

The man's face reflected so much suffering and pain and remorse she could tell he was condemning himself all the while and wanted nothing more than to lie down and die.

As he followed Mary Kay around the hanging clothes, the man matched her movements exactly, doing nothing to close the distance between them. For every step she took to the right he took a step to the left. If she made a dash to the other side, he made a dash. It all seemed absurd, as if taken right out of a Marx Brothers movie. All he wanted was for her to see him. She was just as energetically trying not to. If a crowd had been watching from a distance, they might have been amused by this woman in a skimpy swimsuit being chased around the clothesline by her lecherous, old lover.

Eventually, when she found herself once more on the house side of the clothesline, she made a dash for the backdoor, reaching it easily. Turning back, she saw the man hadn't followed her, hadn't even tried. He was simply standing in the middle of her yard, allowing her gaze to wash over him with the apparent calm of a horse grazing in a pasture.

He obviously wasn't coming any closer, and for a long while, during which she stood facing him in the doorway trying to sort through her emotions, she felt a sort of drain, as if she were giving off energy through her gaze and he simply absorbing it. Then in a medium voice as matter of fact as if she were calling children in for their supper, she said, "I'm going to call the police now."

The man turned away slowly and loped into the seven-foot-high field of corn.

Chapter 2

During the moments that were left of the Sunday morning mass the twenty-foot half circle of concrete in front of the church lay empty. The concrete apron was badly pockmarked, having lost its finish long ago due to a cement shortage when the old church was built. The materials to build the church had been donated, and the man responsible for the poor mix had passed away long before it was discovered his sacrifice had been less than sublime.

A wide crack ran across the slab, starting at the base of the church's double wooden doors, and, if one imagined the crack continuing, it would race across the convent that housed two old nuns, through the old section of cemetery where the markers were bleached and unreadable, across Josephville Road and straight east across miles of corn and soybeans until eventually hitting the St. Louis suburbs and bisecting the Gateway Arch on the west bank of the Mississippi.

A sparrow investigating the crack flew off when one of the church doors swung open, briefly washing the small courtyard with the sound of organ music. The music sounded melancholy, reminding those inside that the world was still a dark place regardless of the early autumnal abundance happening all around them. Four times in the last hour the music spilled out of the cantilevered, stained glass windows lining the side of the church, and inside the people of the small rural Catholic congregation used the music to get them through the monotony of the Sunday service.

According to doctrine, if a person could remain in church at least until communion the Sunday obligation was taken care of, and teenage girls such as the two that now exited could lawfully catch a private smoke against the side of the building, a much more pardonable offense than leaving mass too early on Sunday. In the early fifties the town had been connected to St. Louis by forty-five miles of interstate, allowing Gilmore, Missouri, to grow big enough to be named the county seat. But since its economy remained stubbornly agricultural, the growth eventually leveled off, and now nothing much happened there. It had a population of 2,883 as of the last census, work was beginning on a new co-op across from the high school, and it had a tax base that slowly grew by fits and starts, as if the town itself had a bad stutter.

The doors of the church burst open a second time, and Sy Todd and his wife Darlene were among the first to exit, since Darlene insisted on sitting in the back so people wouldn't notice she hadn't gone to communion. She always complained about the trip to the altar and the long march back in front of all those appraising eyes which was just too much, never mind the cosmic reward. Finally, Sy had quit arguing with her. Once he considered mentioning that if she weren't so guilty of gawking and judging herself maybe she'd be less self-conscious, but after thirty-five years of dealing with Darlene's neurosis, he knew it might be enough to bring on a week-long sulk.

Pete Turner spilled out of the church just behind Sy and Darlene and was the first to catch Sy's eye, looking for permission to approach. Sy watched him come and silently wished he would change course. This morning, he felt somewhat aloof and wasn't up for talking to anyone.

"Can you believe that crazy new priest in there today?" It was Pete's habit to start a conversation devoid of introduction. Sy excused him as he always did but made Pete pay by staring coolly before answering.

"Didn't start off on the right foot, did he?"

"I've been going to church every Sunday since I was six, and I never heard the likes of that before."

"Hello, Peter," piped in Darlene, who had rightfully assumed Peter was going to ignore her and stick to Sy if she didn't interject.

"Why hi, Darlene. We were just talking about the new priest."

"I know, wasn't that just awful?"

"He's lucky he's just passing through. I don't think he'd be able to show his face at St. Michael's again," said Pete.

"I hope he gets over it. He seems to be a good kid," Sy said. Sy wasn't one to leap on other people's misfortune, and besides that, the whole thing made him a little uncomfortable since he rather liked the young priest who was fresh out of the seminary and celebrating mass at different parishes to get his feet wet. He'd just have to get better at reading his audience.

"Going to the game today?" he asked Pete.

"Sure, aren't you?"

"Naw. Darlene's talking about having Mercy and Charlotte over for barbecue."

"You guys do that barbecue thing pretty much every Sunday, don't you?" By saying it in front of Darlene, it was Pete's half-hearted attempt to win permission for Sy to go to the game.

"Yeah, but today we're cooking the dog. Do something different," Sy said. "I already got him skinned and hanging in the garage."

Darlene held a hand against her flaming-red Jackie Kennedy beehive and turned to the side, hiding her smile from Sy. Pete simply blinked, his flat round face showing no understanding of what had just been said. For a moment the three stood there in awkward silence.

Sy was a man everyone liked. Years ago, before he went to work for Templeton Properties, he'd been the only contractor in Gilmore and built for almost everyone in town at one time or another. He had a reputation for being a fair man who knew right from wrong and whom everyone could count on. As a result, any organized function he was to be a part of—and there were a lot—would be put in his hands as soon as he arrived, no matter who else was supposed to be running it. Even strangers would defer to him, often without a word being said.

"You ought to try and come out," Pete finally offered. "Brad Boehmer's pitchin' better than I ever seen him..."

"Yeah well..."

"Course Tony Wilmes says he snucks up that cocaine before the game and in between every inning."

At that point Pete's wife Joy walked up, said an overly gracious hello to Sy and immediately fell to talking with Darlene. With men and women at right angles to each other the four made a perfect square, and since the men and women of Gilmore seldom focused on the same subject, it caused the conversation to be perfectly divided.

"Darlene, I saw Charlotte coming back from communion with Mercy a while ago, and she's getting so cute!"

"He says if you look you can see the outline of a little bottle in the pocket of his uniform."

"I think she's looking more like her mother every day," said Darlene, who was easily complimented and broke into a wide smile.

"If he's that good it means he's got his own steam coming from somewhere," said Sy absently. He wasn't much interested in conversation, devoting more of his attention to casually noting who was still spilling out of the church.

"And how is Mercy?" asked Joy. "That's a beautiful dress she has on. I know she didn't buy that at Burcell's."

"He says you can see a little white ring under his nose by the seventh inning." Pete raised his index finger and traced the rim of a nostril to illustrate his point.

"But don't you think she looks tired? I think she looks tired. Sy thinks she looks tired too."

"Probably dips it in flour to keep it dry," said Sy, with one eye on the church doors. *There's Bill Molitor's wife,* he thought. *Bout to whelp another baby. Bill should be right behind her. Must have gotten cut off by the side aisle. Yep, there he is.*

"Darlene, she's gorgeous! If I had to guess I'd say she's been to that new health club across the highway. It's surprising she hasn't remarried after all this time. She's got every male in town worrying over her like a lovesick dog. But then I can't imagine any of them good enough for her. Come on… let's go over and tell Mercy how beautiful she looks and how wonderful her daughter is. A woman needs to hear those things, and God knows she'll never hear a man say them." With that, Joy threw a quick, serious glance at her husband and grabbed Darlene by the arm, gently pulling her away. "When these boys start talking baseball there's no fighting it anyhow."

"I just think she looks tired, that's all," said Darlene defiantly, her last word on the subject before allowing herself to be led off.

"If he's gonna fry his brain a little flour might be a good idea," said Pete, shaking his head. "It's not like the old days. Hell, you did a better job pitching for Gilmore than Brad with no help from anybody or anything."

"I was usually hung over from Saturday night," said Sy. "That's got to be kinda like doing drugs. Probably helped my concentration or something." Sy watched Bill Kirchner amble through the doors and wade over to the side so as not to have to speak to Father Dieckman. The priest had taken his usual position on the front step to greet his parishioners as they filed out of the church. Saying the mass was the priest's duty, but this was the job he enjoyed, for it was here he could put the screws to people who needed it by looking them straight in the eye and prolonging the handshake. Sy looked for the unfortunate younger priest to be standing near Dieckman, but he was nowhere around.

"He's got a helluva long way to go yet to make the Hall of Fame," said Pete, throwing Sy an appreciative sidelong glance. There wasn't a soul in Gilmore who didn't know Sy was to be inducted into the Gilmore County Baseball Hall of Fame next Monday before the game, and Pete spoke of it with the deference of a kid talking to his best friend's grandfather. Sy had no temperament for praise and acted like he didn't hear it. Pete went on anyway.

"I hear you played even better ball in Korea."

"For the 24th Army Artillery. We were called the Cannoneers," said Sy. "I was a much younger man then." Sy never talked about his time in Korea and wondered where Pete got his information. There was a long pause while Pete waited for Sy to elaborate, but nothing came.

"Well anyway, Sy, you ought to try and sneak out for an inning or two. Just to watch my boy cover second base." Pete could see Sy didn't want to bite on Korea and felt unworthy pursuing such a hallowed subject as Sy's induction into the Hall of Fame.

"He's starting to come on, isn't he?" Sy knew how to feed Pete so he'd do all the talking and Sy wouldn't have to bother much. There was Mrs. Cockburn and her boy Dale, who had a habit of pulling hair out the side of his head whenever he got anxious. It looked like he'd been fretting again, judging by the hint of white peeking through his thick, black hair.

"Hit a two-run homer last Sunday against Foley," said Pete proudly. "That put 'em ahead in the top of the ninth, then he helped finish her off with a double play. Smokin' grounder too."

"What's he batting now?" Out came Tillie Wagoner, Bob Jeter, Mary Methany and all her kids. Behind them came Bobby Capstick, thirty-one years old and still shuffling his feet, cowering like a kid. *He never was right*, thought Sy. *Not from the day he was born.* On Sunday at the game Bobby always had an orange ring around his mouth from a bottle of Fanta. It wasn't there now, but Sy knew it'd be there supplementing his simpleton image by the first inning. God knows Bobby would never miss a ballgame and the chance to shag the foul balls necessary to earn him another soda.

"As of last week, he was batting .318," said Pete. "He still likes to chop at the ball ever once and a while, else he'd be doing even better I imagine."

At that point Marvin Whorley emerged from the church, split off from his wife without saying a word, and searched the area until he spotted Sy and Pete.

"Hello, Pete… hey, Sy," he said, nodding to them both.

Pete and Marvin weren't the best of friends due to an altercation involving Marvin's boys over six years ago. Pete clammed up about his son's batting average, and since Sy wasn't in the mood to enlist conversation there was an anxious moment of pure silence. Both men glanced at the church door to see what Sy was finding so interesting. Finally, Pete muttered something to Marvin about what the new young priest had done, and that got the conversation going.

Sy was thinking about how many Sunday mornings he'd stood in this very place doing this very thing with these very people. His life had become stilted. It came from being so damned responsible. He'd always worked his butt off and towed the line, even as a kid. Always too careful, too calculating. Here he was, sixty-three years old, and while in church it occurred to him that he had only ever made love to three women. Soon he would be an old man, and it would be too late for anything new. He already felt himself getting forgetful at times. Sy never liked to pull into himself but this morning he just let it happen, attributing it to the narcotic effects of high mass. While in church his irreverent thoughts had coincided with an indefinite, high-pitched buzzing in his ears, like the whine coming off a TV test pattern.

Pete and Marvin gave Sy all the room he needed. "Good day for a ballgame," Marvin said finally, hoping Sy would pick up that the comment was meant for him.

"Sure is," said Sy, who preferred it be raining cats and dogs. Anything to make this day different.

"Sy's gotta barbecue," said Pete.

Pete's tone made Marvin realize Sy's wife had issued another order. No one understood how a man like Sy could allow himself to be so called upon by a woman like Darlene. Of course, in the old days Darlene was a sight to behold. And perfectly sane to boot. But fifteen years ago her body started menopause, and to this day there was still an internal struggle between the forces fighting to retire her ovaries and those urging her to reproduce. Her female chemicals were being dumped without measure, and the effect was like a car engine badly out of tune. After fifteen years on a mental roller coaster, she finally gave up fighting it. She was sixty-one years old, and the hot flashes were still so intense they would drive her to tear her clothes off in front of the refrigerator. On evenings with friends when her chemicals flushed through her body, causing her to behave like a child, they would all nod, silently agreeing she must be worth it or Sy wouldn't put up with it.

The reality was that Sy considered it a challenge putting up with Darlene. He'd never lost patience completely, although he'd come close. He fancied himself the Gordon Liddy of spouses and vowed to never cave in. A man's will needed a constant workout to stay strong, and as far as he knew, his will had yet to be bested. Besides that, Darlene could never survive without him.

When Sy's gaze floated back toward the front of the church he noticed Clarence Dickersen had slipped out the side door and was talking to Father Dieckman. Sy quickly excused himself and walked over to join them.

Being lifelong friends, Clarence and Sy simply nodded to each other while Father Dieckman quickly tucked his fat Cuban cigar into his mouth to free his hand, offering it to Sy.

"Sy! Good to see you, man! How's your ass for rats?" The priest spoke loudly and was smiling as big as he could without losing his grip on the cigar.

"Got a few I guess," said Sy, his pat response to a question he never really understood, especially since it came from a priest.

"Good, good, keeps you virile," said the priest, pumping Sy's hand and puffing his cigar. The only time Father Dieckman was without his cigar was during a meal or at the altar. Even then it was never far away. He would set it in the censer before mass, where it smoldered, filling the vestibule with smoke long before it was time for the altar boys to fire up the incense. When Father Dieckman circled the altar swinging the incense burner from its gold chain, with a robed youngster desperately hanging on to the priest's arm, Sy daydreamed the priest could accomplish the same thing by throwing back his head and puffing away at his cigar, like the Holy Ghost's own private locomotive.

By now Clarence and Sy were used to Father Dieckman's anything but priestly demeanor, although it was only the two of them who were ever invited to witness it. He and Clarence made the mistake of taking the reverend out to Clarence's duck blind on the river a few times, and now the priest considered the three of them inseparable. The first time out Clarence and Sy were surprised by how crude and lascivious the priest was. Sy knew it was the kind of environment where men could open up, and, Sy supposed, a setting where even priests could lose their piety. Lately, it continued outside the blind, but still only when the three of them where alone, like now. Sy usually shrugged it off, but the arrangement made him uneasy, especially when the change in the priest occurred so near the church.

Father Dieckman was the same age as Sy, but similarities ended there. For starters, the priest was highly educated, much more so than Sy, who'd only graduated high school. Where the priest was rude and cynical, Sy was thoughtful and spare, but showed considerable wit when he did speak. Where the priest was judgmental in assessing his parishioners, Sy always looked for the good in people, even when he defined their character as wanting. While the priest was duplicitous, especially in terms of his faith, Sy's convictions were confirmed by his actions. Dieckman was over six feet tall, grossly overweight, and the only priest in the diocese who still wore the five-cornered miter, which, if nothing else, told Sy he took his own personal symbols of priesthood a lot more seriously than the ones he orchestrated behind the altar.

"What'd you boys think of the kid's debut?" asked Dieckman, punctuating the question with a billow of smoke. With the cigar stuffed into his flat, puffy face, Father Dieckman could have been a brother to Winston Churchill.

"I just hope he gets past it," said Sy.

"Where is he anyway?" asked Clarence.

"After this morning my guess would be he's back at the rectory spanking his monkey," said Dieckman.

The new young priest had been ordained for all of three months. The final leg of his training consisted of spending a week in every parish of the diocese, saying mass and in general getting a feel for how a parish should run. This morning, just after Dieckman's sermon, the hip young priest surprised Father Dieckman and the congregation by announcing that while the parishioners had always confessed their sins to the priests, both priests would now openly and honestly confess to their parishioners. The young priest went first, blurting out that his biggest crime against God and himself was that he couldn't stop masturbating. In a tense, high-pitched voice, he described his fantasies to a visibly uncomfortable crowd who wished he would stop. The halting soliloquy went on for several minutes, until it came to a painful, abrupt end, like a torturer cranking the final cog on the rack. Dieckman took thirty seconds to mumble something about laziness and improper thoughts, then ended with a hurried blessing that was so conservative it dated back to the apostle Paul.

"You made a nice sermon anyway, Padre," said Clarence unconvincingly. "It was nice having an old veteran up there to keep things on track."

"Thanks. But just between you and me, I had no idea what I was going to say until it came out."

"It doesn't matter, long as you can pull it off... which you did."

"Half of 'em were sleeping... I can see it in their eyes. A man doesn't have to close his eyes to sleep. Sy does it better than anybody," Dieckman said, throwing Clarence a wink. "Funny how usually he's right there, turning pages in his missalette, keeping up. Today he pretended he was here while way off somewhere else. I'm probably the only one who could tell." He ended with a nervous laugh and fished an apprehensive look over to Sy, who was again staring off at the church doors, not hearing.

"I'm sure he clung to every word, Padre," said Clarence. "Didn't you, Sy?"

"Huh, what?"

"Good sermon today."

"Yes, Father, it was. Really was."

"Too long though, don't you think," said Clarence, smiling.

"Yeah, too long," agreed Sy.

"Make it any shorter and you wouldn't feel you were getting your money's worth," said Dieckman, pulling the cigar out of his mouth, finally having a reason to be clearly understood.

"Hell, Padre, I'd pay extra to have you lop off about fifteen minutes," said Clarence.

"No, you wouldn't, not really. After all these years of being a priest, I've learned my parishioners want two things... an easy way to get to heaven and a long-winded priest to make 'em feel better about having it so damn easy."

"How you figure we've got it so easy, Padre?" asked Clarence.

"You don't have to think about anything. Slide into church on Sundays, Christmas, and any other holy day of obligation, babble a few memorized prayers, kneel, sit, stand until catatonic, and you've completed the formula. Now let me tick off the list of what's available for extra credit. Let's see... you can finger the rosary, and you can trace the Lord's final agony by bleeding through the stations of the cross. You can always make a novena. You can kiss the statue's feet on Good Friday and give thanks to the holy virgin with the group-think every other Tuesday. You can put in your time at the summer picnic and again at that greasy sausage supper in October. You can donate canned goods to Sister Mary Bulldike and that other pantomime Mother Theresa. Or you can invite the parish priest over for a formal dinner. It's easy. The only other thing is to walk into the confessional at least once a month, blurt out the same six sins you've been blurting since you were six, and you don't have to feel bad about anything. You can literally get away with murder in the eyes of the Church. The only thing you can't do is forget to put a big fat check in the envelope on Sunday."

Sy and Clarence stood silently for a moment, not quite believing what they'd just heard.

"Seems awful strange to hear that coming from the mouth of a priest," said Clarence finally, this time with something of an edge to his voice.

"Priest, hell! All you people coming here is what makes a priest. I'm just the executor. If you all focused your guilt on Ned Durham's dog, why *he'd* be a priest. And it'd be a hell of a lot cheaper. Just throw a few Milk Bones in the basket when they pass it around."

"Maybe if we all just melted down our jewelry..."

"And made a golden catfish? You could set it down by the river."

"There you go."

"You two ought to give it up," said Sy. "We *are* still at church you know, Padre. If anyone overheard you talking like that, you'd most likely lose your job." Truthfully, Sy didn't abide by a priest talking this way at all. For any man, much less a priest, to have those sorts of views on something he'd committed himself to was unforgivable. Sy's own faith was a long way removed from the unquestioned obedience of the past, yet he still believed in the immortality of the soul enough to continue going through with it all. For him, church was something more than simply deferring to an earlier time in his life, when his parents drilled it into his head that Catholics were the only true believers, and all others were destined for eternal damnation. He'd risen above that. In addition to his own personal reasons for going to church there was Darlene, who needed organized religion as much as she needed Sy to be there with her.

"Don't worry yourself, Sy," said Father Dieckman, putting a hand on Sy's shoulder. "I can keep it up... as long as you boys allow it. There's nothing else I can do. I'm too old to be a gigolo." Stuffing the fat stub of his cigar into his mouth, he folded his arms indifferently, resigned to the fact he'd loosed enough rope to hang himself, yet not caring enough to worry.

Clarence and Sy exchanged glances, both wondering what had possessed them to take a priest duck hunting. Clarence looked down for a loose rock or something to kick at, anything to hide from the priest's shame that shrouded each of them.

The priest caught the gesture and shook his head. "Why don't you boys just accept it? I have." Both remained silent. "Look, just forget it. I'll buy you both a beer at the game."

"Sy's not going to be there," said Clarence, jumping on the chance to change the subject.

"What you got going on, Sy? Today's a day of rest you know." Since Sy didn't seem to hear, Dieckman repeated the question.

"Oh, we're talking about barbecuing with my daughter and the grandkid," Sy said absently and then resumed scanning the church doors for the gorgeous young blonde he'd stared at all through mass.

Chapter 3

Sy lived a mile north of St. Michael's church, where the Quiver River chewed away at a tall clay cutbank on the south slope of Enon Hill. The house sat in the middle of a five-acre rectangle off Eisenbath Road, a good eighth of a mile from the river's floodplain, resembling many of the surrounding properties except for a huge orchard out back. In the middle of the orchard an elaborate pigeon coop rose above the trees like a castle surrounded by green, rolling hills.

Inside the coop, the leader of a group of fifteen exotic roller pigeons lifted his feet one at a time, making three full circles in plain view of the others. The rest sat on suspended wooden dowels like students in a classroom, watching their leader go through his gyrations, bobbing their heads up and down as if ducking bullets. Here and there one would impatiently stretch its wings and resettle with a startled shiver. They hadn't made a flight since early that morning and were antsy for the signal to start another.

Seeing the others were pumped and ready to go, the black and white speckled leader leaned his head far over his back and waddled through the six-inch opening. After searching the sky for hawks, he flitted up to the roof with the rest of the flock following obediently. For five minutes they stood at attention in the spring sunshine, and except for subtle movements of a head or foot they could have been decoys. As if startled, they suddenly leapt into the wind, and for a moment the Sunday morning stillness was broken by the flapping of wings. From a distance, flying furiously as they robbed each other's air, it looked like someone had tossed confetti. Soon they were soaring well above the coop's steep, shingled roof, fifteen multi-colored pigeons flapping in unison higher and higher above the fruit trees, each a full wingspan apart and in perfect formation.

Three times they circled their own five-acre perimeter, over Sy's two-story, turn of the century, clapboard house, along the high ridge of multifloral rosebushes that separated Sy's yard from an old, converted schoolhouse, just short of the ballpark at the bottom of the hill to the east, then back over the richly scented orchard near the river. Where the yard got enough sun, they flew over tightly knitted zoysia grass, perfectly trimmed to look more like a living room carpet than a rural backyard. Viewed from high in the air, everything, from the finely clipped hedges marking the contour of the patio, to the blinding white pigeon coop, to the precise rows of fruit trees standing militarily in the middle of the lot, provided a sense of perfect order.

By the fourth lap the younger pigeons were growing impatient and began feinting the signal by cupping their wings ever so slightly, hoping the others would accept their lead. If one of them had the courage to take things just a step further, the rest would follow without hesitation. All were weary of flying in formation and were trembling, barely withstanding the anticipation of what was to come.

Finally, the leader pumped into a climb over an open patch of zoysia, then led the formation into a dive to pick up speed. Fifty feet above the ground he pulled up, and the entire column froze into a lazy stall. For an instant they floated backward, suspended at the pinnacle of a tight loop-de-loop. Suddenly they tumbled down like rain, end over end, spastically yet in perfect unison, until they all caught at once and swooped away in every direction, not three feet from the ground.

Soon the birds began to regroup, settling down one at a time onto the top of the coop, each returning from wherever its chaotic rush of adrenalin had taken it. By the time Sy and Darlene pulled into the driveway, all were accounted for and eager to perform again.

Seeing them take off, Sy grabbed Darlene by the sleeve of her new red blazer, playfully pulling her around the side of the house to watch the pigeons fly. Sy's black Labrador, Shorty, his muzzle gray with age, heaved himself up and limped after them. For the last six of his fifteen years the dog had suffered hip dysplasia, an ailment endemic to its breed. Sy raised him from a pup and named him after Leo "Shorty" Lenzenwiler, who at that time was running for circuit judge and had his poster slapped across every telephone pole in the county.

"C'mon, Darlene, or we're going to miss it."

"Sy Todd, I've seen those damn stupid pigeons of yours do that a thousand times, day in and day out while you're at work," said Darlene, stumbling around the house behind Sy, trying to keep to the slabs of slate that formed a footpath to the patio.

"But this is going to be a good one, Darlene. I can tell. C'mon."

As a boy, Sy loved nothing more than tending to wild, exotic pets. At thirteen, the creatures in his basement consisted of a six-foot blacksnake in a fifty-five-gallon aquarium, a small brown bat, which unknown to Sy was slowly beating itself to death against its bird cage every night, a flying squirrel which shared much the same fate, and a large box of five baby skunks he'd found sleeping in a log. At sixty-three his "rollers" were living, soaring proof that the boy had never completely left the man. Each time the exotic, colorful birds lifted off to perform their bizarre aerobatics it filled him with exhilaration, as if he himself were up in the sky soaring along beside them.

"Why would I want to see it again?" asked Darlene. After she spoke, she paused to leap clumsily onto another slate. "They're just silly old birds with brains the size of a pea. Dumber than chickens. You'll never see a chicken try and commit suicide. The dumbest things chickens do is pick at each other's butts."

Sy smiled, knowing from her tone she was enjoying his high spirits too. It was always like that after church on Sunday, the feeling of having something over and done with—the brief, lighthearted sensation of completed self-sacrifice. Sy took her by the hand, pleasantly amused when she allowed herself to be led through the gate like a girl on a date.

"At least you can eat chickens. These things are only good for flying over your head and turning everything into the bottom of a bird cage. I wouldn't mind getting a big ol' Tomcat to take care of 'em, but they'd probably just crap on it too. If they were chickens, we could eat 'em. I'd be afraid to eat one of these filthy things. After dinner I'd probably lay down in front of the TV and start flopping over backward. A bird isn't supposed to flop until you whack its head off. I bet if you whacked their heads off, they'd just lay there. That's an idea, Sy. Why don't I go into the kitchen, get the butcher knife and you whack all their heads off?"

Sy glanced back, grinning at her playfulness—a pleasant change.

"And let go of my arm," she said, too coquettishly for a woman her age. "I'm not a little girl you have to force into doing anything! It's usually me having to lead you by the hand just to get you out of the house. In fact, tonight we should go out and have a nice dinner. I don't have anything thawed, and if you want to eat at home, you'll need to get back in the car and go to the store."

Sy stopped so abruptly that Darlene had to dodge around him to prevent a collision. In so doing she completely missed the next stone and stabbed the damp zoysia up to the hilt of both high heels. Before she could pull her legs free the rollers finished their stall and plummeted end for end, as if their spines had simultaneously broken. All but one peeled off at the last minute, and the one that didn't hit the ground with a dull, resonant thump. Having knocked itself senseless, it got up, staggered around blindly, then flew weakly to the section of gutter just above Darlene's wrought-iron patio chair, which it promptly desecrated.

"You and your damn crazy pigeons," muttered Darlene.

Chapter 4

"You're sure in a changeable mood today," said Darlene.

"How do you mean, Salome?" asked Sy, stopping what he was doing to direct a blank look at her. Darlene once claimed that her mother had pulled her name from the Bible, and when Sy was in a teasing mood, he would speculate on how her mother may have chosen differently.

Darlene turned her head as if she'd heard an off-color joke that wasn't supposed to be laughed at. She didn't want Sy to have the pleasure of seeing her smile and reached way over for another tomato to cover the dodge.

"First you're sober as a judge, and now you're like a big ol' teddy bear. After church you didn't have two words to say to nobody. When you did it was a snide comment." She carefully sliced the middle section out of another tomato, measured it against the top of the hamburger bun until satisfied it would fit perfectly, then pushed what was left over to Sy, who was shoving leftover tomato parts into his mouth as fast as she discarded them. Like most everyone else he knew, Sy came from humble beginnings, and even though he could now easily afford to be less frugal, the sight of waste of any kind caused the teeth on one side of his mouth to clamp down until he did something to change things. Today, all he could think of doing was to eat tomato scraps.

Sy had to swallow three times before answering his wife. His first attempt at a response looked like a bird tipping back to swallow a large worm.

"Yug guh yug guh guh yug," mimicked Darlene, without troubling to look up from her cutting board.

"Just tired of talking about baseball I guess," Sy stammered. "That's all those guys want to do."

"Sy Todd, if there was ever a man who couldn't tire of talking baseball it'd be you. I've heard so much baseball living with you I'd like to throw up. All my life I dreamed of the chance to throw out the first pitch and turn around and fire it way up over the bleachers."

"I don't talk baseball around you. Only with the guys."

"Try and tell me you and Pete Turner were talking about canning peaches," she said, carefully sliding the knife into the heart of another tomato.

"That's what I said, Delilah, only with the guys." Sy paused to curl his tongue up after a piece of tomato skin lodged in the gap between two back molars, and as he did, Darlene reached over and with one swipe of the knife swept Sy's pile of hoarded tomato parts into the garbage disposal.

The truth was Sy seldom talked baseball. And never in a conversation that included Darlene, since she seemed annoyed that he had once been a star pitcher. Though, depending on him for everything, she resented being in the shadow of a capable man. Whenever the conversation wasn't about her, she grew impatient and rudely changed the subject, even if the talk had been brisk. On occasions when Darlene's medication was off or the moon was full, or her hormones were erupting, or the mood just hit her, she would wade through social situations like a toddler on a rampage and relished saying the wrong thing. She then let Sy patch up any verbal wreckage.

As usual, it was easier to let Darlene believe she was right. Feigning deference, Sy asked what he could do to help with dinner.

"Turn off the potatoes and start cutting them. Square cubes for the potato salad. Exactly one inch."

"What's wrong with rectangles, my Jezebel?"

"Squares mix better."

"We'll tell Charlotte we made rectangles just for her."

"She'd believe you. She'd believe anything you tell her."

"That's why I turned grandpa. To have little girls believe everything I tell them."

"You've got all three of your girls in the palm of your hand," Darlene said. Then as an afterthought she added, "And probably others I don't even know about." The thought of Sy cheating on her set Darlene to purposefully make a few passes too many with the paprika, immediate vengeance for the years of flirtations that suddenly were as apparent as the nose on her face. Sy paid no attention as usual but fell to cutting potatoes a bit longer on one side, so just about anyone would have trouble calling them either squares or rectangles.

When Sy thought about it he decided yes, he was feeling pretty good. He enjoyed his daughter's company and looked forward to her visits. Having adored her as a child he'd grown to respect her as an adult. She was intelligent, understanding, attractive, and to Sy's relief, had turned into one of the most rational women he knew. The two of them could sit for hours and never run out of things to talk about. For as close as they were, Sy always watched for signs of her mother's neurotic behavior, which by all accounts started around Mercy's age. If it were up to Sy, he'd have had a whole passel of kids like Mercy. He was one of eleven siblings, and knew big families formed solid foundations. But Darlene had nixed that idea straightaway.

The doorbell rang just as he began stirring the potato salad. Darlene took the spoon and surprised him with an affectionate kiss on the cheek.

"There's the doorbell, Sahib. Go greet the rest of your harem."

Sy opened the door and blinked twice, as if discovering a couple Jehovah's Witnesses handing out pamphlets.

"I'm sorry, but we don't need any little girls today."

At sixty-three Sy felt like a stud horse that had only recently been put out to pasture. He knew he still had it in him but for some reason life wasn't giving him any more chances. His light-brown hair grew thick and since he kept it short, showed very little gray. He had steel-blue eyes that could stop a screaming child dead in his tracks, and when he moved there was still a subtle elasticity that made other men his age feel self-conscious around him. He knew he wasn't as fit as he used to be, yet he still weighed what was correct for his height, a tad over six feet. In combination with his weathered good looks and self-possessed charm he was still able to pull appreciative glances from women half his age.

Outside by the grill, Sy took pleasure in mentally sizing up the heat produced by the glowing charcoal. Using wood-handled tongs that were five fathers' days old he distributed the coals according to his formula—thirty coals for seven burgers, four apiece plus the extra two for Darlene's medium well. After making his final placement, the glass patio door slid open behind him, slamming into its frame like a guillotine. Mercy rushed through, carrying the tray of Darlene's identical half-pound burgers, plus two cans of beer.

"I've done five hundred barbecues with that woman, and she still manages to piss me off every single time," said Mercy, slamming the tray on the patio table as if covering a snake hole.

Sy and Mercy flashed each other the same sideways glance of co-martyrdom they had shared for years. "Good. You said it. Now we can have our barbecue," said Sy.

"Here's your beer," said Mercy. "You want to hear what she has me doing now?"

"Not especially."

It wasn't a question as much as a command to listen, and Mercy started right in. "She's in there washing each dish right after I use the damn thing."

"She just started that one. Keeps the kitchen from looking cluttered."

"But I feel like I got a contagious disease or something. A kitchen's supposed to be cluttered when you barbecue. That's what barbecue stands for in French, 'cluttered kitchen.'" Mercy watched her father grin and take a swig of beer. "She washed and put away the goddamn paring knife three times before I threatened to jab it in her neck if she didn't let me finish with it."

Mercy and Sy glugged beer as a sign of unity. After all these years dealing with Darlene, saying the words was no longer necessary. Sy thought by now Mercy should know that. Darlene was who she was, and neither of them was going to change her. Adulthood left Mercy with strong convictions that seemed to require vocalizing; in that way she was a little like her mother. Later the glass door slid again, and Darlene stepped out onto the patio wearing a suffering look. She brushed back a lock of dyed red hair with her forearm, exhaling loudly.

"All set in here, Sy. Ready when you are."

"We've got time to take a walk down to the orchard before I put the burgers on."

"I'm so exhausted I should probably just sit down."

"C'mon, Mom… we're taking a walk through the goddamned orchard," said Mercy.

It was the Sunday after Easter, and walking through the fragrant orchard with his granddaughter unsteadily leading the procession, the abstraction Sy felt earlier that morning all but disappeared. In its place he discovered a sense of calm euphoria. His wife and daughter had forgotten the scene in the kitchen and were chatting away like the best of friends.

The first tree to inspect was a Yellow Delicious, standing much larger and a full length in front of the other reds.

"Yellow Delicious," said Sy, greeting the tree by making "yellow" sound more like "hello."

Their approach awakened Shorty, who'd fallen asleep in the dust beneath the tree's low-hanging limbs. Now half awake, the old dog's first inclination was to roll over on his back, spread his legs and expose himself. His tail beat the dust as a sign he was so very pleased to see them.

"No thanks, Shorty," said Sy. "You want some of that Darlene?"

"None today," she said, laughing.

"Mercy?"

"Dad, you're disgusting!"

The old dog took a slow, upside-down look around and rolled back onto his side.

They inspected every tree in the orchard. As they walked, they could hear the crack of the bats below the hill, plus some of the more voluble chatter as the teams warmed up.

Rounding the last of the six cherry trees making up the back row of the orchard, they found themselves face-to-face with the white pigeon coop. Due to its size and detailed construction it looked like a carriage house on ten-foot stilts. Sy considered it almost elegant. Everyone else thought it vulgar. Wrapped in white siding that matched the house, its south-facing wall was hinged, folding halfway down like a roadside vegetable stand. Sy had added windows with cypress-green shutters that opened and shut. At either end, just under the roofline were two six-inch exit holes. The eastern exit opened to a wide wooden portico with four Corinthian columns stretching down to the coop's base. The westward opening offered only a flat twelve-inch plank which served as a landing pad, and since it provided more space for maneuvering, became the preferred entrance. The entire structure was finished in gold trim, which inspired Darlene to dub it the Taj Ma Pigeon. Sy called it Wallenda, after The Flying Wallendas.

At the sight of the coop Charlotte lit up, ran over and embraced one of the metal legs.

"Girl, get away from there before one of those dodo birds poops on you," said Darlene.

"Mom, she's okay, they're all gone now anyway. Besides, pigeons don't 'poop' on you… pigeons shit on you. Whoever heard of pigeon poop. It's shit, pigeon shit."

"Well excuse me for being a lady," said Darlene, running to rescue her granddaughter. "Mrs. Potty Mouth," she added, coming back with the struggling Charlotte.

"Did you hear that?" said Mercy, turning to Sy in feigned disbelief. "She called me a potty mouth."

It amazed Sy how fast it could happen, this transition from nice and cordial to the two of them spitting like cats. When he thought of their relationship it saddened him. He felt two people who couldn't take a firm position on how to treat one another didn't know each other well enough. Then maybe he was the only one in the world who could really know Darlene. Well, he tried stopping the roller coaster before. It was better just riding it out. Intervention wasn't necessary until things rounded the corner and turned bitter.

"My pigeons don't poop," he said, refusing to let go of his high spirits.

"Poop poop poop," said Charlotte into her grandmother's ear.

"They sure eat a lot of ground corn for birds who don't pass anything," said Darlene. She looked up at the coop, now framed against a clear, blue sky. "And that thing is such an eyesore."

"Mom, you can barely see it from the house. And besides, it's got a certain... character to it." Mercy turned away from her father to hide her grin. She accidently caught her mother's eye, which got her going too, and for a while they both had to stare at the ground. With this simple act of sharing a joke on the ever-august Sy, they again became civil.

"The rollers like it and that's what counts," said Sy. "There's a guy over in Shelbina who lost his whole flock because of his coop. They just up and left."

"What would cause that to happen?" asked Mercy. "I wouldn't want to be around here if that happened to you."

"I think they just didn't like the arrangement. For one thing the coop was too low to the ground, and there were too many lines running above it. They didn't feel safe, so they left. Flew the coop."

"But don't you think maybe you overdid it, Dad? Just a little?"

"A whole lot if you ask me," said Darlene. "The only thing he forgot was a toilet. If they had one maybe they wouldn't..." Darlene hesitated, looking over at her daughter.

"Shit," said Mercy quickly.

"...all over my patio furniture. When he starts putting up Christmas lights, that's when I call the neighbors and get them to complain. If anyone else built that thing he'd be laughing at it too." For a moment the four of them stood in front of Wallenda, each to their own thoughts, staring up at the raised coop as if it were Olympus.

"It's time to go back and put on the burgers," said Sy, refusing to take any more abuse.

Walking back to the patio he, too, had to ask himself why. He already had a perfectly good coop for them. Then he tore it down and built this monstrosity. It wasn't like him to give something more effort than it deserved. Sure, he was a perfectionist. But that was okay because such drive benefitted the man who could clearly see what was enough and what was too much. For some reason he'd lost that clear vision, as well as the self-control that went with it. The thoughts he had about that woman in church. He never allowed himself to go so far. It seemed repugnant now and caused him to be quiet through most of dinner.

"Here. Here's another rectangle, see? See, Mercy?" said Darlene, positioning the offending spud on her spoon, holding it up to Mercy's face as proof. "I specifically told your father squares, and look what I get."

"Drop it, Mom."

"He does it out of spite. I specifically asked for one-inch squares."

"Did you hear that? A home run I'll bet," Sy said suddenly. Resting his knife and fork hands on the edge of the table, he twisted his head toward the crowd noise coming from the ballpark below the hill. "Did you hear that crack? You could tell it was outta there by the way it sounded coming off the bat."

"Who do you think was up?" asked Mercy, happy that her father was talking again. She and her mother had been clicking along well enough, but she always looked to her father when she wanted a conversation of any substance.

"Had to be Gilmore, because what you just heard, ladies and ladies, was a home-town crowd."

"That's one I would've loved to have seen," said Mercy. She stopped eating and looked at her father as if he were a famous painting.

"I can't believe it's still going on. Must be six o'clock by now," said Sy solemnly, doing a poor job of acting disinterested for the sake of the dinner. "Definitely extra innings."

"Definitely extra innings," said Darlene, bending over to Mercy sarcastically.

"Definitely extra innings," Mercy repeated to her daughter in the same manner. Charlotte bent and garbled something vaguely similar to the left of her highchair.

"One of the Jerling boys would be my bet."

"Which one, Dad? Lenny or Bernie?"

"Lenny. Since coming back from that year in college Bernie's been in a slump."

"He's in a slump? What would cause a person like Bernie Jerling to go into a slump?"

"I don't know. A guy lets his guard down I guess."

Darlene said nothing but deftly laid another incriminating piece of potato onto Sy's plate. At the same time little Charlotte sent a perfectly square one whizzing past Sy's ear.

There was another faint crack, this time with no crowd noise to accompany it. Only a few long honks from a couple of cars. Sy turned from the table and listened.

"Well, something must have happened to him at that college," said Mercy, staring at Sy, waiting for him to say something profound.

"Pete Turner would probably say he's doing drugs."

"If he is, it could be an effect of his slump and not the cause," said Mercy, who was not a big advocate of drugs but was no stranger to them either. "You never had a slump, did you, Dad?"

"Enough to know they're easier slipping into than they are getting out of."

"What do you expect to know about drugs?" asked Darlene, who could delude herself into believing that her daughter was as innocent as her granddaughter.

Mercy ignored her and said, "But what caused you yourself to go into a slump?"

"No idea."

"It must not have been too bad. I don't expect guys who make it into the Hall of Fame ever fell too far." With that thought Mercy put down her fork, relaxed back into her chair and paused, staring at her father adoringly.

Sy only grunted.

"Don't talk about it or it'll go to his head," said Darlene. "Besides, it's only for Gilmore County. Pass the salad over here, will you?"

Now Mercy turned her stare onto her mother, and it registered disbelief. "Mom, Gilmore County is the hottest baseball county in the state, if not the whole Midwest. Abner Doubleday would have ended up moving here. And so what if it goes to his head? He has a right to be proud. I know I am." Mercy looked at her father, and her face flushed.

To take his mind off what was happening down the hill Sy began to clear the table. Mercy saw through the move immediately and because she loved him with all her heart, she gave up trying to hold him.

"Dad, maybe you better go down and find out what's happening."

He feigned indifference for ten minutes as they cleared the dishes, when suddenly the crowd let loose another roar. At that point he walked into the kitchen, announcing that well, maybe he would walk down just for a minute and see what was going on. Heck, if the game lasted much longer, they'd have to turn the lights on. Still acting disinterested, he slowly ambled over to the refrigerator and got himself a beer to go.

Thirty seconds later Mercy ran out onto the patio, still carrying the plate she'd been drying.

"I expect a full report!" she yelled after her father, just as he disappeared behind the big Yellow Delicious, almost at a trot.

Darlene and Mercy were sitting in the kitchen three hours later, and Sy was still not back. They were anxious to see him sauntering back up the hill, if for different reasons. Mercy feared she would have to leave without saying goodbye, since her job as buyer for Burcell's youth department required her to jump up fresh at six a.m. Darlene simply couldn't bear being left alone.

"Just wait around for one more coffee."

"No more coffee," said Mercy, anxiously looking out the window into the darkness beyond. "I won't sleep."

Turning back, she pulled her saucer away just in time to keep more coffee from sluicing into her cup. Darlene wasn't as fast and poured a shallow brown lake onto the vinyl tablecloth.

"Mercedes Jean Todd, this is decaffeinated coffee. And if you pull that stunt again, I'll pop this lid off and pour it all in your lap. What would your father think of that, eh?" Darlene ran to the counter for the dishrag then began wiping at the table, wearing a scowl that would freeze water. Whenever she wanted to make a legitimate threat, she would wield Sy's name like a verbal truncheon, and not only with her daughter.

"Coffee's coffee, Mom. And my name's not Todd anymore."

"This is coffee. It just doesn't have caffeine, sweetheart. And if you don't want to consider yourself your father's daughter that's up to you." She spoke in a way that was overly patient, as if talking to Charlotte, which infuriated Mercy, since patience coming from Darlene was the same as sarcasm. Her mother knew that to get to Mercy she only needed to act like she was lecturing a two-year-old. It was an old formula, and it always worked.

"Decaffeinated coffee is the biggest marketing fallacy our capitalist society's overzealous, paranoid, superficial, boot-licking marketing 'wizards' have ever conjured," Mercy said, heating up more as she spoke. She found her mother's implied accusation concerning family loyalty doubly annoying and spoke rapidly, clipping each word as it shot from her mouth.

"One. They say decaf coffee is 97 percent caffeine-free. I can't prove otherwise, so I'll grant you that. Two. Regular coffee is 90 percent caffeine-free. So yes, there is less caffeine, but more than you think. It's all semantics. If the government tries to clear up the confusion, they eventually take the question to court, where a bunch of highfalutin', overpaid, dumbshit lawyers unleash whole bags of bullshit which so confuses the issue the judge eventually bangs the gavel, calls it an impasse, and gives the coffee people the benefit of the doubt. And half of America goes to bed clenching their teeth, staring at the ceiling with eyes as big as full moons."

"Don't drink it then," said Darlene in a retort as maddeningly inane as Mercy's was pedantic. "And I didn't start calling you Todd again until after you divorced Charlotte's father."

"Mom, *Jeff* divorced *me*."

"Because you always wanted to drive the bus. At least that's what your father says. Which proves you're just like him."

"You can call me Todd again when I change my name back."

"You going to do that?"

"Maybe. I would love to be Todd again. But I'm not crazy about having a name different than Charlotte's."

"You might remarry."

"If I become Todd again, I'm staying Todd."

"Whatever. The thing is, you're still young. You still have that Betty Boop thing going."

"What do you mean, Betty Boop? Who the hell is Betty Boop?"

"A cartoon character from the thirties and forties. She looked like a flapper."

"I look like a cartoon character?"

"Short. Skinny. Round face. Big blue eyes. Your father's curly black hair, but darker—more like *his* father's, actually. And *my* boobs."

"We did get lucky in that department."

"It must be jelly, cause jam don't shake like that!"

"Mom! Jesus."

"That's what they said about Betty Boop. My point is, guys should still be attracted to you."

"If I didn't always want to drive the bus."

"I'm sure there's someone out there."

"Mom, I'm fine."

"I know."

For five minutes they sat in silence, not knowing where to take the conversation. Finally, Mercy returned to the subject of her father.

"Well, Dad's probably enjoying himself down there. All his buddies are there and they're probably having a beer or two," said Mercy, more uncomfortable with her father's continued absence than having to hand victory to her mother by speaking first.

"He should have been back an hour ago," said Darlene, sniffing and wiping at her nose affectedly.

"It was a big game. Takes a while to wind down from those suckers."

"Well anyway, when he gets here be as nice to him as you can," said Darlene. "Ever since he's been thinking of retiring, he's been acting a little funny."

"What does acting a little funny mean?"

"Oh, just funny."

"Now come on… funny how?"

"Didn't you notice how quiet he got at dinner all the sudden?"

"Yeah, but he was thinking about the game."

"It's not like him to change like that. Now he does it a lot. He just hasn't been himself lately."

On that score Darlene could be right, thought Mercy. If her father was doing anything so out of the ordinary that Darlene could notice, there may be something to it. Her father was usually a regular Gibraltar when it came to anything mental. "What's the matter with him?"

"Oh, nothing really."

"What do you mean nothing really. First you tell me he's been acting funny, then you tell me he isn't himself... now come on, is he wearing your underwear or what?"

"Well… something like that..."

"What, what? 'Something like that.' Tell me what you mean 'Something like that.'"

"Well… he..."

"WHAT for crying out loud!"

"Well, he... he's getting all hung up about sex." Having said it, Darlene raised her left shoulder and began rubbing her cheek with it.

"What, you ain't doing the nasty for him?" Mercy looked straight at her mother and smiled broadly.

Darlene raised her head, giving Mercy a smoldering look. "No. It's not that. It's not that at all." Darlene looked down at the table, reconsidering. "Well maybe it's some of that, but it isn't all."

"So, what is it then?"

"Your father's starting to notice other women. A lot. We'll be driving down the street or somewhere, and the durn fool turns completely around to stare at some whore in a short skirt. Or we'll be at the checkout line in the grocery store, and I'll catch him looking at the damn Cosmo."

Mercy tried not to, but her smile automatically changed to a tight smirk. "You callin' Dad a horn-dog?"

Darlene shot another look across the table. Again, she looked down before speaking, strumming her fingers slowly against her coffee cup. "More and more it's some young thing. He'll look at some young girl and get this real serious expression on his face. Sometimes I swear they can't be more than fourteen years old. Now that, that just isn't natural."

This time Mercy laughed out loud. "Mid-life crisis, Mom," she said. "Most men get it when they're fifty. Consider yourself lucky." Mercy picked up her coffee cup, chuckling through a quick sip.

"Yeah… but that isn't all of it either."

Suddenly Mercy didn't like the tone of Darlene's voice. She gently set her cup back down, took a heavy breath and said, "Okay, what?"

"He's taken to walking around the house naked," said Darlene in a rush. Mercy paused with her mouth open, watching the red rise from her mother's neckline, past her nose and on to the top of her forehead before laughing hysterically.

"Mom... it's all right for husbands to walk around their own house naked. I mean Jesus Christ..."

"I'll come around the corner into the kitchen, and there he'll be, looking at me in his birthday suit. He only does it every so often."

"See. There you go."

"But I gotta tell you, there's something strange about it." Darlene crumpled a napkin in her hand, then looked away as if there was something interesting on top of the stove.

"Tell me," said Mercy.

"Whenever he does it, and I mention it the next day, he doesn't remember it."

Mercy said nothing, reaching across the table for the pack of cigarettes in her purse.

"You'd think it'd have something to do with this preoccupation with sex business," said Darlene, growing a little bolder, a little relieved at finally being able to speak. "But it doesn't."

"What makes you say that?" Mercy bit the thumbnail of the same hand that held her cigarette.

"We don't do sex anymore. Not really… I've even tried."

Now it was Mercy's turn to blush. Talking so blatantly about her mother and father doing the act was like hearing a nun fart. Thinking about it objectively, Mercy could see her mother being a little difficult when it came to putting out, but she couldn't imagine her father refusing when her mother was up for it. Her mother might be crazy, but she was still an attractive woman. For a long while both mother and daughter sat in silence, each contemplating what life would be like if Sy wasn't Sy. For Darlene it would mean leaping from Sy to Mercy, like a flea who realizes its incumbent host has nothing left to offer. For Mercy it meant she would never stop crying.

"I hope he's not in a slump," said Mercy finally, looking back out the window into the darkness. "I've never seen Dad in a slump before."

Chapter 5

Shortly after eleven, Darlene sat alone at the kitchen table drinking a glass of warm milk. Mercy had been gone an hour, and Sy still wasn't home. Darlene's thoughts pulled back and forth, alternating between anger over Sy's continued absence and an increasing fear that he might never return. She breathed an inward sigh of relief when she heard him come in through the back door, pass through the hallway, and rush upstairs to the bedroom. She resisted an impulse to follow him, and now that he had come home the tide of anger flowed back in and held. Just as she was about to call out, she again heard his footsteps on the stairs. He walked into the kitchen, just as he had thousands of times before, the only difference being that now he was naked down to a pair of socks.

As was her habit, Darlene had every light in the kitchen on, and the blast of neon reflected off Sy's body like sun bleached sculpture. Like a lot of ancient sculpture a few parts seemed to be missing, and in Sy's case it was his arms and head. Sixty-three years of farmer tan caused his arms and head to be darker than the rest of his body, which reflected no color at all, like the translucent white of a fish's belly.

Sy was at the age where people looked better in their clothes than out of them. He still weighed the 175 pounds he had carried most of his life, but where before his physique was muscular, he now sagged where muscle had been. The thick mat of hair on his wide, well-developed chest had long ago turned a grayish white. Where before his stomach rippled it now waved, each wave overlapping the other until ending in a lipid round of flab just above the groin.

Unaccustomed to the glare, Sy stepped back into the hall until the door jamb shielded his face from the hundred-watt bulbs. When Sy ducked into the shadows Darlene's fear returned. Unable to see his face, she was no longer looking at her husband but a stranger who'd come to do harm. When it happened before it was different, and she'd chalked it up to a nascent streak of lechery. What worried her now was the realization it was not that at all, had nothing to do with being a prelude to sex, or even the flirtatious result of too many beers. It was something else. Something she could not begin to imagine.

The only defense Darlene had against anything so bizarre was suppressing the fact it was there. Without saying a word, which she couldn't have done if she wanted to, she slowly turned her back on Sy and bent to take another sip from her warm milk. Before it even touched her lips the glass began sloshing and instead of her mouth it went to her chin, slipped through her fingers, and fell to the table. Then she simply froze, not having the strength to turn back and face him, and for a while she occupied her vision by focusing on a blue violet from the wallpaper, then allowing it to go slowly out of focus. Soon she again heard the soft, even creaking of the living room stairs.

The evolutionary explanation for fear is self-preservation. But Darlene's brief spike almost killed her. Never mind that Sy was naked. She'd seen Sy naked many times. But this time, even with his face in shadow, she saw the lack of expression she'd missed twice before.

For that one instant she recognized her little brother's sweaty, torpid stare just before scarlet fever took him out of her life forever.

Darlene got out of her chair, pulled the stool from the closet, hoisted herself up over the refrigerator, and reached into the sanctified space she and Sy dubbed the liquor cabinet. By her third tumbler of Dewar's, she had tilted the balance enough to make any further shock to her system negligible. Darlene felt the whiskey take over the way the smell of a freshly lit cigar rolls through a room. She felt its warmth flow down her throat and gather in the pit of her stomach before pouring into her arms and legs. After a moment to adjust, the lids of her eyes lowered, like a bull that finally separates the red cape from the surrounding confusion. As quickly as the alcohol dispelled her fear, she lost any doubt as to the reason behind Sy's actions. Darlene was convinced the entire event was a premeditated attack, a secret diversionary tactic passed on from one generation of testicles to the next. Nothing more than an attempt at fashioning a well-subjugated housewife by keeping her weak and guessing. It was clear she had to strike back, putting an end to this testosterone-fueled behavior before it went any further.

Sy came back to himself, and, realizing Darlene had just seen him naked in the kitchen, he rushed into the shower—the quickest way for a man to feel comfortable unclothed, in addition to being the best excuse he had at the time. When he emerged, wrapped in their largest towel, Darlene was sitting on the edge of the bed, waiting for him. As soon as she saw it was the old Sy walking back into the room, back to normal except for the way he would not raise his eyes above her knees, she understood the tactic needed next.

Whereas Sy's eyes had appeared dull and glazed, Darlene's narrowed, showering sparks like a welder's iron. Her mouth didn't seem to be working properly, and three times she had false starts. Finally, after enough stuttering and stammering to make Sy think she'd taken to speaking in tongues, it all blasted out as: "WHAT THE HELL WAS THAT!"

She'd found one of Mercy's cigarettes lying on the kitchen table and lit up. Since it had been years since she'd quit, the slow curl of smoke rising around her beet-red face warned Sy this was a moment to worry about. Darlene's anger he could deal with, but what he was witnessing now transcended anger. It was a critically unstable constitution unable to adjust to a dreadful unknown. For Sy it was worse knowing he wasn't exactly resting on terra firma himself. He had absolutely no idea why he'd done what he'd done, and for the first time in his life he felt confused and helpless.

"HERE! PUT ON YOUR FUCKING PAJAMAS!" she screamed, hurling them so they struck Sy full in the chest.

Shit, she said fuck, thought Sy. He hurriedly picked up his pajamas, turned his back on his wife, and yanked them on. Twice he crossed himself up and almost fell as he struggled to slide his feet into the pantlegs.

"I'M UP TO YOUR TRICKS! DON'T THINK I DON'T KNOW WHAT YOU'RE DOING!"

Just ride it out, thought Sy. *Don't even try to say anything yet.*

"WE DON'T DO THAT IN THIS HOUSE, SY TODD! WE DON'T PLAY MIND GAMES HERE! YOU WANT TO GET THE BEST OF ME, YOU CAN JUST SMACK ME IN THE FACE OR BREAK MY ARM LIKE ANY RESPECTABLE WIFE BEATER! Walking around with all our parts hanging out whenever we damn well please! What's gotten into you? That, that thing I saw downstairs... that's not the man I married! Nice women don't marry men like that! And I'm a good woman, Sy Todd. Too good for the likes of you!"

Sy found it odd that, whenever she got this upset, she acted as if they were just married, even though it'd been thirty-five years since they were newlyweds. Throughout Darlene's harangue he feigned submission. It helped to focus on an area just a bit above Darlene's beltline.

"I COULD HAVE MARRIED ANYONE I CHOSE! But I had to choose you... just because you had a bright FUCKING smile and could pretend you were a lot better than anybody else. YOU'RE NOT FOOLING ANYBODY, SY! AND I KNEW IT ALL THE TIME! I'M NOT THE CRAZY ONE IN THIS FAMILY. YOU ARE!" As she stood next to the bed, her body contorted, as if slowly being impaled by a rod running from her left shoulder to her right hip. With each pause for breath her mouth curled up in misery, a helpless, uncontrollable movement that made Sy's heart thump against his ribs. Sy took a tentative step toward her.

"NO! You stay away from me!"

Cautiously, Sy took another step forward, and she began screaming; wrenching, ear-piercing screeches of the insane. She then stopped just as abruptly when Sy retreated to his spot in the bathroom doorway. She jerked her head as if something were in the window, and when Sy turned to look she ran at him, kicking his shin like a child, then tore back to her spot near the bed. While Sy held his smarting leg, she arched her back and began snarling and hissing at him like a cornered cat, and it occurred to Sy he'd finally lost her. Soon her demons subsided, and a smile came to her lips. When she began to speak again, it came out soft and ironic, like patronizing a child. An electric chill went through Sy's entire body. The voice didn't seem to be hers.

"Mother always said don't marry a man you can outstare. And I can outstare you, Sy." For an instant she locked onto his face, then quickly drew her eyes away. "I always could, and you know it. The only man I couldn't outstare was my father, and if he were here now, he'd have you walking a path so straight it'd rub the skin off the inside of your legs." Then in a dizzyingly mad rush, she returned from wherever it was she'd gone.

"AT LEAST MAYBE THAT WOULD KEEP YOU FROM PULLIN' YOUR GODDAMN PANTS OFF WHEREVER AND WHENEVER YOU DAMN PLEASE!"

Just don't run to your sister, thought Sy. *Don't run to your sister again. I can stand anything… just don't run to your sister*. Darlene was working herself up, and Sy knew any moment there would be too much stress on the old fault line.

"JUST ANSWER ME ONE THING… ANSWER ME ONE THING, AND TELL ME WHAT THIS IS ALL ABOUT!" By the tone of her voice Sy knew it was still too soon to answer anything.

"IS IT A KICK? A big kick, Sy? Life with Darlene getting too boring, Sy? Well look! Look at this...I can do kicks too!" Darlene tore off her silk blouse, pulling it past her elbows. She then fumbled with her bra for what seemed like an eternity before forcing a thumb under the front and snapping it off.

"SEE! LOOK AT ME, SY! I got kicks too! Look at me, Sy," said Darlene. She sat on the bed, put both hands behind her and shook her large, sagging breasts rapidly from side to side. Seeing Sy glance painfully away, she fell to the bed and broke down, purging what remained of her delirium with wave upon wave of convulsive grief.

Sy rushed forward to catch her in his arms, and started issuing the placid, soporific homilies that always eventually brought Darlene back.

Finally, she spoke again, but while she did her chest caught several times, heaving for breath. "Thu, thu, there are plenty... huh... huh... huh... of times I want to see you naked, Sy," blubbered Darlene. "Just don't scare me like that."

"It's okay, honey. It's okay, sweetheart. Everything's going to be okay."

"And just wh... wh... where the hell have you been?"

Later, after Sy found her pills and sedated her, Darlene settled down enough to prepare for bed and even surprised Sy by wearing her two-piece satin pajamas instead of her horrible floor-length flannels, her granny pj's. As she lay on her side, both arms tucked girlishly under her pillow, she was content to watch Sy turn the pages of his book under the reading lamp. It was the only light on in the entire house, and after the stress of the night they were both reluctant to turn it off.

"Sy?"

"Yeah?"

"You were just trying to play one of your silly jokes on me, weren't you?"

Sy turned and gave her his most assuring smile. "I guess I probably overdid it this time."

"Yeah, you sure did," she said dreamily.

"Sy?"

"Yeah?"

"You must be getting old. You used to know just when it was time to reel me in with one of your jokes. You'd set me up, and I'd take the bait just like that. Then I'd be a dumb fish just flopping on the bank."

"I think I was tired," said Sy, staring into his book.

"This time I think you overdid it, and I didn't flop at all. I just laid there real still."

The last made Sy inhale slightly, just silently enough so Darlene didn't hear.

"I won't do it again," said Sy.

"But don't stop reeling me in," said Darlene sleepily. "Please don't stop reeling me in. That's what I love about you and why I married you, the way you can reel me in whenever you want."

Slowly, with her face still toward Sy, her eyes began to close. "And do you know what I do for you?"

"What's that sweetheart?"

"I give you what it takes to want to do it. You see that, don't you?"

"Yes, I do."

Sleepily, as if in a dream, Darlene raised her arm, placing a hand on Sy's stomach. "I can make you feel like that now if you want."

Sy silently closed his book and lightly began to caress Darlene's face. She was as different from other women as a porpoise was different from a fish. She had the same basic streamlining and swam in the same sea, but that was about it.

He let his thoughts grow dim and unimportant, allowing for his subconscious safety valves to work, coating the charred, lacerated edges of his mind the way snow erases the memory of fire. For a while his thoughts came filtered, as through a fine grid that allowed only the most harmless of perceptions. The distant hum of the refrigerator in the kitchen below, the methodical, far-off tick of the grandfather clock in the living room, and Darlene's soft breathing as she drifted into sleep, became the only competition to perfect silence.

Soon his thoughts floated far away, and, like he had done over forty years ago, arrived on a rocky beach in the center of the Korean peninsula.

The day was unusually warm, but the sky was clear, and a light breeze blowing in from the bay chased tiny wavelets onto the rocks in a way that sounded pleasing. It had been a long time since he'd thought of Korea. When he landed there the first time it was during a fierce winter storm, and since the boats could only come in so far to avoid smashing into the rocks, he and his men had no choice but to jump in well over their heads and swim to shore. Sy involuntarily sucked in his breath as he remembered hitting the water, so cold it immediately stiffened a man, reducing swimming the twenty yards to shore to little more than washing in like driftwood. When they finally heaved themselves up onto the rocks only twelve of his original fourteen men had sounded off, and five minutes later he'd already forgotten the names of the two that didn't make it. He remembered little of what happened after that, aside from knowing he'd not been completely dry again for several days.

But this time he was quite alone among the rocks, and Sy felt pleased to have come back under such different circumstances. After so many years of repressing the memory, it was good to return and see the place had a much less violent side to it, and to know that he had in a small way contributed to its present innocence. He saw something moving beyond the rocks, down where the waves dissolved into a short stretch of sand.

Down the beach, walking toward him was a woman. As she came closer, he recognized her. The broad face, the high cheek bones with their daub of red against the creamy white… the wide, penetrating, coal-black eyes, and the single braid that divided her smooth, tawny back like ebony rope against porcelain was Su Lin's. She came up slowly, with her head down, until only five yards away she carefully raised her eyes to his and softly asked if he still loved her.

His mind took a sudden leap and now he was coming back from an all-night patrol. They were just entering the compound, and he was tired and hungry, and there was Su Lin bent low over a small fire, cooking his breakfast. It was early in the morning, and he knew she'd just come from preparing a meal for what remained of her own family, but still she looked fresh and warm and inviting. Soon she brought him a steaming bowl, handed it over gently, then stepped back and sank to her knees to watch him eat. As he dug into the food like a wild animal she knelt there, across from him, yet at the same time closer than any woman had ever come.

The scene changed again, and now he was back hidden among the rocks, high above a river where Su Lin was washing his clothes. She was bent far over, straddling two rocks, reaching straight down to rinse the soap she'd forced into the material. It was only after she'd finished that she straightened up, stretched languidly, and spotted him looking at her. She lowered her head in embarrassment, since it was considered bad form in that part of the world for a man to show a woman such flagrant attention.

She picked up the basket of clothes and started up the hill toward him. When she approached, he saw that it was no longer Su Lin but Darlene. It was a different Darlene, a younger Darlene, from a time when they had first met.

Su Lin was nothing like the woman who lay next to him now. It was nothing for her to get up well before sunrise and tend to her two elder brothers, her grandmother, and her baby sister before going off to the rice fields with her other relatives until dark. Darlene constantly complained she worked too hard keeping up the house for just the two of them, but then would turn around and complain just as vocally that she was bored and had nothing to do. Su Lin referred to him using a Korean word which meant loved one. Darlene had no qualms about calling him a dipshit. While Sy had seen Darlene burst into tears over a faulty garbage disposal, Su Lin once told him, in a voice without emotion to mark the importance of the telling, of how she had witnessed the mortar rip into the group of her mother, father and older brother while she lagged behind. Much later, she had burst into long, heart-wrenching sobs the day he went stateside.

He was young then and had trouble seeing anything from that foreign soil as being relative. At the time of his departure the reality of home had come crashing back in, consuming him in a way that left his relationship with Su Lin as foreign and meaningless as the language she spoke. She had changed him, turned him into more of a man than the war itself, and he had left her with no more emotion than someone kissing his mother before leaving for college. But now, for some reason he couldn't explain, she was back.

Were the two women really that different? Of course they were. He had needed something of himself to erode to marry a woman like Darlene. He'd succumbed to a simplistic way of handling relationships that didn't permit questioning anything. He had caved in, and in, and in, until finally he was too far in to allow a face-saving escape.

Maybe he'd gotten lazy in the way he approached Darlene. Maintaining what it took to win her had been a great challenge. After marrying her he quickly discovered she offered an even bigger one. Maybe she was finally wearing him down. Once, when it was only he and Clarence, Parkers bar and a dozen empty bottles between them, he slipped and mentioned divorce. Clarence agreed that Darlene must be a tussle, but there were some women who were worth it. They had shrugged it off by signaling Angie to bring another couple of salutes to Darlene.

Well, Darlene is Darlene, he thought. And to be Darlene is to be a little bit crazy. There were few men who could handle her. For him, judging the success of the relationship wasn't paranoia as much as a reflection of his own resolve in the mirror of her; like pressing the button on the fire alarm to see if things were still functioning. Admittedly, Darlene was what made things interesting and alive. She kept him knife-edge sharp.

Only now he seemed to be getting tired, and he shuddered to think what might happen if, with the weight of Darlene clinging desperately to his back, he was forced to lay down and rest.

Don't worry Darlene, he thought, bending to kiss his sleeping wife gently on the cheek. *I'm not that tired yet. And yes, I still love you*. Letting out a short sigh, he rolled halfway onto his side to turn out the light, then back around onto his stomach before falling straightaway to sleep.

Chapter 6

It was Sy's habit to get up early Monday mornings. He felt if a guy started strong the first day of work, the next four would come easier. By seven a.m. he'd finished his cereal, the dishes were washed, and his second cup of black coffee sat cooling on the table. Habitually, he dug away at his mouth with a toothpick while reading the sports section.

His intention was to slam his coffee and head for the office before Darlene began to stir, so there would be more distance between last night's incident and its inevitable autopsy. Sy wasn't ready to hash it out with Darlene yet, mainly because his own thoughts were none too clear. Since sitting down with the paper, he had to read entire paragraphs over three or four times before they conveyed any meaning at all.

Hearing stirrings from upstairs, he slammed the paper shut as it crossed his mind to bolt into the garage and speed away. No, it was already too late. He opened the paper again and settled back into the chair. He would greet Darlene casually, even though relaxed was not the way he'd describe himself. But after all the years with Darlene, acting casually in the face of stress was Sy's specialty. He heard the bedroom drawers close, the hallway floor creak in front of the bathroom door, a flushed toilet, and several minutes later Darlene appeared at the entrance to the kitchen.

"You gonna let me have a cup of that coffee, or did you only make enough for yourself again?" Sy looked up as if surprised to see her, then the surprise became genuine. He stared over his paper at the doorway for several seconds, trying to decide if what he was seeing was real.

"It may be too strong for you," he finally said.

As was usually the case after large doses of her medication, Darlene looked like hell. She'd spent two minutes wrapping her hair in some sheer fabric resembling cheesecloth, knotting it at the top of her forehead like a slovenly fishwife. It was what she did when she felt like feeding a depressed state, as if it were necessary for her physical appearance to be in sync with her current mental state. She wore an unflattering quilted housecoat buttoned up to the neck and clutched the lapels with both hands, as if protecting herself. With her face glazed from the night's deep sleep, she looked like an aging seal. She stared hard at Sy before her face fell slack, causing her creases to resemble a topographic map, with lines flowing down the sides of her mouth and closing around her lips from years of smoking. Sy took one look at those pursed lips and prepared for perdition.

He poured coffee for her into a stained mug, which she took before sitting across from him at the table.

"Clothes look nice on you," she said, burying her face in the cup. From the way she said it Sy couldn't tell if it was meant to compliment him for his suit and tie or be a dig about the events of last night. He resumed working away with the toothpick and stayed silent.

It was Darlene's rule that every question or comment between them required a response, even if it was only a grunt. When she saw Sy wasn't even going to do that much, she struck out instinctively, like a crippled snake. "You'd look nicer if you'd get that damn toothpick out of your mouth. It's disgusting."

They sat across from each other quietly, aloof like two dogs approaching a ham bone. Sy reached for the newspaper, pretending to read, feeling the chill of Darlene's stare penetrate the paper. For a while the only sounds in the kitchen were caused by drinking coffee and the humming fridge. Then Sy heard a quick intake of breath, and here it came.

"You wouldn't want to talk to your wife this morning, would you?"

Sy lowered his paper to look over at Darlene. "I'm sorry, sweetheart. What would you want to talk about?"

Darlene gave an affected sniff. "Oh, I don't know. Playing marbles. Canning pickles. American League baseball stats."

"Okay, what's Orel Hershiser's era?" Sy said it with a smile, trying to bring her around.

"Oh, stop it. Just stop it right now."

Sy looked up and saw the puffiness closing in around her eyes. The whites were shot through with a red filigree.

"I've noticed you're starting to look fat." When she spoke, she turned her head as if talking to the refrigerator, and it again occurred to Sy she could be referring to the night before.

"I may have put on a few pounds."

"You used to never be fat. You're getting old." Darlene sniffed and continued to look at the refrigerator. "And you're drinking too much."

The fog in Sy's head verified her last comment, and the coffee was not doing much to clear it. He nodded in agreement but lifted an eyebrow in a way that signaled he was only placating. He appeared to go back to his newspaper. Impatiently, Darlene could not let him get by with only that.

"So why you drinking so much?"

Sy lowered the paper, stared at her, then raised it again.

"Huh, Sy? Why you drinking so much all the sudden, huh? Hey, I'm talking to you."

When the paper came back down Sy looked slightly annoyed. "Look, I know I had six too many last night, but we just couldn't pull ourselves off the bleachers. It was a big, exciting game. People had to let off steam."

Darlene leaned in until her chest rested on the table. "But, Sy, you weren't playing. If you'd been pitching, I'd understand."

Sy's eyes moved up and down the newspaper, as if following columns of type. "I've played enough to know what it feels like to win.

Those boys played one hell of a game. I can't help it if all I can do now is join the celebrating."

"I think the only reason you go down there is to remind people what kind of ballplayer you used to be. Everybody knows you're going into the Hall of Fame. You don't have to keep reminding them you know." Darlene took a drink of coffee to let what she said sink in, then released a truculent breath of air. "Stop trying to steal the limelight from those young men. You already had your day in the sun."

Sy folded the paper shut and opened the next page. "I just sat in the bleachers quietly drinking beer with my friends." For a moment his mind snapped back to Korea. Darlene was targeting him. Just like Charlie.

Darlene snapped right back. "Is that really where you were, at the ballpark?"

"Of course I was at the ballpark. Where do you think I was?"

"I don't know. All I know is you weren't here. Mercy stayed until after ten, wanting to say goodbye."

Outside, a fast-moving cloud darkened the kitchen, then moved on. Sy took a deep breath. Whatever Darlene was to say, he probably had it coming. As he sat across from her at the table, he had a sudden desire to do something big. Anything would do, good or bad—something. Whatever it was it couldn't be done here in the kitchen with Darlene. He desperately wanted out of the kitchen.

"Mercy knows goodbyes don't always have to get said. Least not with us. Say too many 'goodbyes' or 'I love yous' and pretty soon they don't mean anything."

"All Mercy will remember is that you weren't there to kiss her goodbye," snapped Darlene.

After some thought, Sy said, "She'll get over it."

A bank of clouds quickly moved in behind the first one, and inside the kitchen, light pulsed and shimmered like film through an old-time movie projector. Darlene stared hard at the back of the newspaper while gripping the material around her throat with both hands. "Well, she knows you're drinking too much too. She doesn't come right out and say it but, by God, she knows it all the same."

Sy used his tongue to roll the toothpick to the other side of his mouth. "She's just going to have to trust her ol' man to take care of himself." He spoke mechanically and had no interest in getting into it.

Just then the phone rang. Sy jumped up to answer it, pleased to find Mercy on the other end. "Hey, peanut, how ya doin'?"

"Hi, Dad, how are things at the funny farm?"

"Oh fine. We've had coffee and cereal and just strapped on the boxing gloves."

"Bout to duke it out, huh?"

"I keep a hand in her face, but sooner or later she's gonna get inside with that left of hers, then it'll be lights out for yours truly."

Mercy chuckled, then turned half serious, which Sy found slightly irritating. "Well, I'm glad to see you made it home last night. Mom was worried you'd run off with some ballplayer's young wife."

"If I had I couldn't feel worse than I do now. We sat up on the bleachers drinking beer till they ran out." As Sy spoke, Darlene brushed past and headed down the hall.

"That's what I thought," said Mercy. Then Sy heard her start as if to say more, but the phone only hung silent. "You mean you all sat up there drinking in the dark?" she finally said. "Because when I left all the lights were shut off."

Sy hesitated, and during the break he heard a small click over the line and knew Darlene had picked up in the bedroom. He could hear her breathing. "Mercy, I think your mother wants to talk to you," said Sy.

"I was about to say something," said Darlene in a defensive rush.

"Hi, Mom," said Mercy resignedly. She was happy talking to just her father and resented her mother barging in, although it always happened the same way. She never got more than five precious minutes with him alone on the phone. She wanted to press him a little more on what he'd been up to the night before. "How you doing today?"

With Darlene upstairs Sy turned back to the paper but still couldn't concentrate, sure that Darlene was giving Mercy an earful of what happened after she left. He had meant to get Mercy off the phone quickly, but Darlene had taken care of that. If he could have kept them apart for a while there was a good chance Darlene would forget, and Mercy would never have to know about anything.

Soon Sy heard Darlene returning down the hall. She gave him a smoldering look, sitting back down at the table. Sy could see she was no better than before talking with Mercy.

A shadow flitted outside the window. Darlene stood up and went to the sink to look out. The big, blue-mottled pigeon had landed in the center of the patio, goose-stepping toward the wrought-iron table, its head rocking back and forth in time with its feet. When it reached the table, it pecked at the crumbs that had fallen through the latticework the night before. Darlene noticed movement to the right and saw a huge black cat crouching beneath the hedge. It was stretched long and flat to the ground, eyes fixed on the pigeon, so still that if not for the electric play of its tail it could have been a statue. Darlene's frown turned into a tight smile. Excitedly, she watched as the cat took a tentative step forward.

Sy looked up and noticed her smiling. "What are you looking at, Darlene? You look like your heartthrob just walked out of the orchard."

Darlene jerked her arms nervously, gave a weird, high-pitched chuckle, and smiled more broadly. "No, no. More like the soon-to-be ex-heartthrob."

"What? What the heck are you talking about?" Sy got up and walked over to the patio door. When he saw what was about to happen, he pounded the glass hard, causing the pigeon to leap under the patio table, then scramble away in a flurry of feathers. The cat followed the bird's flight, then turned to throw a look of contempt at Sy.

Sy stormed back into the kitchen to face Darlene who was leaning back against a counter, smiling like she was about to bust. "I can't believe you were going to let that cat get my pigeon," he said stonily, his chest heaving.

"Oh, I wasn't going to let it happen."

"Yes, you were. I could tell by the look on your face. You were going to let that cat catch that pigeon and not call me over until it was nothing but a puff of feathers. It was going to be vengeance for last night, wasn't it?" Sy took a few steps forward, resting his hands on the back of his chair. Darlene watched him from across the kitchen, wearing a mock smile.

"Oh? What happened last night?"

Sy's face suddenly fell.

"Go on, Sy. What happened last night?"

"Nothin' happened," said Sy sullenly.

"Nothing happened, huh?" Darlene lifted away from the kitchen countertop, marching back and forth in front of it, gesturing like a lawyer in front of a jury box. A strange calm came into her voice. "Okay, Sy. Okay, if that's what you want to believe. I can deal with that. It just means you're as crazy as I am." She took one step toward him and continued marching back and forth. A sneer crossed her face. "Only, who's the one facing delusions now? Huh, Sy? Who's the one getting the goddamned patronizing look that says reality has done gone completely to shit, and the only thing to hope for is another pill that'll hopefully take the edge off?" She swung her hand up and pointed to her temple like it was a gun. "How's it feel to be a little touched? How does it feel to be curling up inside your skin, to have people roll their eyes and trade knowing glances? You keep sticking with that attitude, and you're going to find out." Darlene stopped marching, arched herself forward like she was trying to hear a whisper, and raised both arms as if drying her pits. Sy clung to the back of his chair and eyed her curiously. The corner of her mouth was starting to twitch.

Darlene's eyes widened, and her voice went singsong like a taunting child. "Yer starting to lose yer shit, and you know it. I can already hear what people'll say. 'There's the house where those two nutjobs live. Sometimes they come out and dance around like they're covered in silly string.'" Darlene raised her arms higher, circling in a wild little pantomime.

"Me, I'm just a little neurotic... maybe a lot. But at least I know it. You... you try and pretend you're Robert fucking Redford, when deep inside I think you're Charlie Manson. A person does what you did last night and that's cer-ti-fide loony."

Sy was taken aback but remembered who the words were coming from and shook it off. He'd let her go, but it was time to cut her back down. "Darlene, I know you're upset, but why don't we just sit back down and try to make a nice morning of it. You worked a little too hard yesterday, and now I think you should rest. Besides, I need to go to work in a few minutes, and I don't want to leave with us like this."

Darlene was ready to shout *There, you're doing it again* when the compulsion suddenly drained out of her like air from a slashed tire. She stepped forward, slumped into her chair, put her elbows on the table, and covered her eyes with her hands. She let out a long sigh and reached for her coffee, which shook on the way to her mouth. "I don't know what's the matter with me this morning," she said meekly. "Too much medicine. Maybe not enough."

"Just give yourself something simple to do today," Sy said placatingly. "Be good to stay a little busy on a day like today, Darlene." Sy slowly moved around his chair and carefully settled back into it. He reached across the table for Darlene's hands and held them between his like a faith healer.

Darlene stared long and hard into the black well of her coffee cup. Judging by the tragic look on her face, Sy knew he had regained the upper hand, and it left him feeling hollow.

"What the hell is there to do?" Darlene moaned. Her head shot up, and she looked pleadingly into Sy's eyes. "Sometimes I get so antsy, Sy, I could just blow to pieces all over the room."

"I know, sweetheart." Sy looked into her face, bewildered, like he'd come upon an upset child and didn't know who she belonged to.

"It's nice outside. Maybe you could take a drive. Go to New Melle and see your sister or something."

Darlene looked up, brushing at her cheeks with both hands. "I guess maybe I could do that."

"If nothing else, just take a drive in the country," said Sy. "I'll be home early. Not feeling too good."

Darlene turned and again addressed her words to the refrigerator. "You can't handle your hangovers like you used to."

Chapter 7

Cities as large as St. Louis have a gravitational pull, which weakens the farther you move away. Travel west on highway 70 out of St. Louis, and on past Gilmore the towns gradually become smaller and farther apart. Eighty miles out you'd eventually discover or at least travel past one of St. Louis's smallest moons—Truxton. If St. Louis's circle of influence were imagined as a dart board, Truxton would only be worth five points.

In Truxton there is very little to do. Half the population lives in trailers. The nearest retail outlet is forty miles away, so shopping is out of the question without planning for it. If you aren't one of the local farmers, chances are the brick plant over in Medellin keeps you busy for at least eight hours a day. If you can afford a satellite dish you watch TV when you come home. If you don't watch TV you can read a book, and if you don't read you sit on the front porch and stare. If that doesn't suit you, you go hunting or fishing.

Aaron Strunk, Lenny Wildschuetz and Aaron's brother Paul had just finished the morning hunt and were at the far end of Lenny's backyard picking doves. The shooting had been good, but they were bored with the cleaning. They leaned on their elbows across Lenny's chain-link fence, not caring how many feathers floated through it back into the yard. Three shotguns, all still loaded, leaned against the fence.

"I could sure use some pussy," said Lenny absentmindedly. The conversation had laid off for too long, and Lenny was always the first to get nervous over silence.

"Here, why dontcha fuck this dove, Lenny," said Aaron. He finished picking his last bird and jammed his thumb in below the breastplate to gut it but instead reached over and kindly offered the newly made orifice.

"You better shoot me a turkey, you turkey. I'd make giblets outta that thing," said Lenny, carefully plucking the remaining pinfeathers on his own bird.

"You're better off getting 'em right after you shoot 'em," said Paul. "That way you can get the dyin' quivers." He leaned out over the fence and spat a big slaver of tobacco juice. Being the worst shot of the three, he already had his few birds picked, cleaned, and wrapped in plastic before the others were half done. All that was left to do was lean on the fence and spit tobacco into the pasture.

"Is shootin' it the only way you can get something to quiver?" asked Aaron.

"What do you mean?"

"I'll bet you never got nothing to quiver in your whole damn life." Aaron played the role of sage adviser for the three of them, even though he'd just turned twenty-two, and Paul was only a year younger. "You ever get a girl to quiver?"

"I seen some quivering in my day. Plenty of it."

"How'd you know it was real quivering," said Aaron, nonchalantly pulling out a string of intestines and slinging them off into the pasture.

"I asked her once and she said so. Besides that, I seen her quiverin' like hell myself."

"You shouldn't be able to see a girl quiver, boy. If you do you aren't going about things the right way. You can feel a girl quiver and sometimes you can hear it, but you shouldn't be looking right at it. A girl don't want you looking right at her when she's quiverin'."

"Musta been finger-fuckin' her," said Lenny, who'd never seen a girl naked other than his sister.

"I don't mean I was looking right at it," insisted Paul.

"Sounds like he was finger bangin'," repeated Lenny.

"Is that what you was doing?" asked Aaron, contempt building in his voice.

"Well, what if I was."

Aaron looked up from his bird and shot a hard glance at his brother. "Boy, you can grab a six hundred-pound Hampshire sow by the ear and get it to quiver if you twist hard enough. No, what you need to do is figure out how to make her want to quiver before you even touch her. You don't go charging right in there with your damn hand."

"She put it there."

"Well, that's different then," said Aaron, satisfied that his brother could at least be somewhat competent when it came to women. After he spoke, he went back to dragging the last of the entrails from his bird.

Paul was pleased he'd been able to stop Aaron short. Aaron was boiling up for one of his lectures, and this was going to be one he didn't particularly want to hear. He mostly put up with Aaron's jabber without a word. This time the lecture was not only *to* him, it was *about* him, and talking to Aaron about him and women got him red in the face. Aaron usually spoke more about things in general—how he felt about layoffs at the brick plant, how it was all due to management sticking to short term goals, and how that was going to have everybody out of a job sooner rather than later. There was another moment of silence, and again Lenny felt compelled to speak.

"These damn livers that sit up here in the rib cage are a bitch to get out," he said.

"That's lungs, not liver," said Aaron. "I can't believe you, Lenny. You been hunting twelve years now, and you still don't know your guts. Me, I could be a doctor by now if I had half a mind."

"Whatever the fuck they are, I'm tempted to just leave the sum bitches." His fingers were too pudgy for digging under dove rib cages, which meant Lenny's birds always had a slight bitter taste. He was only trying now because he had nothing better to do.

"I'd just leave 'em in there then," said Aaron. It didn't need saying because Lenny would do it anyway, but things always went better with Lenny if Aaron gave it his blessing.

Paul walked over to his gun and without warning pumped three rounds into the ground directly in front of them.

Aaron remained calm like nothing happened, but Lenny jerked back like Paul shot him full in the chest. "What the hell was that for?" asked Lenny.

Paul slammed the breech of the gun open, leaned across it and spit more tobacco juice. A wide grin spread across his face. "A man's got to unload his gun sometime," he said.

"Man ought to have the manners to warn somebody too," said Aaron, with little trace of actual annoyance.

In the distance a thin black line undulated above the horizon like a long flying snake. The migrating redwings didn't care where the line went as long as it was pointed generally south, and as they advanced the line rose and fell like a radio wave. If they held their present course the entire column would pass directly over the chain-link fence.

Aaron tightened his eyes, studying the black line as it came on. "Since you got nothing to do why don't you hand me my gun over there," he said to his brother. He crammed the last dove into a bag with the others and reached out his hand.

Paul handed over the gun, and Aaron stood up and emptied it into the column of birds, now directly overhead. Three holes punched through the bird-blackened sky, and when the birds hit the ground it sounded like a brief flurry of good-sized hail. The part of the line nearest the hunters buckled out, like a sudden aneurysm in the sky's flowing black artery.

Aaron calmly handed the gun back to his brother. "Want me to unload your gun too, Lenny?" Lenny shrugged indifferently and leaned further into the fence.

"Hand me Lenny's gun, Paul."

The river of redwings moved off, but one straggler made his way back over them in its hurry to catch up. Aaron swung Lenny's Browning semi-auto behind the bird, followed through and fired. The bird crumpled. Twice it regained altitude when Aaron pumped the next two rounds behind the first. He was easily the best shot of the three.

"Ah, fuckin' lungs!" said Lenny triumphantly, holding up the troublesome organ for all to see before flicking it off his finger.

"Listen!" said Paul suddenly. All three froze and turned an ear in the direction Paul was concentrating on.

"Just what is it you want us to be listening for, little brother?"

"Train!" whooped Lenny.

"It's a friggin' train!" yelled Paul. And then, "I get first crack! I'm the one who heard it!"

"Fuck you! Whoever gets to the depot first!" yelled Aaron. He traded Lenny's gun for his own and ran down the path to the depot, frantically cramming shells into the magazine, dropping some on the ground as he ran.

The depot was what they called the area below Lenny's house where the train tracks ran through, connecting St. Louis to Kansas City. There wasn't a sign of a depot anywhere, but at one time one had sat next to a switching spur that operated parallel to the main tracks. A six-foot-high concrete culvert allowed a small spring to pass beneath the spur, creating a clear little pond between the two sets of tracks. The boys treated the culvert like a cave, and when they were younger the three had fished for bluegill from inside. Now they mostly used it as concealment for firing shotguns, .22s, deer rifles, or whatever they happened to be carrying that day, into the sides of freight trains.

"C'mon you guys!" yelled Aaron. The path to the depot wasn't as worn as it used to be, and they had difficulty making it through the brambles that had taken over. As he ran, a branch from a multi-floral rosebush caught Lenny in the side of the face, ripping his skin in two places below the right eye. The train was coming, and there was no time for lifting the prickly limbs aside.

By the time they emerged from the briars, jumped the rusted out woven wire fence, and raced along the old spur, they all were cut and bleeding from the face, hands, and neck. If they were lucky the train would be carrying cars.

The iron rails and wooden ties that once created the spur were no longer visible, but the abandoned line was clearly defined by a cinder strewn ridge that continued straight as an arrow through woods and fields.

"It's a car train!" yelled Paul between breaths as he raced alongside the others. As they ran, the engine came up directly across from them, twenty yards to the left of the spur, separated by only the narrow branch and a thin wall of trees.

As they ran, the engineer sounded the whistle three times. He'd seen them running along the opposite side with their guns and knew what they were up to. There was nothing he could do at this point but blow a warning, note the location and look for damage at the end of the run.

At the whistle, the three hunters reacted like coyotes hearing the petrified bleating of their soon-to-be-lunch. Pumped by adrenalin, each dove off the embankment like trained paratroopers, then squat-walked under the culvert's concrete roof and set themselves up inside. Aaron dropped to one knee and pulled a bead on a white Southern Pacific logo emblazoned on a peach colored, metal boxcar.

Paul shouted into his brother's ear. "Don't shoot yet, Aaron! I saw cars!"

"Say what?" Aaron's voice shook with the weight of the train, passing so close the ground trembled, like mother earth birthing a volcano.

"CARS," repeated Lenny at the top of his lungs. "A WHOLE FRIGGIN' LINE OF 'EM. CADILLACS, I THINK!"

Aaron held his fire but stayed on his haunches, watching the procession pound by. The two others stood over him with their guns ready. As close as they were, the culvert provided only a narrow window, but the train was going slow, and they would have plenty of time to react.

As it wound its way from its origin in Lubbock, Texas, the train grew larger at every major city along the way. When it hit Missouri, it was a half mile long, led by a series of Southern Pacific boxcars, followed by black tankers up from the gulf, then half a dozen flatcars carrying a mysterious payload covered by tarps that made Aaron's finger itch just watching them go by. Next there was a seemingly endless procession of coal cars, all indigo-red and topped with shallow arcs of black, low-grade bituminous from Colorado. Here and there the coal cars were separated by reefers loaded with beef from Montana and South Dakota. And still the train did not end.

Hidden in the culvert, the three trainshooters waited impatiently for the Southern Pacific to move on. If there were Cadillacs, they would be all the way back, supposedly protected by the caboose.

The train cars rolled by for endless minutes, creating a shockwave of sound that traveled through the ground as well as the air. Suddenly the coal cars ended, replaced by a row of semi-truck trailers that had lost their tractors, reduced to riding piggyback to their final destinations.

A hundred yards away twenty railroad cars loaded with spit-shined new Cadillacs marched into ambush, two abreast all the way back to the caboose. They came stacked three high and five to a row, each bearing a tiny American flag attached to the antennae, as if they weren't just a load of Cadillacs but a government motorcade making a cross-country plug for baseball and apple pie. Each caught a piece of the sun and threw it back from a thousand points of chrome and factory enamel. There were black Coupe de Villes with bright chrome wheels, reflecting the Missouri countryside as they paraded by, white on red, custom four-door El Dorado convertibles, Kennedy cars with doors that swung out from the middle, baby-blue Cadillac limos destined for New York City, Chicago, and Memphis, plus every make and model in between.

The lead automobile was a red Cimarron on its way to a forty-eight-year-old insurance salesman from Pittsburgh who'd been waiting for months. As it broke clear of the concrete culvert, a salesman's dream bought sight unseen like a mail-order bride, its windows disintegrated, and a circle of perfectly round indentations spattered the middle of the passenger door.

"GET THE PINK ONE!" Aaron shouted to the two above him, and instantly the same thing happened to a pastel Sedan de Ville destined for a Mary Kay Cosmetics district manager based out of Charleston.

The third barrage woke a sleeping bum who, hoping to travel in style to Florida, had picked the lock of a white Coupe de Ville back in Dallas. It took a gallon of Port to get himself motivated, and the red leather interior of the car was ruined by vomit long before buckshot did the same to the outside. When the windows blew in on him, it felt like the wrath of God.

The roar of the train canceled the sound of the guns, making the action inside the culvert look like pantomime. Each time a trigger was pulled a shoulder flew back, a barrel came up, settled, and repeated. For as long as it lasted, the little pond in front of the culvert reflected the senseless assault on the thundering freighter. When the caboose finally rolled by, twenty-seven empty hulls lay smoking on the pebbled concrete floor of the culvert.

The caboose conductor grinned and waved until he was out of sight, even though none of the boys waved back. He was used to seeing rabbit hunters stomping the brush along the tracks, and these three made him remember when he used to take his own boys hunting a long time ago.

Still on one knee, Aaron took a big breath and blew like after a hard day's work. "We put the hammer to those sum bitches now," he said. He rose up onto his haunches, slid open the gun's chamber and looked in to make sure he'd fired every round.

Lenny started to say something but finally just let out a funny little giggle.

"Wasn't a guardrail on any of 'em," said Paul, leaning over to release another huge glob of tobacco juice. "These days they almost always have guard rails."

"We got lucky, didn't we," said Aaron, who looked over and gave his brother a wink.

"Can't say the same for those poor sum bitches who gotta keep driving their old Cadillacs," said Lenny giddily. His voice was a few octaves higher than usual and still rising.

"Let's get out of here," said Aaron. "Shootin' up a bunch of brand-new Cadillacs makes me hungry as a blind coon."

He scrambled from the culvert and stood to give the others a leg up out of the ditch before grabbing an exposed tree root and vaulting up himself. After reaching the abandoned railroad levee he saw that Paul and Lenny were stopped in their tracks, staring at something. Aaron was on top of the cinder track in three strides and froze next to them.

Twenty feet in front of them stood an elderly man, naked except for a pair of socks and black penny loafers.

"I'll be goddamn. It's one of them city queers," said Lenny in a half whisper. For several seconds the boys gaped at the silent stranger as if he had two heads.

"What we got here is an escapee from the loony bin," said Aaron. "Fulton, mister? That where you come from? Fulton?"

The man stood silently, focusing on something just beyond the three others.

Paul caught his breath and coughed spastically, having swallowed tobacco juice.

"What the Sam hell is wrong with him?" he said between coughing fits.

Aaron asked again, "Are you a loony bird, mister?"

"Maybe you better not fuck with him, Aaron," said Lenny. "He could be dangerous."

"What's he going to do, pull a zip gun out of his ass?"

The man continued looking past them but started shifting his weight from one foot to the other. His initial blank demeanor changed to one the boys recognized—fear, which did nothing but encourage Aaron.

"What you doing with your pecker out, mister? You got a woman layin' in the woods back there?" Aaron took a few steps forward, stood on his toes, and looked over the man's shoulder sarcastically.

"I bet he's more likely to *be* the woman," said Lenny, getting bolder with the man's silence. The whites of the man's eyes looked strange, filled with mucus, like a fish when it dies. Suddenly the man slapped both of his hands on his buttocks and pushed his groin forward.

"I don't believe it. Look at the sumbitch," said Lenny.

"Hold it buddy, hold on," said Aaron, now set off. "You may damn well be a looney tune, but you still can't go around shoving your pecker at people."

Paul finished summoning tobacco juice from his throat and gave the man a concentrated look. "Where are your clothes at, mister?"

Lenny looked at Aaron, then at the man, folding the gun tighter into his crossed arms. "Don'tcha talk?"

As they looked, the man's eyes seemed to clear, and his arms fell to his sides. He looked twice from right to left.

"Yeah, he talks with his pecker," said Aaron. "Hey, mister! What's this say?" With two audible slaps Aaron landed both hands on the back of his pants and pushed his hips forward. The man became visibly distraught and looked as if he might cry. Paul dropped his gun onto the cinders, pulled down his zipper and held his penis as if he were going to urinate.

"Same to ya, buddy!" he said. Laughing hard, he shook his penis at the man.

Paul put himself away and picked up his shotgun. The man widened his eyes and started backward, a few faltering steps.

"Where you going, pencil dick?" said Aaron, stepping closer.

"No, no..." said the man fearfully. His face contorted in confusion, and when Aaron kept coming, the man decided to turn and run. But before he did, he glanced back at the boys.

Aaron put a shell in his gun and fired into the trees just above the man's head. "LET'S GET HIM!" The others whooped and fell in pursuit, but since they only meant to scare him, they stopped running after a few yards.

At the sound of the gun the man broke into a wild run, fell to the cinders, scrambled back up, and took off through the thick brambles. Against the shadow of the woods his skin seemed pale, except for a dark streak that ran down both thighs and past his knees.

Chapter 8

Sy sat in a McDonald's parking lot, mildly hallucinating since eleven a.m. A front had moved in, blocking the sun, yet he saw things with unusual clarity, the way a pair of yellow shooting glasses enhances contrast. He felt blissful. Life had slowed down. It was as if he'd taken a large dose of Darlene's Valium. It didn't occur to him to wonder what he was doing at the McDonald's or how he got there. The world had set things wonderfully straight.

All his senses were sharper. He caught every word coming from the drive-up menu's tinny speaker crisp and clear, even though it was far across the parking lot. Everything appeared in perfect focus, without depth, as if the light falling on his retinas was filtered through a narrow aperture. He found he could read the numbers on a gas pump across the street without difficulty, staring moronically as the numbers spun like a slow-motion slot machine. His lips moved as he silently counted the numbers on the pump from thirty yards away. A man dispensed the gas with one hand while leaning against a white Oldsmobile Cutlass, and Sy could make out a dry ketchup stain on his shirt. The man released the handle, and the numbers halted on fifteen dollars exact. The sudden stop unlocked Sy's eyes and sent them drifting away as his head slowly pivoted, until he was looking back over the steering wheel. His face wore the frozen grin of a man who'd been knocked senseless in a boxing ring. As he sat there, he tightened his grip on the wheel with both hands, only because it felt good and solid to the touch—everything pleased him so very much.

What a sweet voice, he thought to himself as the girl again spoke through the tinny speaker. It seemed long ago, but Sy remembered speaking to the menu girl too. In his mind he saw it as clearly as if watching it on tv.

He had chatted nicely with the pitifully plain, buck-toothed girl at the drive-thru window, who smiled wide at something he'd said, then covered her mouth when she recalled what her smile looked like. Her cheeks were dimpled, one side much deeper than the other, and Sy could clearly see where her contact lenses sat on her eyes. The odor of grease, cleaning solvent, and the smell of her shampoo wafted into his car. Everything emanating from the drive-thru window smelled strong and delicious, intoxicating.

How nice it is to be parked safely between the two painted lines, thought Sy, having legally rented the space all to himself for the amazingly affordable price of a double cheeseburger and fries. Sy wondered what had become of the food, then looked down. Sure enough, there it was, in his lap, untouched.

He reached for the hamburger first, slowly rolling back the waxed paper after each bite, exposing only enough for the next one. He chewed languidly. The glare on the windshield seemed especially intense. Sy pulled down the shade just enough so the dry warmth would touch his face but not trouble his sensitive eyes.

An overly plump sparrow landed on the driver's side windshield wiper, looking at Sy inquisitively. The bird was a big male, with a black mask around the eyes that morphed into a rust-colored cap on his head, widened over his back, and spread unevenly across the top of his wings. "I'll call you Jake," said Sy. "Cause you're so damn cocky even when you're fat, like Jake Lamotta." If someone had been sitting next to him, they would have found Sy's words unintelligible. It made no difference to the bird, who only hopped along the wiper blade toward the open window, cocking its head to give Sy a discerning look.

Sy bit off half a fry, reached out and around and tossed the other half onto the windshield, where it rolled down to rest against the wiper in front of the bird. The sparrow took the morsel in its beak and flew behind the car, only to return in a few seconds. Sy went on offering bits of French fries until the bird refused to take anymore. It sat on the wiper blade, staring through the windshield, its chest heaving. Dimly, it occurred to Sy that the sparrow looked healthy for a bird that liked French fries.

The brightness softened, and his awareness began to slowly return, like coming out of anesthesia. The strange opiate dream (and the godlike ability that came with it) cleared, and soon it was no longer a dream at all. Sy sat straighter in the car seat, looking around, blinking, wondering where the hell he was. Fifty yards to the right was the overpass to Interstate 70, and on the other side of the overpass a sign rose high in the air that read "Truxton Oil & Gas." Truxton! What the fuck was he doing in Truxton? A jolt of adrenalin coursed through his body like electricity, and his heart fluttered up to his throat, like a bird trying to escape. He started the Suburban, rolled toward the I70 East ramp, and brought it up to speed. He took a deep breath, desperately trying to think. From the back of his mind rose a nagging sense he had something to do. In a flash he remembered the picnic committee meeting that evening, and with the memory he once again became fully present. He shook his head to clear his senses. He'd been disoriented before, but it was always a brief lapse. Nothing like this.

On the way back to Gilmore Sy pushed the Suburban at such speed other drivers gave him the finger. Somehow, he found himself almost two hours from home, with no idea why. One look at the gas gauge confirmed it. Fear, the kind you had to choke back with the esophagus, was pushing him back to Gilmore. As the vehicle rocketed down the highway Sy bent forward, lying on the wheel, trying to control the mess his stomach was twisting up.

Sy was to head up the St. Michael's picnic committee meeting at Parkers that evening and was going to be late—but that wasn't the reason he was going so fast. He drove flat out because he figured the more distance he could put between himself and Truxton the sooner he could lose the feeling that something awful had happened there.

He ran his hand down his face to try and clear his head. A lumbering eighteen wheeler dumped its air horn in one long, angry blast as the Suburban crossed lanes, and when Sy swerved back he oversteered, almost colliding into the side of an OATS bus. By the look of the passengers' horrified faces, they thought they would die of something other than old age after all.

Sy checked his speed, trying to settle down. What happened back there? He vaguely remembered a train and talking to hunters, but it didn't seem real. He could have dreamt it, right? Had he parked the truck and gone to sleep? He remembered how in his dream he was standing on top of a railroad bed, yet the train passed to his right. It had rolled right past him (he knew it had… he'd felt the earth trembling), with its whistle sounding far off. The trees along the train bed had shimmered as if behind a wall of rising heat. He wasn't frightened until one of the hunters began to speak. His voice sounded deep and synthesized—like talking into a fan.

Sy remembered getting up that morning and confessing to Darlene about sitting in the bleachers drinking beer. Shortly after leaving for work, the car had suddenly filled with the smell of rotten eggs. He remembered a sensation beginning behind his eyes slowly moving down; an intense, boiling energy settling in his groin, lying there, tingling. He remembered wanting to do something; he had to do this one thing, and wouldn't it be wonderful to do it. What was it?

Did it have to do with his dream about the train? He concentrated harder, vaguely remembering running through an endless stretch of brambles that had come to life, slicing at him again and again with branches that were stiff and swordlike. Sy wiped his face again and this time noticed a tiny stinging. For an instant he took his eyes off the road, reaching up and pulling the rearview mirror down to look at himself. At first he was curious, then horrified. Razor-thin cuts crisscrossed the face in the mirror. He became aware of similar, barely perceptible stinging all over his body.

"NO!" Sy's shriek rebounded within the confines of the Suburban as he pounded his fist into the steering wheel, overcome by the dreadful realization he had not been dreaming at all. He knew the meaning of the cuts. For a while he drove blindly, barely able to quiet the panic as the Suburban flew down the highway.

What to do now? Other than check himself into a psych ward, there was nothing to do but continue to Parkers for the picnic committee meeting. As he drove, he felt like life had been knocked off its foundation. The wind blowing in from the side vent did nothing to stop him from sweating freely.

An hour later Sy looked at his watch, grimacing. He had to call Darlene. He had forgotten to tell her about the meeting, and it would be bad enough she had to eat dinner alone. After what passed the night before, she'd be hysterical not knowing where he was. Without taking his eyes off the pavement, Sy dialed and pressed send. If only he could break his body down into some binary code, press send, and zap it somewhere... all the way back to Korea perhaps. The phone only rang once before Darlene picked it up. Hearing it was Sy, she immediately started in.

"I called your office about ten o'clock," she said. "They told me you weren't there. That you might be playing golf with Harry Pittman, but when I called and talked to Harry, he said he hadn't seen you in a week. Where the hell have you been? And when are you coming home?"

"You called Harry Pittman?" Harry Pittman was the president of the investment bank that provided 75 percent of working capital for Templeton Properties. He was the one man so important to Sy's work he never risked introducing him to Darlene, although he knew he'd have to, sooner or later. Harry Pittman was new, and so far, no events with wives had occurred. Sy hoped they never would.

"I was going to leave a message with his secretary, but he was standing right there so she put him on," said Darlene defensively.

Actually, she'd waited on hold for over fifteen minutes. She knew she was never allowed to make such a call, especially having never met the man. But for as crazy as Darlene could be, she was also intuitive; she sensed something was off.

Sometimes Sy thought it was more than just intuition. There were times when Darlene's clairvoyance was just plain scary. It was as though whatever had shaken loose in Darlene's head to make her so unstable had also unleashed some sort of sixth sense. Darlene always referred to it as her "Alarms," but whatever it was, whenever Darlene had one of them, she became so sure of what it told her she'd gamble anything on the outcome. Even if it meant calling her husband's sacred business contacts.

"And what did Mr. Pittman allow?" said Sy, with hopeless sarcasm. He put two fingers to his temple, trying to think. He needed to come up with a good way out of this one. By the smug tone of Darlene's voice, she thought she had something on him. The only approach he could think of was silence, which Darlene would take as anger, and not wrongfully so since she had taken it upon herself to call Harry Pittman. The silent treatment was especially harsh on Darlene. It always gave Sy a victory, but mostly a pyrrhic one.

"He was really nice to talk to and real friendly. He said your secretary must have had her wires crossed because he hadn't seen you. We talked a good long while."

After a full minute of dead air Darlene squawked his name in a panic.

"What did you find to talk to Harry Pittman about?" asked Sy finally, afraid of the answer.

"Oh, this and that. We talked for quite a while about you going into the Hall of Fame. And about your silly pigeons."

"My pigeons."

"Yes. He said he used to have pigeons, too, but that was at least fifty years ago." Then, turning up the sarcasm again, "Back when he was a boy."

"You talked to Harry Pittman about my rollers."

"He asked how many you had, and I told him I didn't quite know… there were pigeons coming and going all the time, flopping through the air and bouncing on the ground like walnuts, but that generally there were about fifteen staying in that monstrosity you call a coop."

"You talked about the coop too?"

"He sounded very interested in seeing it, and I told him I didn't know why… it was the ugliest thing I'd ever seen, except for that house of horrors you all are building over on Kings Highway."

At the mention of the Equitable project Sy's heart leapt. She'd done it again… he knew she would, and he was just waiting for her to say it and she did. Having Harry Pittman think his wife was a flake was bad enough, but her voicing such a foolishly subjective opinion about work matters—that was too much.

"Mr. Pittman is expected to give us final okay on a loan extension for that building within a week," he said tonelessly. Through an act of will Sy kept out any inflexion that might betray what was going on in his head. He would keep his responses pointed, which would communicate enough to Darlene in itself.

"I mentioned maybe he and his wife, I think he said her name was Norma, could come over for one of your famous barbeques and he could see it then, along with your orchard," said Darlene. Sy heard her sniff into the phone, like she did when she felt others were thinking her foolish.

Sy said nothing in response, and the expensive mobile airtime went unused for another minute. It was a signal to Darlene that Sy was extremely upset with her. Sy always stressed how they should use airtime as efficiently as possible, and now the silence was the same as a slap.

"So, when do you think you might want them over?" asked Darlene, who was still quite sure of her recent alarm.

"Just let me handle it, Darlene."

"It doesn't matter to me. We can do it next Sunday if you like. That way they could meet Mercy and Charlotte." Darlene was over her guilt for calling Pittman and didn't give a rat's ass when the Pittmans came over or if they came over at all. She just needed to hear Sy explain where he'd been.

"We'll talk about it after the deal goes through," said Sy, mentally calculating the damage Darlene had done. *Everything was probably just fine*, he thought, *at least in a social sense.* In such initial conversations Darlene's neurosis often came off as innocence, which at times could be endearing. Of course, the bit about the building being ugly probably still went over like a pregnant pole vaulter, coming from the developer's own wife. He would have to call Pittman the next morning and assess the damage.

"Whatever you want," said Darlene. Sy heard another insouciant sniff at the other end of the line.

After another long stretch of silence, Darlene finally broke down and asked the question. "If you weren't with Harry Pittman, what were you doing?"

"The office told you right. I was playing golf, only not with Harry Pittman. It was with a guy who thinks he wants to use me as a part-time consultant after I retire. Any more questions?"

"Just when are you coming home?" she said softly.

"Late. I'm supposed to meet the picnic committee at Parkers."

"Make sure you put me in the quilt stand. But not with Gayla Hendricks," she said, and quickly hung up. Sy cursed under his breath and pressed "end."

Parkers was smack in the middle of old Gilmore and hadn't changed since the day it was built. It sat close to the street, with a gravel apron out front with space for six cars. The bar was an extension of Angie Parker's home, accessed through two curtains connecting it to the main living space. Although the home portion was off limits to patrons, it was known to have no more than three rooms, and about any time of the day you could hear the television, and you knew Angie's husband Bunny was lounging in front of it with a cigarette hanging out of his mouth. When the cowbell above the bar entrance tinkled, Angie would amble in from the other room, rocking side to side on arthritic hips like a pendulum of pain, and you could sometimes hear Bunny go through a bad coughing spell, gasping for oxygen. A year ago, Bunny's emphysema got too far along, and one day the coughing finally stopped.

The bar area was small, having the comfortable feel of a cluttered living room. Parkers was more than just a bar that sold three-two beer. Every wall was covered with handmade wooden shelving lined with everything from canned goods, boxes of cereal, toilet paper, and detergent, to handkerchiefs packaged in plastic, fingernail clippers, pocketknives stapled to cardboard, assorted dry goods, and a latticed wooden rectangle containing every brand of cigarette imaginable. When Angie stood at her place behind the counter, you could barely see her for the chaos that framed her. In one corner a small upright cooler held milk and a few other dairy products, and next to it a squat chest freezer housed many choices of ice cream… on sticks, frozen in cones, formed into sandwiches, and in round quart containers. There were also hot dogs and various other meats, half of which could be counted on to be badly freezer burned.

And of course, Angie sold beer, in longneck bottles. It was the only way the older crowd liked beer. Day after day, Angie pulled longnecks from low metal cabinet coolers with shiny convex doors that slid up with a bang. She popped the caps off using a church key or one of the cooler's built-in openers, then waddled over to one of five square wooden tables scattered in the center of the room and along the front wall. Wherever there was space, the walls supported beer lamps and other marketing paraphernalia that made Parkers a bona fide dive bar. Above the door an eight-member team of Clydesdales stood frozen in mid-step, forever pulling a wagonload of suds behind a horizontal plastic dome heavily yellowed from cigarette smoke. The place was so small Angie's entire inventory of beer stood six feet high along the east wall, while another wall of beer formed a barricade shielding the single stool and doorless bathroom, much like the wall shielding rodeo clowns from the bull. When inventory got low this was the last beer to go, and when that happened you could see a customer's head and the better part of his shoulders when he went to take a leak.

In the morning, before Coon Carter poked his way up the three concrete steps, took his seat near the window and ordered his first beer of the day, Parkers operated as a convenience store. Most people there before Coon were on their way to work, stopping to pick up whatever had become their daily habit.

First there were the construction workers, sun-washed men of all shapes and sizes, thickly layered with muscle, even if hidden by fat. They lined up single file, wearing jeans and T-shirts, ten-eyelet boots, dirty baseball caps, and a look of calm resignation. Angie knew them all by name, greeting each of them as they approached the worn wooden counter holding sodas, cigarettes, chew, pre-packaged cakes and pies, and anything else that might help them present nothing but assholes and elbows upon reaching the job site and climbing out of the truck.

After the construction men the clerical workers came. Quiet, middle-aged women dressed in simple cotton blouses and knee-length skirts that had seen way too much wear but could always be augmented by a tad too much makeup, a single strand of cheap pearls, or a new pair of hose, all designed to strike a balance between a secretary's salary and proper office attire. Working in an office environment, they considered themselves above the likes of Angie, who, along with her late husband, had spent the greater part of her seventy-three years squeezing a living out of nickels and dimes. The women paid for their long, thin cigarettes in silence. It was the final moments they were allowed to be surly, and they appreciated the deference Angie showed with her "Yes, ma'ams" and "No, ma'ams" before they were required to do it themselves for the next eight hours.

After that, Angie sold sweets like candy cigarettes, bubble gum, and chocolate… anything to the rush of kids stopping on their way to school.

That ended at nine-thirty, which gave her a half hour to reach deep in the cooler and savor a cold bottle of Stag before Coon thumped in with his cane. This being her first beer, she would gulp it down in three lifts, then sit and stare into the heavy black ceiling fan that never stopped spinning. It had been there for as long as Angie knew, built of solid cast-iron, and would run forever given a constant trickle of electricity. The fan was anchored to the stamped metal ceiling at a weak spot, causing a constant creaking, which in many ways was worse than the stagnant air it was meant to repel. Parkers would always smell of stale beer and cigarettes, no matter how much the air was swished around.

When Sy showed up at seven, Angie and Coon were having a loud discussion over whether or not Coon had laid Barbara Streisand. Both had been drinking all day and were in a talkative mood. The Windler boys were quietly playing pitch with Charlie Westoff at a table in the corner. Everyone called them boys, but in fact they were fifty-five and fifty-six years old, unmarried and living with an old-maid sister who was the main reason they still ran the family farm so successfully.

There were plenty of other places to hold a meeting, but none so colorful, and after the morning events Sy appreciated the consistency of the place. Parkers bar had looked and felt this way for as long as he could remember. It would stay that way as long as Angie held on.

The other committee members had yet to arrive, so Sy took a chair next to Coon, his back to the window below the Clydesdales. Angie took a long time getting his beer, and when she started over with it, she used her free hand to grab at anything sturdy enough to support her, the counter, the back of a chair, and finally the table. It helped ease the pain shooting up from her traitorous hips.

Sy gulped down the beer like he hadn't had twelve the prior evening, and before Angie could hoist herself back up, he went to the cooler, pulled out another and wrenched off the cap. By the time he sat down again Angie and Coon had resumed their argument.

"I'm telling you, it was back when I lived in New York," said Coon. "I was working for the telephone company then. It was long before she got famous, and she was skinny as a wormed-up dog. I'd take Barbara to the diner at Lex and 74th at least three times a week. Only her name wasn't Barbara then. It was something else I can't remember... but just give me a minute and I will." Coon took another long swig of beer, put both hands firmly on his knees and concentrated hard.

"The sonofabitch took Barbara Streisand to supper three times a week and hasn't paid me for one beer yet," said Angie, waving her hand at the cluster of bottles littering the table. Her hips pained her too much to clear it, and as far as Coon was concerned, he'd just start setting empties on the floor when the table got full.

"If I know Coon he's good for it," said Sy. He took another long, slow pull, then set his bottle down softly.

"Hell, maybe he could call Barbara, and she'd take care of it," said Angie. She swung her head in an exaggerated dip and stared hard into the side of Coon's head. He acted like he didn't hear and continued concentrating.

"When was it Coon lived in New York?" Sy couldn't picture Coon ever having lived in New York City and seriously doubted he'd ever been far outside the county.

"If you believe Coon lived in New York, I'll give you the key to my little villa in the south of France," said Angie, shaking her head contemptuously. Sy saw her head continue to shake, as if after putting it in motion she was unable to stop. Hadn't someone said she'd recently been diagnosed with Parkinson's?

"Don't know what I'd do there," said Sy. "All those girls on the beach taking their tops off? Bor-ring."

"They do that there, don't they," said Angie with a wink. "If I tried that I'd burn these white old duds to a cinder."

"Julie, I think," barked Coon. He turned away from the table, his head twisting hard to the left, like trying to rub an itch with his chin. His mouth fell open, and he gasped for air with quick little sucking noises. Unlike Angie, Coon's involuntary motion was a form of Tourette's. As the two moved together, Sy felt like he was in a clockmaker's workshop.

Coon's wrinkled old neck finally stopped twisting, and his head turned back around. He looked at Angie and Sy blankly. "I think her name was Julie something... naw that don't sound right." With a shrug of his shoulders Coon stopped searching for the name but found his beer again with no trouble.

"You owe me for so many beers I've done lost count," said Angie, thinking a reproach the best response to Coon's foolishness.

"You haven't picked up a god-durn empty bottle from the table all day. All you got to do is count the god-durn things," said Coon, nodding down at the table.

"Hell, Coon, there's only about twenty bottles here," said Sy. "I've seen you drink twenty beers before noon on a bad day." Sy was glad Darlene wasn't there. It was good to be away from her, and she would never take to the two he sat with anyway. He'd completely forgotten about the McDonald's parking lot.

"Well, I aint been drinkin' 'em alone either," said Coon, with an accusing lean in Angie's direction.

"I'll tell you what he's doing," said Angie. She looked straight back at Coon, then crossed her arms and swung her cigarette at him. "He's sticking his empties back in the case thinking I won't notice." Having made her point, she took a big pull off the cigarette and smiled smugly at Coon, who tried acting genuinely surprised at seeing a case of empties at his elbow.

Coon was ten years older than Angie, had only his house on Wilmes Road, his aged black International Travelall, and Parkers to occupy his time. He had no family left, and his only interest besides longnecked beer was the woman who served them to him. He and Angie had dated for six months years ago, when Angie was still in high school, and there were no two better drinking buddies in all of Missouri.

"You know, I used to see her naked all the time," said Coon, deciding Angie needed ignoring. Soon as he finished speaking, his head again tried unscrewing itself from his shoulders.

"Who? Angie?" said Sy, falsely wide-eyed.

"No. Barbara Streisand. Only that wasn't her name then."

"Gotcha."

"Back then she wanted to be an actress, not a singer. I never did see her act, but she used to sing to me all the time. We'd be lying there in bed, high up in my apartment at Lex and 74th."

"I thought that was where the diner was," interrupted Angie with a snicker. She was completely crossed now, arms and legs, sitting higher in her chair. She hooked the thumbnail of her cigarette hand under her top row of teeth and sat there with her mouth open, looking at Coon.

"...at Lex and 74th, and she'd snuggle up real close and sing real soft and pretty, right in my ear. Sometimes she'd make up the song right there on the spot. And it would be beautiful." At the end Coon's voice sort of choked up, and he quickly drained more beer to loosen it. "I was the one who encouraged her to go into singing perfessional," he said finally.

"Bullhockey," said Angie, hoisting herself up from her uncooperative hips, starting her way toward the cooler. By the time she turned to make the arduous journey back to the table, Clarence had walked in and stood next to the others. She turned around using small steps, setting the three open bottles on top of the cooler. Knowing Clarence was a Stag drinker, she slid open the panel to the left.

Clarence nodded to the Windler boys, said hello to Sy and Coon, and good humoredly berated Angie for not letting him get his own damn beer. Angie answered that if a man had to get his own beer he might as well buy it at the liquor store and drink at home. It was only after he sat down that Clarence noticed Sy's face.

"What the Sam hell happened to you?"

"Nothing really," said Sy. "Had a little tiff with a lady's cat is all."

"Was it a Russian Blue, Sy?" asked Angie, who had five cats herself, none of which were around now. "Bet it was a Russian Blue. Russian Blue's get meaner'n hell. Only time they give you any loving is when they want something out of you. Otherwise, you'll never see them."

"Could have been a damn bobcat for all I know," said Sy, feeling a little uncomfortable with the way Clarence was looking at him.

"Must have been a bobcat, by the looks of you," said Clarence.

"I just held it when the lady handed it to me. Then it went nuts."

"If that don't sound like a Russian Blue, I'll—"

"Coon here was just telling us how he used to kiss Barbara Streisand on the lips," Sy interrupted suddenly. Angie wanted to go on talking about cats, but Sy needed to change the subject. Coon just sat there looking dour.

"Is that right, Coon?" asked Clarence, with the same false look of amazement Sy had used earlier.

"Used to kiss her in a good many places," Coon said to the table. "She used to sing to me."

Clarence was about to ask if the fact that Coon was at least thirty-five years older than Streisand ever got in the way but decided Coon had done nothing to deserve such sarcasm.

"Coon, that's something most men would shoot their own dog for. Guess we need to treat you with a little more respect." Clarence raised his beer to Coon and clinked a salute.

"She can warble," added Sy.

"She hadn't got discovered yet," said Coon. After clinking bottles with Clarence, he cheered up a bit.

"Just the same, that's one fine woman. Speaking of fine women, how did Darlene handle that late board meeting last night?" asked Clarence, turning to Sy. Clarence had been with Sy and the others at the ballpark the night before, and he still looked it around the eyes.

"Oh, you know Darlene. Threatened to pull her own head off for half an hour, then settled back down okay."

"I don't suppose she'd believe it if you said the game went sixteen innings." Clarence was the only one of Sy's friends who made other than passing remarks about Darlene.

"What's this board meeting bullshit?" asked Angie.

"We were sitting three rows up, on wooden bleachers. I'd call that a board meeting… wouldn't you, Coon?"

"Only kind of board meeting I've ever been on," said Coon. Just before stopping his mouth with the end of a bottle his head jerked around again, causing him to spill beer on the front of his shirt.

"I bet Barbara goes to lots," said Angie nastily, screwing up her face at Coon like a six-year-old.

"Just stick around," said Sy. "We're about to call the annual meeting of the St. Michael's Church Picnic Committee, the honorable yours truly presiding."

"Sounds like cars right now," said Clarence, leaning back on his chair to squint through the wooden screen door.

"FOUR LEGS!" yelled Angie. "That's the only goddamn original chair I got left."

Outside, car doors slammed, and the sound of footsteps on gravel grew louder before Larry Knaus, Ruthie Turner, and Father Dieckman entered the bar.

Sy pushed another table against the one they'd been using, while Clarence walked over to the back wall, grabbed an empty case, and started clearing the table of beer bottles. Angie grew a little quiet, not used to playing hostess to such exclusive guests, scooted around the table, and sat next to Coon. Drunk as she was, she was determined not to show pleasure at the sudden business. She spent some time focusing on the creaking fan in the middle of the ceiling. "You all get your own beers now," she said. "I ain't as limber as I used to be."

Sy went over and got beers for everyone, writing down how many he had taken on an old calendar hanging above the cooler. The calendar was still open to December—Clydesdales pulling beer through a snowstorm.

When he brought the beer to the table everyone except Ruthie Turner congratulated him on choosing Parkers as the place for the meeting. The last time Ruthie was there she had seen a live maggot drop flat onto the counter from a box of Cream of Wheat. Bunny was still alive and brushed the writhing thing away with the back of his hand and said nothing. Ruthie never forgot it and tried to sit as small as she could on her chair with her hands in her lap, sorry that even her shoes had to touch the floor.

"I talked to Marvin Kaegle just before I left, and he said to tell you he's sorry he won't be here. This is the last night of his son's baseball tournament." Ruthie made the announcement, then set her chin on her chest as if implying she didn't intend to say anything else the rest of the evening.

"Legion team's playing some outfit from Illinois," said Father Dieckman, lighting up a brand-new cigar. "Nobody knows anything about them, but the speculation is we'll do all right if they can get the lights to stay on. I was there last night, and three bulbs exploded for no apparent reason." Sy could see the reverend would be putting on his good face tonight. *Perfect*, he thought. *Priests should act like priests.* He was gearing up to start the meeting and forgot how he had acted like anything but himself only a few hours before.

"Sounds like an act of God to me, Padre," said Clarence.

"He does act for mysterious reasons," said Angie with a nod.

"I think you mean in mysterious ways, don't you Ange?" said Larry Knaus weakly. He'd been laid up at home for several weeks and still felt the effects of cement poisoning he'd picked up for refusing to wear rubber gloves while pouring concrete.

"I don't know," said Angie. "Some things he does don't seem to have much reason behind it either. Excuse my sacrilegiousness, Father." Dieckman only grunted, to convey he wasn't interested in discussing church rubric. Experience taught him those who weren't Catholic, never went to any church, or when into their cups liked discussing ethereal issues. Angie fit all three of those categories, and he wanted to cut her off short. To throw her off, he brought up Sy's face.

"What in the world got hold of you?"

"A cat I met that has it in for real estate people," Sy said quickly, raising his beer.

"A Russian Blue," said Angie.

"Now..." said Sy, clearing his throat for attention. "...we might as well get started. There's a helluva lot to do between now and August third."

"I figured I was here to have a few beers," said Coon.

"Since you're here, you're welcome to throw in your two cents worth, Coon."

Now that he'd been formally invited, Coon scooted his chair closer to the table. If he showed a little interest it was a sure bet he wouldn't pay for another beer the rest of the night.

"You boys are welcome to join in, too, if you like," said Sy, looking over at Charlie Westoff and the Winklers.

"Naw, you all look like you can handle 'er just fine," said Tom, who saw the interruption as an opportunity to take a leak. Standing up, he revealed himself as the thinnest man in Gilmore. With his patched jeans, outdated pearl-button shirt, amateur haircut and shy, introspective attitude, no one would doubt here was a man who might share a sister for a wife. "Just keep me working in the beer stand, and I'll be fine." It was more than the three card players had said in the last hour. Apparently, Tom spoke for them all, because when he returned, they immediately fell back into their game of pitch, silently nursing their warm beers.

"Okay," said Sy. "It's already quarter till eight, so I'm thinking we just concentrate on organizing the dining room for tonight. Before we start talking about who does what, I've got last year's list to work from. I know it's awful tempting to just do the thing the same way, but there are people who've been stuck at the same job three years in a row. It wouldn't be fair to make them do it again." Sy reached into his battered old briefcase and handed out copies of the list. Giving one to Coon reminded him of something.

"Coon, I'm going to start off by taking back what I just said. You got any objection to selling dinner tickets again?" At eighty-four Coon represented the parish's old guard, and when he sat at his little table selling dinner tickets in front of the steps to the school cafeteria, it added color to the whole event. The people coming all the way from St. Louis every year would be disappointed if old Coon weren't there to wisecrack and sell them their dinner tickets.

Coon said no, he didn't suppose he'd mind and could probably do it one more year anyway. The job made him feel important, and he'd consider it a snub giving it to anyone else. He was the "old storyteller," and the dinner-ticket table provided a captive audience.

"Long as the old fart don't start telling people about Barbara," said Angie. "Scuse my French, Father." Dieckman assured the inebriated Angie that her particular idiom was the last thing that needed a pardon. Sy went on, already tiring of being sidetracked and glad no one had asked who the hell this Barbara person was.

"Larry, I figure on you to organize the food supply, since you have that wholesale connection with your brother-in-law. I penciled it out the other day, and we'll need about 1,000 pounds of sliced beef, 1,500 whole fryers, and 3,000 pounds of potatoes—long as we can still take back what we don't use. You'll also be responsible for coffee, tea, and milk. Everything else but dessert comes in a can, and that's handled by the school lunch distributor."

"Shouldn't be a problem," said Larry.

"Ruthie, desserts are on you. I'm thinking if we can get every woman in the parish to bake one pie and a cake that should about cover it."

"I'll spread the word at the next sodality meeting," Ruthie answered softly.

"Padre, maybe you could include this stuff in your Sunday bulletin, eh?"

Dieckman simply nodded, chin in hand. He seemed uncharacteristically distant, barely maintaining enough interest in his own cigar to keep it lit. It was good to see Sy take over, because otherwise the responsibility fell to him, and he didn't feel up to it.

"Oh, and Ruthie, maybe you can make a list of all the girls who can waitress. Last year we took them down to sixth grade, but I'm thinking that's too young. We got complaints from people who had to get their own food. Some of the girls just up and left."

"Clarence, how would you feel about overseeing the dining area," Sy continued. "Greeting and seating and what not."

"Your table, Messieur," said Clarence, bowing deferentially to Coon, indicating with his hand.

"My fuckin' table," said Angie suddenly.

Clarence nodded as if to say *yes, it was* and got up to fetch more beer for everyone but Ruthie, who politely refused on the grounds that she'd been trying to have a child, and alcohol might be a bad idea. After that, Angie announced that she'd been pregnant five times, and that it was mainly due to alcohol in every case.

"Okay, now let's talk about the kitchen. We've had Margie Belkins, Annie Winkler, and Mabel Stuart mashing potatoes three years now, and if they must do it again, I think we're gonna have some lumpy spuds." Mashing potatoes was the worst job in the kitchen, and anyone assigned to the job considered it an indictment of sorts.

"Who's been getting all the cush jobs?" asked Dieckman.

"Linda Durban and Alice Criebaum," snapped Ruthie. "They've enjoyed being outside in the quilt stand for five years, and I think it's time to give someone else a chance."

Now it starts, thought Sy. The nitpicking, the backscratching, and the irrational vendettas. Even a simple church picnic couldn't escape politics. He worried about Ruthie in a position of power, and it looked like he was right. It was no secret that Ruthie and Linda Durban were at odds. Linda's dad was a pig farmer living up the hill from Ruthie and Pete. Five years ago, Pete built a bass lake out back but failed to realize three hundred head of pig shit passed through the watershed behind the house. As a result, the only thing the lake could support was carp. Being a religious bass fisherman, Pete considered a carp nothing more than an aquatic pig.

"What about Nicole Petersen?" asked Larry. One of the most well-off women in the parish, Nicole Petersen lived in a big house on the river bluff, had a built-in swimming pool and did everything she could to flaunt her wealth. Larry was probably imagining Nicole Petersen mashing potatoes with two hands and getting moist potato all over her full-length ermine. He'd been a concrete laborer all his life and had the calloused hands, bad back, and cement poisoning to prove it.

"What about me?" said Father Dieckman, which prompted everyone to look in his direction to see if he was serious. "No, really, I think it would be good public relations for the parish priest to do something menial." Sy shook his head in amazement, wondering what in the world possessed Dieckman to suggest such a thing, and made a mental note to ask him about it later.

Astonished, the others had to agree with him. Clarence noted that, yeah, it wasn't a bad idea, but he should probably wear his black cassock if they really wanted to milk if for all it was worth. "Maybe for a buck apiece we can march 'em past the table and tell 'em they can witness an actual exorcism. The padre could say a little prayer over the boiled spuds, then mash the devil out of 'em."

"Good, it's done then," said Dieckman. Everyone but Sy beamed at the priest, amazed at his selflessness. The simple truth was Dieckman knew he'd have to do something that day, and mashing potatoes would at least get him out of the serious arena, where decisions had to be made and one had to give a damn.

"So that's Linda Durban, Nicole Petersen, and Father Dieckman mashing potatoes," said Sy, feeling like a judge pronouncing sentence. "Let's move on to chicken fryers."

The screen door screeched open again and banged behind Leo Purdy. He was off duty as sheriff of Gilmore County as of the last five minutes but still wore his uniform—white cowboy hat, boots, and sunglasses. After walking in, he greeted the group by raising the fingers of one hand to the brim of his hat, then stood in the middle of the room with his hands on his hips.

"Hell, have a seat, Leo," said Clarence. "But I'll warn you, pulling up a chair means you're automatically on the picnic committee. Kind of like being conscripted or constricted or constipated or some damn thing." Clarence had not only missed dinner, he'd only had a hotdog for lunch. The beer was going to his head. Normally the buzz he felt would be a signal to slow down, but most of the people here were well ahead of him and it didn't matter.

Sy on the other hand realized he was getting drunk for the second night in a row. It wasn't his nature to do that. No doubt he was feeling his beers, but they were doing very little to loosen him.

"I only stopped in for a six-pack to take home, but I suppose I could drink one here with you all," said Leo. He pulled up a chair and sat in it backward. Leaning his arms on the backrest, he took the beer Clarence offered without acknowledging the favor.

"Guess we can count on you and your boys to keep order again this year, eh Leo?" said Father Dieckman.

"I imagine we will. Long as you all know when to shut down the beer stand. As I recall last year it ran a little late." Although a native of the community, Leo took his job seriously.

"Last year, Mike Forde was in charge of the beer stand, and you know how he never likes to see a party end," said Clarence.

"I hear that," said the sheriff, tipping his first one back. "Course there ain't nobody drinking at that hour except the ones who shouldn't be. I keep trying to tell you to serve three-two. The church makes a little more money, the kids stay a little more sober, and I go home early."

"Leo, you know as well as I do this town's full of nothing but Germans," said Clarence. "And Germans would let you mess with their beer about as soon as they'd let you mess with their women."

"Three and two is five," said Leo.

"That's what I'm supposed to be serving here," said Angie. "But there ain't been a three-two beer in this place for years."

"It's a good thing you're on the short arm of the law, Ange," said Leo, who smiled and winked.

"As long I'm here it'll stay that way. Shit, I'll close down first." For as seasoned as the old girl was she'd begun to slur her words. When that happened, everybody knew to humor her. A riled Angie could give a tongue lashing that ripped strips out of a man's pride.

Sy saw they'd gotten done about all they were going to do for the night. Realizing it was done as well, Ruthie Turner rose and, before anyone knew she was leaving, the screen door slammed behind her. When she stood Sy got up too, being the gentleman the beer made him feel like, but he stood quicker than he'd meant to, and his chair went crashing to the floor behind him, almost in unison with the screen door. The sudden combination of noises made the group jump, and for five minutes afterward Angie's head rocked like it rested on a spring.

With Ruthie gone everyone quickly relaxed, and all talk of the church picnic left with her. Everybody but Coon talked at once, and the reason he didn't was because for the last ten minutes he'd been concentrating on numbers scratched out on paper borrowed from the cardplayers.

Hearing Ruthie's car start up and pull away, Sy again stood up and this time headed for the door. "Guess it's time to go out and water the building," he said, still embarrassed about the chair.

For some reason, when Leo Purdy walked in Sy had begun feeling claustrophobic. He wasn't sure why, but Leo's sudden appearance gave him a start, even though they'd known each other for years. Outside it was pitch black, since the moon had yet to come up, and Sy didn't stray far from the patch of light thrown from the screen door. If it weren't for the noises coming from inside Parkers and the sound of his stream on gravel, the night would have been perfectly quiet.

Alone in the dark Sy grew reflective, again, feeling there was something he never got done, and probably never would. *Fuck the goddam picnic*, he thought. This little town and its everyday people had folded him up and stuck him in a box there was no way out of. Somewhere along the way he had made a bad turn. Living in Gilmore all his life, he was past the point where anything here interested him. Life was numbingly dull. *Hell of a time to decide that,* he thought. After shaking himself dry he zipped his pants, stood in the screen door light for a moment, then walked back into Parkers the same way he had since he was a snot-nosed kid.

"So, what's new in the crime world these days?" Larry asked Leo.

"Not much... just glad to see you all still got your clothes on," Leo said loudly. He was tickled to have information only he was privy to, and he wanted everyone to be impressed.

"What're you talking about?" asked Larry.

Knowing the power of the pregnant pause, Leo took another long pull of his beer before going on.

"You know Mary Kay Schleuter, Bert Schleuter's daughter, that nurse gal who lives in Shelbina? No? Well anyway, the other morning a guy walks into her backyard while she was hanging up clothes. Which might not be all that unusual except for the fact he was totally buck naked." Leo leaned back on his chair to survey the room, which caused Angie's eyes to open wide, but he settled back down before she had time to say anything. The news so surprised everyone in the place that even John Windler let out a low whistle.

"Didn't rape her or nothing. Didn't seem to need to. The way it sounds he just stood there wanting her to look at him." Leo paused again, waiting for someone to say something.

"She said he was an older fella. Crazy as a loon."

"The world's just full of screwballs, ain't it," said Angie.

"I been sittin' here thinkin'," Coon suddenly barked. "Figure I been drinking beer since I was thirteen. And, if I were to guess, I'd say I put down an average, now this is just an average—I ain't been drinking every day of my life—of three bottles of beer a day. I'm eighty-three so that's seventy drinking years. If my figuring is right, I've had seventy-six thousand, six hundred and fifty-some-odd beers."

Chapter 9

Sy stumbled out of Parkers, climbed into Charlie Westoff's pickup and spent several minutes trying to get the key into the ignition. He made several stabs at it and tried guiding the right hand with the left but found it still wouldn't work. Finally, he quit trying and sat up to think it through. It was then he noticed his Suburban parked alongside the building, right where he had put it.

By some twist of beer logic, he considered it the pickup's fault for deceiving him, and after crawling out slammed the door hard with his foot. He weaved over to his Suburban and leaned against the fender, head down. After a minute he opened the door and leaned in. He had no business behind the wheel. He forced himself to concentrate as he pulled out of the parking lot, draped himself over the wheel, and drove. There was a chance Darlene was still up and waiting. He was dimly aware of something in the back of his mind, but since it didn't feel like anything positive, he refused to engage it. Whatever it was it didn't want to go away, content to rest there on the periphery until the time came to come forward with its unseemly business. He'd have to eventually bring it up and analyze it to get rid of it, but he'd had too many beers to think about anything other than driving.

Although Sy knew the road, he completely missed the intersection at Windler's bottom and sent the big lumbering Suburban flying off the six-foot embankment. The truck became airborne, the engine racing to an explosively high pitch like a screaming horse that lost its footing and knew it was about to die. Twin beams shined parallel to the field of soybeans, illuminating three feeding deer, which turned and looked toward the vehicle with diamond eyes.

The lights shortened as the heavy Suburban finished its arc, dove into the soft earth, and leaped repeatedly over the tops of soybeans with the grace of a three-ton gazelle. Sy swerved to the right, gunning through the beans for fifty yards and unsuccessfully tried to drive back up to the road. Several times he tried escaping the river bottom and gain purchase on the blacktop, but each time the tires spun out just as he was about to clear the top. Each time he charged the incline it came up at him like a wall, and he unknowingly reacted by letting up on the gas pedal too soon. After settling back into the field for the sixth time, he finally remembered the Suburban had four-wheel-drive. In his hurry to engage it he failed to come to a complete stop, broke the differential in a clash of metal, and it was suddenly useless.

He turned out the lights, lowering his head until it rested against the steering wheel, and took several long, deep breaths. *As a younger man I could do this,* he thought. "As a younger man I could handle my liquor," he whispered out loud. After a while he raised his head resignedly, flipped the lights back on, and inched along the field's perimeter until hitting a narrow dirt contour that led him out of the field and back up to the county road.

After that he did his best to think of nothing but driving. Even though he was on good terms with Leo Purdy, he didn't know any of his young deputies, and if one of them were to arrest him for drunk driving Sy had the suspicion Leo would probably have to back the guy up. Once discovered, he'd be obliged to pay the Windler boys for three acres of prime beans.

Before Sy pulled into his drive he turned off the headlights to keep them from shining into the bedroom window and waking Darlene. As an added precaution he parked near the street, knowing that when he wasn't home Darlene slept very lightly. The sound of a car door could be enough to cause her to sit bolt upright in bed and start fabricating scenarios until she finally convinced herself of one of them and called the police.

Sy had driven the rest of the way home with his window open, and the cool night air revived him a little. Still drunk and humbled from running off the road, he didn't feel like going to bed just yet. He bent across the front seat of the Suburban, fishing around in the glove box for a small, three-cell flashlight.

When he raised the trap door in the floor of the coop and swung the thin beam across the row of roosted pigeons, they woke with a start. A few flapped to the other side of the coop for a safer vantage to see what was happening. One began to coo loudly, nervously sounding the question that spoke for them all—*Why is it you're here disturbing our sleep so late at night?*

Convinced that all fifteen birds had come home, Sy lowered himself back down through the trap door, relieved to escape the fetid, dust-filled air of the coop. The fresh night air rushed in around him and down into his lungs, and he drank it as hungrily as he had the beer that evening. In the darkness he missed the last step, stamped his foot solidly onto the hard-packed earth, and cursed. Arching himself up from under the coop his face shined in the glow of the bright full moon. It appeared low on the horizon, perfectly framed between two large apple trees, which seemed frozen in the cool, iridescent light.

Upstairs in the bathroom he glanced at the mirror, saw the cuts and stared at himself. Entering the bedroom he quickly put on pajamas in the dark. When he gently slid into bed next to Darlene she rolled over, put an arm across his chest, and sleepily asked how the picnic meeting had gone. Sy whispered his response to the ceiling so she wouldn't smell beer.

Darlene fought her drowsiness, determined to wake up. She had promised herself earlier that before the day was out, she'd apologize to Sy for calling Harry Pittman. Sy would have preferred she roll over and go back to sleep, because in addition to his chaotic state of mind, the room was spinning.

"I'm real sorry, Sy. You know I didn't mean to spoil anything."

"You didn't spoil anything. I'll call him first thing in the morning, and if there are any wrinkles to iron out, I'm sure it won't be too tough."

"And I'm sorry, too, that businessmen can't behave like real people and not be put off by one innocent phone call."

After Darlene's last remark Sy rolled over and sighed. She could never bring herself to peel off an apology 100 percent. After a few minutes she spoke again.

"Sy?"

"Yeah?"

"How did your other meeting go, the one with the guy after you retire?"

"Oh fine. Just fine." In the dark, Sy reached up and rubbed his fist into the socket of his right eye. "We're supposed to meet again in a couple of weeks. He's got to go back and talk to his board or something."

"What's his name? I meant to ask you."

"Carmichael. Jim Carmichael." It was the name of a sports columnist in the *Post*, and since Sy said it without thinking it hadn't triggered any alarms. Yet.

"Carmichael. I don't think we know any Carmichaels."

"We know one now."

"How long they been living here?"

"About three months, I think. Why all the questions? Go back to sleep. You were sleeping so nice, and now you're going to have yourself all wound up tight as a drum."

"I'll get up and sleep in the guest room if I keep you awake."

"No, I want you right here where I can get to you." Sy rolled over and put his arm around his wife, being careful to keep his head well above hers. Darlene returned the gesture by tucking her head snugly into Sy's shoulder.

"Why would you want that? Why would you want to sleep next to a woman who doesn't even know to keep her mouth shut?"

"Cause otherwise I'd be the one who couldn't sleep. I don't sleep worth a damn when you're not here with me."

"That's nice. I love it when you say nice things like that." She leaned up and kissed him on the mouth, and Sy held his breath until she rested her head down on his chest. For a while she was quiet, and Sy thought maybe she had gone back to sleep.

"Where was it you met him at?"

"Who?" asked Sy. His head was starting to pound a little, and he wished Darlene would just go on to sleep.

"That Mr. Carmichael. Where did you meet him at?"

"At his house up on the bluffs. We talked on his patio overlooking the river and had those silly little sandwiches that make you feel like a pig if you eat more than three. When he got up to go to the bathroom, I jammed three more into my pocket and ate them later. Now go on back to sleep."

"Oh, you didn't. Did you really?"

"Sure. Small as they were they were pretty damn good."

Darlene giggled and kissed him twice on the collarbone. Judging by the irregular breathing he felt on his skin, Sy knew the questioning wasn't over.

"So did you meet his wife?"

This time Sy waited a little longer before answering. "No, but I met her cat."

"You met her cat?" In the darkness Darlene raised up on an elbow, and Sy could feel her face close to his. "What do you mean, you met her cat?"

"As soon as I walked in the door it jumped out at me from a landing on the steps. It got me in the face pretty good, Darlene."

"You mean it scratched you?"

"Scratched the shit out of me."

"Oh, you poor pumpkin! Are you okay? How bad is it?" Darlene raised a hand and with her face still very close to his began gently stroking Sy's nose and cheeks and the sides of his neck. "Ooh that nasty cat," she whispered softly. "I can feel a scratch here on your cheek, just below your eye."

"Yeah, she got me pretty good there."

"What did you do to make it angry, Sy?"

"Didn't do a thing. Just walked in the door and it got me."

Darlene turned her hand over and continued tracing Sy's face with the back of her fingers, placing small kisses wherever she imagined another cut. Fluidly she rolled onto him and began to move, and Sy could feel the weight of her breasts sliding across his chest.

There was nothing forced about Darlene's move, which meant there was no better opportunity to get things back on track. Darlene was seldom this forward. After all the years they'd been together he could count on one hand the number of times she had initiated sex; yet he was no more excited than if being licked by a puppy.

Darlene's breathing changed to quick, deepening gasps, which made Sy doubt he was in bed with the right woman. Before he could stop her, she traced a hand down the front of his pajamas and slid under the elastic of his waistband. Sy let out a soft moan, and in the darkness Darlene could not tell that it wasn't from pleasure.

With her hand still under his waistband she raised herself up on one elbow, and Sy knew she was looking at him there in the dark, probably perplexed. Then she did an incredible thing. She began inching herself toward the foot of the bed, pulling at his pajama bottoms as she moved down, and did something she hadn't done in over thirty years of marriage.

Sy would have given anything to feel differently. After failing himself so completely that day and drinking too much beer, Darlene's newly discovered sensuality was completely lost on him. Finally, she gave up, heaving herself above him, resting her hands on either side of his shoulders.

After months of nothing, it crushed Darlene to realize that nothing was going to happen still. She had been planning this since her call with Sy that afternoon, replaying it in her mind until she genuinely wanted it. She thought maybe the reason Sy was acting so unnaturally lately had something to do with her not being as fanciful in bed as she could be, and all he needed to change back into his old self was a little more attention from her. She knew men had build-ups, but she never knew how strong they could get until Sy started parading around naked. She was surprisingly excited to help Sy, but his lack of response left her feeling foolish and unwanted.

For Sy, it was an awkward predicament, and if he didn't say something soon Darlene would probably burst into tears.

"Hey, Darlene. I think I had six more beers than I should have tonight," he whispered finally.

Sy could sense her face just above his, and as he waited for a response, two drops of moisture fell out of the night, landing on his cheek. He felt her tremble and collapse into his arms at the same time he reached up for her, and for a while they both shook from the power of her long, convulsive sobs.

"You never want me anymore," she sputtered. "You used to want me all the time. You're acting funny, Sy. Sex kinda funny. I thought it was because I wasn't doing enough for you, but that isn't it, is it? You don't want me even in no nasty way. And now you're drunk again for the second night in a row. What's wrong with you, Sy?"

Sy stared straight ahead as if in a trance, and after Darlene finally quieted down, he silently mouthed the words "I don't know" into the darkness of his bedroom.

Chapter 10

Sy laid in bed with his face to the window, watching to see if the morning would advance into anything beyond a diffused gray. Normally he would have been up long ago, but there was a dull ache at the base of his neck, and he knew that if he went vertical he'd be able to take his own pulse off the booms in his head. It had to be late. From where he lay, far from the dresser, he couldn't begin to make out the numbers on the alarm clock. He'd already gotten up once around six and shut it off, but after hitting the bathroom he had crawled back into bed.

Judging by the light outside it was time to get up and then some. He brought his right hand up and curled his fingers, making a small peephole over his left eye until he narrowed his focal point enough to see the numbers on the clock. He'd seen a native from the African savanna do the same thing on a National Geographic special. Squinting through his fist, the nearly naked hunter was able to spot a small dart in the neck of a warthog, and now Sy used the same technique to see that it was already seven-friggin'-fifteen, and he would be late for work.

Sy eased out of bed so as not to wake Darlene. He considered the possibility she was not actually asleep, but only pretending due to what had happened during the night. Drunk as he'd been, he remembered everything. Standing up on the cool hardwood floor, he glanced over at his sleeping wife and grimaced. Her breaths were long and steady, and in her sleep, she looked more at peace than Sy had seen her in some time. *God, let her sleep*, he thought. He was in no condition for such a test as her waking up would be. He walked over to the dresser, chose suitable clothes and put them on in the bathroom. Before dressing completely, he opened the medicine cabinet and took three aspirin. He closed the cabinet but then opened it back up, staring at Darlene's medications. They filled an entire shelf and included everything from Hydrocodone for her persistent headaches and cramps to a full bottle of Seconal, which she seldom took. Sy shook out a Valium, swallowing it and the aspirin without water. He considered putting another in his pocket, but it was the first time he'd done such a thing and felt guilty. The cabinet door swung slowly shut of its own accord, and when his face appeared in the mirror, he cursed. He grabbed his toothbrush from its place on the wall, and when it fell into the sink he cursed again. Pressed for time, he barely brushed—just enough to alter the taste in his mouth. Walking out the front door, he took a few steps down the driveway, bent to pick up the newspaper, and climbed into the Suburban.

Sy's office was in St. Charles, a town on the Missouri River just outside of St. Louis County. Located halfway between St. Louis and Gilmore, St. Charles had seen rapid growth, providing the opportunity for Sy to earn a good living while still enjoying a rural lifestyle. He liked the work he was doing there and the money that came with it, but the drive back to the bucolic land where he grew up made I70 feel like the portal to paradise.

Sy regretted getting to the office late, but once there he settled in, spending the morning with his door closed. He made a few calls to review progress on a couple of his more important projects but spent an equal amount of time just looking out the eighth-floor window at the Missouri, catching the sun in the distance, and imagining, as he often did, the tired crew of the Lewis and Clark expedition pulling up at the end of their first full day on the river.

At eleven, Harry Pittman called and suggested lunch. They met for burgers at a blue-collar bar in an old section of St. Charles called Dogtown. The restaurant was Sy's suggestion, and while at first doubtful of the casual atmosphere, Pittman quickly relaxed and seemed to enjoy himself. He supposed they were slumming, had found the idea delightfully different, and quickly adopted a non-business attitude, which worked in Sy's favor. Mercifully, he didn't ask about the scratches.

After discussing local sports, Sy introduced the topic of the Kings Highway project. He was relieved when Pittman said nothing regarding Darlene's comment about it being a monstrosity. Pittman did in fact speak of his conversation with Darlene, but only in glowing terms: how he'd been impressed with Sy's wife, and how he'd like to meet her someday. Talking about Darlene with Harry Pittman made Sy nervous, so after sufficient time had passed, he excused himself, saying he had business to attend to, which seemed to disappoint Pittman, who graciously said he understood.

After walking out and shaking hands, Sy didn't make it back to the office. Sitting in the Suburban in the parking lot behind the bar, he dialed his secretary and told her not to expect him that afternoon. He had outside business. As he had done the day before, he rolled out onto the highway and found himself traveling to nowhere in particular, only east this time, toward St. Louis. As he drove, he realized he had no idea where he was going, but it didn't seem to matter. He was racing away from whatever it was that had caused the cuts on his face, and it was only the driving that was important.

As he drove, the worry he'd been repressing swooped in, consuming him like a blast of radiation. What's going on? What's so dramatically off kilter that it would cause him to act so insanely? How did he get those cuts all over his body? He knew it wasn't a dream, since they were all over him. It made sense to assume he'd taken his clothes off again. But who saw him? And how did they react? And why, why, why, why, why oh why on God's green earth did he do such a thing?

Was a stranger sharing space in his brain? Some shadowy alter ego, come to abuse his body just enough as to not destroy it? Well, it would destroy him if this continued. A person like him, ever in control; it would certainly be the end of him.

He'd always had that James Bond kind of precision about him. Whatever he was in control of usually turned out well. It wasn't that he was born under some benevolent, watchful star, or had a lifetime agreement with Lady Luck. No, good fortune rolled his way because he took the time to think things out and cover all the bases. Nobody else he knew made the effort. It was that simple.

Now he just had to make a bigger effort. He would fight it. Next time he would fight like hell against whatever was happening to him and win, then it would never happen again. Like a cigarette addiction—you had to stop cold turkey. Nip it in the bud, as Barney Fife would say. Sy set his jaw hard and gripped the wheel until his fingers showed white.

After an hour he exited, traveling north on an uninteresting county road until it took him to a place called Plevna. He drove through the small town, passing its community center, a nondescript diner, and a Sinclair station with a big green dinosaur mounted on a roadside trailer. On a hill in the distance a church spire rose above a clump of huge elms, each looking to be a couple of hundred years old. Before Sy got to the base of the hill he looked to his right, spotting a ballfield. Without thinking he turned the wheel, pulling up to a woven wire fence across from third base.

There was a Khoury League game going on. Sy watched from inside the Suburban for several minutes before getting out and ambling behind the few wooden bleachers to a small concession stand between home and first base. He stood in front of it for a while, idly watching a tall red-headed boy hurling fast, extremely wild pitches at a much younger boy who edged well away from the plate, almost out of the batter's box. "Strike three!" yelled the umpire, a squat, balding man who wore his blue jeans so low the top of his buttocks showed above his belt. The batter seemed relieved to walk back to the dugout. Leaning the bat against the wire fence, he clutched the fence with both hands and entered a conversation with a young woman on the other side. The woman gave instructions, clearly more upset about the boy's poor performance than he was.

"What can I getcha, fella?" Sy turned around and saw the question was directed at him, coming from an old man leaning casually out the window of the concession stand. "What can I getcha fella?" the man repeated patiently. Sy put his hands in his pockets and leaned against the wall next to the window.

"I don't know. Beer, I guess."

"Don't sell beer. This is a kid's game." The old man talked through a toothpick, not looking at Sy but at the players on the field. Sy noticed the man had only one arm.

"Well, what ya got?" asked Sy politely.

"Got Coke, Pepsi, root beer, and orange Fanta." Turning his attention from the ballfield, the old man looked at Sy, sizing him up. "But if you don't want that I might let you have a Stag from my stash. I don't enjoy drinking alone, so since you're the only one here, I'd be glad to offer you one."

Besides having only one arm the man had a badly wrinkled face, a sign he'd spent a lot of time exposed to the sun. "If ya got one to spare, sure," said Sy. He looked inside the window and noticed a Styrofoam cooler on the floor just to the right of a big metal bin. He really didn't want a beer, but it just seemed natural, since after all he was at a ballpark.

"No, but that don't matter none. Don't plan on gettin' myself swacked or nothin'." With that the old man uncoiled from the ledge, made his way over to the cooler and lifted the lid. With the man's back to him Sy noticed the arm had been severed just above the elbow. Sy heard the stirring of ice, and the old man lifted a bottle, tucked it under his stump and used a church key to pop off the cap. He tossed the opener on the counter, pulled the bottle out from his armpit, and handed it to Sy.

"You do that pretty well," said Sy, taking the bottle. He was surprised at how cold it was.

"Done it a few times," said the old man with a wink. "The trick is to do it quick. Otherwise, it'll freeze ya."

Sy raised his beer and said, "Here's to you."

The big red-headed kid struck the last batter out in three straight pitches, and the home team slowly ambled out to take the field. Sy waited to see who would approach the mound and was pleased to see it was the same boy who talked to the woman through the fence. Sy watched the boy go through his warm-up throws and recognized a lot of his own style in the way the boy kicked his left leg up even with his right shoulder, shielding the ball with his body right up until he let go. The boy appeared much more confident on the mound than at bat.

Sy smiled when the first batter approached, and the boy went for the bill of his cap with his fingers before staring the batter down like a pro. On the first pitch the batter hit an easy grounder to the shortstop who bobbled the ball so badly he couldn't make the play.

"I could do better than that with one hand tied behind my back," said the old man. "'Course if I ever found it, it'd probably smell pretty ripe by now." The man snorted loudly at his own joke, and Sy winced more at the sound that bleated from the man's nose than what he'd said. Although he lacked sophistication, the old man seemed genuine, and Sy took an immediate liking to him.

"You used to play some ball, did you?" Being at a ballpark, Sy's mood lightened enough to where he might enjoy a conversation with ol' one-arm.

"Helch, yes, I used to play some ball. Back when I lived in Pennsylvania. Used to play a good bit of it." Sy knew the response the man was looking for but paused to see how anxious the old guy was to talk. By the way he used the stub, Sy assumed the forearm had been gone a long time. He'd seen guys play with one arm before. It amazed him how easy it came to them and wondered if he would have kept on, given the same circumstances. "You play with that one arm?" asked Sy finally.

"Only one I had," said the man. His voice grew stronger by a few decibels, and as he talked the first word of each sentence sounded like a dog's bark. "Weren't no other way. Corn auger saw to that. If it'd taken both of 'em I probably still woulda played. Course I woulda had to play third base... the bag, not the position." The old man let out another hearty laugh, then stopped like a switch had been flipped and went to the Styrofoam cooler.

"How did you go about it?"

The man came back and spoke as if he hadn't even heard the question. "I used to play for the Centralia Blacksheep. Center field. It was the only place they could stick a one-armer. Ceptin' the bench." The old man looked down, considering. Sy heard a loud crack and swiveled his head in time to see a lanky leftfielder run back to make a nice one-handed catch. "Used to catch the ball with one hand..." The old man raised himself and held his hand up like he was catching a ball until Sy turned back around to see it. "Used to catch the ball with one hand... like that kid just did," he continued. "Then I'd quick tuck the glove under my fin like this, an' reach in an' come up with the ball and fire her in. And do it quickeren' most guys who still had both arms hangin' on 'em."

"Is that a fact," said Sy, raising his eyebrows to register the proper surprise. He then raised his beer so as not to overdo it.

"Sometimes when I was angled just right, I'd flip the glove up in the air and snatch the ball when it came out. That was always the quickest way." The old man grabbed at air to help convince Sy it was the most incredible thing Sy had ever heard. "Most people got more parts than they really need anyhow."

The old man thought to himself a while, shook it off, and turned his gaze on Sy. Sy was looking out to the field again, so he stared at him a good long time. *Here's the kind of man you don't see around here very often*, the old man thought. It was the way the guy stood against the window with his jaw set, looking out over the field, weighing things. The old man could tell Sy was the type of person who called on others to try and measure up. Yet he'd lost his fire. The old man noticed his eyes turned blank as he spoke. This stranger come outta nowhere seemed a nice enough fella, but he had something eatin' at him. The old man could tell. He tried remembering when he last saw a man like that. There were those cuts on his face too. He was curious, but after years of dealing with questions about his own deformity he saw no big enough reason to ask.

Sy felt he had disappointed the old man by not acting impressed enough and made up for it by asking how he went about batting. This got the old man talking again, going into great detail how he would stroke the ball using one hand and back it up with his stub if he were called to bunt. "Never clobbered an over-the-fence home run, but I could always dink out a base hit when we needed one," the old man said.

For the next several innings they quietly watched the big red-headed kid fire fastballs at batters like he meant to kill them. In the stands a small group of mothers made up the only spectators, and they watched the proceedings gloomily. The only chatter came from the pitcher's mother, sitting on a bench next to the first base dugout, yelling encouragement to the next batter. Sy took another pull off his beer and asked the old man who she was.

"At's Brenda Lubbert," said the old man. "Only mother here who gives a big rat's ass 'bout who wins or loses. Although the only thing she really cares about is her boy. She talks to him between innings, reachin' in through the dugout fence, rubbin' his head an' whatnot. Ever since the game started, she's been tryin' to convince him that big red-headed kid ain't got nothing goin'. But she ain't doing so good with it. That big kid's got 'em all convinced he's aiming at their heads. Might as well be true too. He's wild as a monkey. Can't believe he ain't beaned nobody yet." The old man drank and shifted sideways, resting his weight on his good elbow. "Threw one clean over the bleachers a while ago." The old man took considerable time hawking up a load of phlegm from deep in his throat, letting it slide out between his lips and onto the ground.

"You can't blame them for being nervous," said Sy. "That boy could ruin things for a kid this young. It's no fun for anybody when you got a boy like that pitching. If I was the other team's manager, I'd be complaining." Sy looked for a manager in the dugout, seeing it was another mother. Judging by the way she slouched on the bench looking the other way, she was oblivious to what was happening.

"C'mon Johnny, SMACK ONE OUTTA HERE!" yelled the young woman by the home team dugout. "That pitcher's nothing but a wuss!"

The big red-headed pitcher looked at her and scowled. He wound up and let fly another fast ball, hitting the batter squarely on the shoulder. A few groans came from the bleacher moms, and a skinny young man wearing a white T-shirt and black glasses ran from the third-base dugout, joining the umpire in making sure the batter was all right.

"Told you so," the old man said to Sy. "By durn, he nailed him good." He leaned back, shading his eyes under the overhang to see how it was handled. As he watched he began absently scratching at his stub with his good hand.

The batter bit his lip, trying his best not to cry, and as he limped off to first base the young woman who'd been doing all the yelling ran up from around the fence, too late to assist in any way. Lamely, she yelled after him to just shake it off. She turned around, gesturing wildly at the umpire and pointing to the pitcher. Sy couldn't hear what she was saying but wished he could. After a bit she went back to her bench, kicking at the ground as she walked.

"Thanks for the beer," said Sy. He wanted to speak to the pretty young woman who had such passion for the game of baseball. The old man said nothing, staring ahead, gently rubbing the point where his empty sleeve was rolled and pinned.

Sy quietly walked up and stopped just behind her. "If somebody doesn't take that kid off the mound and put him on first base where he belongs, you're gonna have more goose eggs on the bench than you got ballplayers," he said.

"Don't I know it," said the woman. She kept her gaze fixed on the field, fingers tightly gripping the fence, without turning to face him.

Sy eyed the curve of her tight jeans until she finally twisted her head around to see who had spoken to her.

Sy's face flushed. He hadn't expected her to be beautiful. Not here in a little two-pump town called Plevna. She looked younger than Mercy, had short, wheat-colored hair pulled back from her smooth face with twin barrettes and large, blue Icelandic eyes that shined like mercury on either side of a perfectly thin nose. Where Sy's face turned crimson, hers went white as a fish's belly, as if blood had flowed from her face into his. As quickly as she had paled, she regained her composure with a shake of her head, eyed Sy curiously, then turned her attention back to the boy who was walking up to the plate, trying for all the world to look braver than he felt. They both watched in silence as the boy took four straight pitches, then flung his bat toward the dugout and ran to first.

"They should all do just that," the woman said under her breath. "They should all just take the walk and learn that big bastard something about pitching."

"That wouldn't teach them anything," said Sy. He nonchalantly walked up to the fence beside the woman and wove his fingers into it. "It's important they learn good habits when they're young. They'd be wasting their time, doing nothing but walking around the bases like it was some kind of cakewalk."

"Yeah, I guess you're right," she said. "But goddammit, that big galoot's gonna wind up and really hurt somebody." She stomped her foot hard into several inches of pea gravel carpeting the area beneath her.

"All they need is for one kid to get a good solid hit off of him," said Sy. "If somebody could send a hot line drive back at the mound that would be all it'd take." The woman shot an inquisitive glance at Sy, who kept his eyes directed on the field.

"Won't do any good to shake him up," she said. "He's already as wild as he's gonna get."

"It's not for him… it's for your boys here. If somebody could show them that pitcher isn't the devil himself, they could settle down and start stroking the ball. Especially after that kid got nailed while ago."

A boy swinging a bat just in front of them put on his helmet and marched toward the plate. He was still swinging the bat as he walked, trying to put on a brave face. Another boy, much smaller, got off the bench and walked over to choose a bat. Sy recognized him as the pitcher. "That's my boy," said the woman quickly. "C'mon Timmy, smack one down his throat!" The boy looked up and smiled bleakly. He took his time choosing a bat and started swinging it jerkily in every direction. His mother moved a step closer, giving him further encouragement.

"He puts his pants on one leg a time, Timmy. He ain't nothin'. Just look at him. He's one of them oddball redheads. You know how they smell funny don'tcha." The boy kept swinging the bat and shot his mother a sheepish grin. She had another idea and whispered urgently. "Pretend he's naked!" The boy convulsed his shoulders to show he found it funny, but this time didn't turn around.

Suddenly Sy surprised them both by speaking to the boy. "Timmy, why don't you get a smaller bat?" The boy looked surprised to hear his name spoken by a stranger and stopped swinging to squint at Sy. His mother looked at Sy, too, and asked why he should do that. Sy put on his friendliest face and continued talking to the boy. "You need to get around on the ball faster, Timmy. Pitcher's got pretty good steam." The boy looked questioningly at his mother, who first looked at Sy and then nodded for him to go ahead. The boy walked over, chose another bat, then stood in front of Sy like he didn't know what to do next.

Sy leaned farther into the fence, looking brightly at the boy. "Your mom's right about not being afraid of that guy, but you gotta treat him with respect. If you don't, you're only fooling yourself. He's throwing hard and he's wild, but you'll be okay if you stay loose. You gotta stay loose so you can get outta the way of the ball. If you're loose, you got nothin' to worry about, okay?" The boy blinked at Sy and nodded. "Now. When that ball comes, imagine you're watching it in slow motion. Think like you're playing softball. Can you do that?"

"I think so," said the boy. The boy's mother started to say something then thought better of it.

"When that big softball comes floating in, don't take your eye off it," Sy continued. "Follow it all the way in until it meets your bat. And you might want to choke up a little."

"Like this?" said the boy.

"Even more. Up until it doesn't feel natural anymore, then back it back down a bit."

"Batter up!" Sy looked up in time to see the previous batter sauntering down the first base line. The umpire and catcher were both looking their way. The boy turned and headed for the plate.

"Timmy!" The boy stopped and turned to Sy expectantly. "Get down and roll on the ground."

"What!" said the boy's mother. She looked at Sy as if he'd just gone mad. The boy squinted like he hadn't heard right.

"Just get down and roll," Sy repeated. "Loose, remember? Makes you good and loose." The boy looked at Sy questioningly but then hit the ground like he'd been shot, rolled back and forth a few times, then jumped up and ran to the plate. The visiting team hooted like a bunch of baboons. The boy's own team members stayed quiet but looked at each other like they couldn't believe what they just saw. A woman's laughter echoed from the bleachers and died out.

Timmy's pretty mother turned hotly toward Sy, her face flushed with anger and embarrassment. For a second Sy was afraid she might try kicking him. "You trying to make an ass of my boy?"

"If I'm wrong, I'll apologize to him," said Sy. "And to you too," he said as an afterthought. The woman just shook her head, pulled away from the fence, and walked around to the other side of Sy, closer to home plate. "C'mon, Timmy, clobber one!" she yelled at the top of her voice, then flung herself at the fence.

Timmy took three check swings in front of the pitch, then sent the ball sailing well over the left fielder's head with a sharp crack. "WHOOOEEEE!" yelled the boy's mother, jumping up and down like she was on a pogo stick. The home dugout emptied as the boy's teammates ran out to congratulate the runners as they rounded third and headed home. Finally, Timmy came around, running so hard he almost tripped, but he managed to step proudly across the plate well ahead of the ball. The team danced jubilantly as Timmy fought his way out of the crowd and up to Sy. "Hey, thanks!" he said, beaming.

"You just gotta stay loose," said Sy, shaking his head up and down, grinning until his mouth hurt.

As the game continued Sy walked back to the concession stand, bought two Pepsi's against the old man's insistence he have another beer, and rejoined the young woman on the bench behind the fence.

"You know he's gonna make like one of them holy rollers every time he steps up to the plate now," said the boy's mother.

"It was just to distract him. I could have told him to waddle like a duck, and it would have done the same thing."

"Thank God you didn't do that," she said. "He takes it hard enough when people laugh at him the way it is." She turned to smile widely at Sy. "For whatever reason, I think he could have jumped out of the way of a bullet there if he had to." She maintained her smile and shifted her gaze down toward her crossed ankles, raising them off the ground.

"Good thing it's only Khoury League," said Sy. "They're not shooting real bullets yet." Sy examined her profile and again was embarrassed by how she made him feel. Ashamed, maybe. She was definitely younger than Mercy.

"Brenda Lubbert," said the woman suddenly, offering her hand with her palm up, like she wasn't used to a formal handshake.

Sy took her hand crossways in his, shook it limply, and told her who he was.

"You seem to know something about baseball Mr. Todd... or at least how to teach it." Now that introductions had been made, it was the woman's turn to be shy, which wasn't her nature.

"I used to play a little ball..." Sy caught himself about to start bragging and swallowed some Pepsi to suppress the urge. He moved his foot back and forth in the pea gravel, something he'd been doing at ballparks for a long time. He felt his chin with the palm of his hand, wishing he'd taken time to shave that morning.

"Crap," the woman said suddenly, as if she'd just remembered leaving a burner on at home.

"Beg your pardon?"

"Uh, you sat in some crap. I forgot to warn you about the bird crap when you sat down."

Sy raised one side, noticing a spot of white and green paste on the back pocket of his slacks.

"That's not crap," he said, remembering a similar point made recently between Mercy and Darlene.

"That's shit. Bird shit."

"I was gonna say shit, but I didn't want you thinkin' badly of me," said the young woman. She raised her chin, shaking her hair out. "You probably already do, the way I was screaming my head off a while ago."

"It's good to see a little fire at a ballgame," said Sy. "That's the difference between watching it on TV. Getting all caught up is the reason to watch a game in person."

"Yeah, but this is little league."

"It's the same game no matter how old you are. For these boys, it's a chance at being something other than an invisible kid. Not much different than the pros. If the players take things seriously, so do the spectators. Age doesn't matter." Sitting there, next to this pretty woman, Sy concentrated on being charming. It used to come naturally, so it was odd being conscious of it. He took a swig of Pepsi and held the bottle low between his legs to appear nonchalant.

"No matter how interesting things get I need to get a better handle," she said. "I'm always losing my shit. My mom used to tell me that all the time. 'Brenda, you're losing your shit,' she'd say. Only after I was old enough to be said 'shit' to, of course. My mom wasn't the kind to talk that way to a kid." She leaned back, stretching her arms languidly above her head, then peered through them at Sy. She wore a tight-fitting T-shirt, now raised to expose a flat abdomen. "You know what

I'd say back to her?" Sy grinned, shaking his head no. "Groovy, Mom. That used to be my favorite word back then… groovy." Sy watched the young woman's eyes sparkle as she spoke and found himself completely taken by her. She was a girl in a magazine ad who had come to life.

"Can't you say it anymore?"

"What, groovy? I don't know... why don't we find out." She lowered her arms, planting her hands squarely on her thighs. "Say something to me." Excitedly, she swiveled to face Sy and brought her leg up to rest on the bench between them. She wore a half grin, and Sy thought to himself he'd never seen eyes so alive as hers. Sy rested his hands on the bench, slowly looking around the ballpark, until his eyes settled on the wooden scoreboard beyond first base.

"Your team is down six to three."

"Groovy," she said, not taking her eyes off Sy. She sucked in a quick breath, delighted.

Sy found he couldn't look at her with more than a passing glance. She took another breath, exhaled, and said, "So, what you doing here? Got a son playing?" She gave him a playfully shrewd look. "Grandson?"

Twice Sy started to respond but didn't know what to say. He had no idea why he was here instead of the office. "I don't know. I was just driving," he finally said. "Saw the game and pulled over. Can't resist a ballgame."

"Even little league, 'cause it's just as honest as any, right?" After speaking she held her lips slightly parted, preparing to either talk again or break into another smile.

Sy shook his head up and down vigorously. "Especially little league. I think it makes me feel like a talent scout or something. Waiting for the day I see one of them on TV. There'd be something nice about watching a big leaguer you once saw carry his glove on the end of a bat."

There was commotion on the field, and Sy and the woman looked up to see a boy from the opposite team trapped in a hotbox between first and second. The second baseman faked a throw, then threw to first where the runner was tagged out.

"You know any big leaguers?" asked the woman.

"Yes, ma'm," said Sy. "One. Person I used to play ball with in the army. Right fielder named Arnie Johnson. Moved around the big leagues for about five years. Wasn't a bad ball player, but the first time he fell into a bad slump he never came out of it. He started drinking and finally died on some street in... Detroit, I think it was." Sy thought a minute about the man he used to know and found he didn't care anymore.

"That's so sad," the young woman said. To change the subject, she playfully reached her foot under Sy's legs and erased the trough he'd made in the pea gravel. They looked at each other and smiled.

"I went to a big-league game once," she said. "When I was fourteen my grandpa took my brother and me to Busch Stadium for my brother's birthday. The Cardinals against Cincinnati. I was so excited just being there, although I don't remember much, except that the only run the Cardinals scored was a home run by Orlando Cepeda. I remember wanting to get his autograph, but we were so high up, and I was scared to go all the way down by myself. But I didn't want my grandpa to go with me either. Grandpa wore his overalls." For a moment she stopped talking, thinking about something. Sy motioned with his hand to go on.

"He used to call me 'peaches' 'cause my hair was kinda that color then. That's a nice thing to call somebody isn't it?"

Sy nodded.

"Grandpa was a farmer all his life and hated going into the city and being around so many people. It took an hour just to park the pickup. He didn't know what was legal and what wasn't. But he was also kinda poor and since somebody gave him free tickets, he couldn't not go. I loved my grandpa a lot, but I do remember him being a little tight. I also remember being embarrassed that night because he wore his overalls. They were brand new, but still overalls. I didn't sit next to him I was so embarrassed, and I didn't even talk to him, or people might think I was with him. That was so mean, don't you think?"

"I wouldn't worry about it," said Sy. "He was probably wound up so tight from being there he didn't notice." Sy thought about all the times he had taken Mercy to Busch Stadium. It was never a major event such as the one he just heard, but they always had a good time. He'd gotten many autographs for Mercy.

"It was the only time I've been to Busch Stadium, and I haven't been back since."

Sy heard her giggle. One of the boys in the dugout bent to scoop up a practice ball rolling in from the third baseman, and before it reached him it hit a stone, bouncing up and smacking him in the face, but not hard. "YOU GOTTA BE QUICKEREN THAT!" she yelled.

Sy sat back on the bench, realizing how much he was enjoying himself. After such a shitty beginning it had turned into a decent day, and now he was sitting next to a pretty woman who seemed to like talking to him. It was all innocent enough; no reason to worry about anything. There was the age difference and that certainly helped make their sitting together more kosher. Not only was she pretty, she had a strong energy he found infectious. She didn't seem highly educated but not dumb either. Flighty, maybe, but not dumb. Soon she spoke and surprised him again.

"You know you got an awful strong aura?"

"A strong what?"

"Aura. You got an awful strong aura."

"Jeez," Sy said. "I'm really sorry, I didn't have time to shower this morning."

"No. Really. When I first turned around and saw you a while ago, I thought I was going to pass out."

"Yeah, that's the effect I have on most women," said Sy. He sucked in his breath and exhaled, raising himself from the shoulders in a mock exaggeration of pride.

She leaned in, speaking with more emphasis. "Each person has their own aura. We all have one, but only some can pick up on 'em. I've got a strong aura, too, like you. Could you tell when you met me? Sy looked at her and shook his head no. "Then how about this. Have you ever been able to tell when something's gonna happen? Or when somebody else is thinking about you?" Sy shook his head again. "Well, I can. I got this third nipple like my grandma. Without elaborating, the young woman sat up straight on the bench, pointing just below her right breast. "She had a strong aura too. Oh, it isn't gross or anything. It just looks sorta like a mole." She noticed Sy blushing about the nipple and felt the need to let him know everything was all right.

"In general, it isn't much fun. Most of the time I'd rather not know things. The worst of it is when you're lying in bed at night. You're lying in bed at night, you know, all by yourself, and suddenly you know somebody's thinking dirty about you. It just kind of fades into your mind the way the title of a movie comes up at the show. You can tell it. They're thinking dirty about you, and God knows they probably aren't just thinking. Sometimes I can tell when there might be three, four guys laying in their beds, thinking about me at the same time."

"You're a pretty woman," said Sy. He was a little taken aback by the subject and began wiping his mouth with a finger. "You've got to expect guys to think about you like that now and then." He wasn't completely sure how to respond to what the woman was saying. He only knew that if she could indeed pick up on things, he hoped he hadn't given off some signal as to what he himself had been thinking. He tried clearing his mind and watching the game.

"Maybe," said the young woman thoughtfully. "But I just wish I didn't have to know about it." For the first time she tried picking up on what Sy was thinking but found she couldn't. He had a big aura, and there was no way she was able to cut through it. She stopped trying and spoke again. "I bet you're one of those people who can pretty much do whatever you set your mind to, aren't you?"

Sy turned to her with a look of amusement.

"Like right now you don't want to talk much, so you don't. You got no need to make conversation just out of nervousness like a lot of people. Well, me, I'm like that too. I can make myself not eat for three days when I see my jeans are getting too tight. Nothin' but water for three solid days. Bet you could do that, too, if you set your mind to it."

"That can't be much good for you," said Sy, amused.

"You any good at stare contests?" asked the pretty young woman. "I bet you are, with the aura you have. Tell you what. Give me a week to practice up, then we'll meet back here and have a stare contest. Timmy plays the same time every Tuesday."

"That'd be groovy," said Sy.

Chapter 11

By evening, Sy had settled down on his patio with a glass of iced tea. So as not to arouse suspicion from Darlene, he'd made it home near his usual time and was now meditating silently. He had come home tired and was content to do nothing more than sip his tea and listen to the sounds of the American Legion game as they rose from below the orchard.

It was by far the warmest evening of spring, and Sy drained the glass quickly. Even though he wanted more he was too tired to get up and refill it. Instead, he tilted the glass way back and chomped a big ice cube with his back teeth. He should water the lawn or weed some flowers or finish spraying the fruit trees or something, but at the time none of it seemed important.

He heard footsteps coming around the side of the house and heard Mercy say, "Let's see if Grandpa's back here." Mercy rounded the corner, matching Charlotte's small steps and walking with her head down, holding her daughter's arm. It melted Sy's heart, watching them come around the corner like that. When Mercy finally looked up, she was surprised to see Sy sitting there.

"Can't you hear the doorbell from back here?"

"Only if you're listening for it. And hello to you too."

"God, we must have stood at the front door for fifteen minutes."

"That's fifteen minutes I could have been playing with snicklefritz here," said Sy, throwing a playful sneer at his granddaughter.

"You all by yourself? Where's Mom?"

"She's at a Lady's Sodality meeting and won't be back until ten." Sy reached into his glass and tried to fish out another ice cube. Mercy stood for a minute with her hands on her hips as if her father were a stranger needing to be sized up. She wasn't sure what kind of mood she'd caught him in.

"Want me to get you some more tea?"

"That'd be nice of you."

"You want another tea or a beer?" She walked over, kissed Sy on the forehead and took the glass out of his hand. "Me, I did nothing but take shit all day, and I'm going to have a beer."

"Naw, tea would be fine."

As Mercy was about to turn away, she stopped and looked hard at her father. For the first time she noticed the scratches all over his face. "What the hell happened to you?"

Sy saw where she was looking and reached up and brushed self-consciously at his cheek. "I had a run-in with this cat. It's all so silly… I don't want to talk about it, okay?"

"But wha... something scratched the piss out of you!"

"A cat," Sy answered quickly. "Ask your mother. I told her all about it." Sy bent toward his granddaughter and sneered in her face, hoping Mercy would drop it. She furrowed her brow for an instant, then shrugged her shoulders and walked away.

After Mercy walked into the house Sy spent the next couple minutes having a stare contest with his granddaughter. He'd been thinking about stare contests since meeting the young woman that afternoon. What was her name again? At first Charlotte looked at him inquisitively but then realized it was a kind of game and did her best to stare back at him. Then Sy made a loud farting noise between his lips and Charlotte gave up with a giggle, wobbled over and threw herself between Sy's legs. Soon the glass door slid open, and Mercy leaned through with one hand on the door and another on the inside wall of the house.

"I don't see any sign of cooking in here. Have you not eaten anything?"

"Your mother said there was pizza in the freezer."

"Do you want me to heat it up for you?"

"No, I don't feel like eating anything. It's too hot."

A little later Mercy came back out with a plate of cheese and crackers, as well as a fresh iced tea and a beer. When she returned, Charlotte turned and faced her mother hostilely from between Sy's legs, in a way that suggested she was claiming him all for herself.

"Here, you gotta have something, Dad. Good Lord, you'd think you were watching your figure or something." For a while they picked at the cheese and crackers in silence and watched Charlotte, who had wandered off and seemed to find something interesting at the base of the bushes along the patio. She was bent over, poking at the base of them with a stick.

"What do they do at those sodality meetings anyway?" asked Mercy. "I've never been to one, but I keep imagining all those women sitting around clucking like a bunch of hens."

"Oh, they do a lot of things. Organize the quilt club. Decide whose turn it is to clean the church or the rectory. Things like that. But mostly I think they trade recipes. Every time your mother comes home from a sodality meeting, she has a new recipe for some kind of salad. Should change the name to Lady's Saladity."

"Half of those recipes are nothing but pure garbage. Some of 'em she should just throw out. Remember that one she made last summer that called for wilted lettuce?"

"It probably would have been pretty good if she wouldn't have taken wilted so seriously."

"Rotten lettuce salad. God, I'm getting sick just thinking of it," said Mercy.

"Your mother's just trying to keep from getting bored. It's important for a woman your mother's age, else she spends too much time worrying about having to let her pants out or if her roots are showing, or if her new glasses make her look old."

Mercy brushed her long hair back with a forearm, and for a while they both sat there thinking of aging women and rotten lettuce.

"So how you two getting along these days?" She asked the question and then quickly raised her beer, to have something to hide behind if she appeared overly nonchalant. Sy was taking another drink of his tea as she asked the question, and it caused him to hold the glass to his lips a little longer than he'd intended.

"Oh, we're both still stubborn as hell. About the same as always." Then to cover up the thinness of his response he added something as an afterthought. "Had to patch up another situation today that she plowed through like a bull."

"That's not too surprising. What'd the old girl do now?"

Sy told Mercy about the incident with the phone call to Harry Pittman and explained how he'd met with him that day to discuss business, but more than anything to see what he had to say about Darlene. He told her that as it turned out Pittman seemed genuinely taken with Darlene and had even brought up the subject of their having dinner together.

A rabbit quietly appeared at the edge of the orchard, taking advantage of the fading light as well as the random apples that had fallen beneath the trees. Charlotte spotted it and waddled off with her stick to try and get a poke at it. A little later the ballpark lights came on, and as darkness fell, they formed a halo of light rising above the orchard like dawn.

"Want to go down and watch the game?" asked Mercy brightly. "I'd consider it an honor to sit with you on the bleachers, instead of having you nod from the pitcher's mound like we used to do. I felt like a kid in a concentration camp, always watching you pitch from the other side of wire mesh." As she looked at her father, Mercy pulled at an ear like a shy little girl. It was something she fell into when alone with her father and could do nothing to stop it. "Sides that, it's not every day a girl gets the pleasure of sitting next to a Hall of Famer. You all ready for next Sunday? How does it feel being the chosen one?"

"Like being crowned the King of Hearts on Valentine's Day," returned Sy, unsmiling. "Kinda silly."

"I'd think it'd be an honor. I know I'm tickled as shit."

"Hmmph."

"So you wanta go down or not?" asked Mercy after a moment of silence.

"It's kinda nice to just sit here, isn't it? Besides that, it's only a Legion game. More interesting to sit and listen to a Legion game and imagine what's going on rather than actually seeing it." It was a lie, but he'd already seen one game that day and that was enough. He produced a toothpick from his shirt pocket and idly picked at the area between his real teeth and the partial plate he'd worn since catching a line drive back to the mound twenty-five years ago. He seemed focused, so Mercy waited for him to speak next.

"You were too young to see me play Legion ball, weren't you?"

"Dad, I wasn't even born yet. How the hell could I?" Mercy turned her head and knitted her brow. She was a little annoyed with the solemn change to his voice and wondered where the question was going to lead. She suddenly realized Charlotte was out of sight in the orchard and jumped up and yelled twice for her to come back.

As she trundled off and disappeared into the orchard after Charlotte, Sy saw one of the rollers return from some mysterious mission and gently settle itself on the ledge at the entrance to the coop. It took several minutes for the bird to admit the day was over, and when it finally waddled through the small opening to roost it did so reluctantly, pausing to look back several times, as if hoping the sun had not gone down but had simply disappeared behind a heavy cloud.

When she returned with a squalling Charlotte, Mercy put her to bed in the guest room, and for a long while they could hear her fitful screams from the patio, even though Mercy's old bedroom was on the second floor and faced the street.

"So is every night game a Legion game?" asked Mercy.

"No, sometimes it's Khoury league, but Khoury league games won't stir up that much noise. That's a Legion crowd. Those kids get to drinking beer, and soon they're all hootin' at the umpire or at the other team or at each other. Night's the only time they can play. The Hard Road League's got the field all tied up on Sunday, and everybody works during the day."

"What about Saturdays?"

"Saturday's the day you gotta get something accomplished. It's not a day for just kicking around." To her dismay Mercy noticed Sy getting solemn again like he was trying to before. She decided to stop trying to talk him away from it. She'd never seen her father wallow in the dumps before, but that didn't mean there was anything wrong with him doing it now. He was only human, and maybe in a way it was good for him. Still, she had to wonder how long he'd been out here moping, and it occurred to her that maybe this wasn't the first time.

"Legion ball is probably when a guy is at his best," he said, staring down at the glass in his hand. Mercy saw her father hesitate, unusually embarrassed, yet determined to go through with it.

"Why is that, Dad?"

"When a guy's young like that he doesn't have so many things pulling at him. All a guy had to do was play some decent ball."

"You're starting to sound like a sorry old man," said Mercy teasingly. "Like you should be sitting in front of some barber shop."

Sy answered as if it weren't his daughter talking, but a stranger he didn't need to look at. "You know I didn't have one over-the-fence home run hit off me during my entire Legion career?"

"You mean you used to walk everybody? Just kidding." It was Mercy's last attempt to keep Sy out of the gloom, but it flew right past him like a fast ball.

"Did you know they retired my uniform?"

"No!"

"Yeah. I dare you to go down to that field right now and find some young Legion buck wearing a jersey with the number thirty-two on it."

"Where'd they retire it to?" Mercy was a little surprised to hear they'd retired his uniform and made a note to question her mother on it later. Of course, it had to be true. A man like her father didn't lie about something like that.

"I don't know. They just took it off the books or something." Sy didn't know what had become of the uniform. He just knew it wasn't hanging up somewhere for public display or anything as important as that. And they certainly didn't give it to him. He was pretty sure retiring a uniform just meant they didn't delegate the number anymore. If during a game anyone were to ask why there wasn't a number thirty-two, someone would tell them and that would be enough.

"I used to have this change-up that would get batters so disgusted they'd want to take themselves out of the game," said Sy. "I'd bring it in underhanded so they couldn't see it coming. It would usually be when they were expecting a fast ball, and all the way until the very end I'd put everything into it like a fast ball. Then I just wouldn't let go of it. As it was about to leave my fingers, I'd suck it back in and it would come on so slow it looked like I was lobbing a watermelon." Sy sat there numbly, running his fingers over the rim of his empty glass. The words came evenly and without emphasis; he could have been describing his method of cutting the lawn.

"The trick wasn't so much in knowing how to throw a change-up as when to throw it. I could read a batter's mind and know what he was expecting to see and then do the opposite. Like I could see if a guy was winding up tight like he wanted to cork one over the fence, I'd throw him a melon, and he'd get so tangled up trying to stop his swing and start it again that he'd miss the whole damn works."

"And then he'd have to bend down and pull up his shorts in front of everybody," said Mercy. She was starting to warm up to her father's reverie. She loved hearing people from her father's era talk about the past and usually got information about him second hand, from her mother or their friends. Her father lived in the present and had too much energy to dwell on what was behind him. For whatever reason he was opening up, and she intended to hear it all.

"You had to be a good pitcher, because when I watched you play you ran like a herd of turtles," she said, feeding him. "They used to throw you out at first from center field." Mercy heard her father make fun of himself saying the exact same thing, and now she brought it up as test to see if he was digressing into fantasy. If he could handle a little candor, he was probably all right.

Sy looked at his daughter and smiled thinly. "The pitcher doesn't have to run. Doesn't have to hit for that matter, but I could generally hit the ball pretty good. I didn't hit it as often as some, but when I connected, I'd give it a pretty good ride." Mercy was relieved to hear Sy speak realistically about his running ability, but it was a kind of backhanded admission, and she was still uneasy with her father's sudden aggrandizing.

"If Legion ball was your peak, I regret missing it—you pitched like a machine during Hard Road," Mercy said. Sy stopped to muse a little more, moved the toothpick to the other side of his mouth and started digging in a new spot.

"They used to call me a 'mature pitcher' by the time I played Hard Road. I couldn't out-throw younger pitchers then, but I had a whole sack full of pitches that were pretty damn deadly if you knew how to use them together."

Sy stopped talking and went to work with the toothpick. The contentious spot was way in the back, and he held his mouth open wide as he worked away at it. Mercy heard him click his partial plate out with his tongue and then click it back in.

"I remember one Sunday playing this team called the Silex Clowns, which was pretty appropriate when you hear what happened. We were beating them six to nothing in the seventh inning so there wasn't any pressure when I came up to bat."

Mercy knew the story her father was going to tell. She'd been very young, but it was one of those few frames of time a person clips out and stores perfectly intact. It was the name of the team that had done it.

"We knew we were going to win, and I guess I felt a little showy and took three big cuts the first three pitches. The first two I foul-tipped, but I sent the last one way out toward center field, and it felt good, you know, like I could tell I sent it pretty good. But when I got halfway to first, I could see it was going to be short of the wall, and I kicked it in to at least make sure I got a two-bagger out of it. I should have stayed on first, as slow as I run. Roy Ohmes was coaching first and tried to hold me up, but I went for second anyway. I knew the game was all sewn up and just didn't care. But then when I rounded first I heard the plate umpire yell 'Home Run!' and I knew the ball couldn't have been in the air all that time. But everybody is laughing and spilling out of the dugout, and their pitcher throws his glove down all disgusted, and when I pass the shortstop, he's just standing there looking at the ground and shaking his head." Sy's voice became a little more animated, and he was coursing his palm over the stubble of his chin, trying to suppress a smile.

"The center fielder had circled under the ball, but instead of making an easy catch, it struck his head and bounced over the fence. I didn't see it happen, but it was funny because when I rounded first, I remembered hearing what sounded like two coconuts clunking together."

As her father told it Mercy remembered and wondered why the scene had never occurred to her since. She was a little girl and had been in the stands watching and saw it unfold. She remembered seeing the ball go over the fence and feeling sorry for the center fielder because everyone was laughing at him.

They both laughed, if for different reasons. Sy because of all the jokes that followed for weeks afterward and Mercy because it made her remember what it was like to be five years old with pigtails and sit on wooden bleachers and drink orange soda which you had to hold with two hands while watching your dad play baseball.

Sy leaned forward, as if he were about to reveal the formula for nuclear fusion.

"You know when I was really at the peak of my game?"

Mercy shook her head no.

"When I played for the Cannoneers."

"The Cannoneers? Who the hell are the Cannoneers?"

"The 24th Army Artillery's baseball team."

Mercy knew her father's Korean tour occurred shortly before he met her mother and that it was a deeply mysterious part of her father's past. All he'd said was that it snatched him prematurely out of Legion ball, and he'd tried to make up for it by playing over there.

"You were the hot dog over there, were you?"

"There were some guys who said my pitching was what helped me make the youngest master sergeant in Korea. Our CO was a nut for baseball and never missed a game. I didn't lose one the entire year and a half I was there. I got that write-up in *Stars & Stripes*," said Sy calmly, as if that sort of thing happened every day.

"I know. You've got it framed and it's hanging in the hallway. But you never really talked about it. You didn't lose one game the entire time?"

"Not one... I was on a roll in Korea." Watching Sy's face, Mercy settled back further in her chair and slowly crossed her legs. Sy had gone back to staring at his glass. "And it wasn't just baseball either."

Mercy realized her father was about to spill his guts about Korea. She was insanely curious and wanted to help pull words out of his mouth, but at the same time wanted to postpone it for as long as possible, for his sake. There was probably a time when her father should have talked about Korea, but that time was well past, and she felt something malevolent behind this late confession.

"What kind of a name is Cannoneers for a baseball team?" she asked, trying to stay on baseball, not war.

"It's a pretty good one if your CO named the team after the big M115 eight-inch howitzer. And if he happens to be your team's biggest fan. And if it means he can get the nine starters out of going on patrol because you've got a big game against the 26th. We all thought it was a beautiful name. I'd have let him call us the butt lickers if it got me and my guys out of patrol duty."

"Patrol was bad?" Mercy blurted, but when she saw Sy's reaction she regretted asking. His face changed three times. Through sheer force of will Sy regained control, and, trying to be offhand, said, "I was a pretty simple guy until Korea." He jumped up to flip a switch near the patio door.

Earlier that spring Sy had installed an electric bug zapper, the kind that surrounded a lightbulb with an electric grid. Two seconds after Sy turned it on the first insect hit it and fizzed into oblivion. "Hey, you want another beer or something?" he asked. She nodded without speaking and he said, "Yeah, I'll have one too."

Just inside the patio door he stopped. "You smell anything funny?" he asked.

"No. Why? Should I?"

"No. No, I didn't think you would."

It seemed a long time before Mercy heard the door slide again, but he was back with two beers as well as something of his old spirit.

Mercy had no idea how to restart the conversation and stayed quiet. Sy popped open his can of Busch and took a long pull. When he next spoke, he wore a mischievous grin that Mercy welcomed.

"You know, if you think summer's hot in Missouri it's a piece of cake compared to Korea. In Korea it'd be a hundred and five degrees. And if it was any more humid it would have been like being underwater. The record while I was there was a hundred and fifteen. And that day the only people that didn't sweat were the ones that were COW."

"COW?"

"Casualty of war," said Sy. "Dead." He took another swig before going on.

"There was no escaping it. The only river was high up on this mountain behind camp, and before it came low enough to do any good it changed course and watered the gooks. Only they weren't called gooks back then. We called 'em Charlie. Like in Viet Nam. We'd sleep in the shade during the day and do patrols along the river at night. Patrol was the only time you had a chance to swim, but since Charlie was everywhere, I'd only let two guys go in at a time while the rest stood guard."

"I don't imagine they did cannonballs either."

"Even with only two guys you didn't jump into the river... you just kind of slid in. And you didn't make any noise once you were in." Sy stopped to take another pull of his beer, and when he set it down on the wrought-iron table Mercy heard the tinny clink of an empty can.

"There was a master sergeant from the 38th, Lloyd Murdoch was his name. On the first night he lets all his guys go in at the same time. He was dying so bad to cool off himself he went in with 'em. Lloyd told them to stay good and quiet, but all they could think about was the water and they just didn't stay on their toes.

"No matter how careful they were I guess they made a little noise, 'cause after fifteen minutes Charlie lobs hand grenades into the river. There was this one kid... a kid from West Virginia who couldn't swim and was just sittin' up against a tree when it happened. He later told me he heard about five plinks into the river like rocks and then all the sudden the water erupted."

Mercy looked for any sign of angst in her father but saw none. She was amazed by the story but was too worried about Sy to show what she felt. All she could think to say was, "God, that sounds awful."

"Weren't my guys." Sy shrugged and drained the spiders out of his beer and set it in front of Mercy with a look that said it was her turn to get more. "A guy only has enough feeling in him to take care of his own. Clark Gable One was pretty shook up about it though. I know because since he was the only one left of the squad, they gave him to me."

"What in the world is a Clark Gable One?"

"That was the kid's name. Clark Gable Farby, I think it was. It was odd because I already had his older brother under me, and he had the exact same name. We called 'em Clark Gable One and Clark Gable Two to keep 'em straight."

"You mean to tell me he and his brother were both named Clark Gable?"

The memory made Sy grin. "There were a lot of weird things that went on in Korea, and I think most of them happened to me. Clark Gable One and Two were from the hills of West Virginia, and the way they told it their mother went to the movies for the first time and never dreamed a man like Gable could exist." Sy shrugged again, pushing the empty can further toward Mercy. "Everything over in Korea was happening pretty fast, and you didn't notice anything like that for too long."

Mercy got up to get two more beers, still puzzling over why a mother would use the same name twice.

When she came back Sy went on. "One day I had this idea. If we couldn't go to the water, maybe we could bring the water to us. Excited, Sy raised his beer and held it, like he didn't know if he wanted to drink or keep talking. "I had Clark Gable One and Two, Freddie Forde, Miles Wilson and some of the other guys cut down a couple hundred stalks of bamboo, then chop 'em in half, lengthwise. It took a couple weeks to tie 'em all together, but when we were done, we had this water trough that came all the way down from the top of the mountain. At the very end we had this piece of split bamboo with holes along the bottom that we hooked in crosswise for a shower."

"Naw, you didn't... really?" Mercy was delighted, although not surprised, at her father's ingenuity. He'd always been smart, but what was most impressive was the way he could get other men to act. He was a born leader, and long ago he told her the story of how they had made him sergeant the week he was inducted. They were in a hurry to find sergeants and simply went down the line of men and made each one read from the Bible. It was something in his voice. In the way he could read without stopping. He was only nineteen at the time.

"It sounds like they had you in the wrong outfit, Dad. They should have put you with the engineers, building bridges or something."

Sy only shrugged.

A huge June bug zeroed in on the bug zapper light and wedged itself into the electric grid. The sharp burn of electricity continued for some time before the low current fried him off. Below the orchard an elderly woman with a high-pitched voice rooted for the next batter and clapped her hands hard enough to be heard from the patio.

Mercy looked up and followed her father's gaze to the dome of light above the orchard. She felt close to him now, happy he was confiding in her.

"I guess you're old enough I can tell you about this Korean girl who used to wash my clothes."

Mercy sent an ounce of beer down the wrong pipe and tried to keep from coughing until her eyes watered. Sy waited politely until finally it came bursting out.

Still not over her coughing fit, she strained to get the words out from deep in her throat. "Tell me about her." Not once had her father intimated that he was a sexual being. In fact, he and her mother rarely embraced in front of her. Stoicism lifted him above such acts. One time when she was sixteen, she tried sneaking out the front door without a bra, and he simply looked over his paper and said, "Finish dressing." That was the closest they'd come to discussing sex, and she marched back into her room and sheepishly slipped into a bra as if commanded by God himself.

"She was from the village that joined the compound. About seventeen at the time and the prettiest thing in the whole Korean peninsula." Mercy had stopped coughing by now, but before he spoke again Sy coughed twice.

"Everybody had their eye on her but once it was known she was mine they left her alone."

Mercy was incredulous and could not keep from showing it. She had been resting on an elbow, and now her entire forearm went dead, slapping on the table.

"She was yours? Wha... what'd you buy her?"

"No. Course not. I mean she was with me. I mean we were together for a while." Sy was showing more embarrassment now than

Mercy had ever seen from him. For a while they sat looking down at the table. Sy coughed twice more. "No, I didn't buy her... but we were sure as hell sold on each other."

With another burst of resolve he looked Mercy straight in the eye and told it all in a rush, as though if he were to stop again, he wouldn't be able to continue. He told how he'd hang his shirt, pants, and socks outside the tent so the sweat could dry while he slept. And how he'd wake up and find everything still hanging outside the tent, but freshly laundered. He talked about how, whenever he walked into the village, the people living there would run up to greet him, smiling and trying to get closer. It bothered him that Su Lin would bow her head and refuse to look at him. He knew it was her laundering his clothes. He would sit in the shade with the old men and pass out cigarettes, and they would all be very solemn and nod knowingly at each other as they smoked. Occasionally, they would indicate how fine a girl Su Lin was and peer over at Sy through slitted eyelids. Su Lin would never be seen then, but Sy knew she was always close by. And one day, while smoking with the old men, he caught her looking at him from behind an oxcart, and she knew she'd been caught. The next time she brought him his laundry she delivered it inside his tent and did not leave until Clark Gable Two woke them up gently and said the patrol was to begin in fifteen minutes.

"Before I left, I managed to ask her in very bad Korean why she never wanted to look at me. And you know what she said?" Mercy shook her head no, breathless. "She said she was unworthy."

Sy sat there looking so dispirited Mercy thought she would cry. Finally, she managed to say, "You had to leave her there, didn't you."

"Yep." Then in a way that sounded like it took years to convince himself, "That was all part of the war, you know?"

"It sounds like it was a real sad thing to have to do, Dad." Mercy wanted to reach over and touch her father but only went so far as to extend her arm and let it drop. She tried to imagine her father married to an oriental and living in Gilmore in the mid-fifties but found she couldn't.

"It wasn't the worst thing I had to do while I was there."

Here it is, thought Mercy. *Here comes what he's been building up to.* While outwardly she appeared attentive, inwardly she was about to buckle. If not for the fact she inherited half of her father's resolve she might have. He had withstood so many of her own emotional storms over the years, she owed it to him to stay strong for this small wash of his. At the same time, she had no idea how far this might go.

"I killed a hell of a lot of people."

Mercy gave her answer a lot of thought before she spoke. "I can't think of any war where people weren't killed, Dad. And it was their job to kill you. Thank God you were smarter than they were."

"Yeah. Thanks be to God," said Sy dully. Then, "I don't think God had much to do with what went on over there."

The bug zapper atomized three mayflies and sent another big June bug writhing to the patio. Sy stared at it for a while and then swung a leg over and squashed it slowly, with a long, audible crunch.

"If he was anywhere near there, I'm sure he would've made us all play by the rules. And he would've benched some of the real crazy bastards and would've changed some of the things that didn't have to happen the way they did.

"I wouldn't have had to fall in love with a girl and then not be able to stay with her." Sy raised an eyebrow and shot a quick glance at Mercy.

"Maybe you wouldn't have wanted to. Maybe life in the US would have changed her."

"Clark Gable Two might have been killed in a helicopter, but it didn't have to happen on his way back from leave." Again with the eyebrow. "That first day back after vacation is always a bitch, isn't it?"

"Yeah. A real bitch." Mercy spoke softly and stared ahead, a verbal backboard simply bouncing the conversation back to her dad.

"And we wouldn't have had to spend three days of June, 1953, playing cards and shooting Koreans as they were trying to retreat, stacking their bodies like they were bags of sand. Sy glanced over again to check her reaction.

She was taking it, but on the verge of deciding not to. Mercy was vaguely aware that Sy's soliloquy had changed. In the last few minutes his admissions had gone from a cleansing exercise to a source of titillation. He was trying to shock her.

It occurred to her everything her father said so far could be a lie, and it scared her so badly she didn't know what to do. As if from a distance she heard herself give only the most cursory replies. At the same time her father was getting more forceful with his declarations, as if whipping himself with words.

"We did that. It was one of the days we had Charlie on the run."

Below the orchard a wall of cold air moved into the sunken ballpark, changing the temperature by fifteen degrees within minutes. An entire bank of lights between the left and center field fence began exploding like popcorn, spewing shattered glass all over the outfield. Mercy turned to her dad, wide-eyed.

"Thermal inversion. Cold air hitting hot bulbs. It happened the other night too."

"Okay…" said Mercy blankly. "Go on."

Without looking up from the table Sy took another drink of beer and stared at the can before continuing.

"We blocked off their only means of escape, and for three days an entire company walked into our laps, in twos and threes, since they'd been busted up for so long." Sy spoke with more emphasis but mechanically, sounding rehearsed, as if he were reading from a script.

Below the hill the lights above the grandstand were next to react to the sudden thermal inversion. Thousands of fragments of glass rained onto the tin roof that shielded the spectators.

"As soon as they rounded the bend in this big, high granite wall, we'd let 'em have it. I had Melvin Hakenwerth posted on top of the wall so he could radio ahead, and we wouldn't have to stop the card game until the last minute."

"Did you?"

"We shot the piss out of 'em for three days, and after the first morning got tired of burying them so we stacked 'em in rows." Sy's gaze held on the ballpark lights that were still on. They reflected strongly in his eyes, which were heavily glazed, looking like he'd had twelve beers instead of two.

"Each stack eventually got about eight feet high. It was the first thing Charlie'd see when he rounded that wall, those stacks, and after a while we thought it was real fun to wait and see Charlie's face when he rounded that corner. We'd calmly stand up, let 'em see us, wait a while longer, then shoot the fuck out of 'em. They had no place to go, and we shot 'em like rats."

Next the lights behind the visitors' dugout went, and if it were July instead of June one might have thought it the finale to the Gilmore fireworks display. From the patio the light above the trees no longer formed a perfect arc but had pieces chopped out of it.

"Yeah?" said Mercy. He had used that word and now she was certain it was no longer her father who was speaking. It was some stranger who had scratches all over his face.

"Once one of 'em came around the corner all by himself, and when he sees he immediately raises up his hands and starts squealing like a hurt dog. I stand up and walk right up to him and suddenly he starts acting like a prisoner, but I just walk up and shoot him in the head with my pistol 'cause Clark Gable One had just drawn an inside straight and I'm pissed."

On the patio it was still warm, and a single bead of sweat made its way down the side of Sy's face, past his ear, down to his jaw, and finally hung beneath his chin, waiting for the first movement to shake it off.

"My goodness," said Mercy.

"The third day we had to stop because by then you could smell what was going on all the way around the wall, and Charlie could tell it too. He stopped coming around to visit."

Below the hill the popping finally stopped, and the glow above the orchard had all but disappeared. It was being replaced by the halo of the full moon, which had almost cleared the orchard trees and continued to rise a little to the west of the ballpark.

Chapter 12

The next morning Sy got to work early. Everything went smoothly until ten o'clock when he ended up in a meeting he didn't want to be in. While having breakfast, Harry Pittman had found a one-column article buried in the editorial section concerning the possibility of a laborer's strike. Harry had been burned by unions on a previous project two years ago, making him wary of the Kings Highway project. He called the meeting while driving to work, and Sy and Peter Marshall rushed to Pittman's downtown St. Louis office in the rain. They knew the purpose of the visit was basically to do nothing more than hold Harry Pittman's hand.

For the fifth time Pittman asked Sy what he thought of the situation, and Sy was struggling to find yet another way to say the same thing.

"Boog Cook as much as admitted to me the whole thing was only for show." Sy still spoke patiently, having slowed down more each time, until now it sounded as if he were explaining to an eight-year-old child. "Elections are in three months, and Boog wants to be damn sure he stays president. Those were his exact words. He told me a month ago to expect a lot of fake rumbling, and frankly I expected more than this. When your PR department is basically a bank account number you can get the papers to publish anything you want. It's too dangerous for him to stick his neck out now and call a strike. He just threatens one, to make voters think he's a man of action. After he wins, he'll have nothing to prove for a while. We've got smooth sailing for at least two years, and if the project's not done by that time, we'll be far enough along that unions won't matter.

Sy had seen investors react like this at least once with every project and was expecting the same from Pittman any day. Although far from finished, the twenty-story downtown office building had just been topped out, and now the frantic search for renters had begun. It always went slow at first, until you got that one major tenant. Once that happened the rest would fall in line. So far that major tenant hadn't materialized, and that was the real reason for Pittman's nervousness. It was still early and Sy wasn't worried. Loans floated and loans sank, and he'd yet to sink one.

When Sy explained what he thought was enough he turned the conversation to golf, knowing Peter Marshall would be happy to carry it. As president of Templeton Properties, Peter needed to contribute something to the meeting. He knew little about the project and had fumbled a few times before he finally quit talking and allowed Sy to handle it.

Harry and Peter immediately found common ground, which was the Bellerive Country Club. Sy wasn't a member since it cost over fifteen grand a year to join. He backed away and only listened selectively as Peter took the conversation over.

"If you can stay just above the trap that sits in the middle of the dogleg, you've got a clear shot," Sy heard Peter say.

"Maybe we should go out there some afternoon and knock a few around," said Pittman. He sounded relieved to no longer speculate on business failure.

At some point during the meeting the rain stopped, and the clouds momentarily parted. Sy sat in the middle of a column of warm light slanting down from a tall, narrow window. In the humid stillness of the room he began feeling sleepy. Deep in the inner sanctum of Pittman's office things became quiet and churchlike.

Sy fought to stay attentive until Pittman got a call that went on for twenty minutes. At first it annoyed Sy that the call didn't seem important, and that Pittman made no move to dismiss them. After a while he didn't care anymore, just sat enjoying the warmth from the window and floated away. Peter set himself to mapping out the Bellerive golf course on the back of a legal pad.

Sy leaned further into the heavily padded leather chair, drifting patiently. The warm, hypnotic light made him want to doze off. Soon his eyelids lowered and his head fell forward. He caught it just before it fell off his shoulders and onto the floor.

Pittman only continued talking into the phone. "Uh huh... Uh huh...Yeah... Uh huh... Yeah, well let's talk about that, Jack, because I..."

Sy heard the soft click of the door behind him, and Pittman's secretary walked in with a tray of coffees. She looked to be about twenty-five, had short blonde hair that curled around one side to expose a delicate looking ear, and was tall, like a fashion model. She wore a professional looking gray jacket and skirt, a white blouse with a narrow, close-cropped collar which showed only a hint of gold necklace, and a pair of black patent leather heels that rose so high off the floor they couldn't be anything but painful. Before she left, she smiled at Sy, revealing a tiny beauty mark at the corner of her mouth.

After the door closed behind her, the room filled with the strong, undeniable odor of rotten eggs. It quickly grew so overwhelming that Sy's nose started to burn, and his eyes brimmed with tears. It was as if someone had dumped tear gas into the air vent. He raised his arms to rub his eyes and found it odd that he couldn't feel either of his hands. Odder still, Peter wasn't reacting, and at first Sy thought he was trying to be polite in the presence of a major investor. Sy was on the verge of saying something, but when he looked at Pittman, he was still in the middle of his conversation, casually chewing the end of a pencil.

He had smelled the rotten eggs before. He had no idea what it meant, and before he could think any further, he was suddenly blinded by an intense light that erupted from behind his eyes. His mouth parted and went slack. For a micro-second the roof had blown off the building, and Sy was looking straight up into the sun with both eyes open. The flash was a key that opened him up and allowed something strange and irrepressible to bore into him. He felt his body warming up. He was heating up quickly now and could feel the warmth rising from his feet like mercury and past his knees and through his genitals and further on. He heard a small, annoying buzz in his ears and tried swallowing hard to get rid of it. In his mouth there was the taste of blood.

Sy tried to speak but it came out a deep gurgle which no one heard. In his confusion he began to panic, afraid to do anything but resign himself to silence. A trickle of sweat gathered between his shoulder blades, traced down his spine, and was absorbed by the top of his pants upon reaching his beltline. Eventually, things stopped swimming, and, except for the slight mechanical buzzing in his ears, returned close to normal. But the thing that had invaded him was still there. It became an ache that pulsed in and out, and when it expanded outward it demanded he do something he did not want to do.

Sy fought to clear his mind, pushing the thing to the perimeter of his skull, where it thinned like membrane, fragile but refusing to leave. It stayed there weak and thin, waiting patiently for Sy to wear down. Sy's concentration broke, and the thing began expanding inward once again. Sy bore down but drove it less further away.

He tried finding strength in thinking of the people who depended on him. He thought of Darlene and how radiant she looked when she was playful and smiling, but the thing inside him wanted him to do again what he'd done to her, and now he saw her become bewildered, then crying in anguish. He tried focusing on Mercy's face but remembered what he'd told her when he just barely smelled the eggs yesterday—and the way that he'd told it. Remembering, he grew hopelessly lost, and the thing began closing in tighter and tighter until there was only a small circle of Sy left, and then only a glimmer… and then that, too, disappeared.

When Sy left the room, he appeared disengaged, and Pittman covered the phone, stating that Sy was entitled to feel bored and apologized for the interruption. Peter covered for him by saying the only thing left to talk about was the back nine at Bellerive, and he could handle that all by himself. But as Sy backed out of the door with his raincoat on his arm, Peter looked at him oddly and was about to ask if he felt well. Once out of Pittman's office Sy walked straight to the elevator, missing the coy smile from the stylish secretary.

By the time Sy reached his Suburban he was breathing hard. Initially, he remained behind the wheel, hoping that if he sat still for a while the rotten egg smell would go away, and he wouldn't have to continue. He sat slumped against the wheel, staring down, reading the odometer over and over. Fifty-four thousand, six hundred fifty-one and two-tenths, he kept repeating, silently moving his lips as he counted.

The buzzing in his ears increased another degree. He got out, walked to the back of the Suburban, and opened the rear door. He moved aside his clubs and golf outfit, dug further back, and pulled out a small toolbox. He opened the toolbox and removed a small pocketknife that was all but rusted shut.

His first stop was a Shell station less than half a mile away. Even though his tank was three-quarters full he pumped in another five dollars' worth, and when he paid the cashier behind the glass, he asked for the bathroom key.

When he walked out from behind the Shell station, he was wearing his khaki raincoat buttoned all the way up and carried a brown paper bag stuffed full. It had begun to rain again, much too hard to even consider playing golf, but judging by the lime green showing incongruously beneath his expensive raincoat he had changed into his seersuckers. In the bag were his navy suit and trousers, his white oxford shirt, his red striped tie, his underwear, and what remained of his green golf pants.

He drove north on Hanley Road for another two miles before turning east on Highway 70. It was mid-afternoon, the highway was not crowded, and he drove without incident. The further he drove the more his face took on a maniacal grin, and if someone had looked at him in passing, they would have thought he just remembered something absurdly funny.

After crossing the Mississippi on the Martin Luther King bridge, Sy drove thirty minutes into Illinois, then took Route 15 south into Belleville. He rolled up to a red light and stopped. The rain had become a light mist, and behind the intermittent stroke of the windshield wipers Sy was hunched close to the wheel, holding it firmly with both hands at two and ten. His smile remained but it had stiffened, like a wax sculpture.

With the bad weather darkness would come early. As Sy drove up and down the streets of Belleville, the damp, sunless sky darkened evenly, as if the city were gently sinking. Sy drove aimlessly. Each time he slowed for a light the hiss of his wet tires died quietly. His favorite cassette was in the stereo, but he didn't bother to turn it on, and except for the sound of his wipers against the windshield, everything inside the black Suburban was deathly still.

Sy saw a middle-aged woman with a young girl step off a bus and disappear down an alley. He gunned the Suburban down the damp street, through a long yellow light, turned left and parked along the curb. As he stepped out, he was still wearing the wooden, sardonic grin, but a corner of his mouth began to twitch and curve down.

In ten steps he was at the opposite end of the alley the woman and girl had slipped into. He looked nervously up and down the street before going in. Positioning himself beside a dumpster with his hands stuffed deep inside his pockets and his head down, he understood no more about effective concealment than an ostrich.

If Sy had been less focused on the girl and the woman, he might have noticed a fourth person walking the rain-swept streets with him. When Sy stepped out of the Suburban and into the alley, a man, looking to be around Sy's age, followed him in. The man had been walking as aimlessly as Sy had been driving, but unlike Sy, he seemed fully aware of his surroundings and enjoying his walk in the rain.

Seeing Sy step out of the truck he stopped in mid-stride. Dressed the way he was, with the lapels tightly buttoned and collar turned up tight, the man sensed something was off with this guy, even though the dampness was heavy enough to warrant a raincoat. He was, after all, wearing one himself. Watching Sy duck furtively into the alley he felt compelled to follow. From where he stood on the rain-soaked sidewalk, he could plainly see the other fellow take his position near the dumpster.

Ten minutes later Sy was still holding his place by the dumpster. The mist collected on his trench coat, coalescing into beads of moisture, and his hair hung down on his forehead like a short row of stalactites. The sardonic grin changed to a puzzled look, and after a while Sy walked out of the alley and on down the street.

He operated from a small part of his brain that worked only by rote—reacting to street-crossing lights, a rushing ambulance, a begging mutt—paying little attention to anything else. The rest of his brain seemed to be sleeping. The world had stopped turning, and he was on hold.

Weather kept people off the sidewalks, and except for the few cars that shot ambiguously past, Sy wandered alone. At one point he followed an older woman, but just as Sy thought about approaching her she entered a tavern. Before the door swung shut behind her, Sy caught a glimpse of people huddled around a dark bar trimmed in red vinyl. Briefly, he heard an anguished Patsy Cline singing "I'm crazy for trying," but the door closed and cut the song off.

As Sy made his way down Main Street Belleville, the streetlights came on and reflected off the wet blacktop. The wind picked up and pushed the fine mist horizontally, causing a screen door to bang unevenly against the wall of a house. Up ahead Sy caught a glimpse of a large rat scurrying into a storm sewer and gave the gaping hole a wide berth as he passed.

Across the street, the man who had been tracking Sy walked briskly to catch up. Like Sy, he was dressed for business in a brown slicker, the only difference being he wore rubbers over his dress shoes and sported a brown fedora. His fists were planted deep in his pockets like Sy, and occasionally he stole a furtive glance across the street. He had recognized something in Sy's dress as well as his demeanor. Except for the hat the guy across the street was a mirror image of himself.

Both men walked directly across from each other for two more blocks until Sy turned his head stiffly and noticed the other man. Sy suddenly sped up to get ahead. The other guy did the same, and now it was a footrace to the cross street. They reached it at the same time and, as if on cue, they both made hard turns—one left, the other right. They met in the middle of the street, stared at each other for two seconds, and snapped open their coats at the same moment. Aside from Sy's pants being bright green and no hat, they were dressed exactly alike. They wore pantlegs strapped just below the knee. And not a stitch more.

An unexpected ecstasy coursed through Sy's body upon feeling the cool air and wash of another's eyes on his skin. But after a few seconds, when he dimly realized he was being required to provide the same service, the feeling all but died. He shut his coat with his hands still in his pockets and glared at the man as if he'd belched loudly at a friend's funeral.

The man in front of Sy held his coat open wide, curiously holding his breath, then sucking air in quick little spasms. He cocked his face to the side with a devilish look that seemed to say *How you like these, my man?*

The man held his coat open a bit longer, then tugged it closed in sudden resignation. "Jesus what's a man gotta do to snake somebody these days? I thought it might be interesting, snakin' a snaker... But hell, it was like looking at myself in my own damn mirror!"

Agitated, he turned quickly to the right, then back at Sy. "Goddammit! Everybody starts wanting to show their dicks, and soon there won't be anybody left to look at 'em."

Upon seeing the other man's nude body, the buzzing in Sy's ears subsided to a low-level hum. As the buzzing decreased it left him a bit more lucid. Still, Sy could only stare. He realized his mouth was hanging open, and he felt himself redden until his face wanted to burst.

The man looked to be the same age as Sy. Though he tried to sound menacing it didn't come off that way to Sy, knowing he was naked under the coat. Unlike Sy, he was overweight with thick, black body hair starting at his neck, carpeting his chest, tracing the curve of his inflated belly like mountain conifer, and finally disappearing under his overhanging belly. Beneath all that hair he was white as a pearl.

With a hint of a southern drawl, he said, "Goddamn whole world's turning queer as a three-dollar bill. I thought I was the only pree-vert for a hundred miles, but there you were airing out your goddamn pecker like it wasn't getting enough oxygen." The man looked away disgustedly and then turned back. "You gonna talk or just stand there trying to think up a good excuse why you got rubber bands holding up your pants?"

"I… embarrassed," Sy stammered.

"Well, you shouldn't be. Looked to me your equipment's as good as anybody else's." The man squinted and studied Sy closely. "You ever do this kind of thing before?"

Sy looked sheepish and shook his head. "No… not this way."

"I thought you seemed new at it," said the man. "Although your technique isn't bad."

Both men looked around surveying the night, trying to act nonchalant, like two people whose dogs are taking a crap at a busy curb. They were still standing in the middle of the street.

"Might as well call it a night," the man finally said. "Nobody's going to be out on a night like tonight 'cept the friggin' weirdos like you and me." He turned to walk away, thought for a second, then turned back and said, "You want to get a drink?"

The rotten egg smell was still there but had abated somewhat. Still, he was too confused to say yes or no to the man's offer—or much of anything else for that matter. Following the man down the street his awareness grew, as if slowly waking up from a long operation. Maybe this guy carried some clue as to what was happening to him.

He couldn't believe he had just met another person doing this terrible thing. Wasn't he the only man in the world sick enough to perform such a disgusting act? Knowing others were doing it, too, heartened him, in some strange way. Unlike Sy, the man knew what he was about and showed no sign of self-abasement. He kept a step and a half ahead and didn't break stride until they came to a drab little beer joint called The Sheriff's Office. As Sy followed, he buttoned his raincoat up tight, including the very top button of his lapel, which caused his head to sit strangely atop the coat like it had been placed on a shelf.

They entered, and fifteen pairs of eyes turned their way, perceived no immediate threat, and went back to focusing sullenly on glasses of beer. A stale cloud of beer and cigarette smoke hung thick in the air, and everything was glazed in a thin, sticky film. In front of the door an unused pool table stood like an altar. As Sy made his way around it, his shoes stuck to the floor, and each step sounded like he was unzipping Velcro.

Sy and the man made their way through the heavy atmosphere, their long business coats and dress shoes making them look as out of place as a couple of Zulu warriors. When they slid into the second-last booth from the back, a middle-aged, painted waitress with a short skirt and legs cratered by cellulite came over to take their order. She wore a realistic looking badge on her shoulder that said "Deputy Sheriff," and it might have passed for the real thing except she'd taped the name "Cathy" across the middle.

"My my, we don't see many hotshot businessmen like you all in here. Last time we seen nice businessman coats like that was when the ATF boys come in and nailed us for paying off on the poker machine. You boys ain't from the ATF now, are you?"

Sy looked up in a way that pleaded with her to stop talking, but she took no notice. She swept a wisp of drab blonde hair out of her eyes, and Sy noticed a good inch of black roots. Her eyes were sunken and dark, giving the appearance of heavy mascara, which she didn't wear. The waitress took her time lighting a cigarette with both hands and flipped the lit match into the ashtray between them. She took a deep puff, brought an arm across her bulging belly and grabbed her elbow, holding the cigarette well aloft. Sy was about to order a beer when she spoke again.

"We don't see many businessman raincoats like that in here," she repeated. "My boyfriend Dennis wears raincoats, but they ain't near that big, and they're a hell of a lot more fun to put on."

"We'll have two Busch beers with our raincoats, please," said the man across the booth.

"Bottle or draft, sweetheart?"

The man gave Sy a questioning look, and Sy only shrugged. "Draft," the man said. "Frozen mugs if you have them, please." When the woman left, he began surveying the bar in such a way Sy couldn't tell if it had his approval or not. He turned back to Sy and reached his hand across the table. "Bernard," he drawled. "Bernard Belmont. And it's an honor to meet another man of such spirited interests." He pronounced Bernard with the accent long on the second syllable. Sy responded with his first name only.

"Sy. That's an unusual name for an exhibitionist," said Bernard. "Most of the time we're named something fruity, like Constance or Philip. Course they'll try and tell you a name's got nothing at all to do with it. But it surely does. Hearing a name shapes people's perceptions, and they reflect those ideas back to you, defining who you become. It's like passing a virus." The man stopped to give Sy a wide smile, then spoke again.

"Now what's the first thing you thought when you heard me say Bernard?"

Sy only reddened and shook his head.

"Most people I'm introduced to say stuff like 'museum curator.'" The man laced his hands together and put them on the table. "And what I got to show 'em belongs on display, so there you are. I pity the poor sons a bitches named Jim or Bob or Alan. They don't ever know what in hell to become."

Sy stopped listening after the man called him an exhibitionist. It was the first time he'd heard the word since this whole business started, and it caught him by surprise. Thinking about it he supposed well yes, he certainly fit the definition of exhibitionist. But to be a real exhibitionist it had to be a way of life, and it just wasn't that. Not at all. For him it was only because of the rotten egg smell, and maybe it would happen one more time and stop. Then he remembered the intensity of the struggle he'd had with himself that afternoon, and he was suddenly very much aware of being naked beneath the raincoat.

Reaching into an inside pocket, Bernard produced two expensive Cuban cigars and offered one to Sy. After clipping both with a small, gold-plated cutter he produced a Blue-Tip match, struck it flagrantly across the table, and held it up to Sy. At first Sy refused, but Bernard was insistent, saying he'd let the match burn his fingers if Sy didn't come around. Sy took the cigar, leaned in and puffed hard, twirling it with his fingers to get the big cigar stoked, and as he did Bernard spoke again, in the same tone he would use if he were delivering a lecture on physics.

"One thing you gotta do is make sure of who you're snakin'. For instance, you shouldn't have been going for me. Guys old as us are mostly no good. They'll either just grin at you and shake their head or not even acknowledge you and walk on. And that's the worst thing that can happen. You get all pumped up, and the person just walks off like you're invisible. It doesn't hardly seem worth it."

"But you... you were… trying to show yourself to me *too*," said Sy hesitatingly. He hadn't smoked a cigar in a long time and was beginning to think he could enjoy it.

"Yeah, that's true," Bernard said, holding the fat Cuban with all five fingers, puffing meditatively. "But only because I was hard up." He took another puff and blew three smoke rings, each perfectly controlled to pass through the one before.

"Young guys are the best. They see another man's tube steak, and it scares the hell out of 'em. Like they're afraid they might end up liking it or something. Either that or they get afraid there was something about them that made you want to show 'em in the first place. Yeah, they put on a hell of a show. First their jaw drops, then they turn all red in the face and start sputterin' like a goddamn pressure cooker. They get all worked up, mad as hell and start yelling. That's when you know you're doing some good. That's when you can really enjoy snakin' somebody."

Bernard took another big toke, and Sy imitated him.

"But the problem is they'll hit you. Darlin' young bastards get so agitated they try and take a poke at you when they don't know what else to do. Only drawback to snakin' young guys is they almost always smack you. Now where's that fuck-pig of a waitress?"

"Can't you call it something else?" asked Sy. "That sounds vulgar."

"What, snakin'? You'd prefer I said paraphilia, the medical term for what we do? No, snakin' sounds more like what you're doing. Surprising people. It always surprises people to see a snake. What you need is a word that hits 'em in the guts and makes their stomachs flop over. For example, you don't ask a woman to masturbate you… you have her *jack you off*." Bernard raised his cigar hand high and gyrated like he was on a bucking bronco. "And those floppy things between their legs? They're not labis majora... they're pussy lips."

The waitress walked over and sloppily set down two mugs. She surprised Sy by picking up his cigar from the ashtray, jamming it in her mouth and taking a big pull.

"There, you see," said Bernard. "She knows something about the element of surprise."

"You boys are buttoned up so tight you look like a couple a prudes," she said. "Do a girl a favor and show her more of what you got."

"Only if you do the same for us, sugartits," said Bernard brightly. Too dim to think of an evocative reply, the woman set her tray on the table, reached up and undid three buttons of her blouse until the top of her bra was exposed.

"She's just looking for a big tip," said Bernard behind his hand, acting as if the words weren't meant for the woman's ears.

"Hell, I'd want more than the tip," said the waitress. She reached over her tray and tried unbuttoning Sy's lapel. "Let's loosen you up here, baby. You look as up tight as my ex-husband."

"NO!" yelled Sy, loud enough to get a glance from every table around them. When she reached for the button Sy jumped, slamming his thighs into the table, which sent beer sloshing everywhere. The waitress's tray tipped, sending an empty mug flying. Luckily, the mugs stayed on the table and nothing broke.

"Okay, babydoll, have it your way." She picked up her tray and went off smugly.

"Dumb as a sack of hammers," said Bernard, following the waitress in amazement as she marched off. "But the very definition of redneck coquette."

Bernard took a big swig of beer and continued with his lesson. "The ones you got to be careful snakin' are old ladies. Sure, they'll always give you some helluva good eyeball, but I'm always afraid they'll up and die on me. Where a younger woman will scream her lungs out, old ladies want to just stand there and tremble. You half expect 'em to close their eyes and drop like a bolt slammed in their head." Bernard paused to look across the room and watch the slovenly waitress prod an obese customer in the stomach with a pool cue, as if searching his belly button for chalk.

"Except for this one old gal," he continued, warming up to his own voice. "About eighty years old and sweet as could be. She looked like your old fourth grade teacher, you know? She's wearing this dowdy old dress that shows all her old-lady bulges, cat-eye glasses and thick, white support hose, and she has this wispy white hair that's tied up in a bun. She was coming out of Famous Barr with a big shopping bag, and when she walked into the tunnel to the parking garage I jump out and snake her right there, like a big ol' dog."

To illustrate, Bernard held his cigar low above the table with the fingers of both hands. "Without battin' an eye this little ol' gal marches right up and kicks me in the fuckin' nuts with everything she's got.

Then she slams me on the shoulder with her purse and turns around and walks away like Joe friggin' Louis."

Sy gave out a small laugh. He would have found the story even more amusing had he not been somehow intrigued by it. It was nine hours since the meeting at Pittman's, but the eggs were still there. Sy was more himself, but the strange desire to bask naked in front of an appraising gaze was still faintly there.

"And another thing. You can't be doing it on your home turf. Where is it you live exactly?"

Sy was reluctant to tell him where he lived, but sitting there with the man, talking about the subject so openly, gave Sy a fraternal feeling like he'd never experienced. Even in Korea. Besides that, they'd just seen each other naked. "I've lived in Gilmore almost my entire life... Old Gilmore."

"Good," said Bernard. "Not sure where that is, but you already know about getting away from people who might put the finger on you. First time you sneak up on a guy and he turns out to be your brother-in-law, you're fucked."

"You know, I don't do this sort of thing all the time," said Sy. "Just sometimes the mood hits me hard… like a hammer." Sy picked up his beer and took a nervous sip. "Started just a little while ago, far as I can tell."

"Shit, I'm ready to snake somebody most any time," said Bernard. "Since I was about eighteen. I got half a mind to get some eyeball off that dumb-ass waitress."

Sy turned around and appraised the woman again, this time with an eye for how she might react to seeing him suddenly nude. He noticed her blouse was still undone, and she laughed while the fat man with the pool cue navel tried to pay for his beer by sticking bills down her front.

"Once I snaked an entire Amtrak train as it was pulling out of the station," said Bernard excitedly. "It was perfect. People who ride Amtrak start gawking out the window like they're watching television soon as the thing starts to move. They all filed past me at about a fast walk, and I gave 'em the most exciting scenery they were going to see the whole trip."

Bernard looked straight at Sy as he spoke. His eyes widened and shined like twin moons through the swirl of smoke. "Ladies jumped up and grabbed their husbands. Young girls pointed and giggled like at the zoo. People were smiling and waving and pressing up against the window. All looking at me, spread eagle to the world, wearing nothing but a shit-eating grin. I tell you Sy, it was art. The beauty of it was nobody could stop the train and smack me or kick me in the nuts or give me a rash of shit. It was the longest continuous snakin' I ever did. I just stood and snaked and snaked and snaked for over five minutes. Thought I was gonna blow a nut right there."

"What do you mean, blow a nut?" asked Sy, confused.

"Man, I was gonna spew forth like the windshield washers on your friggin' car."

Sy grew incredulous. "You mean to tell me it was doing that to you?"

Now it was Bernard's turn to be surprised. "You goddamn right. Only problem was the caboose came before I did. Why the hell else would a man want to do something like that?"

"I don't know," said Sy. "It never occurred to me in that way."

"No, you only do it for your nut, you know? I call it eyeballin'. Get it, eye ballin'?"

Whatever small bond Sy felt with the man across the booth changed to contempt. For Sy, whatever it was, it was not sexual... as far as he could tell. He had no idea what it was. Personality disorder? Maybe. Probably. Whatever it was, he needed help. Sy raised his beer and he drank. At the moment he didn't care what it was. He just knew it differed from whatever the fuck Bernard had going on.

"My God, that's disgusting. What you're using those people for... it's only a little above rape."

"Rape? Naw, c'mon... Well maybe kind of like rape, but you're not hurting anybody. Least as long as some senile old lady doesn't flop down and die." Bernard said it matter-of-factly, as if he'd come to terms with the question long ago and was beyond taking it up again. "Besides, half of 'em I wouldn't want to touch with a ten-foot pole. Ugh. The thought of actually having to touch somebody... now that's disgusting."

"What about your wife?" Sy nodded down at the ring on Bernard's finger.

"Leslie? She's seen me naked so many times it'd be like standing in front of a wall."

"No, I don't mean... snaking... her," said Sy impatiently. "What about Leslie? Don't you two, you know, do it the normal way anymore?"

"Are we still making the beast with the two backs? Hardly. Leslie doesn't want anything from me anymore, and she's got nothing I'm interested in."

"You live with a woman, you've got to do it sometime," said Sy. "You've never come back from a wedding dance where you've been laughing with friends and dancing a lot and maybe you both had a little too much to drink? Or you never walk in from work after having a really good day and you find out she's had a really good day, too, and maybe you barbeque on the patio or something, open a bottle of wine and drink it, just the two of you, and then afterwards you go to bed and you're still happy and not at all tired?" Hearing himself talk Sy thought maybe he and Darlene's sex life wasn't all that bad. Not for a couple pushing sixty and sixty-four.

"Why in the pluperfect hell would we want to do all that? We watch TV. We have a couple drinks until the news is over. I stumble up to bed and go to sleep. Staying awake's not worth a fuck and neither is she."

Bernard's face went blank as he brought the mug up to it, then brightened. "Oh, we kiss every once in a while. I give her a big ol' bear hug on her birthday. It's not that we don't love each other or anything. I just can't stand to touch her the other way. I'd rather put on a tin bill and pick shit with the chickens."

"Why do you figure that is?" asked Sy, idly circling the rim of his mug with his forefinger.

"Just seems silly."

"Silly…"

"Well now I can't figure you," said Bernard. "You're obviously still pokin' your wife. What brings a fine upstanding gentleman like yourself out to the streets of Belleville, Illinois, in a pair of inverted cut-offs if it's not about your nut? You making a political statement like Lady Godiva? Taxes too high? National debt too out of hand for you? No, lessee, you're exposing yourself to skin cancer to protest the depletion of the ozone, right?"

Sy took another long drink and ashed his cigar.

"I don't have the slightest idea why I do it, to tell you the truth. I guess it'd take a hotshot psychiatrist to figure it out." Sy lowered his head like a tired old dog, resting his chin on the mug he held with both hands. He began talking again, and the words came out slow and soft and steady, like a religious litany one knows by heart.

"I can tell you I've been pretty unhappy lately. I can tell you life is dull, and things aren't as enjoyable or as effortless. And that I'm starting to feel sorry I gave up so much, just to be everybody else's Rock of Gibraltar. I'm telling you, Bernard, being the strong one isn't what it's cracked up to be. There's just nothing in it. Cept being smug. And what good does smug do you? It gets old. *I'm* getting old. Time is slipping up on me. It's a little harder to get out of bed in the morning. The young guys at work are beginning to question what I tell 'em. They've never done that before… It's harder not to feel pissed all the time. And after all these years it's hard to accept the fact I've got a wife who's bat shit crazy, and everybody knows it."

Bernard sat back in the booth, giving Sy all the time he needed. He knew men who had been in this place before, himself included. He liked this guy and would give him a good listening to.

"Pretty women seldom look at me anymore. But I still look at them. Oh boy do I like looking at a pretty woman. I remember when girls would come up to me all the time, and all I had to do was ignore them and that would make 'em come on more, you know? If I got interested in one, I'd take her to my ballgame, and she'd sit with all the other girls, and they'd watch me pitch and yell real loud and high pitched, like girls do. Afterwards she'd come up to me like a puppy, all flush and excited, expecting me to say or do something profound."

Bernard cleared his throat and Sy stopped talking, expecting him to say something. When Bernard replanted his cigar, the quirky smile was missing.

"You tell *me* why I drove to Belleville. All I know is something inside told me to up and do it. I tried to make it go away, but couldn't. Used to be if there was something I knew wasn't right I wouldn't do 'er. I decided right away that something was wrong or it would hurt somebody else, and that'd be it. I smoked cigarettes when I was younger. Two packs a day. One day I decide it's bad for me and I up and quit, just like that. I used to be so responsible I could carry two, three, or a dozen people. Now I'm thinking I can't even take care of myself. I used to never take another drink after I started feeling 'em. Well, I've been drunk twice this week and it's only Wednesday, and for the life of me I can't tell you why."

With his elbows still resting on the table, Sy drained his beer with his hands. Bernard waved to the waitress, who brought two more without saying a word. Ignorant as she was, she'd been a waitress long enough to spot a serious table and knew to let them alone. When she set the beers down both men hurriedly drank. Sy sat up with his shoulders against the booth, staring pensively at his hands on the mug and continued his soliloquy, with Bernard quietly listening like a priest.

"Lately I been thinking that maybe, just maybe I've been too cautious all my life. Like I've worn this overcoat all along, buttoned up tight like it is now, and all the sudden I'm making up for it."

There was a loud crack, followed by clacking of stone on wood. A white cue ball bounced against Sy's foot. He picked it up and turned it over slowly, as if there might be a message. The fat waitress stood next to him, resting on a pool cue.

"It's not a hard-boiled egg, if you're thinking about eatin' it," she said sarcastically. "It's a cue ball, and we'd kind of like to have it back."

Sy handed it over and apologized. She blew air up over her face, lifting her thin bangs slightly and shook her head while waddling back to the fat man, who stared hard at the two of them.

Still pushed up against the booth, Sy drank more beer, then idly turned his glass on the table. He hesitated, took another drink and said, "Did you ever get the feeling that you want to do something, want it so bad until finally it doesn't make no difference who it affects or why, you just gotta do it?" Bernard nodded knowingly and ordered two more beers. He knew when a man had to talk.

"Like this one guy I heard about," Sy said. "He had to write. This guy was in prison. I forget his name, but he wrote for seven days nonstop, without eating or sleeping. Course he'd never made it past sixth grade and none of it was any good, but he had to do it all the same. They finally took away his pens and paper so he'd eat, and when they came back to check on him, he'd written a full paragraph out of mashed potatoes. Well, that's how bad it gets for me... only I'm not writing. I'm doing something sick, and I'd give anything to make it something else."

Sy felt miserable and didn't care if he offended the man across from him. "I watched this crazy guy once. He was staying at this expensive home for… well it was some kind of insane asylum. He'd go down to this bridge that crossed a little creek on the property. Every day he'd march into that creek and pick up big rocks one at a time, climb out, and stack them on top of the bridge abutment. By the end of the day, he'd have hundreds of rocks, all lined up on the bridge. When they were about to call him in, he'd throw every one of those rocks back into the damn creek. Compared to what I been doing I'd call him a lucky man. I'm feeling crazier than that poor bastard."

"There's a fine line between what's crazy and what's not," said Bernard defensively. "People can act a little crazy one minute and sane as a judge the next. Take me, for instance. I know you think what I do—what we do—is a bit… eccentric. But I'm a long way away from the nuthouse. I may not look like it, but I'm the proud owner of a fine little steel mill in Flat River. We make nothing but hardened steel couplers for McDonnell Douglas, and it doesn't take a whole lot of brains to make it work because we've got a thirty-year contract. Even so, I've got a hundred and fifty people working for me. A guy can't be nuts and handle that many people successfully. Guy does one thing that's a little odd, that's okay. As long as it's fairly harmless and you understand it's unusual. And if nobody finds out, of course."

Sy looked across at Bernard and thought it could very well be true. He appeared as clean cut, educated, and in control as any business professional he'd met. He rested his elbows on the table, put his chin between a thumb and forefinger, and nodded.

All so-called deviant behavior was relative, and if showing your body to strangers was your one thing, maybe there was a way to live with it. Maybe things weren't so bad after all. That realization, in addition to the beers he'd slammed, caused him to feel better, almost pleasant.

"So does your wife know what you're up to?" he asked.

Bernard grinned, bent down, and showed Sy what was under his coat. "Who do you think made these? Elastic around the top, machine sewn like factory." He snapped the band against his leg as proof. "I've been kidding her about starting a mail order business."

"Not every man's wife would be so understanding," said Sy.

"She's all right as long as she knows I'm not a looney," said Bernard. "As long as she can keep driving her fancy car, take her trips and flash her Gold Visa Card, she'll be all right. But she keeps telling me the day I get discovered she'll divorce me. And I can't say I'd blame her."

"You're not worried about getting caught?" Now that Sy felt better he stopped thinking about his problems, concentrating more on enjoying his beer and cigar.

"I expect to get caught eventually. No, I *know* I'll get caught some day. But that's what keeps things interesting. I'm waiting for it. It's what this whole thing is building up to, really."

"You almost sound like you want it to happen."

"Yeah," said Bernard wistfully. "My final expose'. The biggest one ever." His face mellowed, taking on a faraway expression, like men do when considering their dream.

"You know how I'd like to see it happen?"

Sy shook his head no.

"I'd like to see a big picture of me in the newspaper, steel company president, full frontal and lookin' proud."

He frowned and said a little angrily, "Fuckers will probably black out my prick though. They'll have one of those black bars running diagonally across it like when they don't want to identify people."

"It's the only thing they won't be able to recognize," said Sy.

"And by then I guarantee there'll be plenty of people who could recognize it," interrupted Bernard. He said it with so much pride and joy, like he'd just become a father. "It's what my life's been leading up to. The day Bernard Belmont gets to wag his dick at the world."

Sy considered such a thing happening to himself, and it horrified him. Not so much for what it would mean to him personally, which was considerable, but how Darlene would take it. She'd fly to pieces like a butterfly in a tornado. He pictured Darlene scrambling up out of a creek and struggling to place a rock on the bridge above. Then he saw an image of Mercy. She was crying, slowly putting pictures of him in some unused closet.

"For me it's the element of surprise," Bernard continued. "The bigger the surprise the better. It's not worth doing if it doesn't surprise people."

"I'm sure your picture in the paper would be a big surprise," said Sy. "I can see the caption now. 'Steel magnate gears up for huge new erection.'"

Bernard laughed and said, "I knew this kid in high school who liked to surprise people too. Hard telling what he might be doing for kicks now." Sy asked what it was the kid did.

"This kid, Kenny Martin, farted all the time. No matter where he was or who was there. He was great at it. We'd be in class, taking a test. All of a sudden he'd let out this huge fart, the kind that rumbled the desk, and everybody would bust up, including Kenny. It was so damn funny, the teachers wouldn't do much about it. They'd just shake their heads and hide a smile. Other times he'd be in the middle of answering a question the teacher asked. He'd stop talking, lean over, squint real hard and blast one out. Not just a little squeaker either, but one of those big BRIGGADIM, BRIGGADOWOWOWOWs. He had a reputation for it, and you'd be disappointed if Kenny was in class and didn't rip one. Everybody acted disgusted, but they all loved that somebody had the balls to do it. That's what they're going to say about me when the picture comes out in the *Post*… 'That guy had balls.'"

"Even if they can't see them," said Sy dryly.

"Even if," said Bernard. "Hope it's a *big* black bar if they're going to use one," he said, grinning. "I'd be embarrassed if people thought I was a pencil-dick."

"I'm kinda like Kenny," said Sy flatly.

"What do you mean?"

"I can fart whenever I want to."

"Go ahead and fart," said Bernard, nodding at Sy.

"I don't want to."

Both men paused, then laughed uproariously. They emptied their beers and set them on the table. Sy wiped his mouth and burped loud and long. He threw a wide grin at Bernard, who congratulated him on the surprise move, then turned on one side and tried farting with no success.

"Sometimes Kenny's farts wouldn't stink," he continued. "But he would eat stuff that made 'em stink like hell. He always gave the same excuse that it wasn't paying the rent, so he had to kick it out. Junior year we took French and gave him the nickname that stuck until we graduated."

"Okay, what was the nickname?"

"Kenny Coupe du Fromage," said Bernard with an exaggerated French accent. "Kenny Cut the Cheese."

"The boy who wanted to be loved so bad he farted in public," said Sy. No doubt, he was starting to feel buzzed. For a while both men drank in silence.

"You got any other hobbies, besides… snakin'?" asked Sy.

"What you mean? Like building ships in a bottle?"

"I mean real everyday hobbies. Me for instance, I raise rollers." Sy tilted his head and looked thinly at Bernard, like a shy boy trying to tell if he was being listened to.

"Rollers? You talking about those queer little beetles that roll balls of shit all over creation?"

"No. I'm talking about pigeons. Rolling pigeons." Sy went on to tell Bernard all about his birds and their strange genetically induced proclivities.

"I guess I have a hobby, too, although it's not nearly as exotic as skydiving pigeons," said Bernard.

"Yeah, what's that?" asked Sy, hunching forward enthusiastically.

"Fish."

"There. You see," said Sy. "You raise goldfish?"

"I don't raise goldfish, for Christ's sake. *A* fish. I got this gar from out of the river. Sometimes I feed him goldfish though."

"Gar! What are you doing with a gar? Those things get big, don't they?"

"He's about yay big," said Bernard, indicating eighteen inches between his hands.

"How big is your tank? Must take a fifty-gallon for a fish that big. Hundred maybe."

"Naw. I keep him in a ten-gallon tank. Bout this big." Bernard again indicated with his hands, a length just slightly larger than before.

"But that's not near big enough!" said Sy, beginning to slur.

"I know," said Bernard. "He can't even turn around. When I feed him minnows he has to wait until one swims up by his head, then he kinda flips his jaws sideways to grab it."

"Isn't he awfully uncomfortable in there?"

"Yeah, but fuck him," said Bernard absently.

The two men raised their beers, and when they caught each other's eyes they again burst into uncontrollable laughter, spewing beer all over the table.

Facing the pool table, Bernard brought his arm up over his head in a big bear wave. The waitress was looking in his direction but stretched across the table with a cigarette dangling from her mouth, too busy rehearsing the geometry of the shot to pay attention to Bernard's current needs. "That bitch needs to have that stick jammed up her ass," he muttered.

The fat man sidled up behind her, held his arms out wide and threw a few pumps into her rear. Without looking off her mark she rammed the butt of the cue into the middle of his pants, causing his mouth and eyes to open while his beer fell out of his hand, smashing against the floor. He stumbled a few feet back into a stack of empty beer cases and sank onto one. He spread his legs wide while firmly holding the cue in front of him, and his teeth were grimly set.

Bernard waited for her to miss the shot and argue it was the fat man's fault before raising his voice and yelling, "What's a guy need to do to get a little service around here?"

She marched over with the beer like she was the queen of England, who, having found no domestics available, deigned to serve the guests herself. "Funny how you can be somewhere and see more horse's asses than you do horses," she said, very un-queenlike.

Bernard seemed to ignore her and looked at Sy, mock serious. "You know some women are just born smellin' like that. They can wash every crack they got and still have that dog in heat kinda odor about 'em."

"At least we don't go around gettin' drunk with our coats buttoned up like a goddamn straitjacket. You boys gay or somethin'?"

"If we were to gaze upon your visage much longer, madame, we might consider it," said Bernard.

"I'm going to turn up the heat in here and bake you two shithooks," said the waitress before turning around smartly and heading back to the pool table. When she got there, she spoke to the fat man and pointed at their table. The fat man looked in their direction, wiggled his shoulders around, and touched the bill of his cap two or three times.

"Let's slam these and get the hell out of here," said Bernard.

"Place kinda smells like rotten eggs, doesn't it," answered Sy. Both men raised their glasses and drained them quickly.

When they stood to leave, the jukebox was having a momentary respite. Everyone in the bar heard their footsteps on the wooden floor, watching them weave between the rows of tables. The waitress and her pool partner watched them hostilely. Sy was halfway out the door when Bernard turned around and stared at the waitress blankly.

The sound of long loud flatulence resonated from under Bernard's coat and over the floor and into the ears of everyone in the place. Sy saw the back of Bernard's coat waft out ever so slightly.

Making their way down the sidewalk, Sy laughed until he cried and was still wiping at his eyes when they entered the next bar a block away.

Two hours later the air outside the second bar was still wet and heavy, causing the façade to shimmer like a fresh oil painting. Occasionally a car rolled by, and twice someone entered the bar—lone, furtive individuals who could not sleep or had no work to report to the next day. A half-hour after midnight a skinny, black dog slinked out of the alley, climbed the few steps and sniffed the door jamb, trying to identify the myriad of smells coming from inside. Suddenly the door burst open, striking the dog across the bridge of its nose. It yelped and quickly disappeared back into the depths of the dark alley.

Sy and Bernard stumbled out, their arms around each other's shoulders, and maneuvered the three steps to the sidewalk.

"I don't care what yer wife shesh about you, you're the best goddamn snaker this country's ever seen," said Sy, his tongue thick. "I gotta lotta respect for you and your ability."

Bernard looked up and down the street, trying to decide which way to go. His eyes were shining. He had the look of a hungry wolf.

"YOU HEAR ME!" yelled Sy.

"Damn straight I hear you," said Bernard. "And you gotta lotta potential."

"AN' I GOTTA LOTTA POTENTIAL!" announced Sy to the world, swinging his free arm wide. "I like you, Bernard. You're a man who knows what he wants and goes out and gets it. Fuck the consequences."

"I know what I want now," said Bernard. He twisted them to the right, the direction they'd come from earlier, and began surveying the area in all directions.

"KING SNAKE!" yelled Sy. "FROM NOW ON WE'LL CALL YOU KING SNAKE!"

"And I think we'll call you a cab," said Bernard, who seemed fired by the alcohol rather than drunk, giving the impression of being more sober than Sy.

"LOOK OUT EVERYBODY, HERE COMES A KING SNAKE!" Sy fell against Bernard in convulsive laughter, as they stumbled another twenty yards.

Sy fell drunkenly silent as he fumbled at the buttons of his coat. He stopped in front of a clothing store window and snapped it open. Three mannequins displaying the latest fall fashions took no notice of him.

"Look at that motherfuckin' technique, Bernard. Didja see the way I snapped it open? Snap! Bam, here's my nuts lady!" Sy scrunched up, put his fist in his mouth and belted out a shriek reminiscent of Faye Wray. As Sy fumbled with the buttons again he smiled drunkenly, tottering back and forth on his ankles. He couldn't remember feeling so free and was overcome by the world of possibility.

Bernard had kept walking and was thirty yards ahead. Nearing the bar they were at earlier, Sy saw him duck into the parking lot. He picked up his pace and stumbled through the night's damp haze. Upon reaching the parking lot, he saw Bernard standing ten feet in front of the waitress, who was putting a case of beer in the trunk of her car.

Bernard was saying nothing, and she looked at him apprehensively.

"What you doin' still here, you old fart?" she said. "When people old as you can't control their own asshole it's time to put 'em away." She said it with little conviction, becoming more nervous as she studied the silent Bernard. She looked around to see if anyone might be left in the parking lot. She didn't like the man's eyes. They had grown big and hungry and evil. A grin spread across his face that showed every tooth down to the gum.

"Luke," she said softly, as if to test her voice lest she need it.

Bernard seemed to know the scream was coming and took a half-leap toward her, landing hard with both feet. He whipped the coat open so hard the snap of it could be heard clear across the empty lot.

The slovenly waitress began screaming at the top of her lungs, and when she was able to tear her gaze from Bernard's groin she turned to run but was stopped short by Sy, and she screamed again, louder than before. Sy's coat was spread wide in perfect imitation of Bernard.

"Margie?" called the fat man from the bar door. "Margie, you okay?" The sound of her name stopped the waitress's screams. "OVER HERE LUKE! WE GOT A COUPLE PERVERTS!"

Hearing the sound of the fat man approaching on a run, Sy and Bernard folded up and took off down the alley at a fast trot and kept going until they reached the alley near Sy's Suburban. Sy stopped to catch his breath and stood gasping for air with his hands on his knees. He could hear Bernard doing the same behind him, and after several minutes Sy recovered enough to speak. "God, we threw a scare into that fat ass waitress, didn't we!"

When Bernard didn't answer, Sy turned in his direction and saw an outline in the darkness, but it was enough to know Bernard was in trouble. "Bernard!" he whispered hoarsely. When Sy stumbled up to assist he saw that Bernard wasn't in trouble at all and was in fact completely lost in the act of masturbation. Sy looked at him again, shook his head weakly as he stumbled away, brought his hands back to his knees, and began vomiting profusely on the cobblestones.

Chapter 13

Darlene stopped staring at her coffee mug and got up to wash it at the sink. After rinsing, she changed her mind and refilled it. She sat back down at the kitchen table, but after adding cream and sugar she stood up and washed the spoon she used to stir. She washed it vigorously, trying to erase a stubborn stain. By the time she returned to her coffee she found it too cold to drink, and as she set the mug back down, she noticed her thumb begin to twitch. Her nerves were acting up again.

For a while she sat at the table, her hand going from her chin to the tabletop. Her nerves bled energy, the way a severed power line releases electricity into groundwater. She felt exhausted, didn't want to do anything; didn't know where to begin, and nothing felt worth the effort.

At last she went to a closet and pulled out a slim telephone book. Back at the table she flipped through it hurriedly, until finding the section she wanted. She slowly traced the columns of names with her index finger. Carlson, Carlton, Carlyle... but no Carmichael. She tried telling herself it might be unlisted. Sy said they lived in a big house up on "Snob Hill," so they would probably be snotty enough to have an unlisted number. Darlene got back up, picked up the phone and punched 411. After an interminable length of time, she heard someone pick up on the other end.

"Information what city?" came a tired voice on the other end.

"Gilmore," said Darlene. Her alarm grew stronger, and she was quite sure of what she was doing.

"Yes?"

"Carmichael. James Carmichael," said Darlene. She waited, breathless. Her nerves reared up in a wave of electricity that left her tingling.

"I'm sorry, we have no listing under that name," came the tired voice. Darlene thought a moment.

"Do you mean it's listed, but you can't give me the number? Or is there just nothing there?"

"We have no listing for a J. Carmichael."

"Maybe it's a new listing," said Darlene. "Can you try looking under new listings? And expand the search to all of St. Charles County?"

"Just a moment," said the voice. Then, "We have no listing for a J. Carmichael anywhere."

"Thank you," said Darlene dully. She stood next to the phone with her face inches from the wall. After a while she heard a faraway beeping and hung up. Her hand rested on the cradled phone while her mind searched for possibilities. The electric fire blazed just under her skin and left her trembly. Her mind refused to stick to one thought for more than two seconds. Finally, she picked up the receiver again and started punching numbers. For some reason she couldn't get her finger to push the right ones and had to hang up twice. On the third try she heard ringing on the other end, and someone picked up.

"What do you want?" Mercy sounded annoyed.

"Where do you get off answering your business phone like that?" Darlene came off sounding as annoyed as Mercy. Hearing her mother's voice, Mercy's stress level rose, as if Darlene's negative energy traveled the phone wires along with her voice. There were major problems at the office, and Mercy was already stressed enough.

"What do you want, Mom?" Mercy snapped back. "I'm real busy today."

"That's no excuse for being snippy. Not on a business phone. When I worked in an office, I never dreamed of such a thing. My boss would have stood me up and shoved me right out the door."

"I have caller ID." Mercy paused to consider, then spoke more softly. "I'm sorry, but it's crazy this morning. What is it you need?"

"If your father heard you answer a phone like that, he'd..." Darlene was about to lean on her husband and decided she didn't want to. Didn't want his help at all. She heard a loud exhale that told her Mercy had lit a cigarette. It worried her that Mercy was smoking, but she kept from saying anything.

"What do you want, Mom?" repeated Mercy.

Darlene responded in a babbling rush. "I just wanted to tell you I'm not feeling too good. I got up late, and now it's almost noon and I'm still in my housecoat and I don't know what the hell to do. Nothing's working for me today."

"MOM! Slow down! You've got yourself all worked up. Maybe you should just sit down, have a cup of coffee, then get yourself dressed. By then something will come to you. It always does. But first you have to settle down." Mercy's voice slowed, becoming more pedantic as she spoke.

"I've had my coffee," Darlene sighed. "Maybe too much."

"Look, Mom, I've got a lot to do. Is that all you wanted to tell me, that you drank too much coffee and now you're having a bad day? If so, I hope it gets better for you, but I have to go."

"Can we have lunch?" asked Darlene. "Maybe things would go better if we could have lunch somewhere."

"I don't know, Mom..."

"Your father came home drunk again last night," Darlene blurted out. From the other end of the line Mercy heard a sniffle. Her mother was about to cry. "And he was real late for work this morning. He's never late for work."

A silence hung over the phone. "Okay," said Mercy. "We'll meet for lunch."

At night, Dapper Dan's was a drinking man's bar, but during the day they served a nice blue-plate special. The oldest establishment in St. Charles County, it hosted a horde of senior businessmen for lunch and happy hour who treated it like their private club. Inside it was so dark you could barely recognize the person at the table next to you, and no one beyond that. It was how the grayhairs liked to do business, in a corner of some dark bar, drinking, drawing on napkins and teasing out information until late afternoon. Most accomplished more over lunch and a couple cocktails than they would in an entire day behind their desks. There wasn't a fashionable fern to be seen, and the two tiny windows way up front provided the only evidence it was day and not night.

Mercy and Darlene sat huddled in a booth, surrounded by vintage mahogany, etched glass, and worn, smoke-stained leather. They looked so out of place in the testosterone-soaked bar they could have been mistaken for business-class call girls, waiting on an afternoon rendezvous. They were the only women there, aside from a fortyish Vietnamese bartender who bent and poured behind her ornate mahogany altar like an exotic high priestess. She was a stern looking woman, yet made up in such a way the wrinkled old businessmen in their pin-striped suits would sit at the bar and eye her appraisingly.

Darlene stared after the woman who'd just taken their order, insouciantly strutting between the tables back to her position behind the bar. She couldn't believe Mercy had chosen this place and told her so.

"What's wrong with it?" Mercy opened her purse, removed her cigarettes, and placed the purse between herself and the wall. "It's a good, affordable lunch... and close to work, since I've got to get back."

"You don't come here a lot, do you?" Darlene laid her elbows on the table, brought her hands up to her face and looked around apprehensively. "Doesn't seem the kind of place for a lady. I mean a real lady." Darlene dropped her hands and leaned in close. "Don't you get the feeling all these men are looking at you?"

"No matter how hard they look, I'm not going to take my blouse off and that's it." Mercy looked at her mother, and her eyes flashed amusedly. The Vietnamese bartender came back and set a glass of water in front of Mercy and plopped down Darlene's iced tea, spilling some in doing so. Darlene immediately unfolded her napkin, making a big show of cleaning up the spill in front of the bartender.

"They all seem like two-bit con men pretending to be important," said Darlene flatly. "I wouldn't give you a box of chocolates for the whole lot of them. I've been to businessman lunch places. Plenty of them. But they were always filled with gentlemen, not these... I don't know what. This place has no class." Darlene surveyed the bar and shuddered lightly.

"Try not to get yourself worked up, Mom. Let's just have a nice lunch, okay?"

As if to agree, Darlene squirmed in her seat a few times and settled. She took a sip of her tea, winced, then reached for the sugar. As much as Mercy didn't want to bring it up, her curiosity got the best of her, and she asked her mother about what she'd said concerning Sy. Darlene seemed to have forgotten about it, pausing to think.

"Your father's turning into an alcoholic," she said primly, glancing at Mercy for her reaction. "He's been drunk on his rear three times this week."

Worried, Mercy sipped her water. It still bothered her the way he had talked on the patio two nights ago. And that strange walking the house naked business. He was no doubt acting weird. The increased drinking could be a reaction to something. But what?

"You say he was late for work?"

"Didn't leave the house until ten o'clock. After thirty-five years of living with him, this is the first time he's been late for work due to drinking. You should have seen him. He looked like hell. Face all puffed up like a big white dumpling. Still had those scratches too. Worse thing was he wouldn't say a word to me. Just grunted. When two people who've been together that long start grunting at each other like pigs, you might as well ask for the annulment."

"Yeah, I saw those scratches Tuesday night." Mercy picked up a fork from the table and turned it over in her hand.

"Oh yeah," said Darlene, with a quickness that comes from suddenly remembering something. "Wait till you hear about the scratches. He told me a cat got him. Cat my eye. I tried calling the guy's house where it supposedly happened, and you know what I found out? About what Mr. Honest Abe told me?"

Mercy shook her head, oblivious to everything but her mother's painted lips, which machine-gunned the awful words relentlessly, forcing Mercy to press into the wood panel behind her. Mercy's vision narrowed, focusing on those lips, like looking through a tunnel, or the barrel of a gun. Darlene was going to tell her that her father had told a lie.

"That person doesn't exist," said Darlene with finality. "At least not in St. Charles County. Your father concocted this whole elaborate story about visiting this guy and his wife up on Snob Hill, and how their cat jumped on his face and scratched him. Cat my eye."

"Where do you think the scratches came from?" Mercy spoke tightly, from up in her chest, not yet allowing herself another breath. She found it impossible to believe Sy had lied.

"Lord if I know. Probably got drunk and fell into a barbed wire fence. Banged up his truck too. I didn't even ask him about that, but it's all dented up in front, big as you please. It happened Monday night, when he was at the picnic meeting. "Least that's where he said he was."

Mercy stared dumbly down at the fork in her hand.

"He did his naked thing again Sunday night after you left," Darlene added.

Mercy looked up quickly. "Was it the same as before?"

"No. This time I got mad at him. Let him have it with both barrels. He was trying to play that sick joke on me, and I let him have it right back at him." Darlene raised herself in triumphant indignation. She'd completely forgotten the look on Sy's face when he entered the kitchen.

"You know, he started acting kinda strange with me Tuesday night, out on the patio."

"HE DIDN'T TRY AND TAKE OFF HIS CLOTHES IN FRONT OF YOU DID HE!" Darlene almost screamed the words, and all activity stopped at the nearby tables. Heads turned to look.

Embarrassed at her mother's outburst, Mercy sunk her head between her shoulders, then cocked it angrily sideways at her mother. When she spoke, it was through her teeth, in a whisper. "No, Mom, of course not." Having made sure her mother registered her anger, Mercy lightened up. "He just started acting a little funny, like he didn't even know it was me he was talking to."

"Was he drinking?" asked Darlene accusingly.

"No, Mom, he wasn't drinking. Okay two beers, but that was it. He just started talking about a lot of strange things... Korea, for example."

"He hardly says a thing about Korea to me."

"I didn't think so. Do you have any idea what happened to him over there?"

"Just that he played a lot of baseball," said Darlene. "I swear that man could organize a ball game in the monkey house." Darlene was visibly miffed that her husband had chosen to confide in Mercy but not her. As usual he was only thinking of himself.

"By the way he talked it got pretty rough." Mercy shifted the end of the fork she was holding to the other hand and held it between the two. "It makes me wonder if Korea has anything to do with what's affecting him now."

Mercy would have loved to tell her mother about the Korean girl then. Darlene was in one of her moods and needed slapping around. But her mother wouldn't be able to take it, and Mercy felt the frustration that always came from dealing with her mother.

"Korea happened a long time ago," sniffed Darlene. "There were a lot of men in Korea, and none of them are shucking off their pants at the drop of a hat. They may be drinking, but they aren't doing it just to be cruel to their wives."

"You're probably right," said Mercy, who only heard the substance of what Darlene had said, not the intended sarcasm, nor the self-pity. It was a defense reaction, this selective listening.

Though she'd been there many times, the bar seemed foreign to Mercy. The old mahogany booth had widened, the wooden corners that used to fold comfortably around her were cold, hard and barren, like in an empty courtroom. Her mother was seemingly talking from a great distance. In a far corner a juke box played a snappy song from years ago, one she barely recognized. She raised her water glass and saw her mother, now animated, looking toward the ceiling and singing along with the song.

"So, what are you going to do?" Mercy was shocked by her mother's sudden change and only spoke to confirm she wasn't imagining what she saw.

Darlene kept singing along with the music. "Hit the road Jack, and don'tcha come back no mo no mo..." She paused and looked at Mercy brightly. She even smiled. "I don't know. I've just decided it's his problem." She resumed singing and truly did not seem to care.

"Mom, what are you doing?" asked Mercy.

Darlene only continued. "Hit the road Jack... an' don'tcha come back no mo'..." Mercy waited patiently for the song to end. "Ray Charles," said Darlene, when it finally did. She seemed absolutely unconcerned by what they'd just been talking about. "Black musician from the early fifties. Your father and I saw him at the Casa Loma Ballroom. He had the saddest eyes... I don't imagine you ever even heard of him."

"Mom, did your medicine just kick in or something?" *Probably one of those red ones,* thought Mercy.

"What do you mean, dear?"

"We were just talking some pretty serious stuff about Dad, then suddenly you're singing rhythm and blues. Don't be so weird. I'm weirded out enough as it is."

"It's like I said, sweetheart, whatever your father's up to, that's his problem. I've just decided I'm tired of picking up after him." Darlene took a sip from her tea and smiled over at Mercy as if that were the end of it.

"Mom, for all we know he could be in real trouble. After all he's done for us, we can't let him down. He seems to need help, and we're going to give it to him. You and I."

Mercy considered letting her mother have it. It was absurd to suggest she'd been covering for her father all this time. If her mother hadn't poisoned his every chance to succeed, her dad could be the president of the United States. But expecting her mother to be logical was like expecting one of the Burcell store mannequins to recite the Gettysburg Address. She held her tongue.

"You're not going to help him tonight," said Darlene. She spoke spritely, like a schoolgirl. "He's got another one of those silly picnic committee meetings. He'll probably come home so drunk I'll have to pour him into bed." Darlene giggled, then leaned around the edge of the booth in search of the juke box. She was warming up to the old businessman's bar and wanted to hear more music from the old days. She might just stay here a while after Mercy had to leave.

"Don't say that," said Mercy sternly." I don't want to hear you talk like that about Dad."

"It's true though."

"No, it isn't," said Mercy forcefully. "That's not the man he is, and we both know it."

"People change," said Darlene. "Look at me, I'm suddenly feeling a lot better."

"I'm pleased as fuck to hear that."

"Don't talk dirty," said Darlene. "I imagine that bartender talks like that. Those men like to hear her talk like that, which is why they look at her like they do. She probably goes into the bathroom and zips their pants for them. Her way of thanking them for not dropping a bomb on her head when she lived in some heathen place called Play-ku or some such thing." Darlene chuckled and thought herself very clever.

"Here she comes, Mom, so don't say anything stupid," said Mercy. She'd just witnessed her mother go from depressed to loopy, right in front of her. It had happened before, but never so quickly.

Mercy marveled that Darlene wasn't in some institution by now. It was her father who kept her out all these years. Her strong, incredibly patient father.

The bartender approached, springing lightly up the single step to their booth, and set their plates down in front of them. "You want anything else?" she asked tersely, as if serving women was beneath her, one of whom was nothing more than an ordinary housewife. Mercy tiredly shook her head no. Darlene picked up her fork and dipped it into her plate. She grimaced, hugely displeased.

"Oh god, these mashed potatoes are instant," she said. Darlene laid down her fork in the presence of the bartender and pushed her plate into the middle of the table.

Chapter 14

By ten o'clock everyone on the picnic committee had left Parkers but Sy, Clarence, and Father Dieckman. It was now eleven, and the three that stayed on were seriously drunk. Angie had hung in, matching the men beer for beer until ten forty-five, when her tired, bony shoulders finally slumped against her prized wooden chair, her belly buckled out round and distended beneath her white cotton pullover, and her poor palsied head sank down low onto her chest, the first time it had been completely still since six that morning.

Sy gently nudged her awake, assuring her they could hold down the store if she wanted to go on to bed. Angie yawned and said she might go, not wanting to be late for her boys in the morning.

The truth was Sy, Clarence, and Father Deickman couldn't have guarded much of anything. They'd been slamming beer since they walked in, and all three were tight as ticks. Someone could easily sneak in the back door between their trips to the bathroom.

At this stage of the night, they were feeling overly fraternal and argued over whose turn it was to buy. Springing for beer carried the same emotional charge as bestowing a rose on a woman, the main difference being real men never showed appreciation. You just took your beer and maybe went so far as to clink bottles.

"As your spiritual advisor I insist on buying the next fucking round," said Dieckman, who as usual had gone back to showing his true face after everyone left.

"You take care of supplying the guilt and let me handle the means of losing it. All right, Padre?" Clarence was known to be a belligerent drunk from time to time. At this point he was still only dancing around the edges of it.

"Okay… paper, rock, scissors," said Sy, who by now had stopped worrying that he was uncharacteristically drunk again. He slowly began counting before the others could refuse to join in. On three they all snapped their hands out to the middle of the table, palms down.

"Paper, paper, paper," intoned Sy. "We'll have to do her again."

"Mine was a piece of eighty weight, glossy cover stock," said Dieckman. "Clarence's was nothing but a piece of one-ply ass-wipe."

"Worth a hell of a lot more than a slick page from a magazine when you're in a pinch, Padre. Or after a pinch for that matter."

Sy said nothing except to restart the countdown. This time Sy and Clarence came up with scissors, which easily succumbed to the priest's close-fisted rock.

"And with this rock I shall buy thee three beers," said the priest. Putting two hands down on the table to steady himself, Dieckman started up from his chair, sat back down, then headed for the cooler. Sy and Clarence watched him go, wearing half-assed grins and shaking their heads.

"Probably time to go home anyway. Beer's starting to taste bad," said Sy, trying to calculate if Darlene would believe picnic committee meetings could last this long. The truth was he felt like staying all night.

"Let's have the padre turn it into something else, Sy. Whatta ya say, Padre? Can you turn Sy's beer into a red wine? Maybe a fancy Burgundy?"

"You've got it all backward, Clearance," said Dieckman, as if asking permission to land a plane. "I can only turn things into blood. And for that I need to start with wine. Beer just turns into a plasma."

"You know, Padre, you really ought to cool it," said Sy. "Why do you keep it up, this Catholic priest bullshit? You can't possibly be happy doing something you don't put any stock in."

Sy usually remained unchanged by alcohol, but now that he'd flooded his system several days in a row, a barrier had been crossed. His mood was all over the place, swinging from euphoric to sad to self-righteous. Suddenly he needed more than anything to get to the bottom of Father Dieckman's duplicity. Such conflicting behavior, coming from an extremely intelligent, highly educated man caused a kink in Sy's thinking. Sy hadn't gone beyond high school, but his critical thinking ability was on par with the priest, and although drunk, he was determined to not dismiss this religious anomaly until the priest provided a satisfactory answer.

"That sounds like a life story kind of question," responded Dieckman. "For both your sakes I hope that's not what it is."

"Go for it, Padre," said Clarence. "I'm tired of having to carry the conversation." Clarence's last words were lost to Sy and Dieckman, as they were tied to a tremendous belch that lasted all of three seconds.

"I have to warn you I've seen strong men faint dead away from the sheer ludicrousness of it."

Sy picked up his bottle and tilted it toward the priest as a sign he was welcome to begin. As if setting themselves, all three took a big pull off their beers. Sy and Clarence stared at the passel of empty bottles in the middle of the table, both contemplating what it could be they were about to hear.

Dieckman lost his bluster, pausing to decide whether the story was worth telling. When he finally spoke, it came out quietly and less shameless, almost modest.

"I suppose I should start by saying I went into the seminary to please my mother." The priest took another drink, stared at the bottle label, and absently began tearing at it with his fingernails. The ceiling fan hit a lower stride on its own, becoming noticeably quieter. In the last hour the air coming through the screen door had cooled, lending a crispness that makes spring nights perfect for sleeping.

Sy looked at the profane, cigar-chomping man wearing a black shirt and clerical collar. He had trouble picturing the blasphemous priest with a mother.

"My mother was a very religious woman, and like any good Catholic, was overly concerned with redemption." Dieckman started slowly and paused between words, as if having to search a gamut of possibilities before coming up with the next one. "But then like most Catholics, she didn't want to go to a lot of work to achieve it."

"You saying your ma didn't go to church, Padre?"

"Oh hell, she went to church all the time. Sunday mornings, Good Fridays, Holy Thursdays, Sacred Saturdays, Ash Wednesdays. On Tuesday evenings she'd go to church and recite entire novenas to the God-Blessed Virgin Mary. The only reason she didn't go on Monday was because even the parish priests figured they weren't any better than God and needed a day of rest too. When the law was passed you could fulfill the Sunday obligation on Saturday night and then sleep-in the next morning, she'd go both times. I believe she thought it earned her some sort of ethereal extra credit." Here Dieckman paused again, thoughtfully taking another drink.

"No. By saying she didn't go to a lot of work I mean she didn't give one single thought to what she was doing or why. She blindly followed the formula the Church laid out for her, as if it were some beneficent uncle you could completely trust, expecting him to take complete care of you. Uncle Church, with all his histrionic dogma, stipulated that if you follow the letter of the law, plugging in the proper response to every equation he laid out, there's no question you'd be saved. As long as you were a nice little fascist who understood churches needed money, which meant giving generously. The tougher the formulas, the more certain people like my mother were of salvation, and the more control Uncle Church would have over them. If you only knew the huge corporation the Catholic church has become. For Uncle Church, there was never any separation between church and state. It was always state. And a pretty corrupt one at that."

Clarence turned his head to the side, raised his fist to his mouth, and coughed loudly. It was not a natural cough but a forced one, meant to register disagreement without verbalizing it. Dieckman didn't pick it up and went on with his private homily.

"Basically, Uncle Church grew into the huge concern he is today because he preyed on the sheep-like diffidence of his members… the refusal to even try and comprehend anything for themselves."

"How do you account for all the yuppie families joining St. Jude's?" asked Clarence. "Most of those people have college degrees. Some with letters behind their names the length of my friggin' arm, yet they're still dumb enough to believe in the Church. How do you explain that, Padre?" Being drunk *and* a good Catholic, the priest's words had Clarence boiling for a fight. The only thing stopping him was the nagging idea the overly educated priest might have him outgunned.

"Uncle Church got smarter too. Now he reaches young families through their kids, baiting them with highly regarded parochial schools. It's certainly not the religious posturing that brings them in. They're going through the sham of attending Sunday mass to save their children's brains, not their souls. It's just a different way of holding someone hostage to propagate the Church. Come over to the rectory sometime, and I'll show you statistics indicating every family that joined the parish in the last three years has had children who just slipped within the boundaries of preschool."

"Go on about your mother," said Sy, finding the priest's words not a revelation but a relief. He thought much the same way and only went to church for social reasons, certainly not spiritual ones. To buy time Dieckman went through the motions of relighting his cigar.

"Like millions of other good Catholics like her, my mother was paranoid about the gates of hell and wanted to be sure and cover her bases. If by some celestial circumstance all that time and effort and mindless recitation were wiped out by something as cataclysmic as, say, mortal sin, or a confession or baptism that didn't take, there was always one sure-fire way to cover her ass. She could have a son become Christ's earthly clone. She figured sacrificing me to the priesthood put her right up there with the God Blessed Virgin sacrificing her own son. Or that nutcase Abraham, who woke from his own psychosis just in time to keep from plunging a knife into his kid's heart. You should have seen her the day I was ordained. I don't doubt she expected to start floating above the crowd and be assumed into heaven."

Exasperated by hearing such talk, if not the fact it came from a priest, Clarence slammed his empty beer down, scooted his chair hard against the wooden floor, and stomped off to the bathroom. Standing alone in the small john, surrounded by the sharp stench of urine, Clarence rocked on his heels, took aim at a white pisscake and tried to blink himself into clear-headedness. He already decided such talk meant the party was over, and when he reappeared from behind the beer case barrier, he bid Sy and Dieckman a formal farewell and marched unsteadily out the door. Both paused to listen to Clarence's retreating footsteps on the gravel, the sound of a door being slammed, and finally his pickup roaring to life. Clarence gunned the truck through first gear, sending gravel flying angrily against the building's clapboard siding. Slamming into second, a rear tire screeched on the pavement, and again when Clarence made a tight U-turn in the direction of his house.

"Your mother didn't put a gun to your head," said Sy, trying to egg the priest on and forget Clarence. Here was a new Dieckman he'd never seen before. The priest was opening a window and letting Sy peer in. What he was seeing was not a priest gone bad, but a complicated man who wanted no more than to be treated like a fellow human being. Sy found himself genuinely liking the guy for his honesty and was curious to know how far his soliloquy would go.

"No, she did worse. She laid her eternal soul in my hands, just as blindly and self-centeredly as she offered up any other religious invocation. I think I could probably forgive her for wanting anything else of me. If she'd asked me to support her financially, I could have at least contemplated refusal. But to require me to save her everlasting soul! Well shit. That's kind of hard to walk away from."

"Especially if you're only a kid," interrupted Sy.

"Fifteen," said Dieckman. Sy whistled softly.

"Of course, at the time I really wasn't aware of all the irony involved." Again Dieckman stopped and tilted his beer up without taking more than a sip. Sy did the same to show he was still with him.

"I'm not real clear on what you mean by the irony," said Sy. Dieckman had said so much already. Sy wanted to slow him down so there was time to let it all sink in.

"I couldn't save her god-blessed soul... 'cause there's no such thing." Dieckman said it quickly and dismissed it with a wave of his cigar, as if meaning to get to it later. Sy shifted in his chair uneasily.

"To be fair it wasn't all her... In a way it intrigued me to become somebody that special, the person others looked up to and respected enough to offer their unquestioned obedience. Like a spiritual state trooper."

Sy stole a glance over to the priest and saw he had changed. As he talked, the folds of skin around his mouth and cheeks barely formed the words, falling flaccid as soon as he stopped speaking. It occurred to Sy the priest was himself confessing, but to no one in particular. If Sy hadn't been there he'd probably continue talking to the bottle in front of him.

"So, starting from the time I was an uncomprehending, obedient, pimple-faced boy, the priesthood became my life. And was for the next thirty-five, forty years."

"That's a long time to commit to anything," said Sy, shaking his head knowingly. "Especially starting at that age."

"Oh, it was okay at first. My mother came to visit me at the seminary all the time and told me how proud she was and how my work was going to be the most important a man could do. Never mind I was only a teenager with few friends, was growing incredibly fair skinned, and had my own sexual identity threatened nearly every day. I began having doubts about the priesthood early on, but by the time I finally realized it wasn't for me it was too late. I had already put in all that time and was given my first parish. Besides that, I already had priest stink all over me and couldn't wash it off if I wanted to. It's like when a guy's released from prison. Twenty years later he's still an ex-prisoner, and nobody trusts him. Everybody thinks an ex-priest is still going to try and preach to 'em. Or at least be judgmental. So for a long time I went about my business and put on a good face. It wasn't all that tough, since I hadn't yet lost my faith in organized religion—only my orchestration of it."

"What caused you to be like... how'd you get to be the way you are now?" While the priest talked Sy had slipped further into the fog, and when he spoke he slurred his words, dimly aware the priest was doing better at holding his liquor. It didn't occur to him he'd been outpacing the priest two to one. Hoping food would help, he carefully rose and got a Slim Jim from the counter. When he returned, he sat with his legs and arms crossed, his head tilted for a better listen, and slowly chewed the spicy sausage stick as thoroughly as he devoured the priest's words.

"One thing about the seminary, they educate you very well," continued Dieckman. "I handled all the theological discussions easily and even started studying other religions on my own—all the major ones, anyway. I could have graduated interdenominational Yale divinity school! None of that was what started me against Catholicism, but it certainly changed the way I planned to administer it. No, the one thing the seminary did was wake up the scholar in me. After all, it didn't allow for many other outside interests. You certainly couldn't date girls or drink beer with the boys after work or even own enough land to plant a friggin' garden. And since being God's own representative on earth isn't really all that demanding, because people already wanted what you were selling, I had all the time I wanted to continue studying anything I damn well pleased."

"And what pleased you?" asked Sy, knowing he could have chosen better words.

"Neuropsychology." The priest spit out the word as if fired from a gun, then turned a sly sideways glance at Sy for his reaction. "A good fit for a priest, don't you think?"

"Neuro–Psychology," repeated Sy soporifically. In his state he could only express himself by lifting his eyebrows slightly, showing no more surprise than if he'd heard the priest say the sky was blue.

"Yeah. And I haven't been the same since."

"Why is that?"

"One day I realized God was only chemical."

Dieckman took another slow pull off his beer, then suddenly became animated, as if spurred by his own memory. The color returned to his cheeks, and he reached into the circular tin ashtray in the center of the table, retrieving his cigar. He seemed to have sobered up, and while relighting continued talking excitedly, quickly getting ahead of himself.

"That's when I really got fuckin' pissed, you know? You know what it's like to suddenly realize you gave up your youth, your competitive spirit, your chance to become rich and famous, to own a Mercedes and a beach house in Florida and have women—beautiful, full-lipped women with big tattas all ready and willing—and give it all up for nothing? Or better yet, you know what it's like to miss the chance to marry and see your own offspring? And I tell you, Sy, it's the only option for any kind of life after death—to see them grow and play ball and go to a real high school with real teachers who aren't closet homosexuals and date girls and screw and fall in love? And finally live the life you missed out on, even if it was only vicariously through your sons and daughters?"

The priest stopped again and for a moment focused on a corner of the table, one of the few spots that wasn't covered by empty bottles.

"In one fell fucking swoop I was not only unfulfilled, I was robbed. And Uncle Church and religion became as unnecessary as tits on a boar."

"Did you say chemical?" asked Sy thickly. The beer he drank like water was shutting him down, and it took longer to analyze what his dysfunctional senses picked up. He was unsure he'd heard right.

"As chemical as the medication you'd buy for your kid's zits."

Dieckman had both elbows planted, holding his cigar with ten fingers, trying to suppress his excitement. Smoke poured from around the base like a rocket just before liftoff.

Sy squinted hard, wondering if the priest was making a joke. "I'm not sure I follow you, Padre." He referred to the priest using Clarence's favorite term, just in case he wasn't supposed to take him seriously.

Dieckman pulled the cigar out of his mouth to ash it, releasing a huge billow of smoke. The priest looked down at the table while scratching a familiar spot on his balding head and let out a quick, heavy sigh that caused his shoulders to lift and drop. Finally, his head shot back up. He'd found a way to begin.

"Look, Sy, you're Catholic. You heard of the apostle Paul, right?"

Sy nodded curtly as if to say of course he knew who the apostle Paul was.

"Well, besides being a class A, card-carrying poofter the guy also suffered epileptic seizures..." Dieckman stopped to think and waved his cigar in front of his face as if to dismiss what he'd just said. It was all wrong, was a wrong way to start, and he stuffed the cigar back into his mouth and sucked contemplatively for a while longer.

"Have you ever heard of endorphins, Sy?"

"I've heard the word somewhere before," said Sy, screwing his face up and twisting his head toward the ceiling fan in mock concentration.

"Do you know how they work? Endorphins are the body's protective chemicals," said Dieckman. "One example of what endorphins do is runner's high... you heard of runner's high?"

Sy nodded yes, he had heard of it.

"It's kinda like the body's own morphine. When you work yourself too hard, or you get the shit scared out of you, or you're about to have a nervous breakdown, your body squirts out these little endorphin dealies to help calm you down, so you can cope with whatever's fucking with you at the time."

"Kinda like beer," said Sy, raising his bottle to prove he was listening.

"Yeah, kinda like beer," said Dieckman excitedly. He stopped speaking only long enough to take a quick, energetic pull, deciding he didn't really care what Sy thought of what he was about to say.

"The fact is your body puts out a constant supply of that shit, and it's working on you all the time. Twenty-four hours a day. Even when you're not tired or scared or anything. And you know why your body puts out those kinds of chemicals, Sy?" He leaned in, as if taking Sy into his confidence. When he spoke again his voice had an even stronger edge.

"You'd go motherfucking insane, that's why," said the priest, who hadn't waited for or even needed a reply.

"You've heard we only use one-tenth of our brains on a day-to-day basis? It's actually more like one ten thousandth. And the reason why is those fuckin' chemicals. They shut you down, Sy. Otherwise there'd be too much to comprehend, and you'd short circuit." Dieckman stopped a moment to see how much Sy was taking in before presenting something even more unconceivable.

"Each person is at each moment capable of opening up and becoming one with the universe. Sounds fucking crazy, doesn't it? But I swear by God it's true. Or should I say I swear by the periodic table? Too fucking much information would overwhelm the average mind, so the brain and nervous system evolved to shut out most of it using these endorphin-like chemicals, only letting us in on what's necessary for survival."

"Kind of like the governor on a lawn mower," said Sy. It was coming clearer what the priest was saying, and getting more interesting, even if he didn't necessarily believe any of it.

"Yeah, but think more in terms of a reducing valve. Now back to Paul the apostle. You know when he was knocked off his horse by that blinding light on the road to Damascus? Wasn't fucking God telling him to shape up? Nothing unearthly about it at all. His reducing valve just went out on him."

The priest stopped to lick part of the cigar wrapper that had come undone. The pause was a test to see if Sy was really listening and wanted to hear more. It was difficult explaining, and the priest didn't want to go through with it if there was no reason to.

"I'm still listening, Padre," said Sy.

"For some reason Paul's body decided to stop making enough of the protective chemicals. When he got low his brain opened to full capacity, his synapses started firing like batshit, and he saw God.

"Makes life seem kind of meaningless, doesn't it?" continued the priest. "The realization there is no benevolent Father in heaven waiting to let you cash in all your chips. Despite the overdeveloped outer lobes evolution wrapped around our original brainstems, we're still just as chemically operated as the first organic compounds to coalesce out of the primordial soup."

"So, I think what you… a Catholic priest… are telling me," said Sy, "is that what I been prayin' into, ever since I was a little pecker head, is all bullshit."

"The concept of God is fairly recent, Sy. It basically came out of the awareness we all started having at the time our brains grew large enough to be dangerous. Some would call it consciousness."

Dieckman stopped talking and thought for a while. "People like my mother, who believe in religion and its eventual cosmic reward, who really make themselves suffer, what with all the acts of contrition prescribed by the church, and all the pain and agony and guilt and abstinence that goes with it... you'd think it would be easier for them to die than it is to live wouldn't you? When those people are on death's door, they freak out. Why? I mean since they're so prepared. Once you understand how it's all chemical, and that life is essentially meaningless, it's just the opposite. It's more important to live and get everything in you can because after you die there isn't anything more.

"I've seen plenty of devout people die... delivering the last rites and all. And you know, almost to the person, they all suddenly get this intense fear at the end. They thought they were prepared to die, but they weren't. At the last minute they seem to realize there's a chance they were wrong, and that maybe there really isn't anything after all, and all that work and saving up they'd been doing was all for naught. Then they want to live more than anything. Suddenly they want to go back and do it all over… make the most of the only life they would ever have—as if they suddenly opened up like Paul and understood everything I've been talking about."

Judging by Sy's blank non-reaction Dieckman knew he'd gone too far.

"Okay… okay, let's forget all that stuff about God and get back to Paul. He wasn't the only one to have his mind take off like a runaway Audi 5000. What William Blake called 'divine intuition' and Buddha called 'awake' was more apt to be the same shortage of some chemical in the brain. Think about it. All LSD does is block those chemicals that inhibit your brain. Crazy people are probably more tuned in than you or I will ever be. They've got a hell of a lot more receptors popping and buzzing and going off. More than they can handle, and it literally drives them nuts. More normal people, the ones who are cheerful all the time, who seem to have endless energy, the ones you would call 'well adjusted,' probably are, in the chemical sense. Their engines just purr right along with the perfect mix of chemical 'fuel' and don't miss a beat.

"Now take people who claim to have ESP. We can all do it—we're just chemically blocked for our own preservation. The people who are truly clairvoyant aren't. They run out of blocking chemicals from time to time. Or they're missing altogether."

Sy thought of how crazy Darlene could get but dismissed the idea just as quickly. If anything, Darlene's problem was a lack of awareness, not too much of it. Then he remembered her constant "alarms" and suddenly grew more unsure of anything.

"Look at Van Gogh," continued Dieckman. "Here's a man who was overwhelmed by life, usually negative and prone to fits of deep depression. He was most probably at the mercy of his chemically induced whims. He was missing some of his protective chemicals, his 'Alpha chemicals' let's call them. The reason he was so into alcohol and drugs was because alcohol and drugs were the only things that could shut him down and took the place of the natural drugs his body had such a hard time supplying. Yet at the same time his chemical lack opened all his receptors and allowed him to paint the nuts off anything he chose."

Dieckman took Sy's sudden introspection concerning Darlene as a sign of indifference and tried harder to express the importance of what he was saying.

"Chemicals control every aspect of your very existence, Sy. Let me try it another way. Your colon gets too full, you get a chemical message telling you to shit. Too much of that chemical and you'd shit your brains out. Or at least you'd try to. That poor young kid that helped me say mass last Sunday? Could be missing the chemical mix that keeps him from jerking off every waking moment. Dorothy Maddox, that two-ton mass of flesh who lives out by you? She's missing a blocker and eats until her throat finally has to provide a signal, and she starts gagging.

"Then there's that Gottlieb guy who was on trial three months ago for committing forty-seven rapes. Turns out when certain of his chemicals got low, he would have a kind of a seizure, and he'd go out and rape the first person who came along. Maybe back in caveman days that sort of activity was normal. But as man grew more civilized, the people with the chemicals that held the sex drive in check were the ones that survived. For some reason Gottlieb ran low. He'd have just enough to cruise along like normal for a while, then they'd dip below the minimum level, and some poor woman would have him heaving himself up on her as mindlessly as if he were a dog humping her leg.

"Was that guy a sinner? Fuck no. His only problem was he acted like our earliest ancestors did, before the reducing valve evolved. Adam and Eve called that earlier period bliss. But after the reducing valve threw in the chemical wrench the Bible writers called it Original Sin."

Father Dieckman's last remark was too much for Sy, who lived his life thinking will and self-determination was the only true religion, the only viable constitution, and the only basis with which to measure one person's value against another. Now Dieckman was saying it was nothing more than bloodstream that made people the least bit different.

Sy was too impaired to fully realize how what Dieckman was saying might relate to him, but in the back of his mind he knew there was some kind of tie, and he didn't like the sound of it. He stood up from his chair, blinking hard to clear his head. He was frustrated being this drunk again.

In his confused and drunken state, Sy grabbed an empty bottle by the neck, raised it high above his head, and smashed it against the side of the table. It was one of the few times in his life Sy had lost control. Dieckman jumped up out of his seat with a start, not quite knowing what to do once he had, and immediately sat back down, only to stare at Sy, dumbfounded. Sy stood across the table, breathing hard. He looked down at the glass scattered all over Parker's blackened hardwood floor. The jagged neck of the bottle was still in his hand, as if he intended to slice open the first person who came near enough.

"Now," said Sy, panting, "I broke that son-of-a-bitch because I wanted to, not because I'm low on anti-bottle-breaking fluid… okay?"

It dawned on the priest he not only just had seen Sy lose control for the first time, but he was also drunker than he was—another first. The realization helped Dieckman recover, and he began muttering the little homilies that eventually calmed Sy down and brought him back to his seat.

After a few minutes Sy calmed down enough to begin feeling sorry about the mess he'd made. He went through the door into Angie's living area and came out with a broom and dustpan. Sweeping up the brown glass from all corners of the room, he remained silent and gloomy, wrestling with what Dieckman had said, trying to convince himself it didn't pertain to him and the shameless acts he'd been feeling compelled to commit.

He began mulling over what had happened in Illinois. As opposed to every time before, he absolutely remembered showing himself to that fat waitress. True, he didn't remember it clearly—he'd had too much to drink for that. He remembered it though. The fact he remembered might mean it wasn't all coming from smelling the eggs. No. He did it because he was so damn drunk. But doing something because you were drunk was better than some kind of bizarre science fiction mind control. And there was a measure of childish high school camaraderie going on. The eggs were there, he had smelled them the entire night, but the smell was toned down, an electric fence running at very low voltage. You could grab it and feel it, but only a tingle. *But screw that!* thought Sy. For whatever reason, exposing yourself in public was sick sick sick! Thinking about it all day, the memory of last night scared him to death, leaving him mortally ashamed. He spent the entire day locked in his office, inert, frozen to his leather chair in front of the window. It was the memory of what he'd done last night that compelled him to hide beneath a mountain of beer bottles again tonight.

As he pushed the broom across the floor, he found himself repeating what he'd spent all day in his office saying repeatedly. It was only some weakness on his part. Some bout of instability that was a function of old age or stress or simple boredom. He was sure of it. He knew he could beat it if he just bore down. His own force of will got him through his every scrape, and a lot of other people's too. Acting beyond his own control was something the Sy Gordon Liddy of marriages (and life) would not accept. As he worked the broom, his feelings shifted from anguish to self-reproach, and finally to further resolve, which was the only response he'd ever known and trusted.

Dieckman watched Sy silently, not understanding his sudden mood shift but trying desperately to size it up and venture a comment that might help. Before he could do anything Sy stopped sweeping, looked up from his broom, and spoke softly, like a man who'd been beaten well past the breaking point.

"You know, when I was a little kid, I had this habit of picking up my fork from the dinner table, loading it up with mashed potatoes or sliced beef or beans or whatever. And after I'd put it into my mouth, I'd do it all over again, but this time with the fork empty. I'd do it at every meal. Every time the fork went down, I'd bring it right back up with nothing on it and put it in my mouth. My brothers and sisters used to laugh and make fun of me, and my parents would tell me to stop, but I couldn't. It finally got so bad I'd get beat for it, but I kept doing it anyway, for about a year, until they all got used to seeing it and didn't say anything anymore. That was when I quit. I think I was about six. Do you have any idea in the world why I did that, Padre?"

Dieckman slowly shook his head no.

"I never did either. No fuckin' idea why I did that."

Sy resumed sweeping, covering another quarter of the room before stopping again.

"Have you ever done something where…" Sy hesitated for a minute, grasping the broom firmly, one hand above the other, leaning forward to let it take some of his weight. "Did you ever want something so bad, you just went ahead and did it, no matter how selfish, or immoral or unexpected? Like maybe it just overwhelmed you, but you knew it was all right as long as it only affected you and nobody else?"

"Sure, Sy."

Dieckman spoke without conviction. Sy's disposition had changed twice in the last ten minutes, and it was making Dieckman apprehensive.

Sy looked to the side, staring at the plastic tubes of Slim Jims and let out a long sigh of resignation. "Well shit... What I feel like doing now is having another beer. Maybe ten."

Much to Dieckman's relief, Sy got two beers out of the cooler and brought them over, almost cheerfully. For the next hour they talked drunkenly about everything from duck hunting to the church picnic to naming the one woman in St. Micheal's parish they would both like to see naked.

"Say," said Dieckman at one point. "You practiced your acceptance speech yet?"

"What acceptance speech?"

"For the Hall of Fame next Sunday."

"Haven't even thought about the sumbitch," said Sy, picking up his beer for the umpteenth time that night. "Figure I'll jes' wing 'er."

"It's a damn big deal, Sy. You can't just shuffle out there and scratch the dirt with your foot and say 'Aw shucks.' That's not good enough for a Hall of Famer."

"You got any idea where I can get some John F. Kennedy pills?" asked Sy, blinking his eyes and offering up a sudden hiccup.

Chapter 15

The fire had been burning since four a.m. The rain was done but clouds still hung thick and low above the East St. Louis skyline. The orange glow from the sun, still below the horizon, silhouetted the decrepit warehouses and crumbling housing projects that lined the river, and a long, curving funnel of black smoke forced its way up through the orange, vanishing into the heavy night sky. A homeless man slept on the steps beneath the towering Gateway Arch, the blaze reflecting off the river, bathing his face in warm, flickering light. Though his face was swollen, the fire was kind, softening his features enough so one could believe he was once a healthy young man. As he slept the fire blazed on, consuming the mountain of discarded tires that caused the air within a mile radius to smell acrid and unpleasant.

Fifty yards from the flames Arnie Carruthers stood leaning against the hood of his Chevy Blazer, waiting for the sun to rise and make for a better photograph. He was impatient for the light, but the sun seemed reluctant, as if it preferred the opposite hemisphere and was clinging to its final moments there. Arnie wanted to get the shot before anyone else arrived on the scene. The blazing heap reminded him of war, and to capture it properly he needed to get it before the fire trucks came and people swarmed around it like ants. Fire in East St. Louis was a familiar scene, and for the photograph to sell it needed the extra stroke.

Arnie fumbled with his cameras and equipment in a way that gave away his anxiousness. The fire trucks should have been there already. He'd been waiting for both the sun and the firetrucks to arrive for over an hour, and the whole time he could not imagine the sun winning the race. The few people who noticed the fire at that hour felt no desire to report it, secretly hoping it would consume every symbol of industrial decay in East St. Louis, which for years stood silent and wretched across the river from downtown St. Louis like a sullen stepsister.

It wasn't a big opportunity, even for a free-lance photographer. As Arnie waited for the moment, his body bisected by firelight and darkness, he began losing interest, and his thoughts wandered from f-stops and lenses to breakfast and a hot cup of coffee. He got the call about the fire from his sister, who lived in the high-rise apartments across the river and suffered from chronic insomnia which allowed no more than four hours of sleep each night.

Before Arnie started trying to make a living with his cameras, he was an art director for a small advertising agency. Like art direction, his job as a photographer involved grappling with the eye and holding it for as long as possible. His cameras provided more satisfaction, if considerably less money. To him, each of his photographs was a short story on the human condition, while his ads had been nothing but For Sale signs with a twist. He needed a more creative outlet.

When he began pursuing photography, he was fully motivated, but shortly after investing in equipment someone made an analogy that had him feeling defeated before even getting started. After excitedly explaining his recent commitment to a Washington University professor, a man Arnie long respected, the professor sarcastically responded… wasn't it funny how a medical student had to go through eight years of post-graduate work and four more years as an intern before he could call himself a doctor, but anyone who could afford a decent camera could call himself a photographer. The professor was pickled at the time, but Arnie had thought of what he said each time he picked up his cameras, and now his newly chosen line of work was irrevocably sabotaged by imposter syndrome. He'd been at it for a year, still waiting for his breakthrough opportunity. Here he was in East St. Louis at six in the morning, and this wasn't it. He had dragged himself out of bed for the slim chance that something would happen to make the shot interesting, but unless there was the body of a congressman buried in the pile of tires, he was wasting his time. The public hungered for much bigger news than yet another fire in hell.

Air sucked into the base of the fire as if by a giant lung, gasping for more, and in the blast of heat above there was no air at all. The center collapsed and Arnie saw a lick of flame, much higher than he imagined it could go, spear through a vent in the dark cloud of smoke, as if the all-powerful Oz had come back, demanding obedience.

By six forty-five the sky had brightened enough for the exposure he wanted, and Arnie quickly went through five rolls of film, feeling victorious over the caravan of red fire trucks that surely were on their way. After the fire department received enough calls to slouch into action, they finally showed up, not because people had reported a damaging blaze in East St. Louis, but because the fire was belching toxic fumes into the same air they needed to breathe.

Arnie hung around, taking a few shots of firemen at work, unconsciously hoping a flaming Goodyear might come bounding down, spewing melted rubber like a spitting cat, and strike a firefighter or two. He'd be there to record the grisly, Pulitzer-winning aftermath. In the end nothing unusual came about, and he finally stopped trying to capture images no one wanted. It took five minutes to pack his equipment into the back of the Blazer, and it was time for breakfast.

He knew of an IHOP only ten minutes away that was still reasonably clean for East St. Louis. By the time he rolled into the parking lot the fire was a distant memory. Before going in, he grasped the handle of a newspaper machine and jerked it over and down until it popped open with an audible click. Stealing a *Post Dispatch* was his guarantee that if the editor didn't care for his photos, he'd at least get a free paper.

He sat down and ordered the #2: fried eggs, link sausage, hash browns and toast, plus a short stack of Mediterranean fig pancakes on the side. It wasn't until after finishing the meal and growing bored with the editorial page that he noticed a man sitting at the counter, wearing green seersucker golf pants, black patent-leather penny loafers, and a long khaki trench coat. Judging by the curious way he never let his coffee rest on the counter, the man was in an agitated state. He had the newspaper spread open in front of him, and although he stared down at it intently, Arnie noticed the man didn't turn the page.

The expensive raincoat was buttoned up to the neck, with no discernable tie. When men appeared in coats like that this early, they were usually dressed for business, which included wearing a tie. Arnie was positive a tie should still show above the coat no matter how tightly it was buttoned up. This man's neck was long and thin and naked, his head protruding out of the stiff coat like a turtle. Other than too much neck the man was as ordinary as the rest of the people lining the counter—silent, lone men whose best opportunity for adventure was to once and a while eat an exotic international pancake.

When the man got up to leave, Arnie took his time folding his paper, reached into his wallet for a tip, paid at the register and stepped out into bright sunshine. After making note of the man's direction, Arnie unhurriedly opened the rear of his Blazer, looked at the sun again, and idly adjusted his camera down to compensate for the sudden burst of spring. He still wasn't sure he was going to follow the guy, but when the odd-looking businessman looked around anxiously before turning into a dark East St. Louis alley, Arnie started to breathe a little faster, dropping his lens cap twice on the pavement.

He finished loading his camera as he trotted over to the alley. Just before entering, he paused for a quick check, satisfied that everything was correct, and went in behind the man, senses alert, as if going in to finish off a wounded lion.

The strangely dressed man was nowhere in sight, and Arnie quickened his pace. The alley was damp, smelling like rotten meat.

Steam rose from the asphalt, carrying the fetid odor with it. The alley made a sharp bend, and a shaft of bright sunlight reached down between the three-story walls to illuminate overflowing trash bins and piles of garbage tossed to the side. Focusing on finding the man, Arnie broke into a run, taking no notice of the unidentifiable shapes languishing along the walls and in the empty boxes piled in shadowed corners. He rounded another bend and leaped to dodge two mangy curs devouring a redolent meal they discovered behind a dumpster. He turned to make sure the dogs weren't following, then stopped to listen. He heard the clicking of hard-soled shoes and then nothing, meaning they'd either stopped or found a softer base to tread upon.

When Arnie turned the next corner, his pupils dilated, reacting to the rectangle of sun-washed street at the end of the alley. At first, he failed to recognize the figure backed against the wall. The man stood just inside the shadowed edge where the alley opened onto the sidewalk, tight against the brick, as if wanting to sink into it. When his eyes adjusted, Arnie saw the man had his hands thrust in his pockets, peering around the corner up a one-way street, as if waiting to sell stolen watches.

Arnie sucked in a breath, crouched to put a dumpster between himself and the furtive shadow ahead, and crept forward with his palm sliding along the damp bricks until he dared not take another step. Ten yards ahead the man turned to check the alley behind him, and Arnie ducked below the rim of the dumpster. Crouching, Arnie's legs began to burn, and his heart pounded with the thought he'd been discovered. The man turned back, riveted on something up the street, like a dog slamming into point. From behind the dumpster Arnie saw the man crouch and tighten, like a cat stalking a pigeon.

Arnie remained in his crouch until his knees burned. Time stopped. If there were cars they halted just before the alley, and even the pedestrian traffic had vanished.

There came the sound of footsteps on concrete. They came like a knock on a door and then there was a woman invading the backlit rectangle. She was tall and not overly pretty but dressed very businesslike in a khaki trench coat much like the man's. The instant she appeared in the opening Arnie saw the man uncoil like Dracula and open his coat to feed on the gaze of the unsuspecting.

Time resumed and sped up. Traffic whizzed by the lit opening as if overjoyed to be suddenly released. On either side of the street people sped by.

The woman who had stopped twisted her face up horribly. Her screams rocketed down the alley in waves, sounding not like one woman but a hundred as they reverberated from wall to wall down the filthy corridor. Arnie leapt up and ran forward a few steps. With time having returned, only the coat, draped open wide like a sunning vulture, remained static.

"HEY!" yelled Arnie. "HEY, BUDDY!" Arnie's body shook feverishly, and he had trouble controlling his hands. He managed to snap off a few quick shots, then did everything he could to try and get the man's attention. The woman screamed again, and still the coat stayed open. Finally, Arnie ran the last few feet, touched the man firmly on the shoulder, took three steps back, and snapped the picture when the man finally twisted his head around.

Arnie was much too beside himself to catch detail, but the camera took it all in objectively. It saw an alley, a screaming woman, a man's face above a wide-spread coat, and on that face a slack-mouthed stare, as vacant and blind as a corpse.

Chapter 16

Early Sunday morning the fruit trees seemed to know the day would dawn warm, calm, and bright. Long before anything else began to stir they ever so slightly dipped the surfaces of their energy-absorbing leaves to the east.

With the overabundance of rain, the yard had soaked up all it could, and shimmering pools of water were scattered randomly like an ephemeral swamp. Just beneath the grass the earthworms absorbed more water than was healthy and now escaped to the surface, where the early-morning sun would tap them of their excess moisture. On the patio hundreds of them were languidly contracting and stretching to expose their pores, and in their midst a robin hopped an ever-widening circle, scooping them up and tossing them down with each thrust of his beak.

After eating his fill, he flew up into the tree just outside Sy's open bedroom window and began singing of how good the worms were. Inside the room Sy's restlessness had finally quit him, and he slept facing the window. On the robin's second chorus he opened his eyes slowly and blinked. With one big sigh he inhaled the heavy morning air and realized he felt content. The rancid egg smell was gone. It had been very strong the day before. So strong it had carried him away, and he couldn't remember what had happened. But now it was gone, and like each time before, when it had gone away it left him with a feeling of well-being; whole and sure and more relaxed than he could ever remember. He looked out the window and smiled at the bird flitting among the leaves of the sweet gum at the side of the house. "Good morning, bird," he whispered. He'd only been awake a few minutes and wanted to lie there and enjoy what time he had before Darlene stirred.

While lying there smiling at the sound of the bird something else crept into his consciousness. He couldn't smell the eggs, so it wasn't that. But somewhere inside his brain a warning signal was going off. It was like hearing a battle in the distance, knowing there was a chance you might have to get involved. The battle was still far away, so he chose to ignore it and enjoy the bird in the tree. As he watched, it cocked its head side to side, puffed up, then belted out its joy in rapid undulations of its chest and throat.

After a while Sy slid out of bed, put on his robe, and looked over at Darlene, who was sleeping heavily but wore a frown, and Sy was curious as to what she was dreaming about. After slapping on house slippers he padded into the living room, opened the blinds to the patio and nodded in appreciation of the day. Since he was up early, he decided to grant himself the luxury of coffee and the newspaper in his pajamas. He might even have some eggs and toast before starting on some yard work.

Tearing his eyes from his prized orchard, he padded into the kitchen and arranged for coffee, two spoonfuls more than usual. This morning, he felt good, almost giddy, and wanted to present himself with such a gift. After the hi-test coffee started to go, he turned to the business of eggs and toast, and when the blue flame ignited and flared beneath the skillet, he lowered the handle of the toaster and knew he had time to go for the paper.

When he opened the front door, he was pleased to see the paper rolled round and tight and laying in the middle of the driveway. He consciously praised the paperman for his excellent aim, which could only have shown better if there were a big, red bullseye painted on the spot where it landed. Sy picked it up and waved to an early-rising neighbor who honked as he drove past, and Sy skinned off the thin wrap as he turned back to the house. He thoughtfully stuck it into the pocket of his robe as he uncoiled the paper to read as he walked.

The first thing his eyes rested on was a headline concerning yet another dire problem in the Middle East. The next caused his legs to buckle. His momentum swerved him several feet askew, and he fell to his knees in the grass at the edge of the driveway. If anyone else were awake at that hour, peering out their window, they would swear they were witnessing a heart attack.

The thing that struck him down was a large color photo on the front page. It showed a coat held wide open as seen from the back, a glimpse of bare leg and fake pantleg through the vent at the bottom, a woman with a scream on her lips, and his own head planted firmly on top of the coat, looking back at the camera with the mindless stare of a congenital idiot.

Sy tried to get up but found he couldn't. He managed to slide back toward the driveway on his knees and one hand. It was like the weight of the universe had descended onto his back and was trying to shove him into the damp earth. The other hand gripped the paper, which he held aloft like a torch. The paper seemed to have an energy of its own, like kryptonite. It beat Sy down by radiating wave upon wave of debilitating remorse and guilt and insurmountable shame.

Still on his hand and knees, Sy crawled up the driveway and fell onto the front porch, hidden from view by the surrounding shrubbery. He lay on his back breathing heavily for several minutes, staring up at the white overhang, deep in shock. As he lay, things began to close in. The shrubbery near his head became watery and arched over his head to peer down at him. The white porch ceiling grew closer until it hung above his face like an interrogation lamp. Why did you do this? Why did you do this? He felt like cellophane was wrapped around his face, blocking his mouth and nostrils until he could no longer breathe. Soon the edges of his vision turned an opaque gray, the gray moving to the middle, turning darker, until he saw and felt nothing at all. Inside the house there was the smell of burning eggs, but the only response it provoked was a thick cloud of smoke roiling up from the skillet and filling the kitchen.

Ten minutes later Darlene woke to the sound of the fire alarm and came rushing down the steps into the kitchen coughing and gagging from the smoke. Combined with the searing vapor of burning Teflon it affected her like tear gas. After wrenching open the door to the patio she grabbed the handle of the smoking skillet and flung it outside, where it flew through the air like a crippled frisbee. She quickly turned on the exhaust fan, and flapping her arms in desperation, made her way through the burning haze to open more windows.

Eventually she made it to the dining room, where she saw a hazy figure appear through the drifting smoke, surprised to see it was Sy. He was sitting at the table holding his head. The first thing to occur to her was that he was still in his pajamas, which came as more of a surprise than not being able to see across her own kitchen.

When she spoke, the words came out in a burst of anger. She no longer thought about his pajamas but the damage the smoke was bringing to her immaculate housekeeping. "Sy! Your breakfast was burning! Couldn't you see that? You ruined my best frying pan... and God only knows about the furniture and the curtains! Sy!"

He turned to look at her and she stopped cold. Sitting in silence, oblivious to the smoke curling around his head, Sy looked more dead than alive. There was no energy in his face at all. The smoke was stinging his eyes, causing them to well-up, yet he held them open, impervious to the pain. His eyes might be open, but Darlene could tell he wasn't seeing anything. When Sy finally recognized Darlene, his eyes opened even wider and showed white with fear. Darlene had never seen anyone, much less her capable husband, register such a look of terror, and in sudden sympathetic response her bottom lip trembled, and she started to cry. Sy was the first to speak, and when he did her tears came harder, and the thread that held her world together so tenuously popped like a bad fuse.

"Darlene... I need help." It was all he said, but the hopeless way it was delivered told much more.

"What is it, Sy?" she asked in a breathy whisper. "What's happened?" Darlene walked toward him slowly.

Sy turned away and refused to speak again. Darlene inched forward and extended her hand toward the weighted shoulders and withdrew it quickly. Below her breasts she could feel her stomach twisting, making her nauseous.

"Is it bad, Sy?"

He rolled the crumpled newspaper tighter into his fists, as if holding a baseball bat and needing better purchase. By the way he gripped it she knew the paper was the reason for Sy's strange behavior, but when she reached for it, he pulled it deep into his abdomen. He sat like a sullen child and refused to look at her.

When Darlene finally put a careful hand on Sy's shoulder, then reached down and closed on the tightly rolled newspaper, Sy broke. He covered his face with one hand and fell to weeping piteously and without restraint.

"It's not me, it's not me, that's not me," he wailed through the mass of fluids draining from his eyes and nose.

The paper shook in her hand, and it didn't require one of her "alarms" to tell her that once she opened it life would never be the same. She understood nothing but knew the glue that held it all together had dissolved, and she felt herself hurtling away.

She stared at the page, recognizing nothing. Then slowly, like a misty sunrise, the truth invaded her clouded senses. It was too much, and mercifully her mind lapsed into shock. She slumped into the chair across from Sy, and the circuits of her mind closed into the deadening safety of complete mental collapse.

In the time that followed, the smoky air settled to the floor and lay there, heavy as mud. Sound traveled only a few feet from where it originated and plummeted into the absorbing muck. Only the ticking of the living room's grandfather clock was strong enough to persevere, and even it wasn't heard by the two mannequins sitting at the dining room table, exhibitions in their own museum.

In the non-conducting air, the phone did not ring but shook, as if the scene inside the room had given it a chill. After the third vibration the message machine kicked in and a sarcastic, confident Sy said no one was home but if it was urgent enough to demean yourself by speaking to a machine go ahead and do it now. The voice that answered was Clarence's, and for as talkative as he usually was, he sounded hesitant.

"Uhh... yeah, Sy, this is Clarence. Say umm... you haven't seen this morning's paper by any chance, have you? There's a picture of a guy on the front page I swear looks just like you. Uh... judging by what he's doing he's not the best guy in the world to look like either. Well, uh, listen, give me a call when you get home... on second thought forget I called."

A little later the phone vibrated again. The sound of Peter Marshall's nervous voice broke across the still life of Sy's kitchen. "Uh, Sy? Listen, can you meet at the office today? I know it's Sunday, but I think we may have something pretty important to talk about. Uh, I just got a call from Pittman, and he... well I'll wait and tell you when you get in. Uh, come in whenever you're able... whenever you can... I... I'll see you then."

Seconds after the answering machine rewound, the phone shook again, and Sy's tireless voice repeated its message. The voice that came on wheezed of emphysema, originating deep within the chest. "Hey, Sy! How the fuck's it going man? I was able to get your number 'cause I gotta friend at work knew who the fuck you were. We just got off the line at Calgon, and now we're havin' a coupla beers. You know Calgon? The fuckin' soap factory, man. We make everything from your wife's bath beauty beads to soap on a rope for homos. We always say if you got no hope in your soul put some soap in your hole. HAH HAH HAH! That's our motto man. We just spent all fuckin' night makin' that pink liquid soap you see in the public shitters. Nobody knows it, but it's whale come, man, and you're fuckin' welcome to come over and donate any time you want. Hey, why don'tcha c'mon over right now and have a beer with us. Us perverted motherfuckers gotta stick together. Or maybe we'll come on over to your place, huh? We'll all take turns throwing a fuck into your old lady."

The answering machine beeped, announcing the caller had hung up. Sy let out a short, high-pitched whine, like a hurt dog. Darlene sank further into the chair, hugging herself harder, as if already submitting to an invisible straight jacket. The phone shivered nervously a few more times, but the callers hung up, and Sy's recorded voice echoed throughout the kitchen, speaking to no one.

Though his mind was functioning, connections were incomplete and often lacked substance. Trying to concentrate, his thoughts flew off in a hundred directions. He saw a kaleidoscope of colors in varying shades of brightness, an image from his past, heard a voice that was once his. In a moment of clarity, he heard a neighbor mowing grass.

Slowly, Sy's awareness returned, like a wild carnival ride sliding to a stop. His eyes returned to the photo under the newspaper's masthead, below the blurb quoting a circulation of over 500,000 satisfied readers.

Sy tried convincing himself it was some horrible practical joke, that someone had used that new photoshop software to make a fake front page with his head on another's body. Realizing the picture was what it was, the only solution was to move away. Take early retirement and move away. That was it. That was the thing to do. He imagined himself living in Seattle or Maine or some other distant corner of the US, as far away as he could get from the violated center, now tainted with the kind of spill even time could never wash away completely.

He became aware of a soft popping sound, looked beyond the hand on his forehead, and saw his expressionless wife opening and closing her mouth like a fish. With some difficulty he stood up, dismissing any further conjecture about his future by returning to a standard from his past—taking care of Darlene. He walked into their bedroom, shook out four pills and poked them one at a time into her mouth as she popped it open. He tilted her head back, forced water between her lips, got her to stand, and carefully led her back to their bed, where she curled herself up with a hand over her face. Sy brought the blankets gently up to her neck, then sat at her side, idly moving his hand up and down her flannel pajama sleeve. He stared hard down at the floor.

How could such a tightly controlled life as his become so equally out of control? He thought of the conversation with Dieckman, who would probably claim it was some sort of deficiency. If that were true, maybe he just needed to eat more bananas. There were a lot of good things in bananas, and maybe he should start eating more of them. That was it. He would start eating bananas at every meal, and maybe that would provide what his brain needed. Everything would be all right again. But first he had to think about leaving and how he would find the strength to do that.

He considered how he should go about selling the house, since moving was the only solution. The thought of moving made him think of his beloved orchard and the prized pigeons living in the middle of it, and how hard it would be to leave them. Maybe he wouldn't have to. Maybe he could bring them along. Raising pigeons wasn't like having a stable of horses.

Later, before the knock on the door, he thought of Su Lin. He could see her lying on a mat at the end of his stare, showing a timid smile, gently beckoning with a wave of her hand.

When he finally heard the knock, it had become very insistent. He walked slowly past the kitchen, into the living room, then stood at the door, unsure if he should open it. When Mercy's voice came through, he hesitated another moment, turned the knob, and swung the door open.

"There you are!" Mercy had braced herself, but her eyes still widened when she saw it was her father who had answered the door. She pulled herself up as straight as possible and stared at where the middle of the door had been. An uneasy silence followed. Mercy was sloppily dressed in a T-shirt and Zubas, having left her apartment in a rush. For a while both father and daughter uncomfortably looked away, feeling like strangers. Finally, Mercy looked up. "Can I come in, Dad?"

"Of course… absolutely," said Sy, shaking his head clear. As she walked past him, he brought his fist to his mouth and awkwardly cleared his throat. Mercy marched straight into the kitchen and got busy. Sy followed but stopped short and stood sheepishly in the dining room, grabbing the back of a chair for support. When he had opened the door, it had been a look of bewilderment that greeted him, but now Mercy was taking charge and Sy could hear her footsteps on the kitchen tile. The steps grew louder, and she marched into the dining room holding a tray of coffee, juice, and sweetbreads. Like her mother, she had a habit of preparing for anything serious by first doing something mundane.

"Sit," she commanded. Sy welcomed his daughter's rare subversion of his authority and slid into a chair obediently. After they were both seated, she folded her arms across the table and said, "Talk to me."

"What do you want to talk about?" asked Sy. His gaze swung across her face, stopped for an instant, then rested on a corner of the table.

"First I want to know what the hell is the smoke about?"

"I burned breakfast."

Mercy waited for more explanation, but none came. She raised her chin, touching it with her fingers. She studied him through lowered lids as if she were a lawyer deciding whether or not to take a case.

"Okay... Now I want to talk about this." She pulled a folded newspaper from her purse and laid it on the table between them.

Reaching back into her purse, Mercy produced a package of cigarettes and had trouble extracting one before lighting it and releasing a big puff of smoke out the side of her mouth. She unfolded her arms and crossed them again and waited for Sy to respond. He had nothing to say about the photo and no energy to tell her that. It would be almost as bad to say he remembered nothing at all about the incident.

"That's the kind of thing sick people do," said Mercy, in her most commanding business voice. "Are you?" Sy didn't respond and began wagging his head haplessly between his shoulders like a sick animal.

"Are you ill, Dad? Do you need help?" In contrast to her father's subdued demeanor, Mercy was highly agitated and spoke quickly. Her father remained numb and Mercy pounced, barely comprehending her own words.

"Goddammit! Goddammit! I'd think you'd at least have something to say! But maybe you've decided action is more important than words!" Realizing she was screaming, Mercy stopped abruptly, sinking back into her chair resignedly. "Do we need to call a doctor, Dad? I think we need to call a doctor."

"No... I don't know..."

"Well, this sure says differently." Her outburst over, Mercy calmed herself and gestured toward the paper on the table.

"You've seen it?" Sy shot a pleading glance at his daughter and then lowered his eyes.

"Damn right I saw it. Along with everybody else and their dog."

"What are you going to do?"

"What am I going to do? What am *I* going to do? It's not me who made the front page of the *Post Dispatch* this morning. It's not *me* who enquiring minds want to know about! Since you ask *me*, I'll tell you what *I* think we should do. Start calling around and find you a good doctor, that's what. One who can tell us what's going on in that fucked up head of yours."

Sy leaned in far over the table, covering his face with both hands. When Mercy saw him do it her heart gave a leap, and she started to cry.

"You can't do this to me, Dad. I'm sorry, but I'm not going to be able to handle it. I see this photo this morning and the first thing I think is I've been cheated. I've spent all my life trying to find a man just like you. And now I find out the yard stick I've been measuring with wasn't calibrated correctly. When I was sixteen and you started letting me date... I had an entire list of attributes that I'd run through whenever I'd meet a new guy. But basically, I only had three options to consider—better than, worse than, or the same as. As who? As you. Eventually I quit doing it. The most any of them could do was 'worse than.' Only one came close, and that was because he dressed the same. He was handsome, witty, and rich, and all he could manage was 'dresses like.' And now for you to just up and... do this..."

Mercy took a large gulp of air, causing a buildup of phlegm to catch in her throat. She balled her fist, raised it to her mouth and coughed uncontrollably. When she was done, the muscles in her face, neck and arms strained against her skin, which was soaked with tears.

Sy sat with his head bowed submissively. Mercy stopped to consider and smoke her cigarette. She crossed her legs and began to rub her knee with the palm of her hand.

"Mom says you've been flashing her, too, for about two weeks now. I'll assume that's when this whole business started." She looked at him questioningly. Sy started saying something but only shrugged.

Mercy leaned desperately across the table, her eyes bleeding tears. "Dad! Can't you tell me something? Give me some reason why in the world you're acting like this? Tell me what's eating at you? I mean my god, do you know what you'll be giving up… what you've already lost? Goddammit, Dad! This is right up there with child rape and bestiality. Is Mom not putting out enough? You probably don't know it, but that's what she thinks. Please tell me it was a big bet you lost or some crude joke that backfired or you were driven by the mob or something... anything, just so we can look you in the face and not be nauseated. I mean when I think of men like in that picture I think of fat, balding guys with blow-up dolls for wives, with spit running down their chins and the pockets cut out of their pants. Goddammit!"

A broad grimace pulled at her slightly parted lips, causing her cheeks to puff up under her bulging eyes. Each time the words stopped her mouth was left quivering, like a worn-out car running in neutral.

"Dad, you're the backbone of this family. You're the only one who could ever handle things. The only reason Mom and I have any independence is because of that big safety net you've got stretched out under us. Because it's always there we can be as cocky and stupid as we want. All my life I've been bouncing around. The only reason I've made it to where I am is because you always moved the stumbling blocks and located the goddamn land mines. You go bonkers on us, and Mom and I don't have a chance in hell."

"I smelled the eggs," he blurted out, as if explaining everything.

Mercy dabbed at her eyes with a Kleenex she pulled from her purse and sniffed twice. "What do you mean you smelled the eggs?"

The phone rang again, and Sy leapt up like he'd been hit with a cattle prod. Mercy jumped back in her chair, wide-eyed, as if expecting him to rip off his clothes and expose himself. Instead, he took three quick strides to the phone, wrapped the cord around his hand and yanked. The jack erupted from the wall and hung like a limp, dead flower. When he returned to the table he spoke as if the entire matter might be behind him. Killing the phone had made him more present,

"When I smell the rotten eggs my willpower dissolves. I fight it and fight it and fight it, but it wears me down until I can't fight it anymore. My mind just gives up, and the rotten eggs take over and then it's not me anymore but someone else. Somebody who pushes me aside, does exactly what they want and leaves me nothing to say about it." Sy began to slowly pace between the dining room walls across from Mercy. "And your mother and I are just fine," he said wearily. "Good as we ever were."

Mercy sat and watched her father's helpless pacing. He was like a captured stray dog, nervously padding out its final hours, as if it understood swift adoption was its only hope for escaping the incinerator.

Mercy continued dabbing at her eyes, more mechanically now that the tears had slowed. She was at least relieved to know her father might not be totally responsible for the despicable image on the front page of the paper. It dawned on her that he had entered another stage in his life, possibly requiring similar attention as her mother. For him it was worse because he had no one to prop him up. The tears came again, but this time because she couldn't imagine her father wanting to live in a world he couldn't control. She'd always feared her father aging, but shrugged it off, pretending the time to worry was still a long way away. But the time for worry was suddenly here. The morning paper had documented its arrival.

Mercy looked at her father through bloodshot eyes. "Why does it have to be taking your clothes off? Couldn't you just fall on the floor and have a fit or something? At least that would be respectable."

Sy only shrugged and looked away. The thing that had festered for weeks had finally consumed him, leaving him weak and empty. Now that people knew, now that he was here, discussing it with his daughter, he was feeling oddly calm. It was like stepping out of the St. Jude's confessional, instantly relieved of a very grave sin.

He sat on a chair near the wall, hunched over his crossed legs, unable to say anything more that Mercy would understand. He remembered leaving Darlene on the bed upstairs, curled up inside herself and trying to disappear.

"Why don't you go check on your mother," Sy said, as tranquilly as if he'd asked her to put away the dishes. "I don't think she's taking this very well."

"Shit, I forgot all about Mom. She knows?"

"Yeah. She knows."

"How's she doing?"

"Badly."

Mercy leapt up with a low moan and ran out of the room. She was thinking that, with all her faults, her mother was at least predictable.

After she left, Sy sat alone in the room, thinking how bad things happen to people who least deserve them. The people who work the hardest were the ones hit by what they so diligently sought to prevent. The man who monitors his cholesterol dies of a heart attack. The woman who checks for lumps eventually finds one. For years he'd fought against his wife's insanity, and now he apparently had developed his own. If insuring against evil brought it on, maybe one would be better off not worrying about anything. Like the goddamn lilies of the valley. Vulnerable, but wild and extremely alive.

His thoughts were suddenly interrupted by loud, Middle Eastern music coming from the patio. Curious, he stood and walked over to the patio door. The repetitive, undulating rhythm seemed to come from a dream, and Sy half expected to see a troupe of Bedouins resting in the orchard.

Instead, he saw a large black boom box sitting in the center of his patio. A woman's bare leg, coming foot first, snaked out horizontally from the edge of the sliding door frame. It hung there, twisting, allowing every strand of muscle to present itself. The leg drew back, then came out again followed by the rest of the body. There in front of Sy was not a clan of encamped Bedouins, but a bejeweled representative, her belly protruding obscenely beneath a thin purple veil that hung from the middle of her face. She wore castanets on the thumb and forefinger of each hand, which she snapped continuously, while ridiculously attempting to meet Sy's eyes in a provocative stare.

Sy could only look at the stripper in amazement, unable to move. On the other side of the chain-link fence, snatches of color moved kaleidoscopically behind the row of multifloral rosebushes.

The dancer quickened her pace along with the music, leaping clumsily around the circumference of the patio. At one point she slammed her shin into a wrought-iron patio chair, stumbling into the low hedge surrounding the patio. She heaved herself out of the bushes in a rush to catch up with the music, completely forgetting the alluring stare, replaced by a sincere look of pain. She performed the rest of the dance with an obvious limp.

When she passed in front of Sy, she performed three half-hearted pirouettes, which magically caused all her outer garments except a G-string to fall to the concrete. She leaped at the patio door, pressing her body against the glass, her breasts moving in time to the music.

"What the fuck's going on here!" The voice was Mercy's, and it came from just behind Sy.

Mercy hastily undid the latch, grabbed the sliding door's handle with both hands, and fired the door open so hard that the glass shattered.

As Mercy descended, the dancer grew wide-eyed and turned to run. Before getting far she tripped over the black boombox, performing an extremely unexotic sprawl on the concrete. The blow to the boombox sent batteries across the patio and stopped the music. White with rage, Mercy pulled the dancer up with her left arm and met her chubby face with a strong right cross, sending her sprawling to the pavement once more. With her nose bloodied and her face streaming tears, the exotic dancer ran in the direction of the multifloral rosebushes, each of her fleshy buttocks arrhythmically pounding out the cadence of her stride.

Still in a fit of pique, Mercy scrambled to pick up the strewn batteries and began firing them after the retreating dancer. As she watched the retreating girl, Mercy noticed movement behind the rosebushes and in an instant was up against the impenetrable barrier, flinging epithets at the people retreating behind the dancer they had commissioned.

After screaming herself hoarse, Mercy turned back toward the patio, out of steam and totally dejected. She kicked at a few of the remaining batteries, picked up the dancer's strewn garments, and handed them to her father through the shattered glass door.

"Mom's completely out of commission," she said.

Chapter 17

That afternoon Sy resigned from work, listed his house with the only agent in town who didn't know him, and spoon-fed Darlene mashed potatoes while she stared up at him in angry silence. She still wasn't speaking, having either lost the ability or simply refused to do it. Either way, for a chatterbox like Darlene, not talking indicated something seriously wrong. The last time Sy checked on her he found her curled in a fetal position, thumb hooked in her mouth. She had no desire to move and lay in bed like a stroke victim, alternately glaring out the window or at the wall next to it, and whenever Sy entered the room she glared at him.

Mercy stayed until late afternoon, trying to get her father settled and her mother mobile. Both seemed to have aged horribly over the course of a few hours, but what concerned her was the way her father would sigh loudly every few minutes. He seemed to be making progress until he spoke with Peter Marshall. He had talked to Peter brokenly, saying little more than if it was all right he'd like to take his retirement now instead of in nine months like he'd planned, with no more explanation than that. When Peter immediately agreed to the decision, Sy was devastated. After the call, his loud exhales became more frequent. He'd start telling Mercy something work related, then stop mid-sentence, remembering.

He spent the rest of the time indoors, in front of the broken patio door, looking longingly at his lost orchard and the fifteen colorful pigeons floating gracefully above it.

Mercy tried everything she could think of to coax him away from the patio door but finally gave up. She was no psychiatrist and who's to say it wasn't right to let him alone, allow for his own internal mechanisms to find the open wound and form the scar tissue that would allow him to heal. What she did know was she needed professional help deciding what to do. Whatever course of action, the prognosis didn't look good for either of her parents. But it was her mother who needed immediate attention, so Mercy called the urgent care hotline. The nurse confirmed she should take Darlene to the emergency room as soon as she could. *They would probably just increase her medication*, thought Mercy, which was what they usually did whenever Darlene had a collapse. She didn't mention her father's problem. Not yet. The real challenge for any doctor would not be Darlene. It would be diagnosing the strange connection between a rotten egg smell and exposing one's genitals to unsuspecting people. For her father's sake, she vowed to somehow get to the bottom of it.

Three times someone knocked on the front door, which sent Mercy peering out from behind the curtains. Each time there was another van parked across the street with a small dish antenna on top. To protect them from further onslaught by the St. Louis media, which was attracted to scandal like sharks were to blood, Mercy tried making the house unapproachable. Curtains were drawn, shades were pulled, and the phone was left where it lay, unhooked and inoperable. A gloom descended upon the house like a wake that was pitifully attended.

The tiny Todd family had drawn in, peeling away layers of social contact like a bad onion, to salvage what was left.

Except for the pigeons soaring above the orchard or Shorty's restless reconnoitering around the house in search of Sy, the place looked abandoned. With all the rain the grass was higher than Sy ever allowed. No yardwork had been done since the business with the egg smell, and it looked as if the house's inhabitants had left hurriedly for an extended vacation, making no arrangements for upkeep.

The big sugar maples in the front yard threw shadows that loomed closer to the house as afternoon turned to evening. The front door opened quietly, and after saying a hushed goodbye to her father, Mercy left to check on Charlotte, who was with a neighbor. When the door closed behind her, she surprised herself by emitting a suppressed shout of freedom. She got into her car and quickly drove away from her very first installment of filial duty.

After Mercy left, Sy knew nothing more to do than wander into the bedroom and find Darlene. There she was, fully awake on the bed, staring at the ceiling with her mouth parted, as if witnessing the imperial realm of heaven. Sy left to wash his face, then came back and sat on the bed next to his silent wife. Before saying anything, he waved his hand over her face and didn't get as much as a tightening around the eyes.

Sy pulled back the covers and slid in next to her. Eventually he began engaging in one-sided conversation, the way a hurting child will speak to a dog.

"Do you think we've done badly up to now, Darlene?" Sy wasn't looking at her but stared at the same spot in the ceiling. "Lately I've been thinking there are things we should do... after we get past all this." He pushed out his lower lip with his tongue like he had dipped tobacco and started again.

"We always talked about Europe... but I've been thinking we should say to hell with Europe and go on an African safari or something... while there's still something over there to see, you know?" Sy continued looking up at the ceiling and began absently rubbing the side of his nose with his index finger.

"It's probably more like we didn't try, eh? Never took the time to figure out how to go about things. For instance, I never bought you one of those slinky nightgowns, did I? I tried once but after I got to the store, I couldn't walk in. All those women standing around, with me going through those fancy lace underthings with all the straps and ruffles, and those women probably thinking I was the one gonna wear 'em." Sy chuckled at the idea of wearing such a thing. "Do you think it'd be too late to buy you a slinky nightgown, Darlene?" Sy crossed his arms behind his head, accidentally brushing Darlene's face, but she didn't even blink. Sy went on wistfully, as if they were lying on a blanket in a meadow.

"Can you even remember the last time we went away together? Don't say that night at Clarence's cabin last summer. That doesn't count, since we came back home in the middle of the night because of all the mildew." Under the blanket Sy's foot moved back and forth like a pendulum.

"You know, Darlene, maybe a little mildew that night wouldn't have hurt us. Just you and me all alone like that, we shouldn't have been thinking about mildew or bugs or anything. We could have taken a long walk around the lake. I remember the moon was big and bright and romantic, like a harvest moon. It wasn't the harvest moon, but close. I remember the grass on the dam was freshly cut, and you could really smell it after the dew dampened it a little. We could have sat on the dam there under that big ol' moon, and I could have kissed you the way I should have been kissing you… and maybe you would've wanted to kiss me back the same way.

"But I'm sure the grass would have been way too wet, or the blanket too thin, or you'd have thought there might be a snake around." Sy let his eyes wander over the ceiling, rolling out his tongue and caressing a corner of his lips. A big bluebottle fly buzzed loudly back and forth across the still room, and Sy's eyes followed it. For a while it hovered over the bed, then zeroed in on a window and bounced between the curtains.

"I guess what I'm saying is a person can get too set and live too strict," said Sy. "Pretty soon it gets real boring without you even knowing it. And I think that's when it starts to be the most dangerous, Darlene. I think there's something inside a person that can't be convinced otherwise, and if you don't do something to spice things up, that part of you will, whether you want it to or not." Sy's face fell flaccid, and the tiredness spread down his neck and into the rest of his body, which suddenly grew heavy. His voice softened even more, hovering just above a whisper.

"Lately, I been thinking what it'd be like for you without me around. I really don't think you'd have it so bad, Darlene. You still got your looks. You could easily find somebody who would want to do more than just babysit you. Make you do things... buy you something sexy... he'd make you start living, and you'd begin to feel better about yourself."

Sy stopped talking for a moment and hoisted himself up on an elbow to see if Darlene was getting any of it. Reaching out, his fingers touched a thick rivulet of saliva running down her neck and into her pillow. He slowly lowered himself back down and again opened his eyes to the ceiling.

"What if something were to happen to me, Darlene? Maybe you could find that other guy who'd have the guts to help you live. It might take a little while, and I wouldn't want you doing it too soon. But say, just for instance, one day I decided to clean the Browning... it's been in the closet for so long it probably needs it. What if someday I was cleaning my shotgun and the rag I was using got tangled up down near the bottom, and I pulled it away to get it loose. And what if what it was tangled around was the trigger, and maybe I forgot it was loaded and it just went off... And what if it happened out at Clarence's cabin and you wouldn't have to find me and you could just go on with some other guy and you could be happy again like when we first met."

Chapter 18

Mercy returned as the evening was turning into night. She rang the front doorbell several times and when there was no answer, let herself in with her own key. Finding Sy idly sitting in the kitchen, she was filled with anger and relief.

"Why didn't you answer the damn door?" she demanded.

"Thought you might be somebody else," said Sy, not even attempting to return her gaze. Mercy studied him grimly. How did her father come to having to make a statement like that? "You look terrible," said Mercy. "And what the hell are you doing with that?" On the table in front of him was a freshly opened can of beer.

Sy just looked at her and shrugged listlessly. "It's okay for a guy to have a beer at the end of the day when he's retired."

Mercy dropped her purse into a kitchen chair. "You look like you might have been drinking ever since I left. Have you?"

Sy finally looked up at her with a blank expression. "Nope. I waited until I got thirsty. Now that I'm retired, I got a new rule. No beer before I need one. I walked past the refrigerator a while ago and realized I was short something."

Without saying a word Mercy reached for his beer, marched to the sink and poured it out. She fired the empty can into the trash like she was killing a snake.

"Here's a new rule for you, Dad. No more drinking until we get you straightened out." She had her hands on her hips and looked as if she'd just scolded a child.

"Since when do you start giving me orders?" asked Sy. It was a weak vestige of the man he used to be, had no power, and Mercy ignored it.

"Is Mom any better?"

Sy shook his head.

"Why don't you go shave," said Mercy. "Just because you're retired doesn't mean you can start looking like a bum."

"I'm a celebrity now too. Celebrities can do what they want, and nobody questions them."

Mercy looked down at her broken father and for an instant felt like bursting into tears, throwing herself around his legs, and begging him to return. But this morning she had cried enough, and now she had to be strong if her family was to be salvaged.

"Shave," she said, pointing down the hall.

All his life Sy was the one to give the orders. Now he seemed to have no trouble taking them and trudged obediently down the hallway like a timid dog.

As she watched him go, Mercy felt a wave of loss, as if her father had died. Worse, this stranger had cruelly appeared, wanting to change her lasting image of him. When he stopped to open the hall closet, obviously mistaking it for the bathroom door, Mercy felt she was going to faint and bit her bottom lip hard until it began to bleed.

When the bathroom door finally closed, she followed down the hall to her parents' bedroom. The dark curtains were pulled tight, blocking all light except for a thin line that crossed the floor, traveled up the bed, and ended on her mother's expressionless face.

After Mercy surveyed the room, she snapped back the curtains and pushed the window open as far as it would go. The air in the room hung heavy and dank. If she couldn't freshen it quickly, she was going to faint for sure this time.

"Mom, it's me, Mercy." When Mercy touched her mother's shoulder the eyes recognized her. Her mother was back from wherever she'd gone but still wasn't talking. Instead, she opted to communicate with only her eyes, and when they looked at Mercy they narrowed with disgust, seeming to say *This whole thing with your father really stinks, doesn't it?*

For the next ten minutes Mercy struggled to dress her mother, who could only assist weakly, due to another charge of pills Sy had thoughtfully provided. While she was bent over, struggling with her mother's shoes, Sy appeared and stood in the doorway, waiting politely.

"Okay, Dad, grab her by the other arm, and let's get her out to the car." She spoke with authority, having no idea how long she would be able to sustain it.

"Let me open all the doors first," said Sy. Mercy quickly looked up, but he'd already turned to go. She was surprised to hear his old voice, and the first reliable thing he'd said all day.

When Sy walked back into the room, Darlene glared at him, daring him to try and touch her. When he attempted to grab her under the shoulder, Darlene slapped his hand away, turning to Mercy for support. Mercy nodded her father on, and he quickly spun around, walking just ahead of them, looking self-conscious. As the small procession wound its way slowly through the house, Darlene shuffled stiffly, holding her head arrogantly erect like a stricken queen. For once she could claim more respect than her husband and was enjoying the dubious honor all alone.

Mercy belted her mother into the passenger seat, walked around, got behind the wheel, started the car, and drove off quickly. As they pulled out of the driveway and into the street, Darlene stared hard at her husband standing in the yard with his hands in his pockets, looking like someone just told a joke he didn't understand. As they drove off, he forced a smile and waved, then missed his pockets three times before finally crossing his arms, watching the car disappear down Enon Hill. He stood there a while, unsure what to do next, then saw a car turn onto his street in the direction of his house. He turned and took a few tentative steps toward the door, then thought better and loped around the side, let himself through the gate, and quickly melted into the labyrinthine shelter of his orchard.

Inside the coop the air was hot and dry and dusty. After climbing through the trap door in the floor Sy folded the upper half of the south wall down on its hinges, allowing air and light to stream through the chicken wire and freshen the inside. From this vantage Sy could survey the entire orchard plus the outfield below, as far as second base. To his left lay the wall of multifloral roses, guarding the eastern perimeter of his property like coiled concertina wire. Beyond the roses stood the old converted schoolhouse with only its red brick shell, rows of latticed wooden windows, and the rusted wrought-iron steps rising to the main door, the only thing remaining of its original dignity.

In a corner of the coop was a bucket with a board on top of it. Sy turned the board over to have a seat free of pigeon droppings, first reaching into the bucket to retrieve the bottle he'd put there when the coop was built. He never intended to drink it and had only left it there for good luck, the way a contractor will seed the foundation of a new house with silver dollars. Sagging into the corner, he uncorked the bottle and saluted the five rollers that had stayed behind, conserving their energy for the more important evening flights.

"Here's to the biggest bunch of misfits in the entire bird world," said Sy, lifting the bottle high above his head with one hand. "And I'm including the African ostrich, the turkey buzzard, and the dodo, even if he is extinct. You and every squab you squeeze out of your pin-feathered loins keep turning cartwheels and slamming into the ground like you do, and soon you'll be extinct too... like your dead cousins, the wood pigeons, who couldn't tell the difference between a perch and a gun barrel until it blew their asses off." Sy took a big pull from the bottle and screwed up his face. He looked down at the bottle and held it away like he didn't know what it was, then spoke again. "But then I guess banging your head into the ground isn't as bad as banging it against a wall. Least it's softer, and you're not gonna hurt anybody else by it." He uncorked the bottle again and took another big swallow.

An hour later the bottle was halfway down, and Sy was still sitting on the bucket. The sun shined through the trees low on the west side, and everything inside the coup—the new clapboards nailed to the exposed studs, the foul, lice-infested straw scattered across the floor, and the omnipresent floating dust—softened like a chalk still life.

"You guys ever wonder why it is you do what you do?" He directed the question to the five pigeons perched tightly together just under the roof. He had been quiet for so long they'd forgotten he was there, and now they all turned their heads and looked down at him stone-faced, like a feathered Mt. Rushmore.

"Ever worry what drives you?" he went on. "I mean think about it. Every time you go for a nice leisurely flight something tells you to act like the Blue Angels on the Fourth of July. You got any idea why that is? No? Well, I'll tell you." Sy raised the bottle again. With each drink he was screwing up his face less.

"It's because you don't have enough of the right shit floating around in those pea brains of yours to tell you not to." Sy blinked and stared at the opposite wall. His head rocked on his shoulders slightly. "At least that's what the padre will try and tell you. Whenever you run out of whatever that shit is you got to try and cover your heads with your assholes. Well let me tell you something..." Sy was leaning back on the bucket against the wall regarding the birds but now leaned forward with his elbows on his knees, still holding the bottle firmly in one hand. "The secret is to make up for what you're missing with something else." Sy took another pull and leaned over and poured some of the whiskey into the pigeons' watering can.

"Now you guys come on down here, drink some of this, and fly right."

A little later more pigeons flew down, walked through the small square portals at either end of the roof, and Sy greeted them as they wandered in. Suddenly there was an exceptionally loud flapping that sounded like someone slapping their stomach, and the big, blue-mottled male lit onto the platform outside the entrance. As he was conditioned to do, he surveyed the area above and below the coop before deciding it was safe enough to come in. He strutted into the coop with a side-to-side swagger and hopped onto the pole.

Sy gave a short flourish of his hand toward the tank, inviting him to have a drink. "It's the hard stuff, but I made it pretty weak," he said. "Anyway, a guy like you can handle it." The big bird only sat on his perch with his head sunk far into his squat body, looking indifferent, as if determined not to give the uninvited guest the satisfaction of being recognized.

Sy looked up at the big bird and clucked his tongue in appreciation. "You're the head honcho in here, aren't you? Whatever you say pretty much goes." The big pigeon paid him no mind and began studiously pecking at the area between its toes.

"You don't take any shit off anybody," Sy continued. "I've seen you. None of the others take off until you do. Then they match you flap for flap. And if one second guesses you and makes a wrong turn, why he scurries back just as fast as he can. Nobody rolls out early either, not until you tell them. I've seen the younger ones just itching to roll out like they couldn't stand the suspense, but you always hold them. I've never seen you smash up either. You know exactly how much altitude you all need, don't you?" Sy gave the big pigeon a sideways glance, as if feeling unworthy of looking at him full on.

"Some of 'em smash up anyway, but that's not your fault. They just can't see you while they're flipping and don't know when to pull up, and some of 'em are too damn stupid to figure it out on their own, and they're the ones you can't do nothing for. You just can't do it all, can you? Much as you try you just can't do it all for 'em."

Sy shook his head sadly, got up off the bucket, and took an unsteady step toward the big pigeon. His feet felt unusually heavy, and he accidentally kicked the water can with a loud bang, which put all the pigeons up inside the coop. For a moment the stillness was broken by the flurry of wings flapping in the tight space. The birds pounded each other trying to rob their neighbors' air, some of them beating their wings hard against the tin roof, and Sy could feel the movement of dry air on his face. Big Blue hadn't moved, continuing to peck away at his feet. After they'd all settled down again, Sy took another pull and could hear Mercy calling for him from the back patio.

Sy took two more steps toward the big blue, and when he was directly under him offered his finger as a perch. "C'mon, big fella. Go ahead and take a chance," he said. He held his breath to steady his arm. "That's it, loosen up a little. You can't be careful all the time."

The big blue cocked his head from side to side, as if trying to surmise what Sy was up to. He tentatively placed a foot on Sy's finger and closed firmly. Sensing Sy was going to remain steady, it carefully pushed off with its other foot, stood on Sy's finger, and puffed out its chest.

"That's it," said Sy, stroking the pigeon's head with fingers that felt thicker than usual. "You got to act confident in front of the others... even in your ignorance."

Sy took a few careful steps backward, returning to his own perch on the bucket. He took another big pull of the whiskey with his left hand and softly exhaled fumes into the bird's face. After observing him a while, the bird turned around and with his back to Sy, released a watery droplet to the floor between Sy's legs.

"That figures," said Sy with a flourish of the bottle. "A friend tries to help get you drunk and you turn around and shit on him. Just keep having your fits. See what I care."

Sy thrust his arm up as if releasing a hunting falcon, and the big blue pigeon settled back onto his perch in three unhurried beats. Immediately it started doing a dance to alert the others it was time for the last evening performance. It lifted its feet high into its chest, one after the other, then turned three complete circles while raising and lowering its head, as if he had once flown to Haiti and studied calypso. The rest of the birds imitated Big Blue, and Sy stood and did the same. With the bottle in one hand and both arms held out wide, Sy raised first one knee and then the other as high as he could, while thrusting his head up and down like a strutting turkey.

"Well, the red red robin goes bob bob bobbin' along," he sang out, waving his arms to keep his balance. After reaching the opposite wall, he turned back, continuing the dance, singing even louder. "Well the red red bobbin' goes rob rob robbin' aloong!"

The pigeons had put up with Sy's visit for too long to pay him much attention now, and they were all too excited about the prospect of doing their rolls to concern themselves with such erratic behavior. But when Sy began turning circles in the middle of the coop and fell hard against the clapboard wall, causing the entire structure to sway, they panicked and tried to fly out at once. From outside they looked like paratroopers on a training exercise, diving one behind the other out of the coop's porthole, then catching themselves on opened wings and swinging off in tight, rising curves.

Sy sat back on the bucket, only moving enough to bring what remained of the bottle up to his lips and drink. Except for himself, the coop was empty, and the only thing moving was the patch of light coming from the west exit, which crept slowly across the ceiling as the sun receded. Soon the light would be gone and submerge Sy in total darkness.

Below the orchard he could hear cars arriving for the Sunday night Legion game, and when he knelt down, stretching his neck over the half wall, he saw the outfielders far below, warming up on pop flies.

Suddenly he was aware of someone just beneath him and heard Mercy call his name in a shout that brought him off the floor. Steadying himself with the crap-covered perch above his head, he held his breath, afraid to move. He peered cautiously over the edge of the half wall through the chicken wire and saw Mercy step out below, oblivious of his presence. He saw her stop and call for him a few more times and then she continued through the orchard toward the ballpark, thinking he might be there watching the game. Sy followed her until she disappeared beneath a large peach tree, swallowed up by a dome of heavily laden branches.

Shortly after Mercy left he noticed more movement. Shorty appeared from beneath the coop, stepped out a few feet, then turned and looked up. For a while he stared up at the coop, not moving. Then he sauntered back under, sniffed at the ladder and laid down patiently in the dust beneath Sy.

Standing unsteadily inside the coop, still holding his grip on the perch, Sy felt disoriented and twisted his head rapidly from side to side and blinked. He had wanted to yell out to Mercy that he was up there. He was up there and planned to stay, and she wouldn't have to worry about him anymore. He would just live up there, and everything would be okay. The message made it all the way to the top of his throat, but a pair of hands folded around his neck and choked it back down. As he stood, he blinked three more times into the trees below. Mercy was back, but what had become of Darlene?

"It'd be just like her to want to stay in the hospital," he whispered.

Sy was not so far gone he didn't realize he was drunk, and since he knew he was drunk he allowed himself the scalding remark about his stricken wife. Using the same reasoning, he began kicking at the wall beneath the chicken wire with his right foot, blow after blow until the boards finally gave way and his leg popped out. His leg dangled outside the coop, bare of the pantleg, which had remained inside. He felt pain shoot up through his spine and into his head despite the alcoholic caul which up until now had cut out almost everything.

Hanging onto the overhead perch with both hands, he was able to kick the hole bigger with the other foot, free his leg, and stand up. Standing there in the center of the cramped coop, his chest expanding with every breath, teeth clenched, and blood pouring from his exposed calf, he felt like a soldier during a lull in battle, anxious to deliver more death yet too full of adrenalin to consider the possibility of his own.

For the moment he had nothing else to vent his hostility on except himself. He switched the bottle to his other hand for a better grip, drank the last of it, and shattered it against the far wall.

A slow smile broke across his face. He'd thought of something else to do. He bent carefully from the waist and let his arms swing from his shoulders as if to loosen them. He put his right arm behind his back like a speedskater and studied a spot on the wall. He shook his head three different times, pretending to shrug off the signal. Then he uncoiled and wound up as if delivering a pitch. But when he raised his left leg high for leverage, he threw himself off balance and went crashing backward into the wall and fell to the floor in a pile. For a while he lay on the putrid floor with his shoulders to the wall, surprised. Slowly he raised himself up on an elbow.

It was his heart. He had taken too much whiskey in too little time, and as a warning to stop doing it immediately, the muscles of his heart pulsed and fluttered. Everything grew dark. Shapeless blots of light danced across his vision. Instead of becoming frightened, Sy let his body go slack and waited for it to come. He laid very still, hoping it would come and banish the wicked egg smell for good. To his dismay the erratic heartbeat slowed, and he soon began feeling less dizzy. It was the very act of resignation, the calm acceptance of an end to the madness that saved him. Sy lay there for some time with his eyes closed, at once both relieved and dejected that the black curtain had raised, leaving him once again surrounded by the heavy closeness of the pigeon coop's interior.

At its peak, he tried to peer through the blackness, to open up and feel its dimension, but he saw nothing and knew there was nothing more to expect. Sy slitted his eyes and for a long time tried to conjure the blackness, but he could come nowhere near the nothingness he'd been so close to before. After a while he opened his eyes and laid on the floor very still, feeling his head rock with every beat of his heart, which now pumped annoyingly strong and smooth, showing no sign of remembering anything of its mad rush toward oblivion.

Chapter 19

Sy woke on the ground below the coop, with Shorty lying next to him. It was late enough into the night that dampness covered the grass, and the only sound was made by crickets. At first, he had no idea where he was and, feeling the earth cold and damp against his back with the still night air pressing heavy against him, he experienced the sensation of having been buried alive. As if in agreement his body refused to move, and it was only after a gust of wind rocked the fruit trees that he recognized his surroundings and was able to turn his head slightly. When his knee finally came up, pushing freely into the air, the shock wave of being buried alive crested, and he was relieved to know he was still above ground after all.

He rose on his elbows, and fountains of pain exploded in his head, vivid eruptions of silver and gold and red, and suddenly being above ground no longer held such promise. The whiskey had gone through his brain like solvent, leaching it of everything required to link mind and body. What it left was one convulsive issue of pain.

The exertion of leaning on his elbows caused him to tremble. He collapsed onto his left side and vomited violently. Shorty jumped away.

A little later a huge white opossum loomed out of the darkness to cautiously investigate the strange thing curled next to a putrid mixture of smells. Shorty barked, which sent the opossum scurrying to the safety of an apple tree, from which it watched the man rise slowly to his knees and stumble across the lawn and into the house.

Putting his hands on the walls for support, Sy stumbled to the end of the hall before pulling up short in front of the framed article from *Stars & Stripes*. Squinting, he leaned in and studied the image of a younger Sy standing on the mound, smiling confidently, with "Cannoneers" emblazoned across the front of his uniform. Briefly, he raised his hand to touch the glass, then made his way to the bedroom and into the adjoining bathroom.

He stood leaning over the washbasin, peering into the mirror at a man he could not recognize. The man stared back at him with swollen, piggish skin, pale as the porcelain below. The left eye was shut, surrounded by angry purple, the result of falling through the trapdoor of the coop to the ground below. Sy found he couldn't look at the face in the mirror without the rest of him recoiling in a wave of nausea. He pulled himself away, then stood hunched quietly in the shower, knowing that any expansive movement would trigger another fit of pain. After turning off the water he fell naked onto the bed and was soon sound asleep. In a few hours the sun would rise and present the entire Midwest with its most idyllic version of morning light. If his head had been clearer as he passed through the dining room, Sy might have seen the note from Mercy propped on the table.

> Dear Dad, I had to check Mom into the hospital today. The doctors say she's had a severe shock and needs monitoring, but she should be able to come home in a few days. I had to tell them what happened. I felt they needed to understand. She's still not talking, but she did feed herself this evening which I take as a good sign.
>
> I don't know why you are doing what you've been doing. But I am trying to understand it, so we can get it stopped. I know it's not like you to do this sort of thing and can only imagine the pain and embarrassment you must be going through. I'm sorry, I know you probably

didn't want me to, but I spoke to the doctor about you anyway. He seemed to have a thought as to what might be going on when I described what was happening and mentioned the egg smell and he wants you to come in for some tests. He mentioned several possibilities and said it was very uncommon but might be treatable. Above all you should know you are not crazy, just very physically ill.

I don't know where you are right now, but I do hope you are safe. And I want you to know both Mom and I still love you very, very much. Love Mercy.

Chapter 20

Four hours after Sy finally made it to bed, the big, blue-mottled pigeon went into his pre-flight strut. The others had gone off to feed, and there were only two young birds, barely more than squabs, left to witness the performance. Though they'd been flying for little more than a month the two were ready and eager to test their wings against their leader, and when Big Blue flitted up to the narrow port and stepped out, they fought to be the next to exit.

Big Blue wasted no time and soared down to a yard above the ground to calibrate the distance, then pulled up hard and pumped himself skyward in ever-widening circles. The two others followed him obediently, pressing close, one at each wing, so when the time came, they would not be caught off guard.

As if meaning to taunt the younger birds or at least teach them patience, the old male rolled through a few slow wide turns, once in a while going into a lazy stall that sent the two young birds standing on their tails. Each time, instead of careening over and plummeting down, he would bank hard and pull out, starting another wide lazy turn. Following close behind him, the two young birds craned their necks, as if wanting to get his attention and ask just what the hell he thought he was doing.

He sensed he'd taken them as far as they would go and after a particularly long stall, in which he'd spread his wings wide and coasted like a descending angel, he pumped the air, sending himself flapping head over tail toward the ground below. The two young birds instantly did the same. In his playfulness, the big, blue-mottled male failed to pay attention to his internal altimeter, and when the ground rushed up to greet him, he wasn't able to decline the invitation. He'd made the miscalculation a few times before, but this time he was unlucky enough to hit a rock instead of the soft cushion of earth. And since his fragile neck had broken in the fall, it was his last mistake. The two untrained young birds followed him all the way down like remora, tottering drunkenly on the ground before launching themselves back up to the coop. The big, blue-mottled male twitched a few more times, then lay still on his flat granite pyre. Just as the sun was rising over the coop he was discovered by the opossum, who proudly dragged him off into the orchard.

One week later the Hall of Fame induction ceremony was about to commence. It was to be held in advance of the game, yet it was still too early for anyone to show up for it, except for a small group of Sy's friends. Clarence, Angie Parker, Coon, Pete Turner, Father Dieckman, and Marvin Whorley sat clustered on the otherwise empty bleachers, from time to time glancing up at the lone microphone standing on the pitcher's mound like a thrown spear.

"I sure don't get it," said Pete Turner, shaking his head. "Guy like Sy, got everything going for him... about to retire, and now getting inducted into the damn Hall of Fame. It just doesn't make sense for him to do what he done." Pete was sitting on the bleachers with both hands under him, his head sunk gloomily between his shoulders.

"A guy don't up and do that kind of thing all the sudden," said Marvin Whorley excitedly. "I think he must have been queer all along. And now we all see the plain naked truth." He was the only one to laugh at his joke, opening his eyes wide like something surprised him, bellowing out a long mulish guffaw. When no one else laughed he knew the others were taking things seriously and there were no more jokes to be made. He turned to the others one at a time, measuring their reactions.

Clarence was leaning back, resting his arms on the next highest bleacher. He turned slowly from below and sent a long sour look up at Marvin, and when Marvin's roving eyes finally fell on Clarence, he quickly looked away pretending it hadn't registered. Clarence turned back and spoke calmly in the direction of the empty outfield.

"You all can think what you want, but that wasn't Sy who done that. Least not his real self." He didn't hope to convince anyone, wasn't trying to convince anyone of anything, but just spoke matter-of-factly. Yet for those who were listening, there was also a soft, hurt quality to his voice like at a funeral. "Sy's the most upstanding guy in Gilmore," he continued. "In the whole damn county for that matter... and I think at least for today we should forget what happened and think about the only man I know who could throw an eighteen-inning no hitter."

"God, do I remember that day," said old Coon, carefully reaching into his mouth with one finger to scour out the plug of tobacco he'd been working on all morning. "A playoff game against Stanton. Spent the whole day throwing knuckleballs." Coon bent low over the space between the bleachers, positioning his mouth like he was taking aim. Slowly the spent wad of tobacco slid out of his mouth, dropped down through the bleachers, and landed squarely on old Shorty, who had come down for the action but was now sleeping in the dust. When the watery ball of tobacco hit him, he looked up with a start and then settled back down to sleep some more.

"It was a regular season game against Cape Girardeau," said Clarence, continuing to stare out at the empty ball field. His voice stayed low, yet carried force, the way a man can do when he doesn't much care who hears him. "And it wasn't just knuckleballs. At the beginning it was fast balls fired one right after the other like a damn Roman candle. And a fast ball wasn't even his pitch. I knew right away he was going to have a good game when he started fanning 'em right off with his fast ball. He had a whole sack o' junk he could throw whenever he needed it. You all know that."

Clarence looked around for confirmation. The rest of them nodded knowingly, and Clarence turned back toward the field. "He went to knuckleballs later. But first he just kept throwing them fast balls like he had too much energy and needed to tap some off."

Behind them a big Ford station wagon pulled in with the sound of crunching gravel and parked behind the bleachers. Behind the wheel sat an old man none of them knew.

"Soon as one guy even started foul tipping his fast ball, he'd come in with that Big Creek curve," continued Clarence. "Once in a while he'd slip in an underhanded changeup and have 'em swinging so hard they'd cut a fart you could hear all the way out to center field. I should know, I was catching him."

"If there's anyone to hear a batter fart it would be the catcher," said Angie. She looked down solemnly like all the rest, and when she spoke she raised her cheeks in a way that wasn't a smile and started shaking her head knowingly until she had to use two hands to stop it.

Clarence waited politely to see if Angie was going to say anything more, then started talking again, still staring through the wire fence at the empty ballfield in front of him. "By the top of the twelfth some of our own guys were betting he couldn't last another inning, but he just stayed up there grinning like a damn opossum, firing strikes like an automatic pitching machine." Clarence crossed a leg over his knee. He was slouched so low on the bleachers he could see home plate through the hole his legs made.

"Once in a while towards the end I'd call a time out and go out and talk to him just to give him a rest. I'd walk out there real slow, like to buy time, and he'd just be standing there grinning. We'd stand out there just shootin' the shit about anything and everything but baseball. The first time I walked out I told him I heard Sue Pinter was shooting a big beaver out of the bleachers, and I just wanted to come out and see what it looked like from where he was. Each time I walked up on the mound after that we'd start out talking about Sue Pinter's beaver, the whole while lookin' so solemn and serious the next batter would get all excited thinking we was talking about him. Finally, I'd get around to asking Sy if he was tired or anything and you know what he'd say?" Clarence gave the others on the bleachers plenty of time to respond, but none of them did.

"He'd say, 'Just one more inning,' and then give that shit eatin' grin. I'd just shake my head and flip him the ball, and he'd burn it past two, three more batters."

"Hey, any of you-all know who's playing here today?" It was the old man who'd just driven up in the Ford. He was standing below the bleachers just to the left of where they sat with his hand clutching a bleacher above his head. The man looked to be as old as Coon and wore a red Cardinals baseball cap so worn the bill was almost folded in half. No one paid him much attention except Marvin Whorley.

"Gilmore against Foley," said Marvin, who still suffered from his badly received joke. "But it don't start till one-thirty."

"Good. I'll have time to find me a good seat then," said the old man.

"Whole damn ballpark's yours," said Marvin. He squinted around to get a better look at the old man between the slats in the bleachers. Marvin was surprised at how old the guy looked and couldn't imagine him sitting on a board for long without major discomfort. He was amazed the guy was even allowed to drive. "Is that why you're here so early? Just to get a good seat?"

The old man smiled wide, showing he didn't have a tooth left in his head. "I always get to the park early. Game goes too damn quick otherwise. I could ask you the same question."

Marvin had an open bag of peanuts between his legs and had been eating them like a hungry squirrel. Seeing the man had no teeth, he offered him a peanut just to see what he'd do with it. "Friend gettin' inducted into the Hall of Fame today," he said.

The old man took the peanut from Marvin, held it close to his face, then popped it into his mouth, shell and all. "Hall of Famer, huh?

Who might that be then?" After the toothless old man sucked all the salt from the peanut, he spit it out of his mouth and onto the ground at his feet.

"That would be Sy Todd," said Marvin gruffly. "But I don't imagine that means much to you." The old man seemed weird and was starting to bother Marvin. He turned around so as not to have to look at him and stared off at the Gilmore Gas Company billboard that made up fifteen feet of the left field fence.

The old man's eyes brightened. "Is Todd playing today?"

"Course he ain't playin' today," Marvin said disgustedly, not even looking at the old man. "He ain't played no ball in over twenty years. That's his dog layin' there in front of you though."

"Strange his dog's here, but Sy isn't," said Pete.

"Maybe he's ashamed to be around him," said Marvin.

The old man looked down, reaching his leg way out and and nudged the sleeping Shorty in the rump with his foot. Shorty snapped his head up over his shoulder to see what he wanted. "You sure it's been that long?" asked the old man.

"Longer."

"Well, I ain't ever seen a ballplayer like him. An' I been following the game for over seventy years. Shoot, I even remember when his pappy played."

At the mention of Sy's father Clarence grew interested and turned around to look at the man through the space between the bleachers. He found it odd the old man knew of Sy. Clarence had never seen him before. "Was the old man any good?" Clarence wasn't sure he wanted to start a conversation with the strange old man, but he was curious to know something about Sy's father and asked anyway.

"No. At least I don't guess. I can't remember nuttin' special what he might a done."

"Did he pitch?"

The old man moved closer, rubbed the white stubble of his chin, and peered back through the bleachers, not two feet from Clarence's face. "No, I believe he played second base, if I remember. Maybe outfield. I only remember one thing for sure about Walt Todd. He had the jumpin' fits... saw him flop right down in the dirt on his way to the dugout once."

"But could he hit?" asked Clarence. If someone didn't pitch it was important that they could hit.

"You know, from what I recall, I don't believe Walt Todd could have hit a bull in the ass with a scoop shovel." The old man chuckled, rubbing his beard harder, then suddenly turned, walked around to the front of the bleachers, the part farthest away from the group, and labored his way to the very top with the assistance of a cane. The whole while he continued laughing to himself, muttering what he'd said about the scoop shovel.

For a while the group watched him go to his seat and when he finally settled on the very top board, he turned to look back at them and waved, as if to dismiss a compliment. Pete was the first to speak, and since Coon was the oldest, asked him if he knew the old man.

Coon looked up at the old man suspiciously. "Can't say I do. But if I did, I think I'd be obliged to start praying for amnesia." Coon squinted hard and went to work cranking his chin over his left shoulder, gasping for breath. At the same time his right arm shot out like he was asking for money, and as his head twisted so did the hand, like on the end of an axle. The hand twisting was something new, but for as strongly as Coon twisted it the rest of them knew he'd be doing it for the rest of his life.

The group looked at Coon's new tic for a while and then Pete brought the conversation back to where it was before the old man interrupted them. "So what do you think of what Sy done, Father?" asked Pete. "Being a Catholic priest and all." Dieckman had been unusually quiet and was thoughtfully puffing his cigar, just enough to keep it lit. He leaned forward, rested his forearms on his knees, looked straight ahead, and answered with more reverence than he'd ever applied to any religious ceremony.

"I think he must have been a damn fine ballplayer to make it to the Hall of Fame. I just wish I'd had the parish when he was in his heyday."

Pete looked at the priest like it was the dumbest thing he ever heard. "No, I mean what do you think about him showing himself in front of people."

"I don't know," said Dieckman, who for once, since he'd inherited the parish, seemed to be lost for words. He paused and puffed his cigar again. "I don't think it would do Sy any good for us to even speculate. But it must have been something bigger than him."

Pete whistled thoughtfully and rubbed his legs with his hands. "But why would the good God in heaven want to put that on a man?"

"I wasn't talking about God."

Pete leaned back and whistled again.

Marvin was happy the conversation returned to the latest gossip, already afraid it would die down as soon as it started. "Well, he for sure showed himself to that Schleuter woman," he said. "I hear there's a guy way over in Truxton claims he seen him too. And what I can't understand is that Darlene's still a fine-looking woman."

"I wish he'd done it to me," said Angie, her head shaking. "I been wanting to see Sy naked ever since I known him."

"I doubt the feeling's mutual," said Coon, who covered his dig by hurriedly turning up his longneck bottle of Busch. He was the only one of the group who was drinking, had already attained his routine level of alcoholic insolence, and would tend it like a cookfire the remainder of the day.

Angie shot him a hot glance, then waved at her wrinkled face resignedly, as if shooing a make-believe fly. "I tell you one thing though… he's drinking more than I ever seen him."

"I imagine I'd be drinking too," said Marvin smugly.

Angie looked around at all the others, and her voice took on a note of concern. "I seen plenty of men drink before. And I know when they're puttin' down beer to drown something that's rotten inside. Some men naturally like to drink, but Sy wasn't one of 'em. He only drank to be friendly, and once he'd get as friendly as he wanted to be he'd quit—or at least slow way down. But lately I could tell Sy was drinkin' to kill somethin', and a couple of times I almost felt like speakin' to it... but then it ain't my business."

"PLAY BALL!"

As one, the group turned their heads to the sound. It was the shriveled old man who sat across from them, and he was now on his feet with the help of his cane, bouncing up and down on his old spindly legs and vigorously shaking a fist out toward the ballfield. It was still early, and he was the only other person on the bleachers. "PLAY BALL, DANG IT!" This time the man's voice broke, the last part coming out in a loud, high-pitched croak, which seemed to embarrass him so much he quickly sat down.

A few more cars rolled into the parking lot behind the bleachers. Bob Mussman, the president of the Gilmore County Baseball Association, stepped out of a yellow Cadillac Eldorado, wearing a very official looking brown sport coat, blue plaid pants and brown fedora, which sat tilted on his head as if he'd been gripped by the shoulders and shaken vigorously. He looked up into the bleachers and waved at the group. Given his role in a community that worshipped baseball, Bob Mussman was awarded no less deference than the president of the United States.

Pete shook his head in wonder. "I offered to put him in a Ford," he said. "Shot him a helluva good price too. Big black Town Car, loaded to the gills. Nice and respectable for a man of his stature. Look at what he's driving now. Big yellow pimpmobile, like one of the bruthas would drive."

The group remained quiet, each caught up in their own thoughts. Clarence sighed heavily. His own thoughts were on his friend Sy and had still come to no conclusion. He leaned farther back, resting his back and arms on the bleacher above and behind him. He craned his neck to look at Dieckman. Even though he didn't like the priest all that much he considered him his only confidant, now that Sy was... whatever Sy was.

“Do you know if... can you go to jail for that kind of thing?”

“What, buying yellow Cadillacs?”

“Damn well should,” said Pete Turner.

“No. Taking your clothes off… in front of people.”

“It’s on the books,” said Dieckman. He leaned forward, placing his forearms on his knees. “Indecent exposure.”

“But he didn’t really do anything, did he? I mean if he wanted to do anything with that woman, he sure as hell could have. Her living alone and all. Not that Sy would ever do anything like that.” Clarence tried not believing in what Sy had done, but knew he was guilty—there was the picture to prove it. He’d gone through every explanation he could think of, but nothing held up. Now he stopped looking for reasons and began looking for ways to make it seem a less serious offense.

Dieckman said, “It’s not what Sy did that puzzles me so much as the why of it. I mean people have been addicted to the exhilaration of doing the forbidden since the snake got to Adam and Eve. Sy’s never been one to need anything like that. Hell, he could take the sin of ordinary concupiscence and wrestle it to the ground before it even entered his brain.”

“It’s a sin to piss on somebody?” asked Coon, not understanding correctly. “I ain’t sure, Padre, but it sounded like you just said it was a sin to piss on something or other.”

“Concupiscence. He never let himself get horny,” said the priest.

“Oh... But is it a sin to piss on somebody? I remember we was in Tijuana once, there was seven of us, and we paid a Mexican a buck apiece to crawl down in a hole and let us piss on his head.” They all looked at Coon, then at each other. They never knew for sure if Coon just had a ripe imagination or if senility was finally settling in.

“If you’ve ever seen Tijuana, it was from the bottom of a bottle of tequila you bought at Gasen’s,” said Angie. She pouted her lips and dipped a shoulder toward Coon spitefully, like a six-year-old girl.

"We was there with General John J. Pershing," said Coon petulantly. "And we all pissed on this poor bastard's head until it run down his face and into his clothes. Once and a while that whole deal still comes up and bugs me."

"I'd sure rather be pissed off than pissed on," said Marvin, who as usual was easily amused by Coon, and now tried to egg him on.

"I always said I'd rather be pissed off than pissed on," said Coon. He was hard of hearing and hadn't heard Marvin steal the line he always delivered after the Tijuana story. He had no idea why no one laughed like they always did and grimly returned to his beer, vowing to remain quiet in the presence of such an unappreciative crowd.

"That's sick," said Marvin, feigning indignance. "To want to piss on somebody's head like that."

"You never did anything that was a little sick?" Dieckman seldom talked to Marvin Whorley directly since he always thought him a bit of a buffoon. Today, after a few of the crude remarks he said about Sy, Dieckman found him especially irritating.

Marvin thought about Dieckman's question a while then turned his head as if to dismiss it. But after a minute of silence he turned and said, "Aw, I did it with a cow once when I was thirteen." It was as if he hoped saying it casually would lift the onus. After saying it, he had no idea why he'd made the confession and wished he had it back.

"You did what?" said Dieckman. The entire group turned to look at Marvin in disbelief, then back at the priest for his reaction. Dieckman seemed to be taking it professionally, as if he were one on one in the dark confessional, where little he ever heard surprised him. Sometimes something would though, and it was being occasionally floored that kept confessions from being such a tedious affair. Marvin started talking fast, trying to backpedal, but it was far too late.

"It was my cousin Tony from my mom's side of the family got me to do it. Said a cow was just like a woman only you didn't have to talk to her afterwards." The rest of the group wished Marvin would just shut up, but he was driven to talk now, hoping the truth of what he'd just said would be diluted in the flow of words. "When you're that age, you're so bound up with pressure nothing seems too outlandish. I remember him laughing the whole while I was doing it. Afterwards I felt bad for a week, and it worried me sick he was going to tell somebody. Haven't thought about that for a long time. Don't know why I thought of it now."

"You didn't piss on her head first, didja?" asked Clarence, who finally stopped brooding when the conversation made the surprisingly sharp turn at deviance and rolled right in to bestiality.

"You probably done things like that, ain't you, Pete?" Marvin was desperate to switch the attention from himself and turned to Pete Turner like a drowning man lunging for a buoy. "You can't tell me you never did nothing that was maybe a little bit off kilter?"

"Jeez, I'd have to think about that one," said Pete slowly. He enjoyed Marvin's discomfort and tried to decide if it was worth coming to his rescue. "I certainly never diddled no cow!" Pete looked over at Marvin and smiled broadly in the face of his embarrassment.

Perhaps Dieckman's role as confessor allowed the others to even contemplate such openness. More likely, it was that a man who was about to be made local hero, a man they all respected, had widened the parameters of what was acceptable behavior. Now that the venerable Sy Todd was a known exhibitionist nothing shocked them. Each member of the group searched their own history for something to tell. Angie was next, and in her mind, she followed Sy's lead more than Marvin Whorley's.

"I remember when I was a little girl," said Angie. "I was the only girl in a house full of brothers... I had seven of 'em, and I was third from the bottom. Figure in all their friends and there musta been about twenty boys in the neighborhood." Angie's head shook up and down, as if she were counting them. "I was about four years old. Every other day they'd corner me out in the barn and try to get me to take my pants down and let 'em see."

"Let 'em see what?" interrupted Coon.

"If you must know, back then I called it my 'inky,'" said Angie, nodding primly at Coon like he was a small child who required tact.

"Sounds like a good name for a squid," said Coon. "Maybe you should have called it your 'Squid.' That'd fit it closer."

Angie tightened her mouth and gave Coon an audible slap to the back of his head, staring at the area she'd struck before continuing her story. "After a while it made me feel special to have something they all wanted so bad, and I used to strut around in front of them like a cat in heat. Course there was nothing in the world that would make me do it. Pudd Winkelman even offered me a dime once. I told him that wasn't near enough... I'd need at least a dime from each of 'em. Well, the next day he gets 'em all together and they do it. They each come into the barn with a bright shiny dime and all together that was more money than I ever seen at one time in my life." Angie stopped talking, put both hands on the bleacher to take some of the weight and rocked gently on her ancient arthritic hips to ease the pain and get her circulation going again. She raised a hand and began stroking her long graying locks with her fingers, preening for the crowd, as if she were four years old again.

"Did you do it?" asked Marvin.

"Damn right I did. I was a little scairt, but I'd given them my word and couldn't back out. I pulled my skirt way up WHOOOH! above my butt, scrunched down there in the hay and pulled my panties down round my ankles like a goddamn whore. They all bunched up to look but stood away like a bunch of scared steers staring at a blacksnake. Didn't know if they wanted to run up and stomp me or hightail it away. Afterwards a bunch of 'em come up asking for their money back, but I held onto it tight." Angie raised her clenched fist above her head to show exactly how she'd done it. "After that they come around by themselves at one time or another. And for the price of a dime, I'd show 'em what they wanted to see. Sometimes, if I liked the guy, I'd do it for free. Got to where I kinda liked doing it, you know... just to see the look on their faces."

Angie beamed when she finished her story. Everyone chuckled and smiled at her appreciatively, unsurprised to learn she'd begun her wanton ways at an early age. The only one not smiling back was Coon, who was busy digging in the pocket of his worn-out overalls. Finally, he extracted his burled old hand and with a flourish reached it up to Angie.

"Here's two bits to keep your damn pants on, woman," he said. Angie shot out her hand and slapped him again, in the same spot as before. Coon acted like he didn't feel it and took another sip of beer.

More cars were arriving, and the bleachers slowly filled. Along third and first baseline a few uniformed players tried hiding their nervousness by playing lazy games of catch. Bob Mussman finished talking to two men who were the umpires. They'd yet to suit up, but even without their official gear they still looked authoritative, watching everything intently like off duty policemen. Bob turned away from them, took a few slow, dignified strides out to the pitcher's mound, and without a hint of embarrassment began chanting numbers into the microphone.

"Pete, what about you?" said Dieckman.

Pete looked pleadingly at the priest, a little surprised to be called out, but he knew what Dieckman was doing and dutifully told his story. "Well, there's only one thing that comes to mind. It doesn't have to do with sex though. Least as far as I can tell.... I used to like killing cats. I'd see a cat, 'specially if it was out in the woods, and I'd just up and blow it away."

"Cats are the only other creature on earth that kills just for sport," said Marvin pedantically. Now that his own confession hung out there a while, he was a little proud of it and secretly hoped no one would be able to top it. "They usually have it coming to them."

"I'm sure some of 'em did," said Pete. "Specially any ol' cat you find out in the woods like that."

"Okay… Pete used to shoot pussy and Angie used to show hers for a dime," said Coon. "What else we got?" All but Dieckman were appalled by Coon and again looked to Dieckman for some sort of priestly reaction, which never came. He simply twirled his cigar in his mouth, looking faintly amused. Angie gave Coon another slap to the back of the head, only lighter this time.

"There was this one cat," said Pete quickly, not to be outdone by the others. "There was this one big ol' tom used to hang out in the neighborhood. Nobody owned it... it was just a stray. One day me and the neighbor kids buried it up to its neck, and I ran over it with the riding lawn mower."

"Shit," said Clarence.

"With the blades running," Pete added hastily, in case the others missed the point.

While the group spent a moment silently pondering shredded cat heads, two human heads appeared above the home run fence in center field, just above "WILMES DRYWALL." As the group watched, two teenagers scrambled up the backside of the fence, positioning themselves precariously on top.

"What the Sam hell are they up to?" said Marvin curiously. The two were attempting something but were having trouble at it, and soon the group stopped watching them.

"What kind of report do you have for us, Clarence?" asked Dieckman. "Wild man like you probably don't know which story to tell first."

"Tell one about sex," said Angie. "I like juicy stuff about sex best."

Clarence started without hesitation, having decided early on what the story would be, but then his voice faded quickly. "When I was a kid..." Leaning back into the bleachers he ran a hand over his face and began again.

"My story's kinda like the one Coon told about that guy—"

"Only difference is it's probably true!" spit out Angie. She took another swipe at Coon's head, but he expected it, dodging neatly. Clarence waited to see if Angie was going to try again, and when she settled back, still staring hard at Coon, he went on. "When I was a kid, I remember playing all alone in my sandbox one day. I remember pushing my tractor through the sand and making that sputtering noise that kids do. I had my dad's two lunger John Deere down perfectly. When all the sudden my mom comes running out of the house all wide-eyed. At first, I thought I'd done something bad 'cause she jerks me up out of that sandbox by one arm. But she throws me on her shoulder, turns and runs to the house faster than I ever thought a mother could. Now I'm looking over my mother's shoulder, back at the sandbox, and there's a naked man standing there right next to it."

"Even as a little kid I wondered about that guy," continued Clarence, shifting his legs and casually crossing them the other way. "I wondered why, instead of getting all excited and running away, nobody brought him clothes to put on."

"He was totally naked?" asked Pete, incredulous.

"Wasn't me," said Coon. "I was with Pershing, pissin' on Mexicans."

"Totally naked," continued Clarence. "I thought about the naked man a lot that day, and how lonely he must be, everybody running whenever he came around. Finally, I went out to the garage and gathered up a bunch of my dad's old work clothes and hid 'em in my room. The next morning, I got up early and brought 'em out to the woods, hoping I would find him and give 'em to him. I didn't see him, so I just left 'em there, piled neat on an old stump. I couldn't understand why it was everybody was so scared of him when all he needed was some clothes to put on." Clarence crossed his legs back the other way again and ran his fingers into his hair, a signal the story was over.

"Maybe we should put together a clothing drive for Sy," Marvin said cautiously, looking at Clarence. Clarence didn't seem to hear and continued sitting back on the bleachers, silently musing.

"Maybe Sy's needing something else," said Father Dieckman resignedly.

"I don't suppose Sy's coming to accept the award, is he," said Pete, directing the comment at Clarence.

"Um, what?" asked Clarence. "Sorry, I didn't hear you."

"I said I don't imagine Sy's gonna come to accept his award."

"No. Mercy called me last night and asked If I'd do it for him."

"Is *she* at least going to be here?"

"Said last night she was going to try. I don't know where she is. "

"Well, his damn dog's come anyway," said Marvin, searching the bleachers to look for Shorty. The dog was no longer there, leaving only the powdery oval of dirt where he had lain. "Maybe we can just tie the damn award to him, and he can bring it up to the house," said Marvin.

Behind third base the visiting team had taken over the dugout and were milling about, playing catch and swinging bats to loosen up. Behind home plate the two managers exchanged rosters as well as a few friendly barbs, judging by the way they slapped each other on the back, raking the dirt with spiked shoes. Behind the concession stand Bobby Capstick picked out a sturdy empty soda bottle case. It would be a while before the game started, when foul balls would be hit. He badly needed an orange Fanta now, and collecting bottles was the only way of earning one until the game started.

Clarence noticed Bob Mussman signaling him to come but at the same time pointed to the outfield, shaking his head. Clarence leaned to wave back and heard an audible surge ripple through the crowd, which by now had grown large.

When Clarence looked in the direction Mussman was pointing, he saw the two teenagers in center field had finished their work and now a long wide banner, poorly painted in red letters yet painfully readable, hung from the fence in plain view—"SHOW US YOUR STUFF SY!"

"Those little shits," said Dieckman between clenched teeth.

"Marvin, can you run out and tear that goddamn sign down," said Clarence, as he eased himself up off the bleachers. "I got a speech to make." With that he started down the elevated rows of boards to join Bob Mussman in front of the dugout.

Chapter 21

In Gilmore there were two options when it came to getting your trash hauled away. You could go with GSD, the municipal sanitation department, which was cheap but horribly undependable, or you could opt for the more expensive Sanitary Services, which was privately operated by two brothers, Harold and Phil Hepperman. Harold and Phil started Sanitary Services based on the idea that a successful business requires a better product and saw no reason why the trash trade should be any different. What made their product better was their exclusive street-to-door service. They figured correctly that people despised having to haul their trash out to the curb, and Harold and Phil were making good money doing it for them. Sanitary Services operated early in the morning, while most people were still sleeping, which left the brothers free to run their primary business, a Johnny-On-The-Spot franchise. The JOTS business sat on three acres just outside of town, enclosed by an eight-foot cyclone fence, and from the highway you could see the rows of plastic portable toilets standing up on end like soldiers at attention. To the Heppermans, the refuse business was a natural extension since they were already adept at carting away stuff people no longer had any use for.

Although built on a fundamental marketing principle, the brothers didn't run what one would call a modern operation. A year ago, they had paid cash for a beat-up old Mack, just before the city drove it into the very landfill it had helped create. Having seen the angel of death rising up on a wave of methane, feeling its foul breath waft through its leaky radiator, the old relic seemed to catch a second wind and chugged along fairly dependably, as if the truck knew it needed to fill in the waiting grave before being swallowed up by it.

"OKAY HAROLD, TAKE 'ER AWAY!" yelled Phil from his perch on the back of the dilapidated old garbage truck. "BUT THIS TIME DON'T POP THE FRIGGIN' CLU—" Before the words were out of his mouth his nervous brother revved the engine of the big Mack and released the clutch with the finesse of a guillotine. As the big truck lurched forward Phil lost his grip and flopped onto the pavement like a rolled newspaper.

"GODDAMN YOU, HAROLD!" Phil leapt up quick as a cat, ran to catch up with the truck, scrambled up onto the running board, and leaned in, screaming directly into his brother's ear. "IF YOU CAN'T DO ANY BETTER THAN THAT LET ME DRIVE THE SON OF A BITCH!"

Harold nervously looked from his loud brother to the street in front of him. "It's my turn. You drove last time," he said.

"This ol' gutwagon's on its last leg, and you're dumpin' the clutch like a bucket of warm piss. If you can't treat the equipment any better'n that we gotta keep you at the dumb end of the goddamn rig!"

"I thought you adjusted this clutch last week," said Harold.

"The clutch is fine. It's your goddamn brain needs adjusting."

As Phil held onto the rearview mirror his stringy, shoulder-length hair lifted from under his dirty baseball cap, flapping like the ears of a beagle. He bent down, looked close into the mirror, and picked at what bits of breakfast remained between the deep gaps in his discolored teeth. The face in the mirror was gaunt and sallow, supporting a heavy beard, which even a corpse could grow. Phil was not yet a corpse, but he certainly looked like one. He drank Old Crow, a bottle a day, and his lean, leathery body had long ago given itself up to subsisting on whatever nourishment fermentation left behind. Only forty-three years old, he looked to be sixty yet managed to heave eighty-pound garbage cans high over his head. As the day (and his drinking) progressed, the liquid fire engulfed the whites of his eyes, converging on dilated pupils like a slow-moving brushfire.

Unlike his older brother, Harold drank only beer, evidenced by his huge, distended belly, which caused his belt to disappear between gelatinous ridges of fat. Beneath his piggish, dull-gray eyes a succession of jowls slung from side to side in time with his ponderous waddle. After taking a step, he would pause half a beat in preparation for the next one, waiting for the fat hanging from his body to stop moving and not throw him off balance.

Where Phil was as tall as he was thin Harold was as short as he was wide. Where Harold was meek and seldom became bellicose unless it involved beer or food, Phil was scrappy and didn't hesitate to scream opinions at whoever was handy. Beyond being incredibly lazy, Harold had no will of his own, usually going with whatever his brother pressed on him. The only thing that associated the brothers at all was the shared enterprise as well as their pervasive stench, which for the most part was more offensive than the garbage they handled.

"YOU JUST PASSED THE HOECKELMAN'S," Phil barked angrily. "YOU GOTTA BACK UP, YOU GODDAMN FOOL. I SWEAR IF YOU JUST TILTED YOUR HEAD A LITTLE YOUR FUCKIN' BRAINS WOULD RUN OUT YOUR EARS!"

As if believing what his brother had said, Harold pulled himself erect and covered his left ear with a filthy paw. With his other hand he searched for reverse, which he finally found after shaving down every other gear in the transmission. Phil leaned in farther, screaming loud enough to be heard over the whine of reverse.

"GRIND ME A FUCKIN' POUND WHILE YOU'RE AT IT!"

"If you can't find 'em, grind 'em," said Harold, trying to act strong despite his growing nervousness. If his brother would only give him some peace he could do his job, he was thinking. Since childhood it had always been the same—Phil lashing out at Harold until Harold became so unnerved he actually did something worthy of reproach. This time was no different, and even though Harold diligently monitored both mirrors, his round pig head rocking back and forth like a metronome, he hit the Hoeckelman's mailbox a foot above the ground, causing it to swing a hammer blow to the concrete driveway. Without saying a word Harold stopped the truck, hurriedly scooted to the opposite end of the cab, got out, walked around to the back of the truck, and took over Phil's post on the rear running board.

After taking a frustrated swipe through the window at the retreating Harold, Phil flung the Hoeckelman's garbage into the back of the truck, including the newly devastated mailbox, and leapt behind the wheel, too white with anger to say anything more to his disgraced brother. After another loud grinding of gears, the old Mack lurched forward, lumbering heavily down the street like an old circus elephant.

The truck moved another three blocks before stopping in front of Sy's ranch style house. Since neither brother bothered with the newspaper, they were unaware of the reason behind the house's vacant look.

"Don't bother being quiet," called out Phil as his brother heaved himself up the driveway. "Looks like Mr. Sy's on vacation."

With the finesse of a beached walrus, Harold bent down and rolled the garage door open. Since his brother had suggested Sy was on vacation Harold was surprised both cars were still there and squeezed between them to reach the door leading to the back patio.

As was his habit, Harold briefly sorted through the two bins for whatever might be deemed useful. Finding nothing of value, he eased himself into one of the patio chairs. Since no one was home it would be all right to take a little rest. A short break between now and when his brother would start impatiently laying on the horn was worth the tongue lashing that would come. He enjoyed looking at Sy's orchard and hoped those crazy fucking pigeons would do their thing like he'd seen them do before. *If only he had a beer and a sandwich,* he thought. *Then everything would be perfect.*

As he sat with his eyes closed, hands folded over his huge belly, happily soaking up the pleasant view, he thought he heard the soft spitting of a cat. Comfortable as he was, he took no notice of it. When he heard it a second time, he just rubbed his massive chin and settled deeper into the chair.

"HURRY UP, BLUBBERGUT!" Coming from the street, Phil's voice sounded far away to Harold and certainly not yet urgent enough to bring him out of the chair.

"Psssst. Psssssssssst!" Again he heard the sound of the cat, louder this time, and when Harold turned his head to look, he estimated it must be sitting just around the corner of the breezeway joining the house with the garage.

"PSSSSSSSSST! PSSSSSSSSSSSSST! HEY, YOU!"

Harold jumped. With both hands clutching the arms of the chair he turned, staring hard at the corner of the breezeway. He'd heard angry cats before, but this was the first time he heard one talk.

For a minute he thought about getting Phil, but there was probably nothing there. It was the wind or something, and if he made Phil come all the way up the driveway, he'd think it was a ruse to get him to bring back half the garbage.

"PSSSSSSSSST! PPSSSSSSSSSSSSSST! HEY, BUDDY!"

There it was again. No mistaking it. Somebody was back there, just around the corner. Harold slowly rose out of the chair, which followed him up before clattering back onto the concrete patio. The noise set Harold off with a jerk, and his corpulent body shook. A ripple of gooseflesh coursed up his arms and down his back and legs.

"Who... who's there?"

"Come and find out," said the voice in a hoarse whisper.

"Wh... why would I want to?" asked Harold. His increasing fear muddled his thoughts more than was usual. He wished his brother was there to make the decision for him.

"JUST COME AND SEE FOR YOURSELF. IT'S NOT GOING TO HURT YOU!"

The old Mack's air horn sounded off in three quick blasts. Harold welcomed the familiar sound; knowing his brother was not far away made him a little bolder.

"What do you want?" he asked. "Is that you, Mr. Sy?"

"I JUST WANT YOU TO TAKE A LOOK... IS THAT TOO MUCH TO ASK?" The voice came again, louder and more urgent. It would likely break into a yell if Harold didn't do what it wanted. He hesitated a few seconds before taking a step forward.

"PSSSSSSSSST! HEY! OVER HERE!"

The same lack of control that caused him to eat three sandwiches at once, now prevented Harold from leaving. Before making another move toward the sound he stepped sideways and leaned against the breezeway wall, not two feet from the corner.

"Why is it you be wantin' me to look at somethin'?" he asked, his voice higher than usual.

"YOU'RE THE ONLY PERSON HERE!"

Harold's eyes opened wide, and his breathing labored. His heart beat as if leaping from a trampoline, reaching high into his throat. For one of the few times in his life he was fully focused and couldn't have eaten a Hostess Cherry Pie if he held it in his hand. "Mr. Sy ain't gonna like it, you messin' around his house like that," was all he could think to say.

"MR. SY ISN'T AROUND!"

The response was so quick and fierce it set Harold back half a step. "You sound like the debil hisself," said Harold. "I ain't gonna take no look at you, 'cause you don't sound in no right mind."

"THEN YOU'LL WONDER THE REST OF YOUR LIFE WHAT THE HELL WAS BACK HERE!"

Dimly Harold saw the logic in that and advanced a step forward, just short of the breezeway corner. It sounded like the voice was just around it.

"If you want me to look at you, why don't you jes step around and show yeself?"

"I CAN'T!" came the reply.

"Why... why is it you can't jes step aroun'?"

"I'M ALL TIED UP!"

Harold grew perplexed and studied the patio while searching for a proper response. Finally, he said, "You mean somebody's got you tied up?"

"NO!"

Harold stopped again to think. The man didn't sound in no right mind. If no one tied him up, how could he be tied up at all?

"Then what you mean, sayin' you're all tied up?"

"I TIED MYSELF UP, YOU STUPID IDIOT! COME AROUND THE CORNER AND YOU'LL SEE!"

The air horn blasted again. From the street, seemingly miles away, Harold heard his brother call him a lazy son of a bitch.

"What'd you go and tie yourself up for?"

"BECAUSE I LIKE IT! NOW COME AND TAKE A LOOK. HOW CAN ANYBODY HURT YOU WHO'S ALL TIED UP!"

The person around the corner again said something that seemed reasonable to Harold. Inching himself closer to the voice he reached out, wrapping his hand around the corner of the wall.

"THAT'S IT, NOBODY'S GOING TO HURT YOU!"

At the last minute his courage left him, and Harold wished for all the world that he wasn't alone. "How 'bout I get my brother to come look at you too? That way there'll be two of us to look at you."

For half a minute Harold heard nothing, and his fear was replaced by disappointment, thinking the strange voice had gone away. Then suddenly it was back, still no more than three feet from him, just around the corner.

"NOBODY CAN SEE ME BUT YOU. YOU'RE THE ONLY LUCKY ONE!"

"Why the shit would I be lucky?" said Harold, his voice rising even more, just on the edge of breaking.

"STICK YOUR HEAD AROUND AND SEE!"

With that Harold had enough and with a quick intake of breath, flung his head around the corner all at once. What met his eyes caused them to open wide and turn his fat face white as a ghost.

There, stretched tight against the screen of the sliding patio door was Mr. Sy, wearing a wide sardonic grin and nothing else.

The thing that horrified Harold the most was Mr. Sy shouldn't have been grinning. As promised, his legs were tied to the two bottom corners of the door. His hands were hanging from loops of rope attached to the top corners, splaying him out like a freshly skinned animal. Firmly pressed against the screen door, the mesh flattened his nose, and his face threatened to push through it. Horridly fascinated, Harold's gaze moved down from the frozen grin, falling onto Sy's chest, which stood away from the screen only because clothespins were fastened to each nipple. Harold gave out a high-pitched whinny, like a frightened pony.

"GOTCHA!" said Sy, with a look of rapture.

Chapter 22

As Clarence made his way down the wooden bleachers the Gilmore High School Marching Band struck up a rapid cancan, making up with volume what they lacked in harmony. He had no idea what he should say on Sy's behalf and decided the best thing to do was keep it short. A man like Sy deserved more, but look how he'd gone and ruined it. *You can never tell what a person will do*, thought Clarence, stepping off the last board. Things go along nice enough, then boom, you're at the bottom of the barrel. But Sy had never been anywhere near the bottom. Not once in his life. He'd been in control since his parents lifted him out of the cradle for the last time. If something like this could happen to Sy, it could happen to anybody.

But jeez, what a strange thing to happen. Taking your clothes off in front of strangers. *It could be worse,* thought Clarence. He could have gone nuts and started killing people. That sort of thing happened too. The only person Sy was killing was Sy… and maybe Mercy… and Darlene. He had talked to Mercy that morning, and she cried over the phone. Damn! That was the hardest conversation he ever had. Didn't have a clue what to say. He'd known Mercy since she was a little girl bouncing on his knee. She treated him like an uncle, and now when she needed him, he didn't have the words. Only a handful of the right words was all that was required, yet his mind was blank. The time would come when Clarence would have to say words to Sy. Should he joke with him? Make light of the whole deal with a few witty observations about birthday suits, catching cold, or joining a nudist's camp? Maybe don't say anything. Just be there when Sy wanted to talk about it and listen and nod knowingly at whatever explanation there was. *That's the better route*, thought Clarence. *Just be there.* Maybe they could sneak off to Parkers when no one was around. Let Sy spill his guts if he needed to. Or not say a damn thing about it if he wanted to do that too.

Clarence walked behind the concession stand thinking his thoughts. Turning the corner, he almost ran into Bobby Capstick with a case of empty soda bottles, and they each did a little dance before deciding on which side to pass. The six-foot-two man–boy mumbled something resembling an apology, then rushed to the window of the concession stand, slamming the bottles down hard.

Shortly after Clarence left to give his speech, Phil and Harold Hepperman rounded the bleachers and walked down the narrow gravel lane between the lowest bench and the woven wire fence protecting the spectators. Upon recognizing the small cluster of Sy's friends high in the bleachers, Phil yelled across the crowd.

"Where do you suppose the guest of honor's at huh?"

"He's not going to make it today," shouted back Deickman, irritated that such a slovenly human being as Phil would talk this way of Sy.

"Well Harold claims to have seen him early this morning while fetchin' his trash. ALL of him."

Harold took a quick pull of his beer and shook his multiple chins in vigorous agreement.

"While we're sitting here making over him, he's probably got his dick out waggin' it at somebody," Phil said, snickering. When he looked up again, he noticed it was the priest who had responded. "Scuse my language, Father, but we now know the kind of man he really is."

"Hang on a minute!" yelled Deickman. He stood and slowly eased down the bleachers, picking a path through the spectators, his face stone but growing redder with every step. Upon reaching Phil, he grabbed the garbage man by the collar, threw him into the fence, and raised a fist like he was going to clobber him. Phil looked at the priest's face, then down at the collar around his neck.

"You wouldn't hit a man, would you, Father?" said Phil, smiling. Dieckman paused. He turned to see the crowd above him looking on in stunned silence.

"I can excuse the language, but there's no excuse for you, you piece of shit."

Knowing he had crossed a line, the priest released his grip, lowered his arm, and walked away as if he would never come back.

When Clarence stepped through the opening in the wire fence, Bob Mussman met him in front of the dugout, shaking his hand weakly.

"If you have anything to say after accepting the award you're welcome to," he said, staring into Clarence's face as though it were a funeral instead of an awards ceremony. "Since I'm the master of ceremonies you can leave it all up to me if you want. I know I'm obliged to say something..." Mussman shook his head, and both men stared at the ground between them in awkward silence.

This whole damn mess is so queer to people they can't get a grip on it, thought Clarence. "I imagine I'll say something," he said gravely. "Sy was a damn fine ballplayer."

"That he was," said Mussman, clearly relieved that Clarence unknowingly gave him permission to cut his words short. "Well, we better get started before those band kids get winded. Just stand here and relax until I give you the high sign to come out to the mound."

As Mussman stepped onto the field, the band picked up the pace to alert the crowd, which broke into loud applause. Clarence found it heartening to see everyone rise to their feet. When Mussman stepped up to the microphone he paused a while to let the crowd play out, then raised his hands for silence.

"Hello everybody!" Mussman spoke directly into the microphone but was interrupted by a loud scree of feedback. He stopped as abruptly as he had started, fixing his eyes on the offending speaker while a soundman turned it out of the path of the other one. Mussman cleared his throat to begin again.

"I think you all know why we're here today..." Mussman's dignified approach was again broken before it started.

"TO SEE A BALLGAME!" Yelled someone from the visitor's area behind third base. Mussman noted where the voice came from and threw the same glance he'd given the faulty speaker only seconds before.

"Yes, that we are," he continued again, still staring hard at the source of the catcall. "But first we're going to honor the man who showed everyone in the county how to play the game. For a period between 1952 and 1967, he brought major league quality ball to Gilmore. And all of us old enough to remember are honored by it." Mussman coughed into his fist to give himself time to find something else to say.

"When this man was on the mound, it was not just a rivalry between two teams, but a show of personal strength. It was no longer some no-count honky-tonk ballgame... it was a presentation of our champion against all comers. On the days when he wasn't pitching, and those were few, the excitement just wasn't there, and Tom Townshend in the refreshment stand would get more attention than what was goin' on in the field! AM I RIGHT, TOM?" Mussman paused as a ripple of laughter rang out across the bleachers. Tom Townshend, the ballpark's one and only groundskeeper, bent far out of the refreshment stand window, nodding in vigorous agreement.

"So, without further ado, because some of you are anxious for today's game to start..." Mussman shot a withering glare toward the voice in the visiting crowd. "I would like you all to join me in welcoming SY TODD INTO THE GILMORE COUNTY BASEBALL HALL OF FAME!"

As Mussman stepped away from the microphone his announcement was met by an eruption of loud cheering mixed with the clanging of a few scattered cowbells. From the parking lot behind the dugouts cars came to life with horns blazing, and for a few minutes the Gilmore County ballpark sounded like the streets of New York City. A few boys in blue jeans and white T-shirts stopped their pick-up game behind the cars, running up to watch. The Gilmore batboy climbed the ladder to the base of the scoreboard and danced a jig. All around the fence people were standing and clapping their hands, shouting encouragement at Mussman.

At the park entrance people were still pulling in off the blacktop, first stopping to pay Butch Wilmes the two-dollar cover charge. After putting the money into an old cigar box, Butch handed out a flyer with Sy's picture.

When the applause finally dissipated, Mussman again stepped close to the mike and in a gracious voice that didn't quite cover the nervousness he felt, announced that Clarence Dickersen should now step forward to receive the award.

Clarence stepped out of the home team dugout and as he crossed the first base line on the way to the mound, he had a distinct feeling, a premonition of some sort, that he was about to sustain a blow to the head. Upon seeing Clarence heading for the mound the crowd again erupted. When he reached the mound Clarence shook hands with Mussman, accepted the oversize gold cup, then sheepishly waited for the noise to die down. It pleased him to hear the loudest noise coming from the small circle of friends he'd just left, led by Angie's raspy croak and convulsive fits of coughing. The ovation continued as if it would never stop, and Clarence concentrated on standing like a castle guard, proud and erect, to publicly honor his best friend in the manner he deserved.

As Clarence's eyes wandered over the blur of the crowd, he was surprised to see Mercy and Charlotte standing by themselves under a tree, far beyond the visitor's dugout. He gave them a tilt of his head to show they'd been spotted, and Mercy returned the acknowledgement with a small wave of her hand.

For as unabashedly vocal and quick with a joke as Clarence was socially, he was an unproven orator, his confidence sliding down through his feet and off the mound like melting butter. Slowly the applause wore away and then an empty silence fell on the ballpark as Clarence fought to think of a way to start. Since nothing eloquent came to mind he turned to the relative safety of convention.

"Thank you... thank you very much," he finally stammered. After another long pause he started in again.

"I know that if Sy was here, he'd be as proud to accept this award as I am to accept it for him."

"WHERE IS HE?" The voice from the visitor's side came strong and clear, and a hushed murmur went through the crowd as every head on the bleachers simultaneously turned to try and spot the heretic.

Clarence stole a look over at Mercy, who was looking down past her crossed arms, gently caressing the ground with her foot. He went on. "Sy Todd was one hell of a ballplayer. He was a starting pitcher who could hit as well as he threw. A hitter who could field. And a reliever who could throw strikes right off the bench. But more than that he was a true sportsman... who could have as much fun playing a losing game as he could pitching a shutout. If there was ever a player for our up-and-coming boys to model themselves after, it's him."

"THOSE WHO CAN AFFORD RAINCOATS!" yelled the voice from behind third base.

The crowd reacted again, while Clarence could only stare glumly into the microphone. Here and there people stood up from the bleachers, leaning to get a better look at the heckler. Seeing no one was going to defend Sy's honor, old Angie leaped from her place on the bleachers, raised her fist high over her head and screamed, "HANG THAT ASSHOLE BY HIS NUTS!" causing another wave of laughter to filter across the bleachers. Angie primly returned to her seat, like any woman of breeding would do, and, after she settled, Coon reached over and gave her an appreciative pat on the leg.

"I saw Sy play more ball than all of you out there put together," Clarence finally continued. "If anybody knew what kind of star he really was, it was me. I used to catch him."

"DID YOU CATCH HIM WITH HIS CLOTHES OFF?" Again, the voice of derision sailed out, covering Clarence with a wave of humiliation. This time the angry rumbling from the bleachers was matched by laughter from the opposing team.

As the laughter continued, Clarence's face turned red as the baseball caps lining the Gilmore dugout. The players grew tense as the attack against their hero continued, and as they fidgeted the red caps bobbed up and down like a musical score. While the reputation of his lifelong friend sank, Clarence's anger began to rise, and what had started out as deep embarrassment became a seething fury of released emotion. It was apparent the formality of the occasion had been lost and, instinctively, Clarence knew the only way to save Sy's reputation was by clearing the air. When he spoke again his voice was level and firm.

"As you all know by now there was a reason Sy couldn't make it here today... and for the life of me I can't give a clear description of what that reason is. What I *can* tell you is that the man you all saw on page one of the Post Dispatch... is not the man we came to honor today. And on behalf of that man, and the family that loves him, I would ask you to clear that picture from your minds.

"Now there's a gentleman seated over to my right... who doesn't seem capable of doing that. He seems to think the only reason people have problems is to provide for his own entertainment. I ask you, sir, to please stand up and entertain all of us for a while."

Without hesitating, a large, heavy-set man dressed in a loose Hawaiian shirt and baggy shorts stood up from the crowded bench on the other side of the visitor's fence. He wore his hair cut close to his oversize head, accentuating the wide-set jaw lining the bottom of his face, which was cocked mockingly to the side.

"I seem to recognize you, sir," continued Clarence. "And quite frankly most of what I know about you has slipped my mind, seeing as how you're nobody special. I mean you've never been inducted into anything, have you?"

The man shook his head no, cockily tilting it back as if to imply the fence was the only thing saving Clarence from a sound beating.

"Let me think a minute," Clarence went on. "I've forgotten your name, but—"

"MARK HAGGERTY," broke in the large man, continuing to stare at Clarence with a contemptuous smile.

"Mark Haggerty, yes that's right. Thank you very much, Mr. Haggerty... and now I remember you. You're a bricklayer on one of Pat Bergman's crews. Am I right?"

"YEAH, THAT'S RIGHT," shot back the man, who, while maintaining his hard-ass demeanor, showed a hint of puzzlement.

"Yes, thank you very much," said Clarence. "Because now that I have a frame of reference, it helped me remember what I was trying to think of. As I recall, there was an incident not long ago between you and your wife's sister, which involved more than picking out your wife's birthday present together. Just whose baby is your wife's sister about to have Mr. Haggerty? Can you tell us anything about that Mr. Haggerty?"

Once again the crowd came to life, but instead of laughter a chorus of loud boos coursed across the empty ballfield. The large man stood as if unfazed, then slowly unfolded his arms, stepped stiffly across the bench, and into a new Ford pickup. He slammed the door, revved the engine wildly, spun the pickup out of the parking spot, through his wall of dust, and disappeared between the cars. The final proof that he had even been there was the sudden shriek of tires hitting the pavement.

"Thank you for your contribution to this afternoon's entertainment, Mr. Haggerty."

Clarence turned away from the mic, then whispered between barely parted lips, "Even if it isn't true." The time to say anything more had passed, and after offering another lame "Thank you," he walked off the mound, carrying the huge trophy by one handle, nearly dragging it across the dirt infield.

While heading for the dugout with his head down, he heard a growing swell of sound. One by one the spectators were rising to their feet, clapping and yelling for the hero who was nowhere to be seen. With car horns blaring in his ears, Clarence stopped in his tracks and lifted the trophy high over his head in a show of victory. Waving with his free hand, he turned the trophy toward Mercy, who put her hand to her mouth and blew him a teary-eyed kiss.

Chapter 23

Mercy sat in her parents' driveway for ten minutes, and since it didn't seem like her father was going to come out, she decided to go in. As she stepped out of the car, she heard the front door shut and after carefully locking up, her father sauntered down the driveway. As he crossed in front of the car's headlights, Mercy could see he had at least dressed for the occasion. He was wearing the blue summer sport coat which had become his office trademark. Mercy noticed his shoulders were nicely set, but there was not enough light to see the expression on his face. Sy bent down and got into the car without saying a word. Still standing behind the car door, Mercy shook her head and got in too. They had waited until dark to go to the hospital so as not to be recognized.

Darlene's hospital was on the north side of St. Louis, a good forty miles away, but since it was late the traffic was light. As they rolled through the streets of Gilmore toward the Highway 70 access ramp the conversation was tentative, with neither Sy nor Mercy contributing anything of any real substance. Neither could think of anything meaningful to say, and whenever Mercy made any attempt at a light observation or conversation starter it came out sounding forced and pathetic. At one point Mercy considered saying something about the award ceremony earlier that day but decided it would be best not to mention anything about it.

"What'd you do with Charlotte?" asked Sy finally. It was a neutral question, innocent enough to break the awkward silence. He was looking out the passenger side window with his arms limply crossed over his lap and seemed to barely realize he'd asked a question.

"She's staying with Nancy Stringer until I get back," said Mercy. "Poor kid. When I left her, she was crying her heart out."

"She probably sensed that you were unhappy. Kids can pick up on things like that. Your leaving is bad enough, but when you leave unhappy, they get scared." Sy spoke softly, continuing to look out the window as he recited the words.

"Naw, she was just tired." Behind the wheel Mercy let out a big sigh of her own, as if to punctuate the thought.

"Now that I'm retired maybe I can keep her for you once in a while," said Sy. "Might be a good idea she gets to know her grandpa a little better." Sy thought a while and then said, "No, maybe that wouldn't be such a good idea."

"You damn right you're going to see more of her," Mercy countered quickly. "That's what retired grandpas are for. Just because you're not working doesn't mean you have to sit on a bench in front of some drugstore." Suddenly Mercy swerved hard to miss a large dog that had leaped out from behind a blossoming lilac bush growing close to the road. It was enough to steal her attention away from the conversation, and she drove silently the rest of the way down Azalea Avenue before turning left onto Main, which would take them all the way to the highway.

Mercy waited until they were further along before speaking again. "What are you going to do with yourself, now that you're retired?"

"The first thing I'm going to do?"

"Yeah. First thing."

"First thing I'm going to do is buy a pair of coveralls with a padlock on the zipper." Sy gave the words little emphasis, but the way he stared solemnly at the closed glove box in front of him was enough to convey his mood.

"Oh, DAD!" Mercy promised herself to be strong, but her father had said his dark little joke with such uncharacteristic resignation, such hopeless melancholy that she began to cry, and in the alternating darkness between streetlamps she lifted her hand from the wheel to wipe away tears. Compared to everything that had happened, it was an emotional spike of short duration, and she soon had herself back under control. Biting her lower lip she again resolved to allow herself the release of emotion only when it would not interfere with saving what was left of her family. In other words, when she was all alone. Charlotte had seen her mother cry so much already she had taken to sympathetic crying jags of her own and ran up to hug her mother tightly the instant Mercy's eyes began to fill.

"Do you know who won today?" asked Sy. If he had noticed Mercy's tears he gave no sign of it. Mercy silently prayed this wasn't a lead-in to the induction ceremony earlier that day. She wiped furiously at both her eyes with the back of her hand before answering.

"We did. Seven to six in eleven innings." By the sound of his question, it occurred to Mercy that her father had only asked it to be polite and probably didn't really give a damn about much of anything. "Brad Boehmer went ten of 'em..." she went on mechanically. "They brought Larry Bowman in to pitch 'cause Brad loaded the bases in the tenth with no men out. Anyway, Larry came in straight off the bench and struck out all three batters. Then Marty Cole pinch hit in the bottom of the eleventh and blasted one over the center field fence."

"Sounds like a good game," said Sy blandly.

"It was a great game."

"I didn't get down there," said Sy, stating what was painfully obvious.

Mercy turned left, easing onto the ramp leading to 70 East. Distracted, she forgot to accelerate and smashed the pedal at the last minute, twisting hard to gauge the oncoming lights rushing up at her. When the ramp finally ran out, she swerved recklessly into the stream of traffic.

"You stayed in the house all day?" she asked, after resettling.

"Yeah. Pretty much."

"I made you an appointment with the doctor on Friday, the one I told you about. It was the soonest they could get you in." Mercy took her eyes off the road for an instant and peered into the darkness next to her. "You going to go?"

"Okay."

After a while Mercy was unable to stand it anymore. "So. You're not going to ask me about it are you."

"Ask you about what?" returned her father dully.

"The big ceremony!"

"What ceremony?"

"Dad, you were inducted into the Hall of Fame today. How could you forget a thing like that?"

"Oh, that's right. I forgot all about it."

"Don't you kind of wish you were there?"

"Doesn't matter."

"Doesn't matter? Course it matters. Everybody gets fifteen minutes of fame in their life, and you completely missed yours. All your friends were there cheering for you. Clarence gave a great speech. The whole damn town came out and supported you. You shoulda been there, Dad."

"At this point I wish I were a little less famous." Sy looked down at his knees in the dim light of the dashboard, from one to the other, as if trying to decide which one could go. He stopped and silently studied his own breathing.

"Well, no one said anything about it," Mercy lied.

She looked worriedly over at her father. She now had two zombies on her hands. Guiding the car down the highway to the hospital, she fought to halt the panic. It caused a slow constriction in her throat, like a pair of strong hands. She struggled with her purse to get a cigarette.

A large black Cadillac passed on the left. Trying to lift the oppressive mood, Mercy pointed out the letters of the personalized license plate. "S O F. What do you think that means, Dad?"

"Sick old Fart." Sy answered simply, without taking his eyes off the glove box in front of him.

For the next twenty minutes they rode in silence, each lost in their own private reverie. As she guided the car past the highway's familiar exits Mercy tried to conjure some insight as to what the future might hold for her and Charlotte, and how much of it they would have to donate to her parents. Her father was ruined. She could only assume he would continue changing until she no longer recognized him. And this time her mother might be gone for good. When she visited her that morning she had gone into some kind of relapse—had laid in bed moving only her eyes, not followed any conversation. A nurse said it could be the medication, but Mercy knew better. When she stopped to talk to her father after visiting the hospital she had lied, saying her mother showed improvement.

All the lying, to her dad, to her friends and acquaintances, had Mercy feeling detached. But any disconnection had to be temporary. She had been put in charge of her own mother and father and wasn't allowed the luxury of walking away. Hell, she and Charlotte may even have to move in with them. There was no escaping her duty, and she would have to resign herself to the fact her private life was over. No reward would be given for such selfless behavior. It was all too tainted. No, the only payback for what lay ahead would be a dirty feeling of being cheated. And with that, a lot of self-pity.

As for Sy, he'd already stopped relating to any concept of future. Staring at the passenger window, it became the screen on which he could project his past. He wondered why he never allowed himself to do it before. It was pleasant, this floating away. Securely deposited in the hands of his daughter, he was free to call up memories he'd locked away. Anything to avoid the troublesome present.

He saw himself as a kid, seated on the wooden porch of the old family farmhouse—the homeplace. He was surrounded by his twelve brothers and sisters, and they each held wide slices of homemade bread, spread thick with rich creamy butter, topped with sugar. They were allotted one slice apiece for lunch and they ate ravenously, hard crust and all. After the meal they began the business of teasing, and ten-year-old Sy reached forward, pulling hard on his younger sister's pigtails. She stood up from the step below, grabbed his shoulder, and socked him hard in the chest. He saw himself fall back as the others pounced, tickling him mercilessly. Hearing the commotion, Sy's mother stepped out on the porch looking stern, drying her hands on a huge oversize apron. She was a stout, big boned German who Sy remembered as forever suffering, and when she came out the roughhousing stopped as quickly as it had begun.

Suddenly they all heard the revving of an engine far down the lane that led up to the house. It came from the other side of the raised berm supporting the train tracks, which crossed perpendicular to the lane like a molehill crossing a footpath.

"TANTA GUSTA!" screamed the kids wildly. Sy and his many siblings leapt off the porch, tearing down to where the lane entered the farmyard. Sy's mother chose to remain, frowning and drying her big red hands on her apron, waiting for her sister to pop over the tracks. As the sound of the revving increased the children bristled deliciously, waiting for Tanta Gusta to come flying over the tracks. Tanta Gusta held title to her Model T Ford for all of four weeks and had yet to master upward slopes. Each slanting grade became her own personal San Juan Hill, and whenever one needed doing, she would back down as far as possible, wind out the engine until it was fit to blow, and then dump the clutch. As a result, the car would come flying off the train bed with a good two feet of air beneath it. As the children listened the car's engine stopped racing, and Sy and all the others knew Tanta Gusta had started off. True to form the lumbering Model T suddenly shot over the tracks, whizzing through the air like it had been fired from a cannon. It landed hard on the front bumper, bouncing three times with the grace of a charging rhino that had tripped. Sy's brothers and sisters grew hysterical at seeing Tanta Gusta bouncing wildly behind the windshield, and young Sy fell to the ground and rolled, having to hold his stomach he was laughing so hard.

Sy sat in the car, smiling at the window. He enjoyed seeing himself as a kid again. But soon the vision of him laughing and rolling on the ground faded away, and something else took its place. He was standing in the warm-up box at the ballpark next to the wire fence, languidly swinging a bat. Sy knew the memory. It was the eighteenth inning of his record-breaking no-hitter against Cape Girardeau. He was loosening up, getting ready to bat and felt warm and strong and good. So far, he was the hero of the game. He'd already pitched eighteen solid innings, and everyone was waiting for him to tire, but he knew he wouldn't. He could pitch another nine innings if he had to. As he swung the bat he grinned broadly, aware that all eyes were on him and not his brother-in-law Charlie Schipper who was at the plate. He swung the bat extra hard and with the momentum his entire torso came around until he was facing the fence behind him. There, seven years old and pretty as a button, was Mercy, her fingers tied delicately into the fence, watching him, wide-eyed. Sy lowered the bat, walked over to her, and squatted down to her level.

"Hi, peanut," he said.

"Hi, Daddy," she said, her little girl's voice lilting brightly. Sy saw the admiration on her face, and it almost made him cry she was so lovely.

"You havin' fun out here, baby?" Mercy's little head bounced up and down on her shoulders, causing her pigtails to brush both of her tiny red cheeks.

Suddenly her face broke into worry. "You gonna keep pitchin', Daddy?" Mercy's little girl voice rose high at the end of the question, and her eyes widened more, focusing on him apprehensively.

"Sure, I'm gonna keep pitchin', peanut. Why do you ask me that?"

"I just heard a man say if you kept pitchin' it was gonna kill you, and I don't want you to get killed." Sy wanted to reach in through the fence, wrap his daughter in his arms, and reassure her everything was okay. Instead, he just squatted in front of her and smiled, so terribly pleased that she was his own little girl.

"Don't worry," he said. "I can keep pitchin' forever. Your daddy's having a lot of fun, peanut. I hope you are too."

Mercy shook her head vigorously. "Oh yeah, Daddy!" Sy's smile widened more. His words reassured her. Sy slowly stood up and resumed swinging the bat.

"Daddy..." Mercy looked at Sy coyly and didn't finish what she wanted to say.

Sy completely forgot he would be batting soon and bent back down on one knee in front of his daughter. "Yeah, sweetheart?"

"Can I have money for a sody?"

Sy bent his head closer to the fence, acting like he was pondering something. "Tell you what I'll do, honey. See that big open spot over there between all the cars?" Mercy turned her head around and back, nodding at her father firmly. "I want you to go stand out there right in the middle of that spot... stand right in the middle of that spot and don't move, and I'll hit you a foul ball that you can go trade in for a sody… okay?"

"OKAY!" said Mercy, in a happy yell. She paused to give her father an adoring look, then released the fence and ran to the spot as fast as her little legs would carry her. She had no doubt her father would do just as he said.

As Sy walked up to the plate he saw his little girl standing there, right where he told her to go, looking for all the world like an abandoned child. When he stepped to the plate the bleachers came alive, and he grinned at the pitcher from Cape Girardeau like they were best friends. On the first pitch Sy pulled his bat, swung low, and the ball sailed over the third base line, over the wire fence, over the row of cars, landing directly in front of Mercy, standing there with her arms straight out in front of her as if ready to catch it, her eyes scrunched tightly shut. Sy watched as the ball bounced once over her head, then saw her turn and scamper after it like a little puppy.

Suddenly the scene on the window changed, and there was the Korean soldier he had executed, looking emotionless, with a forty-five-caliber hole in his forehead.

Sy slowly blinked and now saw his own sixty-three-year-old face. While the scene with his daughter had briefly raised his spirits, the image of the Korean soldier had left him stone faced, with no emotion at all. He heard Mercy curse and the vision vanished.

"SHIT!" said Mercy loudly. "I missed the goddamn intersection." Sy turned away from the window, and they rode on in silence. Outside the car, several tall glass office buildings rose up beyond the highway. A thousand individual panes reflected the moon rising above the horizon like a thousand vertical puddles. Sy didn't recognize anything and realized he had no idea what part of the highway they were on.

"How's your mother?" he asked suddenly.

Mercy was surprised by what sounded like genuine interest but hesitated before answering. She'd already told him, not long ago. She shrugged it off and responded directly, telling him the same lie she had before, that Darlene was showing signs of improvement. Feeling bad for lying, she tried skirting closer to the truth. "They got her so doped up she doesn't even try to talk. Either that or she just doesn't want to. Can't tell."

"Do you think she wants to see me?"

"I really don't know. She's been totally uncommunicative."

Sy thought for a while and then bent his head, pinching the bridge of his nose with his thumb and forefinger. "If there's anything I can accomplish after all that's happened, it has to be one thing."

"And what's that, Dad?"

"Get your mother out of that hospital as fast as we can."

"She's had breakdowns that put her in the hospital before."

"Yeah, but this time she's there because of me."

They rode for another stretch without talking. Mercy took her father's change in attitude as a good sign. Then her father said something that caused her to silently swear to never get her hopes up again.

"How's your mother?" asked Sy blankly.

When they stepped into the elevator, they felt a moment of discomfort, alone together and bathed in bright light. As the elevator rose Sy turned to read a notice on the back wall.

"What the hell happened to your face!" Mercy shrieked, slapping her palm across her mouth. It was the first time she got a good look at her father in the light. When he turned his head, she saw the whole right side of his face was purple and swollen, his eye almost completely shut.

Sy looked up and studied her briefly. "Your father's dying," he said.

His response shocked her more than the angry wound and left Mercy too rattled to press further. When the elevator opened onto Darlene's floor, Mercy walked out stiffly, as if trying not to fall. She turned and saw her father acting tentative. After the door opened, he sheepishly hung back. Mercy stood holding the door, giving him a questioning look. When the buzzer went off, he nervously stepped out, surveying the antiseptic hallways as if suspecting a terrorist attack. To Mercy he looked like he was about to jump out of his skin. He'd visited Darlene in the hospital many times but never as the person who'd put her there. Now he wished he hadn't come. Darlene wouldn't want to see him, and his being there might only prove detrimental. Mercy had to keep turning and coaxing him along the corridor like a wary dog, all the while staring at his crushed face. Just as they were about to enter Darlene's room, they met a nurse coming out of it who told them something that relieved Sy's apprehension, if only temporarily.

"She's still asleep, but you can go in and sit if you like," she said, with a big gracious smile.

Mercy did nothing to allay Sy's nervousness. *He deserves to be anxious*, she thought. Actually, she preferred it over the negativism and the cold aloofness he'd shown in the car. At least he was reacting to something. It was a human reaction to be nervous, and Mercy took it as a possible sign of progress, meager as it might seem. But then she remembered promising herself not to become hopeful, and as they entered Darlene's room it was her turn to be aloof. "Here's a chair, Dad. You might as well sit until she wakes up."

But Sy didn't want to sit anywhere. Instead, he did a strange thing. Immediately upon seeing his wife, Sy's demeanor changed yet again. He quickly went to Darlene's side in three long strides and reached for her hand. For a long time, he just stood there holding her hand and peering anxiously into her face, looking as if all it would take would be for Darlene's eyelids to flutter open and their problems would be solved. He bent over the bed, holding her hand as if praying before an altar.

Darlene's hospital room looked more sterile than most. Between the beds, in front of the separating curtain, a small counter stood crowded with tongue depressors, calibrated glass containers, Kleenex, a plastic pitcher of water, and a large aqua colored female urinal. Incongruously wedged in next to the urinal was a thin vase holding a single red rose. Up against the faded-green wall stood a lightly padded visitor's chair, and although there was a bracket for a television coming out of the wall, one had yet to be brought in. Across from the bed next to Darlene was a tall, thin window that afforded a poor view of the employee parking lot. The air was permeated by the usual odor of medicine, antiseptic, and ozone, but in addition there was also the pungent, unmistakable odor of excrement.

Mercy hadn't had time to arrange a private room, so Darlene was sharing hers with another person, a heavy-set woman of about seventy-five with thin, gray hair that hung about her face in long, dirty strands, wearing an open nightgown that exposed all but the ends of her sagging, heavily veined breasts. Her eyes bulged from her face like a frog, and she sat high in the middle of her bed, staring unblinkingly at the family next to her.

"I just had a baby," she said. "A little baby boy." Odder than the words, she spoke in singsong, as if reciting a nursery rhyme.

After the woman spoke, Darlene let out a slow moan, opened her eyes, and blinked a few times. When she recognized Sy her blank look turned to contempt, and she began jerking angrily at her hand, which Sy seemed incapable of letting go.

When he finally saw his wife open her eyes, Sy grew beside himself with excitement, and he started to do a curious thing. It had never been his nature to apologize—he seldom had reason to—but now he did it shamelessly in a long steady flow of meaningless words and breath. A silent Darlene kept pulling at her hand, becoming more enraged with every passing second. Mercy doubted her mother was hearing anything her father was saying. With the way Sy was babbling on, Mercy wasn't sure she was hearing correctly herself. Sy finally stopped his senseless apologies and tried his best to sound positive, as if his words might heal her wounds.

"It's okay, honey," he said. "We been through a hell of a lot worse than this. We'll get you back on your feet again. We'll get you out of here really quick, and you can come on back home, and I'll take care of you just like before." Sy held Darlene's hand tighter and began rubbing it gently between his palms. Darlene finally stopped struggling, but with Sy's last words her eyes opened wider, and her face turned crimson. She raised her other hand and sent it into Sy's cheek with a loud slap.

From the foot of the bed Mercy jumped out of the chair, looking first at her mother and then her dad, her mouth open. She didn't quite know how to respond. Her father hadn't reacted to the blow, so Mercy figured it best to act like nothing had happened. Darlene only lay there, glaring up at Sy as if meaning to kill him with her eyes. After a while the tension in the room grew so strong Mercy felt compelled to say something. Her mother seemed about to haul off with another slap.

"Mom, Dad was inducted into the Hall of Fame yesterday," she said. "Aren't you proud of him?" It had no effect on the glaring Darlene, whose eyes still burned fiercely into Sy's, and still she refused to speak, as if the man wasn't deserving of even that little effort. "No. No, I guess not," said Mercy dejectedly.

Sy seemed oblivious to his wife's venomous attack and even went so far as to sit down next to her on the bed, rubbing the palm of her hand with his, smiling.

"You don't worry about a thing," said Sy again. "We'll get whatever new medicine you need and..."

What cut Sy short was Darlene, suddenly trying to speak. She moved her mouth and jaws like a gasping fish but emitted no sound.

"What is it, Darlene? What are you trying to say?" Sy looked into her eyes intently, trying to read her words in them. He dropped to the floor, resting his elbows on the bed, holding Darlene's hand firmly against his cheek.

"Go ahead, Darlene… you can do it. Nice and slow..."

"Pppppffft," said Darlene, in an exaggerated movement of mouth and lips. She seemed to have spent all her energy with her frustrated attempt to fight off Sy, and what came was more air than sound. Sy put his face closer and urged her to keep trying.

"Just take it easy, Mom," said Mercy, suddenly worried by her mother's insistence. "You don't have to say anything yet."

"C'mon Darlene, what is it you're trying to tell me?" Sy said. Mercy felt he was merely acting and recognized little of his old self.

"PPPPPPPHHHT... PU... PU..." said Darlene.

"Paper?" asked Sy. "You want pencil and paper?" Having no rationale for that being the case, Sy rushed from the bed and ransacked the room.

"I don't think that's what she wants, Dad," said Mercy, skeptically reaching into her purse. "But here you go." Sy rushed back to his wife's bedside, enthusiastically offering the articles with which she was to write her all-important message.

"We're going to name him Herman," said the crazed old woman in the next bed. "Little Hermy Johnson."

"PU... PU... PU..." Darlene said thickly.

"Here, honey," said Sy. "Paper and pencil."

"PU... PU... PU..."

"Dad, I think you better let her alone," said Mercy, now frightened by her mother's single-minded effort to speak.

"Yeah, that's right, Darlene," said Sy. "Paa-per, pa-per." Sy bent farther over Darlene, his face hovering inches from hers, trying to fix the pencil between her fingers. In his excitement over his wife's desire to finally communicate, he knocked the plastic pitcher off the bedside table, spilling water over the tiled floor and along the wall and under the next bed.

"PU... PU... PERVERT!" yelled Darlene.

Chapter 24

He had taken note of the people quietly lining both walls of the church before pulling back the curtain and taking his seat in the confessional, so Father Dieckman knew Mabel Snethen was the last to be heard. As usual she was making a mess of it, and in the dim light entering from the sides of the curtain, she mistook Dieckman's two-handed grip on his temples as an act of petitioning on her behalf. Such concentration on the part of the priest motivated her to search further for sins against God and man, and since she had already gone through her usual list of transgressions, she began making up more.

Mabel Snethen was a widow of forty-five years and had developed more than a few compulsive habits to make up for her loneliness. For instance, she could not relax until her house was immaculate, sometimes repeating the same chore several days in a row. Going to confession three times a week was her latest excess, and now she scrubbed her soul with the same vigor as she did her house.

Mabel whispered toward the dim outline on the other side of the screen with sudden alarm. "Did I say I intentionally ran over the neighbor's cat?" The event happened five years ago, and Mabel wasn't exactly sure whether she'd actually hit the cat, much less intentionally, but went ahead and confessed to it from time to time just in case—usually whenever she was hard up for something to be sorry for.

Dieckman gave a slight nod toward the screened porthole that separated them. "Not tonight, my child," he said in exasperation. He had a new bottle of cognac waiting for him in the rectory and was in a hurry to get to it.

Mabel missed the sarcasm completely and thought harder about what a terrible sinner she was. "I didn't even tell anybody about it after it happened. Is that a sin, too, Father?"

Dieckman held his breath to give himself strength. "The neighbors have already forgiven you for it and so has the good Lord," he said in a rush of air.

Mabel wasn't content with that answer and paused to think. In no time she struck on something else, bowed her head in mock shame, and leaned nearer to the screen. "Yesterday morning I coveted her husband. I was very wicked, Father, and recoveted him when he was watering the grass with no shirt on."

Dieckman lowered his head further between his hands to try and suppress the laugh that erupted as a spitting noise between his compressed lips. "Whose husband?" he finally managed to say.

"My neighbor's, Father. The one with the cat."

Dieckman knew Mabel lived next to a young married couple and visualized the elderly woman watching the tanned husband from her front porch, getting more breathless with each ripple of his back. He could not tell Mabel to go on and hoped she wouldn't notice the way his shoulders shook, trying to contain his laughter. If she mentioned it, he would just have to start braying like a mule. That's all there was to it.

Thinking the last was duly noted, Mabel made a quick sign of the cross and continued. "I committed crimes against God and nature three times," she said, then sniffed and lifted her head brightly.

What, did you use a cucumber on yourself! Dieckman screamed inside his head. He fought to get hold of himself and whispered back. "Are you truly sorry, and promise from this day forward to not profane what your Father in heaven has so generously provided you?"

Mabel answered as forcefully as if she were making a wedding vow. "I am," she said.

Dieckman was insanely curious but could not bring himself to press the issue. "Anything else, my child?" he asked, releasing a sigh to help regain his composure. Mabel was the last penitent, and even though he'd been in a hurry, he now didn't mind listening to a woman who lied in a confessional. It was beautiful irony and at least as entertaining as anything that would be on television.

"And I lied five or six times," she said as an afterthought.

In the last five minutes, thought Dieckman. Then to Dieckman's surprise she brought it to a quick close by saying, "I'm sorry for these and all the sins of my past life, amen." It was always that last bit about all the sins of her past life that made Mabel sure the slate was wiped clean. Each time she said it her spirit soared, and she often felt giddy.

The abrupt finish left Dieckman a little irritated. The confession was starting to get interesting. He shook his head, trying to decide what to say next. He quickly rambled through the incantation that wiped away sin like a divine washcloth and gave her a symbolic penance of five Our Fathers and six Hail Marys.

"Is that all?" she asked. She was apprehensive that absolution would take no more effort on her part.

"And say a novena to the Blessed Virgin," Dieckman added hastily.

"Thank you, Father," Mabel said. She parted the curtains and left, confident the Blessed Virgin would intervene on her behalf. The Lord could have forgiven her himself, but it took a woman to do a thorough job of it.

Dieckman slid his hand out to part the curtains and leave when he heard the kneeler creak again, annoyed that Mabel had suddenly remembered something else.

Dieckman slid back the panel to expose the screen, and when he heard the steady, shallow breathing coming out of the darkness he knew it wasn't Mabel. The breathing continued for some time without anything being said, and as Dieckman waited he oddly felt he was all alone in the dark church. Suddenly the breathing was interrupted by a soft voice. It came out of the darkness sounding thick and barely intelligible, in short bursts like a person with emphysema, but without the wheezing. Dieckman leaned his face closer to the screen. It was Sy's voice.

It was strange to have Sy in the confessional, since he once admitted he didn't believe in it and had never confessed to Dieckman before. On top of that Sy sounded different, and on a hunch Dieckman put his face even closer to the screen and sniffed for alcohol. There was nothing but the musty smell of the cramped confessional, but with Sy's voice sounding the way it did Dieckman wasn't fully convinced Sy wasn't drunk.

"Bless me, Father. I'm a god-fearing, card-carrying sinner," said Sy. The words had to be attempted several times, and when Dieckman finally understood them he was taken aback.

"Sy, what the hell's the matter with you?" Dieckman squinted, trying to view his friend, but the darkness on the other side of the screen was impenetrable.

Sy started in again, as if not hearing Dieckman's words. "Bless me, Father. My last confession was..." Sy's voice tailed off like he had gone to sleep but slurred in again, like starting a record with the needle already resting on it. "...I don't know how long ago. But since then I've been... showing my balls to everybody."

Dieckman forgot he was in the confessional and began talking to Sy like they were at Parkers, drinking beer. He wasn't sure Sy knew who he was. "Sy, what are you doing here, man? Let's get the hell out of here, go over to my place for a drink, and we can talk about it. Okay?"

"Su Lin's waiting for me," mumbled the voice from out of the darkness. "She's got my laundry done... can't keep her waiting..." Dieckman heard a loud thump from out of the darkness and was about to rise out of his seat when he again heard the soft breathing.

Dieckman's mind raced over what he should do. Suddenly he knew Sy wasn't drunk. It was something else. To keep Sy talking he said the first thing that came to mind. "You know what you're doing is a sin in the eyes of the Church, don't you, Sy?"

"Bless me, Father, for I'm a goddamned sinner..." Sy's words barely oozed out of his mouth, and from their direction Dieckman knew Sy was leaning heavily against the wall of the confessional.

"How many did you take, Sy?"

The priest heard a soft sigh come from the darkness and a few seconds later Sy spoke again, but it came out sounding memorized, like part of the confession litany. "I am heartily sorry for making a mess of... and those who I drug along with me... but I couldn't fuckin' do nuthin' 'bout it."

"Sy! Sy! Forget the newspaper, Sy..." Dieckman knelt on the floor and spoke directly into the thin wire mesh that separated them. "You can beat it if you want to. It's what you got inside... it's your spirit that counts! You're bigger than it is, Sy!" Even though he couldn't see him, Dieckman felt Sy sinking farther away into the darkness, and as he knelt, trying to think what to do next, the black void that separated them expanded and became an entire universe.

Dieckman heard Sy say another dreamy, barely perceptible "Bless me..." and then nothing. The slow, meted breathing he had first heard stopped. A loud thumping noise caused Dieckman to jerk his head up straight, and he knew Sy had fallen to the floor.

"Sy!" Dieckman yelled. He rushed out of the confessional, flung the left side curtain back with one hand, and stared down at Sy on the floor. For a while no thoughts came and when they finally did, he simply closed the curtain on Sy's nude body and turned away.

At first, he walked slowly down the center aisle of the church toward the vestibule exit but then began to quicken his pace, until by the time he reached the communion rail he was running at a fast trot. The sound of his footsteps rang out in the empty church and bounced between the walls.

Chapter 25

"Where the heck have you been?"

Sy smiled at the pretty young woman and took a seat next to her on the bench behind the infield fence. He handed her a Pepsi and said, "I dunno. Got caught up with life, I guess. And hello to you too."

"It's been so long since we've seen you. Timmy's finally quit asking about you. We thought you were going to be a regular." Brenda looked up at Sy's face and squinted. "You didn't have that big beard when you were here the last time, did you, Sy?"

"No, Brenda, I didn't. Thought I'd try something different. Be somebody else a little while."

They both looked at each other and smiled, pleased to know that after three months names had not been forgotten. If someone remembered your name after that much time it meant you were meant to be friends.

"You remembered my name and you remembered Timmy's games are on Tuesday. Nice job."

"And I remember we still have a stare contest to get done."

Brenda turned her face up to the blue October sky and laughed. After meeting him only one time three months ago, she found she still liked this man. Not in any sexual way. Not in a fatherly way either. She liked him as a kind, strong human being who had been good for her son.

"That we do, Mr. Sy."

Sy looked toward the field and watched Timmy on the mound, confidently shaking off signals from the catcher.

"How's the boy's game?"

Brenda lit up, smiling proudly at her son out on the mound. "His third season playing Khoury league and it's his best one yet. Nobody can hit him, and he has the highest batting average on the team. Nothing shakes him anymore. Oh, he's had to lay on the ground and roll a couple more times, which was painful to watch. But it worked, and now he doesn't have to do it anymore. He's made a huge turnaround." Brenda looked down and swallowed. She seemed shy. "And let me just say, it's most likely because of you. A man he doesn't even know."

"Good. That's what I was hoping for," said Sy. "It was my plan to help him even more. There's a lot I could have taught that boy."

Brenda heard something in Sy's voice and turned to look at him inquisitively.

"You're sick, aren't you."

Sy felt her looking at him and nodded.

"When I said I got caught up with life, I wasn't being entirely truthful. Shortly after meeting you, I got pretty ill."

"Ill? What kind of illness?"

Sy shifted in his seat and stared at the field a while before answering. It was his first time explaining, and it felt odd. He hadn't planned on telling her. At least not so soon in the conversation. That third nipple of hers had sniffed it out right away. Well, he damn sure wasn't going to tell her everything.

"Right around the time I met you I was beset by seizures. Which was too bad. I really wanted to help your boy."

"I'm so sorry to hear that." Brenda lifted her hand, pulling back a strand of hair that had fallen into her eye. She still wore her hair bobbed, which framed her face and showed how pretty she was.

"They got bad. At least one big one a day, and a few lighter rounds in between."

"Oh hell. Are you getting better? Did you get straightened out?"

"Not entirely," Sy said, a little uncomfortably. "It's an odd form of epilepsy that's hard to treat. Temporal lobe epilepsy, they call it. I take some pretty strong meds that knock it back, but they don't take care of it entirely. There is a possible cauterizing procedure that would probably cure me, but it's dangerous to do because of where the problem is located. I could stand to lose a lot of cognitive function—at least that's what they tell me. So long story short, I recently retired and will be moving to Florida in a couple weeks."

"Why Florida?"

"There's a community down there that may be able to help me. Plus, I'm not getting any younger and figure I better make the move to a warmer climate while I still can."

Brenda didn't say anything but just sat there thinking. She smelled bullshit but didn't feel the need to parse it out. After hearing Sy's news, she subconsciously began pulling back from what had begun as a promising friendship.

Brenda turned to Sy with a pained look and just as she was about to speak Timmy walked up and put his fingers through the fence.

"Hi," he said shyly.

"Hi, Timmy. How's baseball treating you?"

"GREAT! My ERA is two! And I'm hittin' over .350 as of last week! Coach told Mom I'm the best player on the team!"

"Don't brag, Timmy," said the boy's mother.

"He's not bragging," said Sy. "He's just naming stats. But yeah, Timmy, sometimes it's better to let the stats speak for themselves."

Timmy apologized and softened in front of the man who seemed to know such a great deal about baseball.

"But I've been watching you just now, and it does seem like you've earned some braggin' rights since the last time I was here. It's still plenty early, but if you work at it, you might have a chance to really do something, son."

"Thanks," said Timmy, trying to suppress his pride.

"If you do make it to the next higher levels, make sure to control any big feelings. Self-esteem is important, but there can be such a thing as too much of it. It's never all about you when you're playing a team sport… you got that?"

Timmy looked at Sy and nodded vigorously.

"You don't bean batters, you don't charge the mound, you don't taunt the other team, you don't get up in the umpire's face… basically, you don't disrespect the game."

"Got it."

"Right now, I'm thinking you could be a natural. You got the build and the athleticism, but be wary of feeling too big. If you get a big head, you stop listening to your coach as well as your own instincts. Thinking about your *self* causes slumps. Can you remember that?"

Timmy looked at Sy again and nodded vigorously. "Thinking about your *self* causes slumps."

"If you still remember that when the autograph hounds are on you and the sportswriters are calling you 'Tim,' you'll do okay."

"I will. I promise," said Timmy.

"Okay, son. Looks like your last batter just struck out, so you better hightail it out to the mound again."

When Timmy turned to get his glove Sy got up and turned away too. "I'll be right back," he said to Brenda, who, by the look on her face, seemed to think he was leaving for good.

Five minutes later Sy came back holding his Gilmore County baseball trophy. He handed it to the confused Brenda who at first balked and refused to take it.

"I want you to give this to the boy," said Sy. He said it in such a manner Brenda knew it would be pointless to try and refuse it.

"Sy, it's as big as he is!"

"Tell him it's for the most improved player in Khoury league." Sy paused to clear his throat. "Then tell him I said goodbye… and good luck."

Brenda took the huge trophy from Sy and held it in front of her while reading the inscriptions.

"I don't want to drag it to Florida, and there's no one else I'd want to give it to," said Sy.

When she was done reading, Brenda held the big, two-handled gold cup tight to her chest.

"We don't even know you, Sy. Yet I'm dead sure we're going to miss you."

"It's probably that third nipple you got." Sy smiled shyly and wondered what caused him to be so familiar with this woman.

Brenda stood up, raised her face to his, and kissed him on the cheek. Sy reddened and cleared his throat again.

"I guess I better get going. It's a long drive from out here in Plevna." Sy wanted to reciprocate the kiss to the cheek but instead raised his right hand to shake and say goodbye. He guessed he wasn't that familiar after all.

"It was nice seeing you again," he said lamely.

"Wait!" Instead of shaking hands Brenda brought her face closer to Sy's, staring into both his eyes. After a full minute they had yet to blink, and with their eyes still locked, they both began to smile.

Chapter 26

When boarding was called Mercy got up from her seat at the gate, collected the few bags she had brought, and headed for the jetway. The flight attendant took her boarding pass, scanned it, and handed it back. "Enjoy your time in Tampa," she said brightly. Mercy sighed resolutely, thanked the smiling attendant, and walked slowly toward the plane. She made her way past those already seated, struggling to make sure her carry-on didn't smack anyone as she rolled it down the aisle. When she got to row twenty-three, she heaved the bag into the overhead and slumped into the aisle seat. This was her first trip to the Tampa area and would probably not be her last. The forecast for Tampa was a high of eighty-three degrees and even though the entire month of November had been cold for Missouri she was not looking forward to making the trip. Having forgotten to bring a book, she reached up for the in-flight magazine and absently paged through it.

"Been to Tampa before?"

Mercy turned from her magazine and saw an elderly woman sitting next to the window on her right. The woman's long, platinum hair was tied into a tight ponytail, possibly to hide how thin it had become. Her tanned face was heavily made up, which only accented how badly the skin sagged from her birdlike skull. She wore white capri pants under a loose-fitting, blue blouse, and gawdy, cheap jewelry dripped from her fingers and wrists. It occurred to Mercy that the woman was a long-term Floridian, and this was her traveling look.

Mercy shook her head no and hoped that not actually speaking would be a sign for the woman to leave her alone. But it was not to be the case.

"You're looking a little pale, dear. I think sunny Tampa will do you a lot of good. I've been there twenty years and never felt better."

Mercy gave up looking at the magazine, closing it on her lap. *Alright, let's get the chatter over with,* she thought. *Maybe then I can close my eyes and have a nap.* "I'm not going to Tampa for the weather, nice as it may be."

"Are you traveling for work then? I know you don't live there, cause you're *so* pale, sweetie."

"Nope. Just going to see my dad."

"Oh, that's nice. Does he live in the Tampa area?"

"He's in a trailer park in Lutz, which is in Pasco County. He just moved there a month ago. Bought a nice double-wide from the family of a guy who died recently."

"Which park? We live in a mobile home subdivision in Loveland, but we have friends all over."

"It's called Paradise Pines. There's a small hotel on the property, which is where I'm staying. I think the trailer might get way too crowded."

"Paradise Pines… what do I know about that place? It's known for something, isn't it? Paradise Pines..."

"I doubt it's anyplace you'd know of," said Mercy quickly. "It's really small, and from what I know there's nothing special about it."

"Oh! I think I remember something—" But then the thin, elderly woman saw the look on Mercy's face and waved her hand in the air dismissively. "Yeah, you're right. You can't throw a coconut without hitting a trailer park where we're going. We decided on an apartment on the intercoastal—if my husband and I were stuck in a small trailer or RV, we'd kill each other." The woman leaned in and smiled conspiratorially. "He's a pretty big man."

"Well, my dad lives alone."

During the time the plane lifted off and reached climbing altitude the old woman stayed silent, staring straight at the seat in front of her. It occurred to Mercy that for as worldly as this woman tried to seem, she might be a nervous flyer. Mercy leaned out to see if the drink cart had started down the aisle. She would order a double. And maybe catch it again when it came back.

"Did your mother leave us?"

"I'm sorry?"

"You said your father lived alone. Did your mother pass away?"

Mercy turned and stared at Old Lady Chatty for some time, willing her to *Shut up lady, just please shut the fuck up*. She flipped the page of her magazine, responding without looking up, again trying to convey she was in no mood for conversation.

"Mom and dad are recently separated. She lives with her sister. My daughter is staying with them until I get back."

If the talkative old woman noted any frustration she didn't let on. "That's so sad. Two people who have been together all that time… were they together long?"

"Yes," Mercy said curtly.

"It must have been hard for him to pick up and move away from everyone. Especially a granddaughter. He must have a health condition, poor man. Otherwise, why would he go and leave you all?"

Mercy finally snapped. She gritted her teeth together and spoke through tight lips. "YES, HE HAS A FUCKIN' HEALTH CONDITION, AND DON'T EVEN TRY TO ASK ME WHAT IT IS. OKAY?"

The old woman's face fell further than her age had already dictated. "Just trying to be friendly," she said in an ironic, lilting voice.

When the cart came by Mercy ordered two scotches, neat. She slammed them down one after another, closed her eyes, and was soon asleep.

She was woken by the captain announcing they'd be on the ground in twenty minutes, but kept her eyes closed to avoid the woman by the window. The plane touched down smoothly, and when it stopped at the jetway ramp she leaped up, got her case from the overhead, and stepped three paces forward. She had no checked baggage to pick up and headed straight for the car rental counter.

She made the forty-five-minute drive to Paradise Pines after only one stop, checked in to the spare but tidy hotel that sat in the middle of the compound, and finally made it to her room. She laid the case on the bed and slammed her fist into the hard, plastic top. Like her father, Mercy was a problem solver, but life had presented a problem that might not be solvable. At this point she could do nothing but try and understand and give him all the support and love she could.

There was a note from her dad to meet her at the pool, but first Mercy lay down on the shabby bedcovers and closed her eyes. A little while later she sighed loudly, got up, stood in front of the room's full-length mirror, and removed her clothes. After twisting her torso a couple of times to judge how she looked, she took a deep breath and stepped out of the room.

About the Author

Born and raised in rural Missouri, Dan Roettger poured concrete for a living before throwing down his shovel in disgust and attending the University of Missouri, graduating with a degree in journalism. He went on to enjoy an award-winning career as an advertising creative writer and has shelves of cute little statues to prove it. *Rolling Pigeons* is his debut novel but has been a work in progress for a long time. He recently moved back to his rural roots in northern Minnesota, where he was able to put the finishing touches to the book and concentrate on other stories waiting to be told.

www.ingramcontent.com/pod-product-compliance
Lightning Source LLC
LaVergne TN
LVHW091113080826
845145LV00008B/1898

* 9 7 8 1 9 6 2 8 3 4 7 0 4 *